SEDUCTION OF THE PATRIARCH

A DARK ENEMIES TO LOVERS ROMANCE

CAVALIERI BILLIONAIRE LEGACY
BOOK FOUR

ZOE BLAKE

Poison Ink Publications

Blake, Zoe
Seduction of the Patriarch
Cover Design by Dark City Designs
Photographer Wander Aguiar

CONTENTS

INTRODUCTION

Enter the world of the Cavalieri Billionaire Legacy, where love is as treacherous as the secrets they guard.

Each man in this notorious Italian dynasty is bound by duty, honor, and dark desires woven into their very bloodline. The Cavalieri men know what they want—and nothing will keep them from claiming it.

In *Scandals of the Father*, a powerful man's hidden obsession with a young woman threatens to unravel as the dark rumors of his past close in.

In *Sins of the Son*, vengeance and desire pull Cesare back to a shattered past—and to a woman who will never forgive him.

Secrets of the Brother plunges Enzo into a twisted web of family secrets and forbidden love, as he struggles to protect the woman he yearns for most—his late wife's sister.

In *Seduction of the Patriarch*, revenge pushes a Cavalieri man to the edge as he uses seduction as a weapon against the very woman he swore to protect.

And in the electrifying *Scorn of the Betrothed*, a forced marriage meant to prevent a mafia war becomes a battlefield of passions, with Matteo struggling to control his fiancée—a woman as fierce and defiant as him

When enemies turn to lovers, the line between love and hate is dangerously thin.

CHAPTER 1

LILIANA

"enedict Cavalieri."

Two simple words shattered my world.

I pressed my hands between my thighs to stop them from shaking.

My gaze fixed in terror on the polished nickel revolver aimed at my chest. Though slim, there was a chance I could brazen this out.

My tongue flicked out to lick my dry lips. "Please, my name is Maria. I'm sure this is all just a mistake. I have nothing of value to steal."

Benedict leaned his elbows on the table and smirked as his eyes lingered on my mouth. "Maria, is it? I was led to believe Liliana Fiore lived here. Please excuse the intrusion. I didn't mean to frighten such an innocent *angioletto*."

My forearms tightened against my ribs to stifle my body's reaction to such a large, terrifying man saying my real name.

Little angel.

That was me, all right.

Little *fallen* angel was more like it.

With a lift of my chin, I tried to look affronted, yet understanding. "It's quite all right. Mistakes happen."

Methodically caressing the long, vicious-looking barrel of the gun with his fingertips, he gave a slight nod. A tingling awareness spread up my spine, cautioning me that he was still somehow watching me, even with his eyes averted.

Each second of tense silence was an eternity, like cold honey sluggishly pouring from a bottle.

When he spoke, his deep voice shattered the unnatural stillness, giving me a start.

His penetrating obsidian gaze sharpened. "It is a good thing you have cleared up this mistake."

I clenched my jaw to keep my teeth from chattering as I waited to hear what he would say next.

"For if you were Liliana Fiore, who used to work at the Cavalieri offices in Abruzzo, and not Maria as you claim, well then, I'm afraid the rest of our conversation would not be as … friendly."

Dio santo!

In an effort to slide my chair closer to the door, I pushed down on the balls of my feet through my knee-high black suede boots and shifted my weight backward.

My shoulders hunched and I couldn't suppress a cringe at the screech of the chair legs against the old tile floor.

Benedict pointed his gun back at my chest. "You wouldn't be trying to leave our friendly chat, now would you, Maria?"

My eyes widened and I violently shook my head no.

Although he was dressed like a respectable businessman in an expensive cashmere sweater under a wool coat and dark denim pants, I glimpsed inked skin above the sweater's neckline.

Tattoos didn't technically mean he was mafia, but they definitely increased the chances he was.

None of the Cavalieris had ever spoken of a Benedict at the office.

Knowing the concealed dark side of the Cavalieri family, I would not put it past them to have a hidden family member with treacherous connections.

Playing by the rules did not build a legacy of obscene wealth, power, and privilege.

Tapping the index finger of his free hand against his chin, he kept his piercing black eyes trained on me. "What I find fascinating is how much you resemble Liliana."

Bile burned the back of my throat.

He extended his arm and grasped my purse's leather strap.

In a panic, I flattened my palm over the top of my purse.

The corner of his mouth flirting with a smirk, he slowly pulled on the strap.

I firmly pushed my palm down in a desperate attempt to anchor the purse in place.

He exerted more pressure.

Our brief tug-of-war ended when the purse slid out from under my hand and slithered across the table toward him.

With his gaze still on me, he reached inside for my wallet. "I'm certain your *carta d'identità* will say Maria, then we will clear up this slight mistake, and I will let you return to your evening plans with my full apology."

He opened my wallet and stared at my ID which clearly stated *Liliana Chiara Fiore*.

Why hadn't I thought to get a fake *carta d'identità*?

How could I have been so stupid as to use my actual name when applying for that job at Cavalieri Enterprises?

Especially knowing the real reason I was there.

I shot out of my seat and pivoted toward the still open front door and freedom.

"Stop."

My back stiffened as I froze.

But couldn't believe my luck when a male neighbor passed down the hallway at that exact moment.

Imploringly, I widened my gaze and mouthed, *Help me.*

He glanced behind me at the intimidating man with the gun, tucked his chin into his chest and hurried past.

What did it say about Benedict that he wasn't the least bit concerned about the door being wide open where anyone could see him holding me hostage at gunpoint?

Mafia.

That's what it said.

Mafia ... or worse.

Only a truly dangerous man didn't care about the authorities, or a man with so much power and influence he was confident the authorities wouldn't dare approach him.

Madonna santa!

I was in real trouble.

His chair sliding across the tiles had me clenching my fists at my sides.

His boot scraped against the floor as he approached, and it was all I could do not to take my chances and bolt anyway.

It was only my steadfast belief that a man like Benedict Cavalieri was probably a dead-on shot that kept me rooted to the spot.

Then I caught the scent of his cologne, felt the unmistakable warmth of his body heat directly behind me.

My stomach muscles tensed from the sharp breath I took in my struggle to calm the deep tremor shaking my body at his looming presence.

He reached over my shoulder and slowly closed the door. The automatic lock latched with an ominous *click*.

The heavy weight of his gun pressed into my stomach as he wrapped his other arm around my hip and pulled me back against him.

He leaned in close to rasp his next words directly into my ear, the bristles on his unshaven jaw brushing my cheek. "We're going to need privacy for what comes next ... *Liliana.*"

My knees buckled.

If not for his hard embrace, I would have hit the floor. Instead, he tightened his grasp, drawing me closer against his chest with both arms. It was as if I were being held up by a wall of steel that was on fire.

His lips brushed the outer contour of my ear, sending shivers through me. "You really shouldn't have lied to me, *angioletto*. Now you've made me angry."

A tear escaped my tightly closed eyes and slid down my cheek. "Please don't kill me."

His fingers splayed open as he shifted his hand, moving it higher over my stomach, until it was just under my breast. "You will be much more useful to me alive."

Skimming the curve of my breast, his heated palm ran over my body to clutch my throat.

I cried out and wrapped my hands around his wrist, attempting to pull him away.

The pressure of the fingers digging into my flesh increased. "Shhh, little one. I wouldn't recommend fighting me."

Afraid to breathe, I stilled.

He chuckled. "*Brava ragazza.*"

My insides did an odd flip at the endearment.

Traumatized psychosis was the only reason to explain my

response to the touch and condescending praise from this treacherous man holding me at gunpoint.

He ordered, "Get on your knees."

A sob burst through my lips, and I pleaded with him. "Please! Don't do this."

The hand around my throat tightened as he tilted my head back until it rested against his chest. "Make me repeat myself, *angioletto*. I dare you."

Terrified, my knees slammed onto the hard tile floor, my palms only barely breaking my fall in my haste to obey.

Benedict sat on the nearby chair before twisting his fist in my hair at the nape of my neck and viciously dragging me across the floor to kneel between his open thighs.

I lowered my head as he let go, tormenting visions of being defenseless and vulnerable while kneeling before him like a submissive supplicant flashing before my closed eyes.

Fear kept my lungs from expanding. All I could do was suck in small gasps of air, almost ready to pass out from light-headedness.

He forced the barrel of the gun under my chin and raised my head. "Tell me, Liliana ... who ordered you to shoot my brother?"

His Brother? Barone Cavalieri was his brother?

He is going to kill me for sure.

Tears blurred my vision and I couldn't stop shaking. "I swear, I'm not involved in any of this. I didn't even know Don Cavalieri had been shot!"

He shook his head. "Wrong answer."

Maneuvering the gun until the barrel tip pressed against my lower lip, he growled, "Open your mouth."

CHAPTER 2

BENEDICT

*S*he pitched forward with a heart-wrenching sob.

At least, I assumed it would be, for someone with a heart, or gullible enough to buy her cute act.

I stroked her hair before cupping her jaw and gently raising her gaze to mine. "It's a shame I have to break someone so beautiful to get the information I need." I studied her reaction.

Fresh tears filled her gorgeous, almond-shaped eyes as her lower lip trembled.

If I still had a soul, it might have bothered me.

Unfortunately for my *angioletto*, after a lifetime spent in the shadows doing the unholy work of the devil, the only shred of humanity left inside of me was loyalty to my family.

It was my one saving redemption.

Leaning forward, I gave her a chaste kiss on the forehead before smiling down at her indulgently. "It won't work, babygirl."

With a sniff, she swiped the back of her hand under her nose. "What won't work?"

She was about to repeat the gesture when I grasped her wrist with my free hand and guided it to my thigh.

I then reached into my inner coat pocket and pulled out a handkerchief. After giving it a shake to release the folds, I tenderly swept the soft linen under her nose before handing it to her.

"This adorable display of innocence you are putting on for me."

Rising on her knees, she clutched my thighs with both hands and leaned forward to plead, "But I am innocent. Please, you have to understand, this is all just a misunderstanding."

My hand dwarfed hers when I covered it.

She immediately tried to snatch her hand back, but I curled my fingers around her palm, restraining her.

Locking my gaze with hers, I forced her hand higher up my thigh, taunting her. "What I understand is the Biblical retribution I'm going to rain down on the person who dared attack my family."

Liliana yanked on her captured hand with desperation, using all her weight to pull back on her arm, but I wouldn't release it. Relenting, she pressed her other fist to the center of her chest and wept. "Please! You must listen to me. I was just an assistant in the office. Nothing more."

She appeared so virtuous and fragile, a kneeling supplicant.

All she was missing were the strand of rosary beads and prayer book pressed between her palms.

I wasn't fooled.

Releasing her hand, I gave one of her long black curls a tug.

"As amusing as these theatrics have been, little one, I am not a patient man. I will give you one more chance to tell me the truth, before I resort to more ..." I tilted my head to the side, "*traditional* methods."

Her eyes glistened with fresh tears as she clasped both hands to her heart. "You're not listening! I am telling you the truth! You have to believe me! I'm not involved. I only just found out in the papers this evening that Don Cavalieri was shot!"

She cried out when I raised the gun to within an inch of her lips. "Wrong again, babygirl. Now I'm afraid I'm going to need you to open that sweet, lying mouth of yours."

Liliana tightened her full, cherry pink lips between her teeth, tucking her chin into her shoulder with a whimper.

My forearm rested on my thigh as I leaned forward. "There are seven holes in the human body. If you don't open your mouth by the count of two ... I'll pick a different hole. One."

With a shocked gasp, she barely opened her mouth.

"Wider," I barked.

Her lower lip trembled with her struggle to obey.

Losing patience, I wrapped my fingers under her jaw and pressed the tips into the delicate flesh of her cheeks, forcing her mouth open.

Her arms flew up in a vain attempt to break my grasp.

"Lower your arms before I tie you up."

With her shoulders shaking from her silent sobs, she did as she was told.

The gun barrel scraped against her teeth as I pushed it

inside her mouth. "This barrel is over twenty centimeters long. If you don't behave, I will shove every one of them down your tight little throat until you choke, do you understand me?"

She froze, eyes widening as she nodded, grimacing as her front teeth clattered against the hard metal of the barrel once more.

My fingers still gripped her cheeks to keep her mouth open. "Now, this is the last time I'm going to ask *nicely*, were you the one who shot Barone Cavalieri?"

"Mmmnnfrrmooonffmr! Eeeee swuuurarewhe."

My rather unique skillset allowed me to understand her muffled response to be, "No, I swear."

At least I was getting closer to the truth. I released my grip and eased the gun out of her mouth.

"Do you know who did?"

Unlike before, when she'd given an adamant and desperate response, this time she hesitated.

She licked her lips, her eyes drifting up and to the right in a fruitless effort to stall for time before she shook her head.

A desperate attempt at an emphatic, honest verbal response when she had a gun in her mouth for the first question, an evasive, nonverbal response when she was free to speak for the second.

Another lie.

With a sigh, I rubbed my fingers over the sharp bristles on my jaw and stared down at her kneeling form to try to rein in my growing anger.

I'd never been a tolerant man, even less so now, knowing my brother was currently lying in a hospital bed with a fucking hole in his chest.

I wanted answers and I fucking wanted them now.

Years of covert training clawed to the surface as the devil inside of me roared back to life.

The kill or be killed, winner takes all poison I had long ago purged from my blood once more flowed through my veins.

Every single person involved was going to pay for the attack on my family.

No one was safe.

No one—including the terrified little angel quaking before me.

I hadn't earned my reputation for being a soulless, unrepentant bastard because of my forgiving nature. Years ago, I left that life behind and disappeared into the wilds of Northern Italy.

There would be consequences with my return—complicated ones—as I tracked down leads, called in old favors, and did *whatever it took* to get to the truth.

I didn't give a damn.

I didn't start this war, but I sure as fuck would be the one to finish it.

In a flash, my arm flew out.

My fist twisted in Liliana's glossy black curls at the base of her skull so I could wrench her forward until her face was cradled between my thighs.

Ignoring her cries, I forced her head back and caressed her lips with the tip of the gun barrel. "Bad little girls who lie to me get punished," I ground out through clenched teeth.

CHAPTER 3

BENEDICT

*H*er hands scrabbled behind her to grab onto my wrist, trying to prevent my painful yank on her hair.

A tear slipped over her cheek to hit my wrist. I glanced down, mildly surprised it didn't turn to ice the moment it struck my skin.

Enough. She tried to plead with me, but it only came out as gibberish as I slipped the tip of the gun barrel into her mouth, forcing her to talk around it.

There was something darkly erotic about her full pink lips sucking on the end of the steel barrel, knowing her cute tongue was caressing the underside of the long metal shaft.

My cock lengthened down my inner thigh at the thought.

I couldn't remember the last time I'd fucked a woman.

In my previous line of work, women couldn't be trusted, so I learned to make do with one-night stands and escorts. The problem was, there weren't many opportunities for those up in the Dolomite mountain range of Northern Italy.

Liliana was different.

She looked so innocently sweet, almost fragile, like a little doll who had tumbled off the safety of her shelf into a dangerous, unknown world.

But she wasn't innocent. Far from it.

Which was why I didn't feel the slightest bit of guilt using any means necessary to get the information I needed.

Any. Means. Necessary.

"Show me you can be a good girl. Swirl your tongue around the tip of the gun."

Her body stilled, her terrified eyes widening.

With a twist of my fist, I gave her hair a sharp, stinging tug. "You heard me. Do it. Now. Open your lips so I can see your tongue."

Liliana sniffed as her lips trembled.

Inhaling a shaking breath, she opened her lips wider and after a long, pleading look at me, her tongue swept around the barrel tip of my gun.

The sight sent an electric bolt of lust down the length of my shaft.

Santo inferno!

My chest expanded with the deep breath I sucked in to control my urge to unzip my jeans, pull out my cock and shove her pretty mouth straight to the hilt until she choked.

My voice was harsh with need as my thighs pressed into her shoulders, caging her in. "Again."

Her palms pushed against my inner thighs in her struggle to obey me.

The pink tip of her tongue swirled around the tip of the barrel, wetting it until the metal glistened in the dim light of her apartment.

If I were a decent man, I would give her another chance to tell me the truth.

If I were a decent man, I would admit she had been punished enough.

If I were a decent man, I would confess this was no longer about learning information.

But that was the problem—I'd never once claimed to be a decent man. Far from it.

Adjusting my grip on her hair, I pulled her head back slightly. "I'm going to push the gun in deeper. I want you to show me how you'd suck it like a cock."

Her eyes pleaded with me as she tried to shake her head. "Mfrmrmnomrrlwoooeld. Pseelseases. Ssttouuup."

"Please stop? You're lucky I didn't take off my belt and whip your ass before this. Now do as you're told."

Careful to avoid hitting her teeth, I eased the gun further into her unwilling mouth.

Her head jerked and she gagged, her shoulders hunching up close to her ears.

She reached for the gun handle.

My gaze narrowed. "Touch it and I'll bend you over that table and shove the barrel up your tight little ass instead."

Her hand fell away.

I pulled the gun out slightly, then thrust it deeper past her lips. "Suck it."

Her cheeks hollowed as her lips wrapped around the now wet barrel. The shaky, hesitant swipes of her tongue, along with her whimpers, sent slight vibrations along the gun to my hand where I held it tight.

"That's it, my dirty little angel. Lick it. I want you to suck so hard you fucking swallow the bullets."

She whimpered again in response, driving her fingernails into my denim-covered thighs.

The whisper of pain only enhanced my enjoyment of the twisted sight of my gun face-fucking the captive beauty I had tracked down with the initial intention of killing.

Plans change.

Why kill her when there were so many pleasurably painful ways to punish her while using her as a pawn for my revenge?

I pushed the gun in deeper.

She gagged again.

I refused to relent. "Swallow it. Might as well learn now. You'll be swallowing something *much larger and longer* very soon."

Fresh tears coursed down her cheeks.

I pulled back on the gun, then thrust it once more inside her warm, wet mouth. This time feeling the resistance at the back of her throat.

"Are you ready to tell me who shot Barone Cavalieri?"

More whimpers. She reflexively raised her arms to grip the gun handle, but then lowered them, giving me a slight nod.

The light caught the glistening wet metal as I slowly withdrew the gun barrel upward out of her mouth.

Fuck, that was an erotic sight.

Her swollen lips were stained a deep cherry pink. Using the side of the barrel, I rubbed her spit over her mouth until her lips shimmered as if covered in gloss.

I ran the tip of my tongue over the sharp edge of my teeth, already imagining what her mouth would taste like in the moment.

Warm nickel from the gun, salt from her tears, and bitter

orange and clove from the half-drunk *Crodino* spritz she had in her hand when she arrived.

My torso inched forward as I focused on her mouth. Perhaps just a quick taste ....

Liliana choked and wiped the spittle from her lips with my crumpled handkerchief, breaking the spell.

Giving myself a mental shake, I snapped upright before commanding, "Talk, or I put this gun someplace significantly more unpleasant."

Leaning away from me on her knees, she wrapped her arms around her middle. After swiping at the tears on her cheeks, she lowered her head and said, "You don't understand, if I tell you—"

I brushed back the thick cascade of hair blocking her face from my view. Cupping her jaw, I raised her face to meet my gaze. "Baby, we are way past *if*. Tell me."

Her warm breath caressed my hand with her sigh.

I clenched my jaw and forced myself to focus.

Later.

Only a truly jaded and experienced agent could experience having a gun shoved in their mouth and still be able to stick to their false story.

Liliana is good, but she isn't that good.

She may be up to her pretty eyeballs in this mess, but she wasn't the one who pulled the trigger on Barone. Of that I was certain.

That didn't mean she wasn't culpable.

And until I knew to what extent she was involved, she wasn't leaving my side.

Since we'd be in forced proximity, I saw no reason why she shouldn't also warm my bed.

My cock hardened at visions of thrusting between her now swollen and plump lips.

After all, I believed in keeping my enemies close … very close.

CHAPTER 4

LILIANA

I was a dead woman.

Every single thing about Benedict Cavalieri screamed it.

It wasn't just the gun.

Despite being raised in a convent, no one grew up in Sicily and escaped the ever-present, violent specter of the mafia.

They were so interwoven into daily life, people said the *omertà,* the code of silence, with their evening prayers. From the *capo* to the power hungry *capodecina* to the lowliest *soldati,* everyone knew someone in *the family* or *the organization.*

Even the nuns.

In my village, the *homini d'onore,* or men of honor, as they preferred to be called, were more respected than the local priest.

With each religious feast, especially those which honored the Madonna, the patron saint of the Sicilian mafia, the *capo,* his *vice capo, consigliere,* and *reggente,* followed by all the *soldati,* would have pride of place in the procession through the village to the church steps, often shouldering out the priest and deacons.

Once during the procession of *Madonna dell'Annuziata*, the local *capo* was confined to his bed, so the entire procession, followed by every member of the village, detoured to the front steps of his home to pay their respects to him *first* before continuing on to the church.

Violence. Power. Wealth.

The mafiosi trifecta.

Every day was a game of survival.

Lesson number one: learn who had power, who wanted power, and who was weak, having only a tenuous hold on their power.

It didn't take long for me to realize the weak ones were the men who relied too heavily on guns as their primary source of power. They were like playground bullies who became little babies the moment you stood up to them and swiped their toy.

That was definitely not Benedict Cavalieri.

Some men just commanded power, and it had nothing to do with the gun they were holding.

It wasn't just one thing, it was a combination of things.

How he vibrated with dark energy like some kind of villainous magnet.

I was half surprised all the knives in my apartment didn't suddenly stand up on edge and fly toward his open palm like he was that dude in the comic book movie.

Then there was the extreme arrogance and confidence usually only found in someone with obscene amounts of money and power, with the muscle to back it up … or like in ancient kings or gods, of which he resembled both.

Of course, it didn't hurt that he looked like Mt. Vesuvius

decided to stand up, toss on some designer clothes, and take a casual stroll around Italy.

The comparison was apt, since I suspected Benedict shared a similar temperament to a volcano—cold and deceptively calm on the outside, but a molten, primordial soup of rage and feral machismo just under the surface.

But mostly it was in his gaze.

That horrifying, mesmerizing, penetrating, dark gaze.

The man didn't see into your soul, or even see through you. It was like his eyes were two razor-sharp black diamonds that sliced you to ribbons. It was all I could do not to check my body for cuts and scrapes.

I'm not sure how much longer I can hold out without telling him the whole truth about his brother's shooting.

But to tell him would be certain death.

Yet, to not tell him would also mean death.

Despite his Cavalieri blood, unlike his brother and nephews, he wasn't even attempting to appear to be a law-abiding citizen.

The dark silver hoop earring that made him look like a sinister pirate combined with the peeks I had gotten of a tattoo on his chest certainly didn't help.

While he may or may not be attached to the mafia, he clearly hadn't spent his life picking grapes and making wine like the rest of his family.

Perhaps that was why, even after months of playing at being the dutiful office assistant at Cavalieri Enterprises, I had never seen him?

Matteo!

He had to be Matteo's father. I knew Matteo was Enzo and Cesare's cousin, but it hadn't occurred to me to wonder about his father.

I'd had enough on my plate with Barone Cavalieri and his sons and what had been expected of me.

Since everyone in Italy knew about the Cavalieri family, Benedict must have been living deep in the shadows.

I swallowed.

It only proved my theory.

Only paralyzing fear must have kept me from seeing the immediate resemblance to his brother, Barone. They could be twins. At well over two meters, Benedict was equally as tall as Barone. The top of my head barely reached his shoulder.

Although they were both undeniably, insanely handsome with their Roman god-like features, their cheekbones and jaws appearing to have been literally chiseled out of *Carrara* marble. And their silver hair and beards that made them both look like living embodiments of Jupiter after he traded his lightning bolt for a gun.

But that was where the similarities ended.

While Barone Cavalieri was no doubt dangerous and extremely protective of his family, his brother, Benedict, was at a different level.

Benedict Cavalieri is a hired killer.

Of that I was certain … and he knew I was responsible for his brother's attempted murder.

Unless I thought of something fast, I was definitely in trouble.

Keeping my gaze lowered, I forced my mind to focus.

My tongue moved over the roof of my mouth. The metallic tang from his gun still tingled on the back of my tongue.

I squeezed my inner thighs tight as I ruined the neatly stitched square of white linen clutched in my hands, twisting, and stretching the fiber between my fists.

SEDUCTION OF THE PATRIARCH

I meant, seriously, what was that?

The way he pinned my head between his powerful thighs and fisted my hair to force my mouth down on his ... his ... I couldn't even *think* it. At least it wasn't his ... his ... *other thing* ... but still ... it might as well have been.

The way he stared at my mouth the entire time.

The arrogant way he had made no attempt to hide his lascivious thoughts until his fantasy became my own.

I imagined what it would have felt like if it weren't a cold, metal gun barrel but rather the hot, hard length of his shaft being forced down my throat.

I may not be innocent in what he was accusing me of, but I was innocent in other things.

I could only imagine what he would taste like, *down there*.

Would it be like the time I got curious and licked my skin to see what sweat tasted like?

Would he taste like skin warmed from the sun? Like hot salt and musk.

Darn it. Focus.

He was blocking the only door out of the apartment but maybe he didn't know about the back window?

The one over my bed behind the curtain which divided the kitchen and living area from the bedroom in the small studio space.

The window led to a tiny, iron balcony that was so rusted, I never dared step foot out onto it for safety reasons.

But there was a big difference between not wanting to enjoy a leisurely morning caffe on a rickety death trap, and ... oh, say ... running for your life from a mountain of a man, a mafia-ish killer who had a vendetta against you.

I knew it was supposed to have a ladder that lowered to

the ground below. Since I was on the third level, I'd have to hope that was true.

Rocking back on my hips, I held my hand to my neck and cleared my throat. "Could I please have a sip of something, first?"

I kept my facial features as calm and open as possible as his narrowed gaze swept over me.

Without saying a word he stood.

My palms made a loud smacking sound on the tile as I fell back, barely avoiding having the tip of my nose pressed right up against his … his …

I hated how small and submissive I felt down on my knees at his feet, like a worshipping supplicant.

My head hit my upper shoulders from my having to tilt it all the way back just to look up at his towering form.

In a moment of trauma-induced madness, I imagined white fluffy clouds accumulating around his upper arms as if he truly was some nefarious giant getting ready to crush me under his foot like a bug.

Benedict stretched his arm out and stroked my hair, the corner of his mouth lifting. "It really is a shame I may have to kill you. You really are the most adorable liar."

I sank my teeth into my still sore bottom lip in a vain attempt to stop fresh tears from spilling from my eyes.

I guessed it was a small comfort, knowing that before doing the dirty deed, the man who killed me would feel mildly sad about it because I was "adorable."

He slid his gun under his arm into a shoulder holster, then shrugged out of his heavy, black wool overcoat and tossed it over my small kitchen tabletop before easily stepping around me to head to the kitchen sink.

Water wouldn't sting, but my *Crodino* spritz would.

"Not water, can you please just get a glass so I can drink some of my *Crodino* spritz?"

A glass was needed because the top of the bottle was too narrow for what I had planned.

Raising a sardonic eyebrow, Benedict went straight to the kitchen cabinet which held the small juice glasses and retrieved one before turning back toward me.

As he poured the remaining bright orange, Aperol-flavored drink into the glass, it clicked what that small action meant.

He knew precisely where I kept the glasses.

Which could only mean he had taken the time to search my apartment before my arrival.

I cast a quick glance around. My place was neat and immaculate as always.

I changed my mind.

Benedict wasn't a hired killer.

He was something much, much worse. A trained assassin.

Strictly speaking, a hired killer could be anything from a goon with a gun to a loyal soldier in the mafia. A trained assassin was different.

They were highly skilled men who had no loyalty and only a price, usually one so high that no single mafia family could keep them on the payroll.

A hired killer knocked down a door, fired a gun and fulfilled a contract, but a trained assassin?

Benedict held out the glass. "Here. No more stalling."

Before taking the glass, I braced my hand against the table edge and rose. My legs were so unsteady, I kept my grip on the table as I shifted my booted foot backward one step.

His fingers brushed mine when I clasped the glass, sending a frisson of awareness up my spine.

Our gazes clashed when he didn't immediately release the glass.

His hand shifted over mine, caressing down the tops of my fingers and over the back of my hand with his fingertips before allowing me to pull away.

What had been a ruse, was now a necessity.

Careful not to drink it all, I swallowed a gulp of the now mostly fizzled seltzer drink, needing the bitter, sharp flavor to snap me out of the twisted sensual haze this man was weaving around me that was so wrong.

As I did so, I shifted my other foot another step behind me.

I was now lined up with the break in the curtains which led to the bedroom area.

My hand shook so badly some of the remaining contents spilled over the edge of the glass.

Benedict reached for the handkerchief I had discarded on the table, nodding toward me. "Careful, babygirl. You'll stain your skirt."

The irony of him worrying about me staining my winter cream skirt with orange soda when he had been threatening to stain it with my own crimson blood all evening was apparently lost on him.

He was momentarily distracted.

It was now or never.

I forced air into my strained lungs.

The second he turned back toward me, I tossed the rest of the contents of my glass in his face.

And ran as if a beast from hell were on my heels … because he was.

CHAPTER 5

BENEDICT

*A*dorable.

With an amused smirk, I used the wrinkled handkerchief already in my hand to wipe the harmless drops of *Crodino* spritz from my eyes and jaw.

In an uncharacteristic burst of sympathy, I called out, "Ow! Ow! My eyes!"

There wasn't a doubt in my mind my conniving *angioletto* had assumed the bitter drink would transform into an astringent weapon to disable my eyes.

So I gave her a bit of theater, to let her think her escape plan was working.

I tilted my head to the side and enjoyed the view through the curtains of her cute ass shimmying across the top of her bed in her attempt to get to the window which led to the balcony she no doubt assumed I didn't know about.

Not only was she an adorably terrible liar, but her big, beautiful brown eyes also gave away every hint of emotion and intention.

Although they weren't, strictly speaking, brown. That was too common of a description for her eyes. They were a curiously unique color, more like burnished bronze. I noticed the metallic glimmer had shown the most when I was punishing her mouth with my gun.

I wondered how bright they would shine when it was my cock there instead?

Seeing that she had gotten the window open and was preparing to make good on her escape, it was time to clip my little angel's wings.

Liliana had hiked her skirt up, exposing her thighs as she bent her right knee and readied to throw her leg over the windowsill to straddle it.

Her gorgeous red lips opened on a gasp when I strolled into the makeshift bedroom.

"Going somewhere, babygirl?"

With a cry, she bent low and stretched her leg through the open window.

Before she climbed completely through, I said, "Were you aware that the minimum distance for a lethal fall is four stories?"

Her head turned to look out the window down at the dark alley below, then back at me. "This is only three," she said with a knowing smirk.

I placed my gun on her bureau top, not missing how her gaze followed my movements. Then I leaned my shoulders against the wall and crossed my arms over my chest. "My mistake, you are correct."

Pretending to consider it, I said, "From three stories, you only risk serious injury to your spleen, liver, lungs, blunt chest trauma, rib fracture and, it goes without saying, multiple compound fractures to your ankles, legs, and possibly wrists and arms."

She covered her ears with her hands. "Stop talking! You're just trying to scare me."

I chuckled. "No, babygirl. You've seen my methods to scare you."

My foot shifted to the right, adjusting my stance as I ran the heel of my palm over my hardening cock. Fuck, even the way her cheeks blushed a pretty, dark pink did it for me.

What the hell was it with this woman?

Although "woman" was painting it a bit thick. She was probably barely in her twenties. Far too young for me. I preferred my women experienced, with no strings attached. Younger women still had dreams and expectations.

Besides, the only reason why I was even here was because she was involved in the plot to kill my brother.

If I fucked her it would be for a purpose and that purpose wouldn't be to get my rocks off.

It would be to get information or to use her as a pawn to get closer to Dante Agnello who, I was certain, was the one who'd called out the contract on Barone. Period.

She adjusted her seat on the windowsill, gifting me with a quick glimpse of her purple silk panties.

My cock lengthened to a painful degree, my balls tightening. *Fuck.*

Now I was the one who was lying.

Liliana looked out the window again. "Besides, there's a ladder. A ladder that won't hold your weight, just mine, so don't even think of coming after me."

As she said it, she shifted to slide her other leg over the sill.

I rubbed my jaw, then wagged my finger in her direction.

"Again, you make an excellent point, however, you've forgotten an important detail."

Her lips thinned as her fingers curled around the top of the window. "What?"

"I know it didn't escape your notice I knew where you kept your juice glasses, which meant I searched your apartment."

Her shoulders stiffened.

Clearly she was proud of her observational skills, and annoyed to have been found out.

I continued. "What you failed to do was revise your escape plan after learning that bit of information."

Liliana shifted again on the windowsill, failing to hide her frown.

While I knew she was merely adjusting what was an uncomfortable sitting position, all I saw were her slim legs riding a piece of wood.

Thoughts of taking her back to my ranch up north and forcing her to straddle a leather submission horse while I mercilessly stretched her tight ass with my cock by fucking her from behind nearly had me forgetting the reason why I was here.

Shaking off the erotic image, I said, "You should have realized I would have inspected the balcony. The ladder does not reach to the ground. It is a full story short."

Her head turned so suddenly she slammed her forehead against the window sash. Rubbing her injury, she lowered her torso and poked her head out. When she ducked back inside and straightened, she pushed her chin out. "So? I can jump the rest of the way."

I nodded and pushed my shoulders away from the wall, preparing to lunge for her, just in case. "You could. A one-story fall has only a twenty-five percent chance of fatality assuming you avoid a head injury when you land, the chances of which increase given the hour and the darkness outside. Otherwise, you mainly risk various compound fractures to the ankles, legs, wrists—"

"Stop! Considering you're threatening to put a bullet inside of me, I think I'll risk a broken leg."

I curled my fingers around the iron railing at the foot of her bed to prevent myself from just grabbing her. "Tell me what I want to know, and I promise … it won't be a bullet I put inside of you."

A cold breeze through the open window ruffled her curls as she sat frozen with indecision.

After twisting my wrist to glance at my Breitling Chronomat 44 military watch, I warned, "I'm not a patient man, Liliana. Come back inside."

"You don't understand. If I tell you what I know, they will kill me."

If.

There was that word again.

I saw I had more *persuading* to do.

I straightened and backed away a few steps so as to appear non-threatening. "I do understand, *angioletto*. If you come inside we will reach a solution."

One solution was to simply drag her back inside, but it was so much more effective psychologically if she had a hand in her own destruction.

It would eat at her ego and confidence to know she'd had a chance to escape and had blown it.

The next time she needed to make a serious decision she would question her ability to rationalize and make the correct one, leaving her vulnerable to suggestion.

Intimidation and Interrogation Tactics 101.

After another moment, Liliana swung her leg back inside and crawled to the center of the bed.

Stepping forward, I reached over to close and latch the window. *"Brava ragazza."*

Hiding behind her long hair, she stared at her clasped hands and whispered, "What happens now?"

With my arms crossed over my chest, I loomed over her. "Now? Now, you take your sweater off."

CHAPTER 6

BENEDICT

She lunged for the window again.

I reached over the footrail and snatched her around the waist, lifting her high. As she screamed and kicked out, I swung her around and set her on her feet.

Before she could bolt for the curtain divider and then the front door, I slammed her against the wall and caged her in with my forearms. "Settle down."

Her chest rose and fell with her labored breathing. "You said we were going to talk!"

"No, I said we were going to reach a solution."

Shifting her head to the side, avoiding my gaze, she crossed her arms. "I refuse your solution."

Curling my fingers around her jaw, I forced her to look back up at me. "That's not how torture works, babygirl."

Her mouth dropped open. "Torture!"

The side of my thumb swept across her full bottom lip. My earlier form of *persuasion* had stained it a deep cherry pink, how it would look if she had been sipping red wine all night.

At the movement, her lips tightened into a tight line.

I tilted my head. "*Tsk, tsk, tsk. Bad girl.*"

My fingertips applied pressure to the soft flesh of her cheeks just above her jawbone.

She raised her arm and clasped her small hands around my forearm, opening her mouth unwillingly. It was almost alarming to see how both her hands barely fit around the muscle.

She really was just like a tiny, fragile doll.

One I had every intention of breaking.

I pushed my thumb inside, running the tip along the sharp edges of her teeth. "There is no reason to be frightened … yet."

Cupping her jaw, I sank my thumb deeper into her mouth.

Her tongue instinctively flicked and swirled around it.

With great effort, I suppressed the growl which threatened to rumble from deep within my chest and said, "There are countless forms of torture for interrogation purposes. The first step is intimidation."

My hips pushed against hers. "What I'm doing now."

Her almond-shaped eyes widened at the distinctive, hard edge of my cock pressing against her stomach.

When she tried to pull her head back and away, I tightened my grasp. "Then there is step two, subjugation."

I slipped my thumb out of her mouth.

She clenched my forearm, whimpering, "Please, stop this."

Using the tip of my thumb, I traced her upper lip, making it glisten. "That's a very good start, babygirl, but let's see if we can improve on your earlier performance."

Looking to her right, tears filled her eyes at the sight of my gun resting on the top of her bureau.

"Don't worry. I won't use the gun, as long as you are a good girl and obey me."

Lowering her gaze, she nodded.

I knew better than to try and probe her for answers. She wasn't ready to break, yet.

The pad of my thumb caressed her closed lips. "Open your mouth."

With her glistening eyes sending a silent plea, she slowly obeyed.

"Wider. Let me see that pink tongue."

The blush on her cheeks deepened as she tilted her head back slightly and opened her lips wider.

There was something about her mouth that fascinated me. It was so cute and small yet with full, plump lips. It made a man just want to crush them against the base of his cock.

"*Brava ragazza*. Now I'm going to put my thumb back inside your nice warm mouth and you're going to suck nice and hard."

Without a word, she nodded again.

"Say yes," I commanded.

She licked her lips. "Yes," she whispered.

I couldn't quite explain why or what came over me, but then I said, "Say yes ... *daddy*."

Her shocked gaze shot up to me.

A tense silence stretched.

Daddy kink had never been my thing but between her wide-eyed gaze, innocent act, and all the creative ways I planned on using her sweet body like my own personal fuck doll until she had served her purpose in my revenge scheme, it just seemed fitting.

It had been an impulse, but now, the longer she remained mute, the more I wanted to hear her say it.

The more I needed to hear her say it.

Her brow furrowed. "What?"

"You heard me. Say 'yes, daddy.'"

She blinked. "I don't want to call you ... daddy. It's wrong and twisted."

"That's the point." I leaned in closer, my focus on her mouth. "Now say it," I growled.

Inhaling a shaking breath, she said, "Yes ... daddy."

Fuck.

Both my hands wrapped around her neck, holding her captive for my mouth to slam down on hers. My tongue pushed deep inside her mouth, finally tasting her.

She was bittersweet.

Fitting.

As I ground my painfully hard cock against her middle, I ravaged her mouth, tilting my head to the right, then left, swirling my tongue around hers, each time pressing in deeper and more aggressively.

I knew I was hurting her, overwhelming her. I could feel my beard scraping against the soft skin of her cheeks. Knew I was bruising her lips against her teeth as I bore down on her.

I didn't care.

I was a man possessed.

It was the sweetly submissive way Liliana stared up at me with those big doe eyes and reluctantly rasped *daddy* that made me want to do all kinds of depraved things to her beautiful body.

Even common kinky things like a spanking or ring-gag blowjob suddenly took on another dimension of sensual when I considered making her call me daddy while doing them.

She mewed against my mouth as she rose up on her toes.

Whether it was to lean into my kiss or to get away was immaterial to me.

Shifting my left hand down to wrap around her waist, I pressed my palm against her lower back to hold her tighter in my embrace. My need was so strong, I had to remind myself to be careful not to crack her ribs.

This must be the difference between being with an experienced woman and one so sweet and innocent. I wouldn't know, having avoided the young, virginal type my whole life.

Mainly because the good girls tended not to play in the shadows where I lingered.

Perhaps it isn't all an act with Liliana?

There was something intoxicating about her guileless responses to my touch. The shocked little gasps.

The shivers of response that crept over her limbs.

The way her eyes widened then became heavy-lidded and hazy.

Sick bastard that I was, I especially enjoyed the mixture of fear and desire I saw in their depths.

A rush of blood went straight to my cock every time she submitted to one of my domineering demands, or when she lowered her head because she knew she was powerless to fight me off.

Her small hands pushed against my chest as she broke free from our kiss, casting her head to the side, breathing heavily. "I can't breathe. We have to stop."

Surprised to realize I was also out of breath, I reached for the hem of her black turtleneck, equally surprised I had let her leave it on for this long, depriving me of a real look at her breasts. "There is no stopping, little one. Daddy's just getting started."

She opened her mouth to object, but her cry was lost in a swath of cotton as I whipped the sweater over her head.

Her gorgeous, lush curves were pushed high in a simple, purple silk bra.

Stretching her arm out, she snatched the sweater from my grasp and covered her breasts. "How dare you!"

"Welcome to the next torture step. Humiliation."

It was clear she was on the edge, but not quite ready. It was too soon to probe her with questions.

It was just a coincidence that *questions* were the last things I wanted to be probing her with in this moment.

My hands spanned her waist. "Push your bra down. Show me your tits."

"Why are you doing this?"

"You know why."

Christ, she was beautiful.

There was a high flush on her cheeks. Her lips were bruised and swollen from our kiss, and it made me want to punish them even more with my mouth. Her hair was a tangled mess of curls that hung in wild disarray over her shoulders and halfway down her back, and all I could think about was how many times I would be able to wrap its silky length around my fist.

But it was mostly her eyes. Those stunning, burnished bronze, expressive eyes.

"What if … what if I told you …."

The same pretty face I had just been admiring did about seventeen straight micro-expressions which told me she was about to lie to me—again.

My grip on her hips tightened. "Stop. We both know you are getting ready to lie to me. Let me save you the trouble and a possibly worse punishment. Don't."

Her hands twisted in the sweater she was holding.

I ripped it from her grasp. "The bra, Liliana. Now."

She swallowed, the muscles in her throat contracting before she shifted her arms behind her.

"No, not off. Push it down."

There was no explanation for why I was demanding that, I just instinctively knew she would find it more shameful to keep the bra on and only push it down.

Her fingers dug into the band and dragged it down a few inches until curves bounced above bra cups, exposing her blush pink nipples.

Without thought, I licked my dry lips, already imagining their taste. Before I could find out for sure, a teardrop splashed on the top curve of her right breast.

My gaze traveled to her averted face. "Is the ceiling suddenly so fascinating, little one?"

She sniffed. "This is wrong. We shouldn't be doing this."

It was then I noticed the thin gold chain with a small gold crucifix around her neck. I lifted it up against my index finger and swept its cool, smooth surface with my thumb.

Gold didn't suit her.

It was the preferred metal for worship and sacrifices because it did not conduct heat. It was always cool and impassive, as unemotional as a god.

She should wear silver or platinum, something that would warm on her skin.

Having long given up on God, I studied the Catholic symbol as if it were an ancient hieroglyph. Although I didn't begrudge others the comfort of their religious idols and pageantry.

My eyes narrowed.

Was this just another prop? Another layer to her backstory?

It wasn't possible anyone could be this innocent.

I was willing to believe she wasn't experienced in the general sense but she wasn't the fucking Virgin Mary either.

Bracing my forearm over her head, I shifted the gold charm behind her neck, then kissed just under her ear. "Would my babygirl like me to move on to the next step?"

With her gaze trained on the ceiling, she nodded.

I trailed a series of open-mouthed kisses down her neck. "Then ask me."

She groaned and shifted her hips before saying, "Can you just move on to the next step?"

One long, silky curl resting on top of her left breast proved too much of a temptation. I twisted it around my index finger and gave her hair a sharp tug.

She cried out and grasped the strands in a futile attempt to prevent me from tugging again.

"That is not how you ask me."

"You can't mean—"

"Oh, but I do."

"You aren't seriously—"

"Oh, but I am."

"You aren't really—"

"Watch me."

"But it's so—"

"Do I need to warn you again that I'm not a patient man?"

With a sigh, she said, "Please, *daddy*, can we move on?"

Fuck, yeah, definitely my new favorite kink.

In one move, I ran my hands over her body to her waist. Then I lifted her off her feet, sliding her slight frame up against the wall until her breasts were even with my mouth.

Liliana protested, her hands gripping my shoulders.

"Wrap your legs around my waist."

"No! I can't!"

"It wasn't a request."

"I ... fine!"

She did as she was told.

The moment her legs tightened around my middle, I pressed my denim-restrained cock against her core.

Her shocked gasp was like cool water on a hot day.

I opened my mouth and ran my tongue along the inner curve of her right breast, tasting her sweet skin. Relishing how her fingernails dug into my upper arms.

Savoring her softness with gentle kisses on the top curve before using the tip of my tongue to swirl around the nipple, wetting the areole.

Capturing her gaze with my own, I stared at her as I pursed my lips and blew on her nipple.

Her thighs tightened around my waist, her mouth opening and closing several times as if she couldn't form a coherent thought.

Now that I had her complete attention, I leaned in and rasped my next words against her pert, sensitive nipple, still using my breath to tease her. "Do you know what the next step is, little one?"

Her head rolled from side to side against the wall. "No," she moaned.

I flicked the tip of my tongue against her nipple before replying, "Pain."

Her heavy-lidded eyes snapped open as she stared in horror at my open mouth hovering over her nipple. "No!"

Too late.

My lips closed over the tight bud, sucking it deep into my

mouth … before sinking the sharp edges of my front teeth into the delicate flesh.

Liliana screamed and pushed against me, thrashing in my embrace.

Pinned to the wall within my embrace, there was no escape.

My mouth stayed latched onto her breast as I used my left hand to massage her right breast before painfully squeezing it.

Her small fists pounded on the tops of my shoulders. "It hurts! Stop! Stop!"

When I finally released her nipple it glowed the same gorgeous bright pink as her lips. I couldn't wait to punish her pussy as well, to see if I could get the color to match.

She sobbed. "Why did you do that? It hurt."

I kissed the top of her breast, then closer to her swollen and throbbing nipple. "I did it because it would hurt, baby. That was the point."

Her shoulders shook as she cried.

I flicked her sore nipple with my tongue and she stiffened.

"Now ask daddy to kiss it and make it better."

"Please don't touch me. It hurts."

"That's not what I asked you to say. Do you need another lesson?"

"No!" Her fingers tightened on my upper arms. "Please daddy, kiss it and make it better," she whimpered.

After placing a gentle kiss on her nipple, I shifted my attention to her left breast.

Her body trembled with fear just from the swirl of the tip of my tongue around the areole, increasing her dreaded anticipation of the pain.

This time, after pursing my lips to softly blow on her

vulnerable nipple to perk it up and prepare it for my bite, I paused to cast a glance at her terrified stare.

Letting my lips slightly graze her breast, I said, "Do you need me to continue with the pain step, or are you ready to give me some answers?"

The question was slightly misleading.

It implied the pain phase was over.

Knowing I'd missed an opportunity earlier to have my cock deep inside her pussy to feel the vibrations while she screamed, we were definitely not done with the pain phase.

Especially since there wasn't a doubt in my mind my *angioletto* would likely give her new daddy a reason to bend her over his knee for misbehaving before too long.

Yes, I could definitely get into this new *interrogation* role.

Tears streamed down her flushed cheeks. "I'll tell you anything you want to know, daddy."

"*Brava ragazza.*"

I lowered her feet to the floor as I reached for my zipper.

That was the moment someone kicked her apartment door in.

CHAPTER 7

BENEDICT

*B*efore she could scream and let the intruder know of her presence I covered her mouth with my palm. "Not one sound," I warned.

All glimmers of copper were gone from her eyes; now they were a dark, chocolate brown as her gaze swept from me to the bedroom curtains which barely concealed us and back.

Leaning in close, I whispered in her ear, directing her to crouch low between the bureau and the corner, and to not move until I came and got her.

As I reached for my gun and turned to face the threat, she whispered back while yanking up her bra. "Shouldn't I just hide under the bed?"

With an angry scowl, I gestured with the barrel of the gun to the corner next to the bureau. "Don't question me, little one."

I did not have time to explain to her all the reasons why hiding under the bed was the worst option because it was not an adequately defensible position and had limited visibility.

After a quick assessment through the break in the curtains, I waltzed into the main area of Liliana's apartment, tucking my gun into its holster.

Relaxing a hip against the kitchen counter, I smirked. "Three of you? Good, I was worried this was going to be boring."

Each of them was dressed in head-to-toe black, including balaclava head wraps obscuring all but their eyes.

One look told me they weren't professional "button men"—made men designated as hit men—for Dante Agnello. More like a couple of lowly thugs hoping to make their bones within the outfit and become *soldati*.

It was the shoes that gave them away. No respectable button man would wear expensive, woven Italian leather loafers to a fucking hit job. You'd never get the blood out of them.

The question is, why are they here for Liliana if she was operating under Dante's orders?

I knew Dante Agnello and his outfit was involved with this whole mess.

The difficulty was, when I got involved, things tended to get—bloody.

So, a hunch wasn't good enough. I needed proof.

It was my insistence on absolute certainty that had always made me a valuable asset and why certain international organizations, including my own government, chose to overlook my methods.

"Step aside, *nannu*. We're here for the girl."

Nannu. The Sicilian word for grandpa, not the mainland Italian version, *nonno*.

They were definitely Dante's men.

I laid a hand over my heart. "Aw, I don't know what is

more precious. Your cute ninja costumes or the fact that you think I'd be thrown by you calling me names."

One of them raised his gun to within a few inches of my forehead. "Shut up, *vecchio uomo*. You're outgunned. There's nothing you can do."

Old man. Even cuter. I'd have them all crying for their mommies in three steps.

The corner of my mouth lifted. "I disagree. First, I'm going to break your arm." I nodded to the man standing behind him. "Then I'm going to break his femur, followed by his jaw."

I gave the third man closest to the door a scathing once-over. "You are going to run squealing to whatever mate you have waiting outside in a getaway car."

The first man sneered. "That's bull—"

"You're here for me?"

Turning sharply, rage clouded my vision at the sight of Liliana.

Not only had she deliberately disobeyed me, but she was also standing there in her fucking bra, displaying her beautiful tits to these assholes.

The fact that her arms were crossed, mostly covering her chest, did nothing to cool my wrath.

It was irrational and completely out of character, but the blood in my veins pounded out a primal beat of *mine, mine, mine*.

The idea that another man, let alone *three* fucking men, were staring at my possession with their eyes bulging made me want to tear their faces off.

Storming over to the kitchen table, I swiped my wool coat and swept it over her shoulders, covering her. As I closed the lapels over her front, I growled, "Just wait until I get you alone, babygirl."

Her eyes widened as her throat contracted on a swallow.

She was afraid.

Good.

She should be.

The moment I took care of these idiots, I was going to bend her over, flip up her skirt, and tan her pretty ass with my belt.

Goon Number One cleared his throat. "Signorina Fiore? Dante Agnelli sent us to give you safe passage back to Sicily."

Agnelli?

Could be nothing, but how did you get the Don, the *Capo dei Capi*, the boss of bosses of a major mafia outfit's name, the one you supposedly were hoping to impress, wrong?

We responded together. "She's not interested," I stated at the same time Liliana said, "Thank you. I'll get my things."

Pivoting so I could both keep an eye on the intruders while addressing Liliana's apparent confusion, I said, "You're not going anywhere."

Her knuckles were white where she clasped the lapels of my coat to her chest so tightly. "You are hardly in a position to object. You are outnumbered. Besides, it's not up to you. I'm going."

I rubbed the back of my neck. I really was over all this crap. I was past due calling Matteo to get a status update on my brother's condition. Then I wanted a meal, a bottle of wine, a good fuck, and a warm bed. In that order.

And whether she liked it or not, I had decided two of those things required Liliana to be at my pleasurable beck and call.

My fingers dug into her upper arm. "The hell you are. Are you so fucking naive you don't recognize a ham-fisted kill squad? They are not here to offer you safe passage for a job well done. You are a loose end."

SEDUCTION OF THE PATRIARCH

The pretty blush I had put on her cheeks only moments before vanished as the color drained from her face. Again she looked between me and the other men.

Although I had given her absolutely no reason, quite the opposite in fact, to trust me, I found it strangely irritating she was even hesitating in choosing me over these assholes.

She adjusted the collar of my coat, shifting her fist up higher to her throat as she shook her head. "I don't believe you. They are my countrymen. You aren't. And you are the one who has threatened to kill me, not them."

Technically I had threatened her with everything but.

Semantics.

"Countrymen? You're Italian!"

The men to my right chucked each other on the shoulder as they laughed.

Liliana waved a dismissive hand in my face, her lips twisted in disgust. "I'm Sicilian. Only an arrogant Italian wouldn't understand the difference."

Che due coglioni!

Before I could respond, she bolted past me into the arms of the first goon, who slung a possessive arm over her shoulders, missing her momentary wince as he caught her hair.

The second goon pointed his gun at me. "What are you going to do now, *vecchio uomo?*"

I cupped my right fist in my left hand and cracked my knuckles. "Same plan. Except now, I'm going to break your femur and jaw first. Then I'll take care of your idiot friend. Breaking his arm is no longer painful enough now that he's touched what's mine."

When the man turned to comment to his companions, I struck.

He wasn't even worth the trouble of a bullet.

First, I swept his leg, knocking him to the floor. I then stepped on his right wrist, disabling his gun hand as I raised my left leg.

The femur is the strongest bone in the human body. It takes four thousand newtons of force to break it. Fortunately, a man of my size has a stomp of over six thousand newtons.

With that, I slammed my booted foot down on his upper thigh, close to the hip joint, aiming for the greater trochanter, the neck of the femur, its weakest point.

Goon number two screamed in agony as he doubled over and vomited what looked like carbonara all over the tiles.

I grimaced. "Hurts, doesn't it? I hear it's the most painful bone in the body to break."

The man shrieked again which brought up more vomit.

Since I was a man of my word, when he was done puking and had rolled onto his back, I gave him a swift toe kick to the face, breaking his jaw. The upside was he stopped all his caterwauling and passed out.

As expected, goon number three ran out of the apartment like his ass was on fire.

I turned to face the first man, who was clearly rattled by what he had just witnessed, given the way he kept adjusting his grip on his gun.

Not wanting to give my concern away, I studied Liliana out of the corner of my eye.

There was no color in her face.

Even her lips appeared ashen. Her body language screamed abject terror as she kept her wide gaze averted from the goon on the floor and stayed focused on the gun in this other goon's hand. She repeatedly flinched at his slightest twitch.

If you asked me later, I would say I gave a shit because I

needed her alive for my investigation into my brother's attempted murder.

But if you asked me now?

It tore me up inside to see her vulnerable and terrified.

I flexed my fingers, my palm itching to beat the man to a bloody pulp.

The fact that my own actions toward her earlier were merely a distinction without a difference was neither here nor there.

My purpose was just. Theirs was not.

Besides, I never would have truly killed her.

I was certain they had every intention of doing so.

The goon shook his gun at me. "Who the fuck are you, man?"

Progress. I'd rather it be pointed at me than Liliana. "Benedict Cavalieri."

He used the handle of his gun to scratch his head. "What the fuck? You're supposed to be dead." Then he pointed the gun at Liliana. "What the fuck, bitch? He's supposed to be fucking dead."

She pulled herself together enough to wave her hands and say through clenched teeth, "Stop talking!"

My gaze captured her alarmed one. I cleared my throat and mouthed, *Later.*

And there would definitely be a later.

Especially with that little tidbit of information.

For now, I needed to handle our current situation.

Drawing his attention back to me, I said, "Sorry to confuse your already strained intellectual faculties, but you are referring to my brother, Barone."

Frowning, he turned to Liliana. With a head tip in my

direction, he said, "Is he telling the truth? Which one were you—"

"Shut up, you idiot!" cried Liliana.

"Bitch." He lifted his gun and jammed the muzzle between her eyes. "Nobody calls me an idiot!"

Drawing my gun out of its holster, I shouted, "Hey, idiot."

The moment he turned, his gun swinging away, I fired a single shot, catching him between the eyes.

He stayed standing as if nothing happened. Which made sense, his body was probably used to carrying on without his brain anyway. Finally the arm holding the gun dropped lifelessly to his side as he fixed a blank stare on Liliana.

She stood there facing him, remarkably silent.

I was almost a little proud at how well she was taking all the violence. Truth be told, it created more questions than it answered about her life and background.

Then the goon coughed, splattering her face and chest with blood, before crumpling at her feet.

She raised her hands to her face but then stopped. Her mouth dropped open, her chest rising and falling several times before she sucked in a long breath.

I knew what that meant.

The silence was over.

As I went to reach for her, two more men stormed through the door, guns drawn.

Apparently warned by the spineless one.

Something was off. Five, possibly six, men, assuming there's a driver?

To kill one defenseless woman?

They each fired off several rounds.

Glass shards and splintered wood rained down on us both.

Liliana screamed as I lunged to protect her.

Stretching my left arm around her back, I curled my body over Liliana's huddled form to shield her while I slipped my right arm across my middle and returned fire.

Clearly not expecting an armed response, the shooters were caught off guard.

Not wasting the opportunity, I shifted out of the way and yanked a kitchen chair down onto its side. I pressed down on Liliana's shoulder, pushing her onto the floor. Using the edge of my boot, I prodded her hip, shoving her under the table. "Stay out of sight until I tell you to come out."

With a kick, I sent the chair sliding along its side, blocking her from view just as the second man regrouped to peek out from behind the front door he was using as a cover to return fire.

Unfortunately for him, this was an old apartment building in the *Quartiere San Lorenzo.* The exterior doors were made of oak not steel, no more than five centimeters thick.

I raised my gun and aimed at the first panel, the thinnest part of the door. A bullet would easily travel through five to seven centimeters, especially from this close distance. I fired once.

There was a grunt, then a thud, confirming the man hit the floor.

The other man fired off a few wayward shots as he ran down the hallway, yelling into his mobile phone.

Kicking the kitchen chair aside, I wrapped my hand around Liliana's wrist and pulled her out from under the table. "We're leaving."

She dragged her heels. "Wait. Stop."

I rounded on her. "Are you kidding me with this shit, babygirl? They haven't given up. They are coming back with reinforcements. We need to leave. Now."

Her forearms tightened against her ribcage as her fingers curled into fists. "I need a minute to think."

"There is nothing to think about. They came here to kill you. I'm your only option to get out of here alive."

Her head shook violently, rejecting my statement as she jammed her finger into my chest. "*You're* here to kill me too! You put a gun in my mouth and said you were going to kill me! I can't trust you!"

Not giving a damn about the splatters of blood across her cheeks and chest, I wrapped my hand around her neck and yanked her against my chest. "Haven't you figured it out yet, *angioletto*? I'm not going to kill you. I'm going to fuck you. The gun was just practice."

Taking advantage of her shocked gasp, I slammed my mouth down on hers, allowing myself a quick taste before breaking free and dragging her out into the night.

CHAPTER 8

LILIANA

*T*his was madness.

No, it was worse. If it was madness, at least I would have the sanctuary of an unrestrained mind, incapable of understanding or reason.

Pulling back with all my weight, I cried out. "Wait! My purse!"

"Leave it."

He continued to drag me over the threshold and down the narrow hallway.

"I can't leave it. I have no money, no phone. What about clothes?"

He cast an arrogant smirk over his shoulder. "You don't need any of those things with me."

I caught his double meaning but chose to ignore it.

Before we reached the enclosed spiral staircase at the end of the hall, Benedict stopped and raised his palm.

I held my breath.

Angry voices and the sound of boots on the stairs.

Reaching for my hand, he pivoted and raced back toward my apartment.

Instead of going inside, we moved several doors down.

Without even bothering to knock, he took one step back and kicked the heavy door in.

The man sitting at his kitchen table was so shocked he fell out of his chair, spilling wine down the front of his shirt while filling the air around him with a stream of colorful curses.

Benedict pulled me inside and slammed the door shut. As he scanned the interior, he reached into his back pocket and absentmindedly pulled out a money clip.

Peeling off three crisp one-hundred-euro bills he glared at the man. "We weren't here, right?"

The man snatched up the bills and tucked them into the front pocket of his short-sleeved shirt. "I didn't see anything."

Benedict gave him a quick nod. "Balcony?"

The man gestured with his head. "Just past the curtain."

Benedict reached down, righted the man's chair, and clapped his hand on his shoulder. "Finish your dinner. Anyone comes by, you—"

The man said, "—know nothing."

Benedict patted his shoulder. "Good man."

"Anything for the Cavalieris, signor. We are all praying for Don Cavalieri."

I shouldn't have been surprised he was recognized as a Cavalieri. Only fear had kept me from recognizing him immediately as one myself.

At the mention of Barone, my stomach twisted, sending bile rising in the back of my throat.

I lowered my eyes, feeling Benedict's gaze on me but refusing to meet it.

Pounding boots in the hallway cut the rest short.

Benedict wrapped his hand around my upper arm and pulled me through the curtain and into the man's rather messy bedroom.

He moved to the window. After several tries, he couldn't get the crusty old window to open.

Leaning forward, he ordered, "Shield your eyes."

I turned away with a hand to my eyes, while peeking between my fingers as Benedict shoved his elbow through the glass.

He then used the barrel of his gun to knock the remaining shards of glass out of the frame.

After yanking a corner of the blanket from the bed to cover the part we would be climbing through, he turned to me. "I'm going to climb through first. Then I'll help you step through. Be careful of the glass."

I backed up a step. "Why are you doing this? Really?"

"What?"

I flung my arm to the side. "You heard him. Your brother. The shooting. Everything."

He placed a hand under my chin and stared deeply into my eyes.

For one irrational moment, I thought he was going to say something comforting. I was wrong.

"Baby, you have two options. Your pretty ass follows me through that window willingly. Or I coldcock you and carry you through it. What's it going to be?"

I blinked. "I'll follow you."

He kissed me on the forehead. "Good girl."

For a large man, he moved with surprising speed and agility. Seconds later, he was through the window and reaching back through it for me.

There were raised voices in the other room.

To his credit, the man was holding them off with some impressive lying.

"Eyes on me, little one. Give me your hand."

Clutching his oversized coat to my throat, I slipped my hand in his and swung my leg over the sill, grateful at least for the protection of the thick suede of my boots that rose up to just over my knees, even if I was wearing a skirt with only my bra.

Internally I shook my head for the thousandth time. I couldn't believe I was so rash as to step into that mess without first thinking to put a shirt back on.

Mother Superior would be scandalized at my wanton behavior.

I was just so worried one of those idiots was going to blurt something stupid and incriminating out in front of Benedict. And then of course, they up and did anyway.

He pulled me through the window onto the narrow, rusted iron balcony.

I placed my palm against the brick exterior of the building. "Are you sure this is safe?"

"Not in the least."

"Wait, what?"

He turned his back as he used his boot to give the equally rusted ladder a firm kick. The movement caused the entire balcony to shift and groan.

I let out a cry and scraped my nails against the brick, trying to cling to the side of the building.

He called over his shoulder. "Hold on."

"To what?" I fired back. The windowsill was the only option, but it was covered in jagged pieces of glass, the corner of the blanket having slipped off as we stepped through.

After another kick and another terrifying sway of the balcony, the ladder dislodged and fell toward the ground, clanging and rattling the entire way.

Venturing a glance over the rail, I realized he wasn't lying earlier, the ladder stopped an entire story before the ground. "It didn't reach. What are we going to do now?"

He swung a leg over the rail opening and stepped onto the first rung of the ladder. "I'll go first and then catch you."

The man wasn't human.

He didn't even carefully step down the ladder rungs like a normal person with a healthy fear of a super shady ladder that was probably last used in the eighteenth century. He pulled his shirt cuffs over his hands and slid down it like a fireman's pole.

When he got to the end, he leaped the final four meters as if it were nothing.

After he was on the ground he stretched up his arms. "Come on."

Loud voices and shouts came from deep inside the apartment.

I crept close to the ladder but hesitated. "What about all you said about the liver and spleen and broken legs and fatality rates?"

"That won't happen. I'll catch you. You have to start down the ladder. We don't have much time."

After wrapping his coat as securely as possible around my middle, I placed one foot on the first rung and pushed my foot forward until my boot heel locked against the metal bar.

After a deep breath and a supreme effort not to look down, I made my way down several rungs.

"Keep going. Keep going. You're doing great, baby."

My lips pursed as I called out, "You're not looking up my skirt are you?"

There was a long pause. "What answer will get you down the ladder the fastest?"

Before I could reach back to tuck my skirt between my legs, one of the men chasing us poked his head through the window.

"Oh no!"

He disappeared back inside, but then his leg and arm reappeared.

"They're coming!" I screamed.

"Focus on the ladder. One foot after the other."

I was staring so anxiously at the man crawling out onto the balcony that my foot slipped. I slid over a meter before I was able to grab onto one of the rungs.

My heart was pounding so loudly in my chest, I couldn't even hear Benedict scolding me to pay attention.

Shaking, I made my way down a few more rungs before my focus was once more drawn up to the balcony.

My mouth opened but the only thing that came out was a garbled, choking scream—the streetlight shown on the vicious grimace of the man looming over me at the top of the ladder, a gun pointed directly at me in his outstretched hand.

My forehead pressed against the cold iron and I squeezed my eyes shut, bracing for the death shot.

When the loud report of the gunshot came, my entire body jerked in response.

I waited.

Nothing.

SEDUCTION OF THE PATRIARCH

I heard it took a moment for your body to realize you'd been shot, because of adrenaline.

I waited another breath.

Still nothing.

I looked up in time to see the man collapse forward over the railing. His sightless eyes staring at me, blood dripping onto my head from his open head wound.

Risking a glance down over my shoulder, I saw Benedict replacing his gun in his holster and stretching his arms back up, ready to catch me.

A dangling corpse with only half a face that could suddenly tumble over the railing and take me out at any moment was a surprisingly good motivator.

With no more hesitation, I made my way down the remaining rungs until I was dangling precariously high over the ground.

"Jump."

"What if you don't catch me?"

"I'll catch you."

"What if you don't?"

"I will."

"You might not!"

"Baby, jump. Now!"

"You tried to kill me! You could let me fall on purpose!"

His frustrated sigh was caught on the icy December wind. "True."

I tightened my grip on the sides of the iron ladder. "What?"

"Then again, if I let you fall, I won't be able to fuck you from behind because your legs will be broken."

I clenched my teeth. "I'm not having sex with you."

"Agree to disagree," he called up.

"Will you still catch me if I don't—"

Before I could finish, the balcony creaked and swayed again as another stream of blood splattered down my back, some of it oozing inside the coat collar. "Ewwwwww."

In my disgust, I let go of the ladder and fell through the air.

Benedict easily caught me, cradling me like a baby in his strong arms.

For half a second, we just stared at each other.

His lips curled. "Told you so."

My eyes narrowed. "I'm still not having se—"

Tires screeched as headlights appeared at the end of the alley.

He set me on my feet, but I grabbed at his forearms. "The police?"

He shook his head. "Those aren't the headlights of a Lamborghini supercar. That's a classic Lancia Fulvia Sport Zagato."

He grabbed my hand and raced in the other direction down the alley.

"You can tell that just from the headlights?" I called out breathlessly, running to try to keep up while at the same time gathering up the long ends of his coat.

"They are very distinctive headlights."

"So is that bad?"

He looked over his shoulder as he pushed me ahead of him. "Only if you think the car chasing us having superior handling, a lightweight body, and exceptional speed is a bad thing."

We burst out onto the graffiti-covered side street—*Via dei Sardi*. As this was Rome and it was only about nine in the evening there were still countless people bustling about.

I yanked on his sleeve. "Do you have a car? There won't be any taxis in this part of town."

He looked down at me. With a frown, he closed his jacket more firmly over my chest. "It's on the other side of the building, besides, the last thing you want is a car in an urban car chase." He then pulled his money clip out again and selected a wad of bills and pressed them into my palm. "Hold this."

Panic squeezed my lungs. Was he ditching me? At first I couldn't wait to escape him and now the thought of getting through this alone without his comforting strength by my side made me want to curl up into a ball and cry.

"Are you leaving me?"

Without a response, he stepped into the road, directly into the path of an oncoming silver Vespa. Holding out his right arm, he clotheslined the driver, sending him flying off the luxury moped. Benedict reached out and grabbed the left handle before the Vespa raced off driverless into traffic.

He straddled the seat and called out to me. "Get on."

Stunned, I didn't know what else to do but obey. Calling out a quick, "Sorry," to the driver, I hiked up Benedict's wool coat and my skirt and straddled the padded leather seat, scooting up close behind him and wrapping my arms around his solid middle.

The driver popped up and stormed toward us, gesturing wildly as he shouted through his helmet.

Benedict started the engine up and shouted over the noise. "Give him the money."

I waved to get the guy's attention, then pressed the bills into his hand.

With him distracted, Benedict reached over and snatched the helmet off his head. "We're going to need this."

Before the man could start shouting again, the Vespa

surged forward just as the car emerged from the alley. As Benedict wove into the standstill traffic, he held the helmet over his shoulder. "Put this on."

"I don't need a helmet."

"Dammit, Liliana, do as you're fucking told and put on the helmet," he growled.

Startled, I shoved the helmet over my head, throwing up the visor and shouting, "It smells like someone bathed a wet dog in cheese."

"Hold on," was his only response.

My attempt to touch him only as little as possible went right out the window the moment he cleared *Viale dello Scalo S. Lorenzo* and we turned right onto *Via di Porta Maggiore*, just as there was a break in traffic.

We surged forward on the Vespa.

I screamed and clutched at his middle.

As fast as we were going, a hesitant glance over my shoulder after hearing several car horns and tire screeches showed the Lancia Fulvia directly behind us.

I tapped his shoulder and yelled, "They're behind us!"

He squeezed my knee to signal he heard.

There was absolutely no reason—none whatsoever, especially given the life-or-death chase I was currently in the middle of and the catastrophic mess I still hadn't escaped from with Benedict—that my body would react to the intimacy of his hand on my knee.

What was wrong with me? Everything about this was sinful and immoral.

Still, the man was literally the living, breathing definition of the lesser of two evils for me right now.

He was the man who was only *currently* less likely to kill

me *right now* and that was *only* because I hadn't told him everything he needed to know.

And because he wanted to have sex with me. I needed to ignore that small voice in my head.

Thankfully, Benedict making a lunatic left-hand-turn maneuver at the last minute and almost getting us pancaked by a lorry distracted me from that traitorous thought.

He hopped the curb, sending several pedestrians diving for cover as he raced through the open gate of the *Piazza Vittorio Emanuele II*.

"What are you doing?"

He avoided a group of tourists taking evening selfies in front of the strangely macabre central fountain of three men wrestling a dolphin and an octopus by Sicilian sculptor Rutelli, which looked even more grotesque at night.

Just as I breathed a sigh of relief, we swerved to miss a running dog, only to clip the side portion of an ancient rock wall.

I raised my arm and pointed behind me, shouting, "That was the *Porta Alchemica!*"

The rational part of me knew that Egyptian cult spirits were not going to emerge through the solid rock door and drag me through the portal for disturbing their memorial, but then again, when your soul was stained with as many misdeeds and sins as mine was … it was dangerous to tempt God … any god.

Emerging on the other side of the piazza, we picked up *Via Napoleone III*, the car chasing us nowhere in sight.

He made a sharp left onto *Via Rattazzi* which had me tightening my hold on his waist as I wrapped my arms more fully around him.

The man's abs were a solid wall of muscle!

As I was about to pull away, his warm hand captured my wrist and held my arm in place.

After a sudden right onto *Via Carlo Alberto* and a left on *Via dell'Esquilino*, I was hopelessly lost. I did not know Rome well enough to keep up with all of his twists and turns.

When I realized we were in view of the Pantheon, I tapped him on the shoulder, about to ask him where we were going, when a black sedan screeched onto the street from an alley a few blocks ahead of us. There was another round of car horns and the shriek of tires.

I turned to see a second black sedan emerge from a side street behind us.

Somehow I didn't think it was a coincidence.

Benedict snatched my arm and wrapped it more firmly around his waist before shouting, "Don't let go!"

After that everything was a chaotic, intense blur of cars, close calls with pedestrians, famous Roman monuments, dark alleys and side streets, the occasional piazza, and the shouts and annoyance of various tourists and vendors before we finally lost both black cars and pulled up along a tall rock wall along an eerily silent, tree-lined street.

We were still in Rome and yet somehow it felt like we'd left the city behind. There was an eerie, unnatural calm.

Benedict got off the Vespa and helped me alight.

With a start, I realized there was a guardsman's portico carved into the rock wall. A shadow detached itself and stepped toward us.

I inched closer to Benedict who, once again, closed the front of his coat over my front before wrapping his arm around my lower back.

As the man stepped closer, a corner of the black cloak he

was wearing to ward off the winter chill was caught by the wind and flipped up.

There was a flash of the distinctive bright orange, blue and red uniform of the Pontifical Swiss Guard.

What the hell?

I mean ... what the heck?

Benedict had brought me to the Vatican.

CHAPTER 9

LILIANA

I shifted back a step.

Without even glancing down at me, Benedict's arm tightened around my waist as he continued his low conversation with the guardsman.

Having absolutely no idea what they were saying, I assumed I was having a stroke from the shock and stress of everything that had happened in the last few hours.

After all, I did have the blood of not one but *two* men currently drying to an itchy crust on my skin, so there was that. Then there was the whole being shot at and having multiple people trying to kill me thing.

It was fair to say that would rattle anyone, even if you took out the death-defying car chase through Rome only to wind up at the Vatican.

And of course … Benedict Cavalieri.

He should be in his own category.

Benedict, murder, then mayhem, in that order of apocalyptic catastrophes.

It took a moment to realize they were casually chatting in Latin, because of course they were. Because that was what one did when starting up a conversation with someone from the Pope's private security force in the middle of the night at a secret backdoor entrance to the Vatican. Everyone knew that.

Was it possible to actually feel the moment a blood vessel burst in your brain from overwhelming fear and stress?

My breaths came fast and shallow as my vision shimmered with waves and white sparks. The edges darkened.

Fearing I would pass out and be even more vulnerable than I was now, I broke free of Benedict's grasp and took off running down the dark street.

He was after me in less than a second.

It was truly terrifying how such a large man could move with such lightning speed, and so silently.

Wearing his wool coat had been a mistake. "Liliana, stop!" The thick collar of the coat made an easy target, his hand grasping it and tugging.

Barely hearing him through the blood pounding in my ears, I stretched my arms back and let the oversized coat fall from my shoulders and kept running.

Each step of my heeled boots on the cobblestones jarred my leg muscles like a hammer and risked a broken ankle, but I had no choice.

Before I even reached the end of the street, Benedict had grasped a fistful of my hair and wrenched me backward against his chest. His arm clamped around my waist like an iron band.

Using the unmovable wall of his frame for leverage, I pushed back against him and kicked my legs out, reaching my arms up and clawing at his neck and face. "Let go!"

"Stop fighting, you little hellcat!"

SEDUCTION OF THE PATRIARCH

"No! I'm not going to let you leave me to die in some hidden Vatican dungeon!"

He released my hair and snatched at my wrist. "I'm not going to warn you again."

My nails contacted skin, my scream echoing down the street.

He covered my mouth with his palm as he dragged me deeper into the shadows of the rock wall, back toward the shady entrance to the Vatican.

I sank my teeth into the soft flesh of his palm.

He growled but refused to remove his hand.

My teeth latched on harder, until the coppery tang of blood and salt hit my tongue.

He tightened his arm around my ribs, constricting my lungs. "Take your pound of flesh now, *angioletto*. And I'll take mine when I get you inside," he ground out.

Madonna santa!

His dark threat chilled me to the core.

With a gasp, I released my teeth from his palm. He still refused to remove his hand. Instinctively, my tongue flicked out over my dry lips, catching his skin as well.

His fingers tightened on my cheeks but didn't distract from my distinct awareness of the hard press of his shaft on my lower back where he crowded against me.

Another low, grumbling growl vibrated from deep inside his chest.

I pressed my lips between my teeth and swallowed as my stomach twisted.

Maybe there was still a chance of escape. He was a beast from hell, surely he wouldn't be able to cross the threshold onto the consecrated grounds of the Vatican?

Refusing to release me, we returned to the guardsman and

the secret gate, Benedict one-handedly wrestling the coat back on me. I'm sure we made an even more chaotic sight than when we first arrived on the Vespa, but the guardsman showed absolutely no reaction.

Still, I had to try.

The moment Benedict released his grip, I cried out to the guard. *"Please, I beseech you in the name of all that is holy! I've been kidnapped by this sinner!"*

I thought perhaps tossing in some Biblical language would help my case.

I was wrong.

The man's eyes didn't even so much as flicker in my direction.

He continued his conversation with Benedict as if a half-naked woman hadn't just thrown herself at his feet and begged him for help.

With a tip of his hat, he turned and used a massive brass key to open the arched oak door and waved Benedict and me through. A push from behind sent me stumbling over the threshold into the stone hallway.

I tried to dig my heels in, but my ankle rolled when the heel on my right boot snapped off. With a clenched jaw, I ignored the amused chuckle behind me and hobbled a few steps forward.

The passageway had an elaborate, mosaic tile floor featuring various scenes of mythic beasts devouring naked humans surrounded by flames and dancing demons, under a high stone buttress ceiling. The heavy torches in the iron brackets were unlit; instead, hidden recessed lighting gave the space the dim, candlelit feel of a traditional dungeon, yet with a contemporary twist.

A dark figure appeared.

Logically, I knew it was from a side door hidden along the passageway.

In my fevered brain, I was convinced he'd emerged from a hole in the floor amid a cloud of devilish smoke.

The man looked like Lucifer before his fall.

Benedict was tall and ruggedly handsome in that "I've done dangerous stuff so don't piss me off" sort of way.

This man was sinfully handsome in that "power and money corrupts in a depraved" sort of way.

His appearance was all the more shocking given the black Roman cassock he was wearing. Judging by the fuchsia piping along the shoulder cape and down the sides, he was a high-ranking chaplain to His Holiness.

The devil in priest's garb bowed his head to me. Shockingly the corner of his mouth lifted in what could only be interpreted as a sensual smile, his dark gaze traveling over me from the top of my head to the tip of my broken-heeled boots.

His look was decidedly *unholy*.

He reached for my hand. When I instinctively lifted mine in response, Benedict's heavy coat fell open. His eyebrow rose when he caught sight of my purple bra.

He bent his head and kissed the back of my hand, flashing me a quick wink. "Good evening *bella ragazza*, the Reverend Monsignor Diamanti very humbly at your service."

Diamanti?

The man was a Diamanti?

Of *The* Diamantis? As in the House of Diamanti?

Oh my, he was the infamous Arcangelo Diamanti!

The youngest son of the Diamanti family who had been forced into the priesthood. Like most ancient family bloodlines, there was a tradition: the first son inherited the business, the second entered the military, and the third the clergy, whether he liked it, or was fit for it, or not.

Rumors were Arcangelo was definitely *not* fit as a man of the cloth.

I blinked. Apparently the gossip was true.

There was a low, foul curse as Benedict snatched my hand away from Monsignor Diamanti.

It was then I realized I hadn't closed the coat yet.

With a gasp, I crossed my arms over my chest, just as Benedict shoved me behind him, blocking the reverend monsignor's view.

Benedict stepped close until he was chest to chest with the monsignor. "I will snap your neck and toss your body onto the bones of your ancestors to rot."

My hand twisted into the back of Benedict's shirt, tensely waiting for the monsignor's response, afraid to even peek around Benedict's arm.

After a moment, he responded. "So it's like that?"

Benedict's arm tensed as his fingers curled into a fist. "It's like that."

Monsignor Diamanti stroked his left hand down his waist rosary, which looked to be made of precious black pearls. Stopping to suggestively roll his index finger and thumb over one smooth pearl, he captured my gaze past Benedict's shoulder, intoning, "Precious possessions are locked in a vault. Jewels that are still available to be purchased are charmingly displayed."

Wait. Did the reverend monsignor just call me a whore?

Even more perplexing, is Benedict getting jealous over me?

He responded to Monsignor Diamanti's veiled comment. "Consider this jewel a cursed blood diamond and stay the fuck away."

Seriously? Now I'm a curse? I guess that answers the jealousy question.

I snapped, "I'm right here! And I don't have to take this from either of you!"

With a huff, I turned to storm out but only managed to hobble a few uneven steps on my broken heel before Benedict hooked his warm hand around my neck and swept me back under his arm against his side. "You're not going anywhere."

Arcangelo's gaze traveled over me again as he stroked his jaw. "I do love when they have some fight in them."

Benedict's arm pressed me harder against his side, shielding me further from the monsignor's view as he threatened in a lighter tone. "Keep it up and I'll toss you in an unmarked heretic's grave just out of spite."

Breaking the tension, the monsignor laughed. "I forgot how possessive you Cavalieris can be over your sweet treasures. Speaking of which, tell Cesare I will consider it a personal offense if he lets that hack priest from his backwater village baptize his son."

Benedict nodded sagely. "I'll let Milana know you'd be honored to christen her future *daughter* when she's born."

Laughing again, Arcangelo hugged him before resting his hands on his shoulders. "It is good to see you, Benedict. I only wish it was under better circumstances. Have you any news of Barone?"

My shoulders tensed as I tried to pull back.

Benedict kept his grasp firm before responding to the monsignor. "Later."

I lowered my gaze, my cheeks flaming with guilt and shame. I didn't need to look up to know both of them were looking at me.

Arcangelo cleared his throat then turned to walk deeper

into the passageway. "I've instructed my staff to prepare your usual room in my private quarters. I will be otherwise occupied this evening. Although I trust you won't be starved for … *entertainment* … in my absence."

The monsignor sent another intensely inappropriate look at me over his shoulder.

I clutched at the lapels of the oversized wool coat, closing them tightly over my throat as I leaned in closer to Benedict's hip.

Arcangelo's lip curled in a smirk before continuing to speak to Benedict. "As usual no one knows you are here except for my personal staff and any inquiries from the police will be ignored."

As usual?

Did Benedict make a habit of hiding from the Rome police behind the walls of the Vatican?

At the end of the hall, another guard sprang to attention and pushed open two polished oak doors which revealed a massive chamber filled with stunning fifteenth century frescoes.

As Benedict pulled me inside, I stared in awe at the decorated walls and up at the ceiling.

The frescoes changed from bright gold, vivid crimson, and azure depictions of the Old Testament with Abraham, angels, and the female muses of art, music, astronomy, and geometry, to macabre scenes of pagan sacrifice dancing around a central ceiling medallion.

It was as if we went back in time and entered a medieval hall.

The worn stone floors were covered with expensive, overlapping Persian rugs. At the far end of the room an emerald marble fireplace was flanked by snarling dragons protecting a massive log already slowly being consumed by bright orange flames that sizzled and popped.

Next to it was a carefully polished brass plaque engraved in bold letters which read, *Sala delle Arti Liberali. Frescoes painted by Pinturicchio. Commissioned by Pope Alexander VI.*

I swallowed past the lump in my throat.

We were in the infamous Borgia apartments.

The private rooms of Pope Alexander VI, otherwise known as a member of the noble Borgia family and father of the infamous poisoner, Lucrezia.

The walls closed in on me as I imagined all the treacherous deeds these deceptively splendid rooms had witnessed.

Every deadly sin had been worshipped.

Every sacrament broken in these six chambers.

No wonder the rooms had been ordered sealed centuries ago, but apparently, with the Diamanti influence, Arcangelo had claimed them for his own private use.

No doubt adding to their already tainted legacy.

Despite the cozy warmth of the room, I shivered and gripped Benedict tighter.

He glanced down at me before cutting Arcangelo off. "We'll talk later. For now, I have other matters to attend to."

My cheeks flamed as Arcangelo slanted him an amused look. "Of course. Enjoy attending to those *matters.*"

He turned to leave, and panic seized my chest.

He may be a priest with an infamous reputation, but he was still a priest in the Pope's service, which meant he was bound by God to help me.

Breaking free of Benedict, I ran to Arcangelo.

Kneeling at his feet, I cried out, "Bless me father for I have sinned. Please, I beg you for mercy!"

Arcangelo placed his hand under my chin. "I just bet

you've sinned. I can think of a few ways you can beg me for mercy."

Before I could respond, Benedict snatched me from behind and snarled at the monsignor. "Leave before I make good on my threat."

I watched in horror as the monsignor, my last hope, turned with an amused chuckle and left the chamber.

Then Benedict said, "The only person you're going to be begging for mercy, *angioletto*, is me."

CHAPTER 10

BENEDICT

Throwing her over my shoulder, I carried her through the main chamber.

Past the *Sala del Credo* with its arched lunettes, framed in gold. I ignored the judgmental stares of the twelve apostles as I crossed into the bathroom chamber.

I knew Arcangelo would not have disrespected me by touching Liliana, but still it angered me that I had allowed him to glimpse her half-naked with her gorgeous tits on display.

The woman was covered in blood splatter, with streaks of dirt and rust on what had once been a white skirt from the decrepit balcony I made her climb down. Her hair was a tangled bird's nest of knots and what was left of her eye makeup was smudged around her eyes. What had I heard it called? A smoky eye?

She looked beautiful.

Like a little broken doll that had been left out in the rain and only needed someone to rescue her.

Christ, I needed to get a fucking grip.

This woman was a liar, a murderess, and who knew what else.

It wasn't like me to fall for the honeypot scam, but it ended—now.

Placing her roughly on the marble countertop between two shell-shaped sinks, I pointed a finger at her. "Don't move."

I crossed to the massive tub flanked by marble columns and turned on the silver swan's-neck spigot. Since it was a deep spa tub meant for six people, it would need time to fill.

Testing the water, I made sure it was hot, but not too hot, and pushed in the drain plug so it would fill. I then crossed to the glass-enclosed shower and turned it on.

Returning to Liliana, pleased she had obeyed me, I reached for her leg.

She shifted it to the left and scooted along the slick marble counter. "What are you doing?"

"Taking off your boot."

"Why?"

I snatched her ankle and unzipped the filthy suede boot and tossed it aside. "I'll start with the fact the heel is broken and work my way up from there."

She gripped the top of the other boot as I wrapped my hand around her ankle. "I want them on."

I tugged on the boot. "You can't bathe with your boots on."

She tugged back. "I'm not bathing."

I pushed her hand away and unzipped it. "Yes, you are."

She tried to zip it back up. "No, I'm not."

"Yes, you are." I yanked the boot off and threw it with the other one.

Before she could object, I wrapped both hands around her

slim waist and pulled her off the counter. Spinning her around, I pushed her hair aside and flicked the latch on her bra.

Liliana cried out and lurched forward. She turned on me, holding her unlatched bra over her breasts. "How dare you!"

"The bra goes. So does the skirt and panties."

Her eyes widened as her mouth opened and closed several times.

I nodded. "I'm glad we are in agreement." My arm stretched out and snatched the bra from between her hands and tossed it over my shoulder.

Pressing her back against the bathroom wall, she slid away from me. "You're a monster."

I shrugged. "I've been called worse. The skirt."

Her left arm stayed over her breasts while her right pressed against her middle, protecting her skirt. "No. You can't do this."

I glanced around the room. "Do you see someone here to stop me? God's own man just abandoned you."

Tears filled her eyes. "Please."

"Save it. Those won't work on me. Take off the skirt. Now."

"What are you going to do?"

I gave her body a scathing glance ... and lied.

"Save the innocent act. I need information from you, nothing else."

She grabbed the tiny crucifix around her throat. "It's not some act!"

Not an act?

She didn't honestly expect me to believe she was a virgin?

She really was going down swinging with this whole false narrative she had created around her innocence.

I stalked closer, trapping her against the wall. "You're wasting your time with that bullshit, babygirl. Now are you going to take off that skirt or am I going to tear it off?"

She pushed at my chest. "Don't tear it off! Please. I'll … I'll take it off." Looking around my shoulder she asked, "Is there a robe I can put on?"

"No."

"A towel?"

"No. Take it off."

A blush colored her cheeks. She lowered her gaze and with trembling fingers, spun the filthy skirt around her hips until the back zipper faced front. With slow deliberation, she unfastened the top button and then lowered the zipper.

Her fingers moved at such a methodical, glacier-like pace, I could almost hear the metallic click of the zipper teeth individually. Finally, the skirt slid over her hips to her feet.

Her panties matched her bra, purple silk.

For some strange reason, it pleased me they were not some scrap of sheer lace or worse, a thong. There was something elegant and, fuck me, almost sweetly virginal about a simple piece of unadorned silk.

Not wanting her to see my rising cock pressing against the fabric of my pants, I wrapped my fingers around her upper arm and marched her to the shower.

Standing behind her, I cleared my throat before ordering, "Take off your panties and get in the shower. After you wash off the blood and filth, get in the tub."

She hunched her shoulders as she wrapped both arms around her middle, trying to cover herself. "Why both? Can't I just take a quick shower and get out?"

"No."

She may not know the toll of today's activities on her

body, but I did. She would be better off soaking in a warm tub for a while.

"Do as you're told. Panties, shower, then tub. And don't get out until I tell you to."

A tremor racked her body.

I pulled my fingers into fists at my sides, resisting the urge to yank her back into my embrace.

She was the enemy. She didn't deserve my comfort.

Her thumbs hooked into the waistband of her panties. As she bent over to remove them, the curve of her ass brushed against my erect cock.

I swallowed a groan.

Christ, she was going to be the fucking death of me.

The irony of my having interrogated some of the worst, most dangerous scum on the face of the earth throughout my illustrious career only to have this little slip of a girl be the one to do me in was not lost on me.

Without looking back at me, the moment the scrap of silk hit the marble tiles at her feet, she opened the glass shower door and scurried inside, hissing as the hot stream of water hit her skin.

Satisfied she was taken care of, I took advantage of her momentary distraction to collect her clothes and boots as I made my way out of the bathroom.

She would be extremely unlikely to escape the high, well-guarded walls of the Vatican without my notice, but even less likely with no clothes.

* * *

WITH THE BATHROOM door partially open as a precaution, I took out my mobile phone and dialed Matteo's number.

He answered on the first ring. "I was getting worried."

"There were complications."

"Anything serious?"

I looked at the ajar bathroom door. "Nothing I couldn't handle. How is Barone?"

There was an angry shout in the background then the sound of a metal tray hitting the floor and more angry shouts, followed by Gabriella's unmistakable voice cursing out all of them.

Matteo chuckled. "Already torturing the nurses. Amara threatened to tie him up if he didn't behave. I won't repeat his response, although I'm now scarred for life. Uncle Barone is a freak in bed."

I laughed. "So things are back to normal."

"Pretty much."

After the shared joke, there was a tense silence as the true reality of the situation settled in.

Matteo lowered his voice. I'm sure it was so the women in the room couldn't hear. "So have you found her yet?"

I didn't have to ask him who he meant.

They all knew I had left for Rome to track down Liliana Fiore.

She was our primary lead into who had shot Barone.

We knew she tried to poison Bianca, so it was reasonable to assume she was also involved in his shooting. She was our only way to link this mess to Dante Agnello and his organization.

That was, if Dante was involved, and I was no longer convinced that was the case.

Either way, we couldn't make a move without unequivocally linking him to it, or we would risk trouble with the other mafia families who would be duty bound to avenge

Dante regardless of how they felt about him or their long ties to the Cavalieris.

I looked at the bathroom door again, listening for the running shower.

For the second time that evening, I lied. "No, not yet."

Fuck.

Guilt twisted my gut.

I didn't know why I lied.

Yes, I did. *To protect her.*

From the moment he had been born, it had always been Matteo and me.

His mother was not someone special in my life, nor was I in hers. When she became unexpectedly pregnant with Matteo it had been her intention to leave him with the nuns at a local convent. I couldn't allow that.

For most of his childhood I was nothing more than a shadow, appearing and disappearing at random. The time spent with him was usually tainted with lies and guilt. When I gave that life up, I swore I'd never lie to him again and I kept that promise, until tonight.

Matteo's voice broke through my morbid thoughts. "Do you need me there?"

I gripped the phone harder. "No, I'll be at the winery tomorrow. I need to explain this in person, not over the phone. This may be more convoluted than we first thought. Keep close to Barone for me. Tell the others I'll have information for them soon."

"I will."

With that I hung up and tossed the phone aside with disgust.

I didn't believe her. Not for one goddamn second.

She was guilty as sin.

She may not have shot my brother, but she fucking knew who did or, at the very least, why.

We had been certain Dante was involved, and I wasn't yet completely convinced he wasn't, but the kill squad mispronouncing his name bothered me.

Still, there was no denying she tried to kill Bianca, Enzo's girl, my future niece.

And I just fucking lied to my son to protect her.

The more I repeated it, the angrier I got at myself ... and at Liliana.

CHAPTER 11

LILIANA

Keeping an eye on the slightly ajar door, I sprang naked from the shower and climbed over the high ledge into the tub, sliding along the black marble reclining side into the steaming water. The oval basin was so deep, my toes barely touched the bottom.

After I lifted higher out of the water to recline on the sloping side, I stared at the ceiling. It was a celestial sky fresco with the various dotted outlines of constellations and what looked like pagan symbolism and idolatry decorating the edges.

I slid lower in the tub until the water lapped at my chin and continued to stare at the imposing black marble columns which surrounded the octagon chamber.

It was hard not to imagine I was bathing in some pagan sacrificial temple later converted into a luxury bathroom.

Everywhere I looked was Christian mixed with Pagan, the civilized mixed with the primal.

Having washed all the blood and grime off my skin and

out of my hair, I closed my eyes and let the warm water ease the tension from my muscles.

There were a hundred-thousand things I needed to worry about, including the thousand different ways I could be killed by Benedict, but for now I was going to shut all of that off and soak in this tub. If I didn't, I would curl up in a tiny ball under the water and drown myself out of hopeless despair.

My eyes flew open when I heard the door slam against the wall.

Benedict stormed into the room.

With nothing to cover myself, I slammed my chest against the side wall of the tub. "What are you doing in here?"

He glowered at me as he took a swig from a glass filled with amber liquid, probably either Scotch or whiskey, before slamming it down on the bathroom counter. He then pulled his shirt over his head and kicked off his boots.

Oh no!

"Stop! What are you doing?"

No wonder every time I pushed against his chest it had been like colliding with a wall of bricks. Despite being in his forties, he was clearly in the absolute prime of his life.

The man was a literal human wall of tanned, hard muscle.

And the tattoo ... oh my!

Over his heart was some kind of Christian occult symbol. It was a five-leaf purple passion flower, named for its association with Jesus and the cross. In its center was a triad crown suspended over a bleeding crimson pomegranate.

Was Benedict Cavalieri a member of some occult Vatican group?

Was that why he was allowed on the grounds through a secret entrance?

My mind spun.

It was also impossible to miss the battle wounds and scars.

It added up to one thing. My instincts had been correct.

Benedict Cavalieri was an extremely dangerous and powerful man.

Still without saying a word, he reached for his belt buckle.

With a shriek, I flung myself backward and slammed my back against the other side of the sizable tub, curling my knees up to my chest.

His dark gaze pierced me as he whipped his belt off.

My lungs ached from holding my breath, watching him fold it in half and just stand there.

I couldn't tell if he was contemplating wrapping the belt around my throat and strangling me to death with it ... or something else.

After an eternity, he tossed it aside.

The air left my body in a rush.

Holding my gaze hostage, he reached for the zipper of his pants.

I licked my dry lips. "What ... what are you doing?" I asked again.

Again, he ignored me.

After lowering his zipper, the waistband of his pants slipped down slightly, exposing the dark blue band of his Calvin Klein underwear. His abdomen had that thick band of muscle over his hips that ended ... I forced air back into my lungs when I forgot to breathe.

It was as if he had his hand wrapped around my throat and was controlling my breathing, allowing only enough oxygen to keep me alive, but not enough to keep me from getting dizzy at the sight of him.

He hooked his thumbs into his waistband and lowered both his pants and underwear.

The moment his cock was freed from the constraints of the fabric, the thick shaft bobbed and bounced between his legs.

My eyes widened.

What was that disgusting phrase I never understood about a baby's arm holding an apple?

I get it now.

Kicking his pants aside, he took several determined steps toward me.

I tried to scream but all that came out of my mouth was a squeak.

Then, breaking eye contact, he opened the shower door and stepped inside. Flipping on the faucet, he threw his head back and let a hot stream of water cover his chest and throat.

It took a moment for me to realize he wasn't coming for me.

Even longer for me to process the illogical sense of disappointment and almost-annoyance I felt at his cold indifference. Had I *wanted* him to pick me up and ravish me?

How ridiculous.

How absolutely ludicrous to think that I would want the man who had threatened to kill me to snatch me up in his big, powerful arms and crush me to his hard chest and force another one of those punishing, all-consuming kisses that made me forget my own name on me.

The idea was beyond stupid.

I watched his large, rough hands clasp the same soap I had touched earlier.

Was it weird I was thinking he was now intimately touching something I had touched?

Inwardly I chastised myself. Yes, it was very weird. Sinfully so.

SEDUCTION OF THE PATRIARCH

Spellbound, I stared at his slightly callused palms rubbing around the soap bar over and over again in a slow, rhythmic pulse until a rich, creamy lather foamed over the backs of his hands and dripped down his wrists.

After tossing the soap back in its ceramic dish, he raised his hands to his chest and rubbed them over his neck and chest in sweeping, aggressive circles. The entire time keeping his head tilted back under the spray.

Between the unsettling atmosphere and the glass shower chamber filling with steam, it was as if I were peering at some forbidden mating ritual of a pagan god.

Without even realizing it, I had unbent my knees and drifted from the far side of the tub to kneel along the sloping edge of the tub which faced the shower wall. Two black marble columns flanked the glass of the shower door, reinforcing the macabre imagery of a pagan ritual being performed on a stage for an enraptured audience of one. Me.

Benedict rolled his neck as his hand moved from his shoulder, over his chest, to his abdomen to his … oh. Oh!

I must have made a startled sound because he suddenly opened his eyes.

With a cry, I fell backward in the tub, splashing water over the side as my shoulder hit the faucet and turned the hot water back on.

Coughing up the bathwater I accidentally swallowed, I pushed myself upright to get my face above water and take a breath.

As I did so, his intense, obsidian gaze pierced me to the core.

If the water hadn't already been hot, I was sure the blush on my cheeks from getting caught staring at him would have boiled it.

I'd shifted to turn away as I covered my breasts when Benedict clenched his fist and slammed it against the shower wall, causing a thunderous clap and making the entire glass wall vibrate.

I froze and turned back to face him.

With one hand braced on the glass wall, he kept his narrowed gaze on me, again moving his hand over his abdomen and grasping his erect cock.

Spreading his legs, his fist pulled on his thick shaft until the bulbous head disappeared into his curled fingers and then pushed through again. Each time his hand moved all the way down to the hilt and back, it increased in pace.

His fingers opened and closed, pulsed, and squeezed his flesh, like the pounding heart of some primal beast.

I became lightheaded as I unconsciously matched my breathing to that strong, rhythmic pulsing.

The water in the tub grew hotter, almost too hot to bear. Swirls of steam gently rose around me as I leaned forward, unable to tear my gaze away from the raw sexuality of Benedict pleasuring himself.

We were a pagan theater of the absurd.

Me watching him watching me.

As his hand movement became more violent, fisting his shaft faster and tighter, harder, and harder, I rose on my knees. My hands moved over the tops of my thighs and I swayed, entranced by the heat of the water and the heat in his gaze.

My hand shifted to my inner thigh, the tips of my fingers grazing my ….

The piercing shriek of a thousand glass shards striking the hard surface of the marble-tiled bathroom floor cut through my sensual haze.

Benedict had thrown open the shower door with such fury it shattered.

He stormed toward me like a raging bull.

I screamed and lunged to get out of the tub.

He swung both legs over the high ledge and landed inside, water flying, before snatching me around the waist. Pressing my back against the sloping edge, he went down onto his knees on either side of my hips, pinning me.

The water churned, splashing over my torso and up to my chin, then back to just below my breasts. I raised my arms to fight him off, but he easily captured my wrists and secured them in one hand over my head.

The menacing head of his cock bobbed below my breasts as he leaned over me and ground out, "Time for another lesson from daddy."

CHAPTER 12

BENEDICT

The plan was to shower and calm the fuck down.

It didn't work.

The moment I saw her staring at my cock with her pretty mouth open as if she were begging for a taste, I snapped.

The new plan was to drive my shaft so deeply down her throat she forgot to breathe.

I would use her sweet little body to assuage my anger, lust, and guilt.

I had no fucking idea why I almost died protecting her tonight.

I should be wanting vengeance.

I should have gotten the answers I needed and let that kill squad do my dirty work for me and put a bullet in her head. There was no way to rationalize why she was different from any other interrogation target in my career.

That was a question for later when my cock wasn't hard enough to pound nails.

Now, rational thought wasn't possible.

Now, there was only a driving, feral need to dominate her.

She pulled on her wrists. "Let me go!"

"Not going to happen, babygirl. I'm beyond pissed off right now, so that mouth of yours is either going to talk or suck my cock. Your choice."

Her legs kicked out between mine. "They'll kill me if I tell you anything! I can't!"

I pressed my thighs into hers to stop her kicking. "Can't or won't?"

She pushed her chin out. "Won't."

Leaning up, I thrust my hips toward her mouth. "Let's see if you remember that lesson I taught you."

She turned her head from side to side trying to avoid me, but her lips brushed the head of my cock with her struggles, only spurring me on further.

"You don't understand!"

"I understand just fine. Open that mouth for daddy."

She blushed furiously at my continued use of the kinky word. "Please, I'm not like this! I'm a good girl. I've never—"

Tightening my hold on her wrists, I said, "Well, now you're being daddy's bad girl—and bad girls get punished."

With another stubborn tilt of her chin, she thinned her lips between her teeth and turned her head away.

"Have it your way."

Straightening my knee, I grasped her waist and pulled us both beneath the torrid water.

After a second, I wrenched us above the surface, then wedged her shoulders between my thighs on the sloping wall of the tub.

With her dark hair plastered to her cheeks, neck, and breasts, she opened her mouth to gulp in a gasp of air. "How dare y—"

Taking advantage, I pushed my cock between her lips.

She cried out as her tongue swept under my shaft.

Glaring down at her, I said, "I gave you a choice. Talk or suck. You chose not to talk."

Her mouth tightened around my cock in an effort to force me out of her mouth.

I thrust deeper into her warm, tight throat.

Her shoulders hunched as she gagged.

Then sank her sharp teeth into my shaft just below the head.

Letting out a howl at the sharp sting of pain, I pulled free.

Before she had a chance to gloat, I pulled us both under the water again.

When she came up gasping for air, I swept her wet hair out of her eyes and grabbed her jaw. "Are you going to bite my cock again?"

She coughed and spat out some bathwater. "No."

"No what?"

She sniffed as she swiped water from her eyes. "No, daddy."

Fuck. I didn't think it was possible, but my cock got harder the moment she said daddy.

There was something about forcing her to submit to that kink, knowing how humiliating and wrong she thought it was, that really did it for me.

"*Brava ragazza.* Now are you going to open those lips and suck my cock like a good girl, or do I flip you over and drive it deep into your pretty little ass?"

She shook her head.

I pressed my fingers into her cheeks. "Use your words."

"I'll be a good girl."

I angled my head toward her, cupping my ear.

She brushed back a wet curl that clung to her cheek. "I'll be a good girl, daddy."

With my hands around her ribcage, I flipped our bodies. Resting my back on the slope, I cradled her between my raised knees. Cupping my hand on the back of her skull, I guided her mouth to my cock. "Open your mouth. You've been warned what will happen if you bite my cock again."

Her big eyes blinked several times before she nodded, then her full lips opened as she lowered her mouth over the head of my cock.

It was easily the most erotic thing I had ever seen in my entire life.

My God, I was almost twice this girl's age and yet her sensual innocence, even if it was just an act to throw me off, was affecting me like nothing I had ever experienced before.

And considering the life my jaded ass had lived, and the fact it was a damn miracle lightning hadn't struck me the moment I had stepped.onto consecrated ground, that was no small feat.

She was infuriating and intriguing at the same time.

One moment I wanted to wring her neck, the next I wanted to pull her close and kiss her.

I couldn't decide whether she was a sweet innocent caught in a vicious game and in need of my protection, or a vicious, conniving bitch deserving of punishment.

She hesitantly wrapped her fingers around my shaft and then slipped just the tip of her tongue around the head. It almost made me think she had never sucked a cock before.

After giving her a moment of freedom, I pulled her hand free and used my hand on the back of her head to push her mouth all the way down onto my shaft.

Her eyes widened, her palms pressing against the tops of my thighs in resistance.

"Move your hands under my knees," I commanded.

She whimpered but slipped her arms between my legs, where I pinned them to her sides with my thighs.

As the hot water lapped between her shoulder blades and my calves, I eased my cock deeper into her throat with each thrust.

I stroked her hair away from her face. "That's it, swallow my cock like daddy's good little girl."

Her mouth tightened around my shaft at my degrading encouragement.

Grasping her wet hair, I pushed in deeper, feeling the press of the back of her throat against the sensitive head of my cock.

Liliana gagged, trying to pull her mouth free.

To cease her struggles, I slipped my hips down the marble tub slope, easing my body deeper under the water and completely submerging her head.

She tried to flail her arms, but I kept them pinned against her sides with my legs.

After a second, I shifted up until her head broke the surface.

Pulling on her hair, I tilted her head back and off my cock, letting her breathe. "Don't take your mouth off my cock again without permission, understand?"

She breathed heavily in and out several times before rasping, "Yes, daddy."

Fuck, I could definitely get used to this.

Swiping my thumb over her now swollen lower lip, I said, "Good girl, now take a nice deep breath because this time I'm pushing it down your throat."

Barely giving her enough time, I thrust in. When I reached the tight band of muscle at the back of her throat, I wrapped both hands around her head and gently pushed my hips up, breaking past her resistance. Her throat contracted around my shaft.

Her body jerked and trembled as her lips stretched around my thick length.

Still I pushed.

Her whimpers sent vibrations up my shaft straight to my balls which tightened from the delicious, erotic sensation. Her cheeks hollowed, her tongue struggling to move around the intrusion.

My gaze captured her beautiful bronze eyes pleading with me to release her.

The pressure increased along my shaft as I pulsed my hips, driving my cock in and out of her mouth.

I was so fucking close to coming.

Goddammit.

With another curse, I pulled free of her glorious, tight throat.

This was supposed to be a punishment.

A lesson.

A domination.

A brutal, physical demonstration to her that she was on the wrong side of a twisted game of winner takes all.

That she was nothing more than a pawn to be used and discarded.

The plan had been to prove to myself that my actions earlier had been a fluke, a rare misjudgment, and that I was back on track in making her pay for the part she played in putting my family in danger.

Fuck that plan.

I wanted to make her come so hard she shattered the rest of the shower walls with her screams.

Only then would I find my own release.

Clenching my jaw against the primal impulse to drive back into her warm mouth, I wrapped my hands around her waist and slid her body over mine.

Wrapping my hand behind her head, I crashed my lips down onto hers and thrust my tongue inside, devouring the unique taste of her sweet essence mixed with my own musk.

I had never in my entire life kissed a woman after she had sucked my cock. There was something deeply erotic and intimate about doing so that I had never needed or wanted to share with another woman.

Liliana's mews barely registered under my bruising kiss. In my zeal to capture more of the sensual moment, I drove my thigh between her legs.

It was as if I wanted to crush her small body into my own, absorbing her into my rib cage, a reluctant Adam reclaiming Eve into his body, where she would be safe, forever, and only his.

The obsessive, borderline psychotic, thought alarmed me.

It must be the fucking setting.

It had to be.

I moved my hand over her slick back to cup her ass, tilting my head to the right, giving her no mercy as I continued to feast on her mouth.

Rolling her onto her back, I positioned her on the reclining edge of the tub and kept her from sliding down with the press of my weight between her thighs.

The heated water lapped over our bodies, spilling over the edge from the still running faucet.

Liliana pushed up on her elbows and craned her neck to view the damage. "The water! The floor!"

I kissed the top of her right breast. "There's a drain in the center. Lay back."

"But—"

Pulling her nipple into my mouth, I sucked it in deep, using the points of my teeth to tease the sensitive nub with just a hint of pain.

"Ow! Ow! Ow!"

After releasing her nipple, I growled, "Lay back, I said."

My hand caressed her left breast as I kissed her stomach, then her lower abdomen, before I pushed my shoulders between her thighs.

Her torso shot up again. "No. Stop! You're going to hurt me again."

The water teased the bottom curve of her ass as I spread her thighs open. She had the prettiest pussy I'd ever seen. Soft downy curls and a peek of pink the same color as her lips.

"No, babygirl," I rasped as I kissed along her inner thigh. "I'm going to lick your sweet cunt until you scream my name."

She placed her fingers over my lips. "No. You don't have to. I don't want you to."

Capturing two of her fingers in my mouth, I sucked them deep, running my tongue suggestively between them before releasing them. "I didn't ask your permission."

She tried to shift her hips and move away but the slick surface of the tub just had her sliding back down toward me.

This time she covered her pussy with both of her hands. "Please, just let me get out of the tub."

My gaze narrowed. "The answer is no, now lie back before you make me angry and I decide to shove my cock back down your throat."

Thrusting her lower lip out, she slowly slid her hands away from her pussy.

Yet the moment I leaned my head close and pressed my mouth to her cunt, her hips bucked and she covered herself again.

"I can't! I'm sorry! I don't like you touching me!" she cried.

Her body trembled from my touch. Her mouth responded to my kisses.

I didn't even have to push my fingers inside her pussy to know I'd find it slick with cream just from the way her lips opened, and her pupils dilated every time I growled "daddy" and made her open her mouth for my cock.

She wasn't fooling me for one goddamn second.

This was just another one of her fucking lies.

And I was done.

Time to force the truth on my lying *angioletto.*

CHAPTER 13

LILIANA

*B*efore he could respond, I swung my leg over his head and slid into the water before scrambling to the other side of the tub.

The waters, darkened by the ebony reflection of the marble, swirled around Benedict's lower abdomen as he turned to face me, a vengeful Neptune rising out of the ocean depths to seduce an unwilling Melantho.

I slipped under the swan's-neck spigot and partially hid behind the mini waterfall. "Stay away."

He sliced through the water toward me, a deep scowl between his brows. "Not an option," he said, reaching over me to turn off the faucet.

I clung to the slippery edge of the tub, knowing I wouldn't be able to climb out without him grabbing me. "This won't make me talk."

No matter what he threatened me with, I couldn't talk.

There was too much at stake.

It was a matter of life and death, and not just my own.

Somehow, I needed to either make him understand that, or escape.

He crossed his arms over his hard, muscled chest. "Baby-girl, you don't seriously think this is still about making you talk?"

Water lapped at my chin as I ducked low to cover my breasts. "What else could it be about?"

In a rush, he lunged for me.

Before the wave of water caused by his forward movement hit my face, he notched his hands under my arms and lifted me against his chest until our mouths were just a breath apart.

"You foolish little girl. If all I wanted was information from you, I could have gotten this pretty mouth to spill every syllable you knew within sixty seconds of you walking through your apartment door tonight."

I pressed the heels of my palms against his shoulders and leaned back as far as his hard embrace would allow. "Then why—"

His hard shaft brushed my stomach.

I'd been so focused on why he wanted me to talk, and why like the stupid, immature girl he accused me of being I wouldn't, it hadn't even occurred to me that his reasons for seducing me would be the most base and primal of all human needs.

A man just wanting to fuck a woman.

I thrashed in his embrace. "Let me go!"

He wrapped his hand around my throat and pressed my back into the wall of the tub with the weight of his body.

My struggles stilled; I focused on drawing the next breath into my lungs.

He towered over me. "I'm growing impatient with the bullshit frightened virgin act."

I breathed heavily through my nose. "Did it occur to you that I really am a ..."

His lips thinned. "That you're a what?"

My teeth sank into my lower lip. I couldn't tell him.

It may have been the twenty-first century for the rest of the world, but in Sicily it might as well still have been the Middle Ages where *the family* was concerned.

The family still solidified connections through Church sacraments like baptism and marriage, especially marriage, and a woman's virginity was sometimes her only asset and her only chance at a home, children, and a family. A woman who slept around was not considered worthy of a decent man.

Telling someone like Benedict Cavalieri I was still a virgin would be giving him leverage to literally hold my future, and any chance I might have at happiness, hostage.

It was also why there was absolutely no way *this* was happening.

Narrowing my gaze, I said, "Did it occur to you that I really am"—I shifted my gaze away as I lost my nerve, but forced myself to finish— "not attracted to you?"

For a moment, the only sound in the room was the *swish* and *splash* of the water as it flowed over the edge of the tub onto the tiled bathroom floor.

Then Benedict slowly tilted his head to the right, his gaze traveling over my face to land on my mouth. His grip loosened on my throat when his hand shifted so his thumb could caress my lower lip.

The corner of his mouth lifted in the ghost of a smile that didn't reach his eyes.

My stomach twisted.

If we had been standing in a forest, this would have been the ominous moment when the branches stilled from the sudden lack of wind and the birds stopped singing.

My limbs stiffened as I braced for what was going to happen next.

He cupped my cheek. "I was hoping you would say something like that."

I blinked. "You were?"

Was it too much to hope that my salvation was at hand? Would he now let me go?

Bracing his hands against the tub's edge on either side of my shoulders, he leaned in close to my neck. His lips gently skimmed the outer whorl of my ear.

Swallowing a moan, I wedged my arms behind me, pinning my hands between the tub wall and my butt to keep from running my fingers through his chest hair. I didn't want to show him the slightest sign that I enjoyed his touch and ruin my chances of him letting me go.

Then he nipped at my earlobe before whispering, "Not that I needed an excuse, but I've been wanting to punish that pert ass of yours since the first time you lied to me."

I gasped.

As my body jerked and prepared to bolt, his fingers wrapped around my upper arms, keeping me in place.

He continued on in that ruthlessly calm voice. "And now you've given me the perfect opportunity."

Before I could cry out, he lifted and flipped me onto my stomach over the tub ledge with my knees resting on the wide underwater bench that ran along each side of the tub. The position forced my ass and hips just above the water's surface.

Benedict fisted my wet hair as he stepped to the side. "Time for another lesson."

I placed my palms on the tiles and raised my torso, intending to push off the ledge, just as his hand struck my ass. "Ow!"

My breasts squashed against the wet tiles as I fell forward, more from shock than pain, as I tried to reach behind me to cover my ass.

"Move your hands or I'll get my belt," he growled.

I strained to look over my shoulder. "Why are you doing this?"

His arm was raised, poised over my ass. "Because you haven't stopped lying to me from the moment you opened those cute lips of yours tonight."

"Wait—"

Ignoring me, his open palm came down on my wet, naked skin with a loud, humiliating smack.

I screamed and squirmed, trying to break his grip.

"The more you struggle, the more strikes I add to your punishment," he warned with another smack, this time to my other cheek.

My mouth opened on a choking cry.

The hot water had already made my wet skin warm and sensitive, so his spanking was sending agonizing spikes of sharp, needling pain over every nerve of my body. I hadn't been paddled since I was an orphan at the convent and even then, the nuns only did it over your uniform.

This was so much worse.

"Please," I begged.

He spanked me several more times, either not hearing me or not caring.

My body rocked back and forth with each strike he landed

with ruthless efficiency, first on one cheek, then the other. Sometimes he would punish my upper thighs, then return to my ass. My legs kicked and splashed, my vision blurry with tears.

After what felt like an eternity, he rested his large palm on the top of my ass, then moved it in a slow, soothing circle before cupping my flesh. "Why am I punishing you?"

I leaned my forehead against the tiles and moaned.

He released my ass and brushed the wet curls away from my face. "What was that?"

I sniffed. "I don't know."

He raised up and delivered another spank.

I cried out. "Ow! Stop! I'm sorry! I'm sorry!"

"Want to try that one more time?"

"Because I lied."

He smoothed his palm over my ass again. "Because I lied—*daddy*," he corrected.

Fuck, not the daddy thing again.

His hand moved lower as he skimmed between my thighs, then over the curve of my ass, then lower still, the tips of his fingers between my thighs again.

I bit my lip, not wanting to say it.

His hand left my ass.

I pivoted my head to look over my shoulder.

And widened my eyes at seeing his raised arm.

I knew what was coming.

I cried out. "Daddy! Because I lied, daddy."

I squeezed my legs together.

This was so dirty wrong. No, it had been dirty wrong back at my apartment.

Here at the *Vatican* it was *literally* hellishly dirty wrong.

He caressed my still throbbing ass. "*Brava ragazza.* We'll

get into all your lies later, for now I want you to beg me to lick your pussy."

My forehead pressed against the backs of my hands where I clutched at the edge of the tub. "I can't say it. It's sinful. Please, don't make me."

He pinched my stinging flesh. "Did you want daddy to get his belt?"

I raised up onto my toes. "Ow! No!"

"Then do as you're told."

I swallowed. "Please ... lick my ... my ..."

A sharp, stinging slap landed on my already throbbing right ass cheek.

I screamed. "My pussy, daddy."

Releasing his grip on my hair, he smoothed his hand down my spine to rest on my back as he moved to stand behind me. His other hand slipped between my legs and pushed them open wider.

My breathing came fast and shallow, my body tensing, not knowing what to expect next.

The hand on my lower back moved over my ass and I hissed at the contact.

He leaned over me and kissed the top curve of my right cheek. "Don't worry, baby. Daddy will kiss it and take the hurt away."

My cheeks flamed.

He pulled me away from the edge, so my breasts and stomach brushed the top of the water. Then he pushed down on my lower back, forcing my hips out before using both his hands to pry open my ass cheeks.

With a cry, my hands flew back to knock his away. "Wait! What are you—"

"Put your hands back on the edge of the tub and don't move them again," he ordered.

My lower lip trembled as I obeyed.

The first warm brush of his mouth was an electric shock to my nervous system. His tongue licked and laved the length of my pussy before he flicked and teased my clit.

Oh no!

Having nothing to compare it with, I didn't know how to process the intense sensation of physical pleasure with the emotional turmoil over what was happening.

No boy I'd ever been with had ever gotten past a little heavy kissing.

To say I'd had a sheltered upbringing would be an understatement so I definitely had never experienced a man going down on me, and my cheap vibrator didn't even come close to the pressure of his warm tongue.

To have a man like Benedict, a man I barely knew, let alone someone who was not a boyfriend, do so was deeply unsettling and overwhelming and yet exhilarating in that risky, rebellious sort of way.

This was wrong. On so many levels. So wrong.

The pain. The punishment. The sinful act.

The premarital sexual contact with a stranger who wanted to kill me.

All of it.

Then his tongue flicked my clit again and I raised up on my toes.

When his hands tightened on my ass cheeks a spark of pain blended with the pleasure, sending me into a chaotic spin of turbulent emotions twisting from arousal to torment and back.

Then his rough, bearded jaw brushed against my ass cheek

as he shifted higher. His warm breath brushed against my puckered asshole. It tensed and clutched.

My eyes widened.

I opened my mouth, but no words came out, only a shocked squeak.

His deep chuckle was his only response as he tightened his fingers, holding my ass cheeks open.

His touch was both intimate and exciting, but at the same time, it was also intensely uncomfortable and humiliating. The way he was pleasuring me from *behind*—how he was *spreading* my cheeks open.

And then the tip of his tongue flicked my dark hole.

"No. Not there!"

His tongue teased the gentle ridges, making my hips squirm.

When he spoke, I could feel his lips move against my sensitive skin. "Does it make you feel like a bad girl to have me lick your bottom hole?"

My cheeks burned so hot, my salty tears stung my skin. "Yes. It's shameful. You have to stop. Please!"

He moved his left hand to cup my pussy so his fingertip could apply gentle, pulsing pressure against my clit. "You're right. It's not just shameful. It's probably a sin."

I groaned, my hips thrusting back against his hand. The water lapped at my nipples with my movement, adding to my pleasurable torment.

With his right hand on my ass cheek, he kept it embarrassingly pried open. He leaned down to flick the tip of his tongue once more against my hole, the bristle of his beard rough where it brushed against my skin.

His warm breath against my overly stimulated skin taunted me as much as his next words. "I'm a very dangerous man and you barely know me. You're a wicked girl for letting me touch you like this."

He pulsed two fingers over my clit as he pushed the pad of his thumb into my asshole. The firm pressure and the taboo nature of what he was doing had me nearly clawing through the marble tiles with a gnawing, aching need.

It was almost pathetic how much of a stereotypically repressed Catholic schoolgirl I was turning out to be. Right down to finding the forbidden erotic, including being turned on by calling an older man "daddy."

I even liked when he spanked me.

He was right. I was a wicked girl going straight to hell.

I bit my lower lip until I tasted blood to keep myself from crying out, desperately trying to deny any of this was true, trying to deny what was happening to my body, trying to deny the effect his touch was having on it.

Benedict wasn't fooled.

He increased the pressure and pace of his fingers over my sensitive nub even more, before rasping, "*Tsk, tsk, tsk.* Only a bad girl would let a strange man lick their pussy."

I lowered my head, hiding behind a cascade of wet curls, as my stomach muscles contracted.

The steam from the water.

His sinful touch.

His dark words.

Everything.

I was so going to hell. I tried to shock myself by thinking of Mother Superior. "Please, stop. The Bible says *For this is the will of God, your sanctification: that you abstain from sexual immorality.*"

He pulsed his thumb in and out of my puckered hole as he continued to torment my clit. "It sure does, which means you really shouldn't be letting me tease your cute little bottom hole like this. So immoral."

I swallowed a moan. It wasn't working.

My thighs clenched around his wrist as my back stiffened. "You have to stop," I pleaded.

I keened and tried to pull my hips away, afraid of what it would mean if I …

"What's that, babygirl? I don't think I heard you?"

"Please, stop," I moaned.

"Was there a *daddy* in there?"

Having no shame left, I begged. "Please, daddy, stop. I can't take any more. This is wrong. You can't let me come. It would be wrong. Please, daddy!"

Giving my ass another spank, he growled, "All I heard was please daddy let me come."

He replaced his fingers with his mouth over my pussy and laved my clit with his tongue. The pressure of the pad of his thumb was soft against my ass.

Unable to resist any longer, I rose on my toes and shamelessly pushed my hips back onto his mouth, a completely wicked rush of pleasure stealing my breath away.

White sparks burst behind my eyelids as a euphoria like nothing I had ever experienced before settled in the center of my chest.

Certainly nothing compared to the feeble orgasms I had achieved with that cheap vibrator I had paid a friend to buy me years ago because I was too embarrassed to get one myself.

I almost didn't hear the rush of water as Benedict rose behind me. "Time to prove what an adorable liar you are, my *angioletto*."

He gripped my hip and positioned the tip of his cock against my virgin pussy entrance.

Unadulterated panic cut through my euphoria like a knife.

I needed to stop him.

I couldn't think straight. Part of me just wanted to tell him I was a virgin and beg him for mercy. Another part would rather die than let him know.

There was no way I was getting out of this tub without him having sex with me.

He was too big, too strong, and way too worked up.

I would never make it to the door.

What if ... no ... I can't.

It was a dark, twisted sin for me to even think about it.

Especially here of all places.

But it wasn't like I hadn't seen videos or read about it in books.

I'd always secretly wanted to know what it would feel like to have a man take me *there*.

The way the man usually had to hold the woman down.

The brute force and primal power on display as he over-powered her and drove in deep— ignoring her cries of pain. Then later admiring how his big, thick cock had opened her tiny hole, as if it were a point of masculine pride.

My thighs clenched as a soft moan escaped my lips, then I just blurted it out. "Fuck me in the ass, daddy."

CHAPTER 14

BENEDICT

*M*y hands tightened on her hips as I stilled. "What the fuck did you just say to me?"

Never had such an erotic plea both excited and angered me more.

Her shoulders hitched, and her back muscles tensed.

I fisted her hair and pulled. "Answer me."

Because of my grip, her body floated back, forcing her ass to grind against my already painfully hard cock. If I didn't get relief soon, I wouldn't be responsible for my actions.

It had been years since I had been on the chase and my blood was already running hot.

I had already denied myself a release to get her off, but I would not hold off for much longer, especially if she continued to say erotic entreaties like *fuck me in the ass, daddy.*

Dammit.

What a deceptive little angel she was.

It was obvious she lacked experience. Either that, or she had some disgracefully selfish men in her life.

But why suddenly try and play the whore after appearing shocked to her core at the mortal sin we were committing with a pussy tongue-lashing?

What was her game?

My gaze ran over the delicious way her waist curved in before swelling out over her hips, how her beautiful skin glistened in this light from the drops of water as if kissed by tiny shards of diamonds. She was bent before me in a completely submissive, vulnerable position.

Anger twisted my gut.

If she wanted to take her chances playing this dangerous game with me, then who was I to say no? Unfortunately, I doubted she would enjoy paying the forfeit when she lost.

When she still refused to respond, I released her hair to wrap my hand around her throat and pull her upright against my chest. I ran my other hand over her body.

Fuck, she felt good pressed against me.

Her head was forced to rest on my shoulder as I squeezed her breast before pinching her nipple. "So my supposedly innocent little angel is really a dirty little whore who likes it rough from behind."

She cried out, her hand wrapping around my wrist. "Wait, I didn't mean it."

I ran my lips along the outer curve of her ear. "It's too late, babygirl. You've started this game. Now I'm going to finish it."

She stilled.

I sucked on her earlobe before gently biting it. "My compliments to Dante Agnello."

Her upper arms stiffened against her ribs as she pulled on my wrist.

My hand tightened briefly around her throat before continuing in a low, taunting tone. "Was it Dante who trained you to play the innocent virgin, knowing it would be the perfect honeypot trap for his enemies? Then, if that didn't work, telling you to switch to a dirty whore willing to fulfill any man's fantasy?"

Her breath came in quick, shallow bursts. "I'm not playing at anything. Benedict, please—"

"I've never been a jealous man, but I'll confess, I find myself curiously *angered* by the idea of another man driving his cock into this tight little ass."

My hand moved from her throat to clasp her jaw from behind as my index finger traced her lower lip. "Was he the only one, babygirl? Or were there more? Did he share you with his men?"

I didn't expect an answer and she didn't give me one.

My finger pushed inside her mouth. Instinctively her tongue swirled around it, trying to push it out. "How many men have you let shove their cocks into this sweet mouth?"

My hand moved over her pussy as my anger grew. "Tell me, how many men have been inside your cunt?"

My jaw clenched.

Somehow, with each taunting phrase meant to break *her*, I was actually pissing *myself* off more.

It was irrational—and that was a problem because I wasn't an irrational man. Ever.

Rational would be not giving a damn if she had one or a hundred lovers.

Rational would be bending her over and driving my cock so deep into her ass she screamed for mercy.

Irrational was feeling my anger rise at being proven right about her innocence being an act.

Irrational was wanting to hunt down every man who had come before me, to put a bullet in their head.

My voice took on a dark edge as I released her throat and bent her forward. My hand moved down her back, then over her ass, which still bore the warm flush from my spanking. "It doesn't matter. Daddy's here now."

I cupped her cheek with my palm before suddenly giving it a hard, vicious smack.

She cried out in pain. "Please! There haven't been any—"

I smoothed my hand over her ass before tracing the seam with my middle finger. Prying her left cheek open, I pushed the pad of my right thumb against her puckered hole. "I'm going to fuck this tight hole so hard, you'll beg for mercy."

She gasped as she tried to clench it tightly closed.

I pushed my thumb in deeper.

She moaned and shifted forward.

A nearby ledge held several vials of bath oils. I reached for the first one. Pulling out the cork stopper with my teeth and spitting it out, I poured the contents onto her lower back, watching the thick amber liquid pool before I drizzled more between her ass cheeks along the seam.

The thick, humid air filled with the sharp, clean citrus scent of lemon and eucalyptus. Raising the vial, I emptied the remaining oil into the center of my palm. Placing it back on the ledge, I fisted my cock and slowly massaged the oil over its swollen length.

With hooded eyes, I watched her hazard a glance over her shoulder. I knew what she saw reminded her of the earlier erotic vision of my hands squeezing and caressing the shower soap into a deep, thick lather, and her reaction to it. Good.

The dark water swirled only to about my upper thighs, exposing my thick cock, giving her a good view as I stood behind her with my legs spread.

I winked. "Getting a good look, babygirl?"

With a gasp, she whipped her head forward, hiding behind her hair.

Wedging my cock between her cheeks I used the tip to swirl the oil around her entrance, preparing her.

Inhaling a deep breath, I watched intently as her skin whitened and the soft edges around her clenched hole smoothed as I pressed the head against her entrance.

She bucked and immediately tried to escape.

Anticipating that, I grabbed her hair, anchoring her in place. "You're not going anywhere. Remember, you're the one who wanted to play."

Positioning my cock once more at her entrance, I thrust forward.

She clenched it closed as tightly as she could, but to no avail.

With firm, relentless pressure, I broke through her resistance.

Her fingers curling into tiny fists, her short, keening yelp cut off, as if the shock of feeling my cock inside of her had stolen her breath.

My hand twisted in her hair, wrenching her head back while I pressed my open palm down on her lower back. Then I shifted my thighs until they brushed against the backs of hers, allowing my cock to slip in a little further, breaking past her tight ring of muscle.

This time, she did cry out. "Take it out! It hurts!"

Without saying a word, I pushed in deeper until her tight hole had taken half my length. Her muscles clenched and unclenched around my shaft like a fist.

She pulled against my grasp on her hair. "It's in too far!"

Raising my arm, I spanked her ass cheek with my free hand. "I'll show you too far."

ZOE BLAKE

With that, I thrust in, to the hilt.

My abdomen connected with the soft flesh of her ass as my balls slapped her pussy. Looking down, the beautiful sight of her tiny hole stretched around the thick base of my cock nearly had me blowing my entire load deep inside of her right then and there.

I pulled back slightly and drove in again, then again, as I pounded into her without remorse.

Relishing her body's unrelenting grip on my cock. It was like nothing I had ever experienced before in my life. I couldn't explain it.

It was almost as if ...

Her body shook as she cried, "I can't do this. Please, you have to take it out!"

Cazzo! Santo inferno!

I pulled out slowly, suppressing the urge to thrust back inside her tight warmth when I saw the way her tight hole had stretched open from the girth of my cock.

I turned her around.

Grasping her face, I ground out, "You foolish little girl, of all the damn things to lie about."

It was clear her previous experience did not extend to anal sex.

There was no denying the rush of primal satisfaction I felt at being the man to take her tight cherry.

Followed by the overpowering need to make this right for her, since I had every intention of bending my pretty captive over and shoving my cock deep in her ass as often as possible in the near future.

Her limbs shook and a whimper was her only response.

"Put your arms around my neck," I ordered, pushing my

fist against the spigot to turn the hot water back on as I moved us to the center of the spa tub.

Shifting lower to my knees I submerged her in the soothing hot water, just to above her shoulders.

As I did so, I wrapped her legs around my hips and moved my hand under her body to reach for my cock.

Liliana pushed away from my chest. "I thought—"

"You thought because you lied and started a dangerous game you couldn't finish that I would show you compassion?"

I positioned the tip of my shaft at her now slightly gaping entrance. Knowing her bottom hole would still be lubricated since the oil would not have dissolved in the water.

Her eyes widened.

"You were wrong. You still have a lesson to learn."

Although I wasn't a sadist, I still was no gentleman.

She was still getting fucked in the ass.

I just wasn't going to plow into her from behind, using the full force of my hips. From this position, the weight of her own body would be the driving force pushing me deep into her.

Her fingernails dug into my shoulders as she still tried to clench her hole and keep me out.

Shifting my hands to grasp her hips, I pushed her downward as I thrust up, impaling her.

She cried out, pressing her breasts against my chest.

Wrapping my other arm around her back, I held her thrashing body close, my thrusts increasing in pace.

Pulling back slightly, ignoring the faint glimmer of the gold cross charm nestled between her breasts, I moved to suck one pert nipple between my lips. After giving the nub a bite, I moved to the other nipple.

ZOE BLAKE

"Come on, baby. Tell daddy where it hurts," I rasped against her flesh.

She whimpered as her fingers curled into my chest hair. "You're inside me and it's too big."

Using the water's buoyancy, I pushed her hips up, slipping out until only the tight ring of muscle at her entrance clung to the head of my cock.

Then I shoved her back down on my shaft, throwing my head back with a groan as her tight sheath clasped around me.

"What's inside of you? Let me hear the dirty words from your lips or I'll bend you back over the tub's edge and fuck you properly again."

She buried her head against my neck and muffled her response.

Reaching my arm up, I pulled on her long, wet locks, forcing her head back so I could pierce her with a dark glare. "Last warning."

"Your cock! Your cock is in my ass."

Pressing a hand between our bodies, I teased her clit with the tip of my finger. "Now be a good girl and beg daddy to come in your ass."

"Do I have to?"

"Do you want me to pull my cock out?"

She nodded, her eyes filling with tears. "Please, daddy. Please, come. It hurts so bad. Please, come."

My balls tightened.

I flicked her clit faster. "Daddy will, if you will."

She grasped my shoulders. "It hurts too much. I don't think I could—oh!"

Her thighs tightened around my hips.

The corner of my mouth lifted. "*Brava ragazza.* Come for daddy, so I can fill your tight bottom with my come."

124

SEDUCTION OF THE PATRIARCH

Her head fell back as she cried out. "Oh! Oh! Oh!"

Her body tensed with her release, her interior muscles tightening around my shaft, sending me over the edge. I released a hot stream of come deep inside her virgin ass. My only regret was I wouldn't be able to watch it drip out of her gaping hole as I did so.

Next time.

If only the release had appeased my growing rage.

CHAPTER 15

BENEDICT

*T*he moment I pulled free of her body, she lunged for the side of the tub.

I wrapped my arms around her from behind. "Where do you think you're going?"

"You're finished with me. I was going to get out and dry off."

I'll never be finished with you.

The strange thought crossed my mind and I just as quickly chased it away.

As cruel as it may be, Liliana was nothing more than a pawn to me.

An erotic and pleasing one, but still, just a pawn.

As soon as this mess was over and those who dared threaten the Cavalieri family had learned their lesson, I would retreat back into the mountains and leave her to her fate, whatever that may be.

Another unsettling thought crossed my mind. That her

grim fate was likely to be either married off against her will to a *soldati* in Dante's crew or killed.

Again, I chased the thought away.

Her fate was not my concern.

My only interest in her was to keep her alive for as long as she was useful to me.

Given the dark direction of my thoughts, my voice was harsher than I intended. "Stay right there."

Turning off the faucet, I stepped out of the tub onto the wet marble floor. The water from the overflow had washed away any of the glass shards from the broken shower door near the tub's basin, but there were still pieces of glass strewn about the bathroom.

Snatching a plush, white terry cloth robe from a nearby gold hook, I shrugged it on. Reaching for my glass of Scotch, I downed the rest of the contents then shook out a fresh black towel and crossed to the tub. "Stand up."

Liliana stretched out her arm to take the towel from the security of her submerged position in the water.

I held it out of her grasp. "What part of stand up was not clear?"

"Can't you just hand me the towel first?"

Once again I held the towel open between my hands. "No. Now do as you're told."

Her brow furrowed, she clasped her arm over her breasts, standing up in a rush and reaching for the towel in the same motion.

I refused to release it. "Let go of the towel so I can wrap you in it."

Her mouth dropped open as she tugged on the top of the towel. "I don't need you to dry me off. I'm not a child!"

I firmly held on to the towel. "There is glass all over the floor. I need to carry you."

She cast her gaze over the waterlogged floor. "I'll just avoid it."

"No."

"Then can I have a robe?"

"There was only one."

"Why can't I have the one you're using?"

The corner of my mouth lifted. "Because I'm wearing it."

Her lips thinned. "You are no gentleman."

She wasn't wrong. "What part of my shoving my cock up your ass made you think I'd act the gentleman afterward?"

Her cheeks blushed a pretty pink. "I hate you."

My gaze traveled over her naked and wet body. "That's a shame. I'm growing quite fond of you."

She gave up tugging on the towel and turned her head to the side. Her voice was low and thin as she swiped at a tear on her cheek. "Please just let me out of this tub."

I hadn't missed the defeated tone. Perhaps I was being too harsh on her.

Without further comment, I wrapped the large towel around her and lifted her into my arms. Careful to avoid the more treacherous areas of the floor, I carried her out of the bathroom and into the attached bedroom.

Padding barefoot into the octagon-shaped room, I placed her on the edge of the polished Gaboon Ebony four-poster bed.

"Don't move or trust me, you will regret it."

After that warning, I went into the bathroom to grab additional towels and a brush. Before leaving the room, I picked up the wall phone and spoke to the staff member who immediately answered and gave the order for a meal I knew they had already prepared to be sent in and the bathroom to be cleaned.

When I returned to the bedroom, she was staring in undisguised horror at the surrounding walls, the towel clutched to her breasts. "Is this room some kind of satanic bedroom?"

I placed the extra towels near her hip. I supposed it was too much to hope she wouldn't notice the graphic, bright crimson and gold frescoes that decorated the windowless room.

With a hand under her chin, I directed her gaze back to me. "Don't look at them. You are far too young."

She frowned. "I'm twenty-five, thank you very much, and I wasn't too young for what you just did to me in that tub!"

After curling my fingers into fists and anchoring them on either side of her hips, I leaned over her. "After what you asked me to do to you in that tub. Say it."

She blinked. "What?"

There would be no hiding for her behind yet another lie. "I want you to say it. In fact, I want you to thank me for it."

Her mouth dropped open. "Thank you!"

"Yes, thank me. I want to hear you say, thank you for fucking me in the ass like I begged you to ... daddy."

Her shoulders stiffened as she inhaled sharply through her nose. "No. I couldn't possibly say such a scandalous thing out loud, here!"

Ripping the towel off her, I spun her body around until she knelt upright on the bed, her ass nestled against my crotch. Wrapping my hand around her throat, I said, "You asked about this room?"

With my other hand over her breast, I continued. "Look

closely, babygirl. The frescoes are compliments of a rather sadistic cardinal from the eighteenth century with rather particular tastes in the bedroom. This was his secret chamber."

The walls were decorated with an extremely graphic interpretation of the Villa of the Mysteries from Pompeii featuring the initiation ritual of the Bacchic mystery cult. Various satyrs and women were depicted in increasingly raunchy scenes including one featuring a woman suckling a goat while another was whipped by a satyr wearing a demon mask.

It was owing to Arcangelo's powerful influence that he made use of the Borgia apartments as his own private quarters in the first place, but added to that, his dark sense of humor was particularly responsible for his disobedience of His Holiness's instructions to have this chamber destroyed when it was discovered, and instead turned it into a guest bedroom.

Her heartbeat pulsed against my palm where I caressed the top of her breast. "You can either pick a fresco panel for us to recreate and get into position—might I suggest the fifth one where the women are down on all fours—or you can be a good girl and thank me."

She swallowed. "Thank you for taking me in the ass like I begged you to, daddy."

I released her throat. "There. That wasn't so hard, now, was it?"

She fell forward on the mattress. Grabbing the towel, she covered herself as best she could. "Why are you being so mean to me?"

I grasped her hair and pulled her back until she was sitting on her knees before me. Reaching for the brush, I ran the bristles over the wet, tangled ends of her hair. "You know damn well why."

I would do well to remind myself of why as well.

Her shoulders slumped. "I can brush my own hair."

My knuckles grazed her soft skin as I adjusted my grip on the thick rope of hair I had in my grasp.

She really had the most beautiful hair. It was a rich, glossy shade of black that fell in soft waves almost to the middle of her back.

If she were my woman, I would never let her cut it.

If she were mine ...

Again my gut twisted with the uncharacteristic urge to not only protect her, but to claim her for my own.

Once more falling for her doll-like vulnerability act.

Goddammit. What the fuck was it with this woman?

Obviously, the fact that I hadn't gotten laid in over two years was affecting my judgment. It was my fault for burying myself in the mountains of Northern Italy away from all civilization.

Tossing the brush onto the bed next to her, I turned and threw open the doors to an antique mahogany wardrobe. Grabbing a set of cobalt blue silk pajamas, I slammed the doors shut.

Tossing the pajama top onto the bed, I said, "Put this on and meet me in the other room. Don't make me come back and get you."

As I stormed away, she called out. "Only the top? Can I have the bottoms?"

"Be glad I gave you anything at all," I ground out on my way out of the room.

* * *

WHEN SHE FINALLY JOINED ME, I was seated at the head of a long dining table in the *Sala dei Misteri della Fede.*

Included in the original Borgia apartments and decorated by Pinturicchio, the stone walls and faded, tiled mosaic floor were overshadowed by the magnificent crown of an arched ceiling depicting the life of the Virgin Mary in brilliant jewel tones.

A sharp departure from the bedroom motif.

I rose and pulled out a high-backed chair to the left of where I was sitting.

Yanking on the hem of the pajama top, she gingerly sat on the edge of the upholstered seat, allowing me to shift the chair under the table.

Before leaving her side, I lifted the crystal wine decanter and poured her a glass.

I lifted my glass after returning to my chair at the head of the table, gesturing with it to the frescoes above us. "I trust you find this art more suitable to your delicate tastes?"

When she tilted her head back, my gaze focused on her delicate throat.

Her neck was so small. My hands easily wrapped around it.

With no effort at all, I could snap her spine before she took her next breath.

She wouldn't feel a thing.

The fluttering of her pulse at the base of her throat caught my attention.

The tip of my tongue moved over my lower lip as I remembered the taste of her skin.

Realized that with even less effort, I could grasp her around the hips and kiss that tantalizing place on her throat while I thrust my cock into her pussy until she screamed my name.

Shaking off the image, I reminded myself of her place by saying, "Although I do find an amusing irony in the repeated use of the lily throughout the room. Don't you?"

She lowered her gaze and stared at her wineglass.

"Liliana. That is a form of lily is it not? Did your parents name you that in the vain hope their daughter would embody the lily's symbolic virtues of purity and innocence?"

"My parents didn't name me."

Her eyes widened. I leaned forward at her admission. "What was that?"

"Nothing."

"Liliana, do I need to remind you what happens when you disobey me?"

Liliana reached for the cross necklace at her neck. "My parents are dead. The nuns named me."

For once, I was certain she wasn't lying. This was no act.

Before I could react, there was a discreet knock at the door. At my response, several liveried attendants marched silently in with silver domed cloches which they expertly arranged on the table before us.

If they thought it odd I was sitting at a table inside the Vatican in only a pair of pajama bottoms while an unmarried young female companion sat next to me in only the pajama top, they were too well-trained to comment.

While they uncovered the dishes and set out the tableware, I thought of her unguarded comment.

Instead of enlightening me, it only increased the mystery surrounding her.

If there was one thing upon which the mafia could be

relied, it was they didn't do certain business outside of the family.

There wasn't a chance in hell Dante Agnello would have trusted an assignment like spying on the powerful Cavalieri family, let alone shooting Barone, to someone who wasn't family.

It had already been a stretch to think he had enlisted a female, let alone someone as young and untrained as Liliana, for the dirty job.

I had assumed that he had because she was more likely not to raise suspicion whereas any male suddenly in our midst asking questions would have.

Now to learn she was a female with no parents?

And worse, raised by nuns, which meant no strong family ties, which in turn meant possibly no mafia ties?

This changed everything.

Once again, I was struck by the possibility that Dante Agnello was not involved.

Which begged the question, how was Liliana involved and who was she protecting by lying to me?

CHAPTER 16

LILIANA

J gripped the edges of my chair seat as I resisted the urge to bolt.

Held captive deep inside the Vatican.

In the middle of the night, half dressed, with no idea where my clothes were. It was not an ideal situation for an escape.

Determining the best course of action was to keep my mouth shut and not give away any more details about my personal life, I watched the staff lift the lids on the platters of food. My mouth salivated. I realized I hadn't eaten since early this morning.

Given the late hour, it was more a selection of *antipasti* and *dolci* than a more traditional three-course dinner.

There was a beautiful platter of *tortino della valle grana*, with the poached *Madernassa* pears swimming in a rich, clove-scented syrup and dusted with the perfect amount of crumbled *Castelmagno* cheese. A bowl filled with piping hot sage fritters dusted with sea salt and another bowl of *spac-*

catelle di pomodori with thick slices of fresh semolina bread arranged around the edge. As well as roasted vegetables and artichokes served with a garlic and anchovy dip.

The one item I was surprised to see was a *torta di ricotta* since ricotta cheesecake was a Sicilian dessert.

Perhaps this was a trap.

My gaze went to the wineglass before me.

So fixated was I on its possibly poisonous deep ruby depths, I didn't even realize Benedict was observing me.

His dark voice cut through my concentration. Picking up his wineglass, he said, "*Vino Nobile di Montepulciano d'Abruzzo dei Cavalieri* from the Cavalieri special reserve, of course. Only the finest wine for such a beautiful woman."

His arm remained suspended as he fixed his piercing gaze on me.

I looked from him to my glass and back.

He gave the glass a slight tip in my direction as I still refused to reach for mine.

I wanted to be the type of femme fatale who could stare a man down, boldly reach for her glass, take a long sip, then toss her hair back as she recklessly laughed at danger like I saw in the spy movies.

But I wasn't.

I would probably be the one who got her partner killed by knocking over a shelf and alerting the enemy during an escape or the one who accidentally activated the pen gun because she tried to use it as an actual pen.

Or worse, I would be the one who was only the voice on the phone back at the office who gave them the boring statistical analysis of the bomb radius and how many people would be killed if the hero didn't act in the next four point three seconds.

It was fine. I wasn't cut out for all that attention and responsibility anyway.

Sometimes books, social media, and television made it feel like the only life worth living was one of chaos and adventure. Like if I wasn't trying to eat a snail on a beach in the middle of nowhere, I somehow wasn't *living*.

What was wrong with wanting a quiet life filled with cozy moments like appreciating a rainy day, or smaller joys like walking through the piazza on market day, or teaching your kids to bake?

I guessed those weren't the grand ambitions of great heroines.

That was why I wasn't the heroine of my own story.

I was barely a side character. It was something I accepted a long time ago. The world could hold only so many heroines anyway. Not everyone could be the queen, someone still had to clean the castle and handle the day-to-day affairs of the kingdom.

It was why none of what I had been asked to do these last few months had sat well with me.

None of it.

The problem was, I hadn't been given a choice.

Just like now.

I continued to stare at the glass of wine, the shimmers from the candlelight reflecting off the wine forming into a skull and crossbones in my imagination.

Kicking out my chair, Benedict latched his foot around the leg and pulled the chair close to his until our knees touched.

He then reached for my wineglass.

My knuckles whitened as I grasped the armrests.

Was he going to force my mouth open and pour the poisoned wine down it?

With his head tilted back, he downed half the glass in one gulp.

He then gave me a wink and took another sip. Only this time he snatched the front of my pajama top and yanked me forward.

His mouth then claimed mine.

I choked as he transferred the sip of wine into my mouth with his kiss.

Having no choice, I swallowed, then sucked in a gasp of air.

He reclaimed my mouth and deepened the kiss. He tasted like wine and faintly of mint toothpaste.

When he released me, I sagged against the high-backed chair, wiping my mouth with the back of my hand.

He chuckled, running his tongue over his lips as if savoring every drop. "Now if it was poisoned, we'll both die."

Astonished by his cavalier attitude, I focused on my breathing while I tried to remember the first signs of poisoning as he picked up my plate and rose to dish out the food.

After he set a full plate in front of me, he did the same for himself, then refilled our glasses and took his seat. Raising his fork, he looked at me. "Do I have to take a bite of everything on your plate as well?"

Now feeling foolish, I shook my head.

As he tore a piece of semolina bread and dipped it in the fresh tomato and caper juice of the *spaccatelle di pomodori*, I pushed my plate aside and reached for the ricotta cheesecake platter. My fingertips had just touched the porcelain edge when Benedict stopped me.

"What are you doing?"

The question confused me at first, then my cheeks heated

and I blinked back tears. "You mean you expect me to just sit here in front of a plate of food and watch you eat while I starve?"

After taking a sip of wine, he said, "What have I done to make you think I'd be so cruel as that?"

My mouth fell open. "Do you want me to list the offenses chronologically or alphabetically?"

His gaze narrowed. "How about both? I'll start. B for Barone Cavalieri. Shot in the chest two nights ago at eight in the evening. Your turn. No, wait, I'm wrong. B is for Bianca. Attempted poisoning." He arched an eyebrow. "How ironic. Now it's your turn."

Bile rose in the back of my throat. Pushing my chair back, I whispered, "I changed my mind, I'm not hungry."

As I stood to leave, Benedict wrapped his arm around my waist and pulled me onto his lap. "You're not going anywhere until you eat."

Scandalized, my body stiffened as the soft silk of his pajama bottoms connected with the bare backs of my thighs and ass, reminding me with excruciating humiliation that I had no panties on.

I lowered my head to hide my discomfort behind my still damp hair. "I'm not hungry."

He tucked the hair behind my ear. "Then we'll be here for a while."

With a dramatic sigh, I threw up my arms. "I don't understand. I was trying to eat when you stopped me. Now I don't want to eat and you're making me."

He tapped the tip of my nose. "I didn't stop you from eating, *angioletto*. I stopped you from eating cake before you at least had some vegetables and bread."

I tried to rise off his lap, but he held firm. "*Multiple* people have tried to kill me today, *including you.* I'll be lucky if I survive the week and you're worried I'm not eating enough veggies?"

"Strictly speaking I opted to fuck you instead."

Averting my face, I fumed. "Will you please let go?" Again I tried to rise.

"No."

"Why not?"

"Because I don't want to."

"That's not an answer."

He shrugged as he reached past me for his wineglass. "It's enough of one for me. Now drink."

"I don't want any."

"I didn't ask if you wanted any, I told you to drink. You need to calm down. The wine will help."

I stared at the wine.

"Babygirl, contrary to popular understanding, there are other holes to get alcohol into the human bloodstream other than just through the mouth."

I snatched the wineglass from him. "What is it with you and *holes*?" Then with both hands I tipped it into my mouth. Taking such a large gulp, some wine dribbled out of the corners of my lips.

He covered my hands with his own as he pulled the glass down. "Easy. That's an expensive, rare wine you're guzzling like a cheap Campari." Leaning forward, he pressed his mouth to mine, flicking his tongue over my lower lip.

At my shocked look, he winked. "Waste not, want not."

He reached around me to fork some tomato and capers onto a piece of bread which he then held in front of my mouth. "Open up."

My lips thinned, knowing at least with this he couldn't threaten me with a different hole. "I don't like capers."

Without saying a word, he popped the piece of bread in his mouth and forked an artichoke heart instead, thoughtfully cutting it in thirds first before holding it up to my lips.

Still I hesitated.

As if reading my mind, his lips nudged my neck, caressing my skin. "There might not be a hole, but I could still bend you over this table and spank your impertinent bottom for disobedience."

My eyes widened at the unmistakable nudge of his hard cock beneath my right thigh.

Benedict gave me a wolfish grin and again seemed to be reading my mind. "And yes ... *that* would follow."

With no more resistance, I opened my mouth like a baby bird and let him place the buttery artichoke on my tongue.

"*Brava ragazza,*" he chuckled as he picked up a piece of fried sage for himself.

After he fed me another piece of bread, this time with only tomato and no capers, and two pieces of roasted vegetables, I asked, "If I promise to eat more vegetables, could I please return to my own chair?"

"No."

"But—"

"No. Tell me about Bianca."

My back stiffened. I reached for the wineglass he had just refilled. I almost never drank and even then, only the occasional cheap red table wine, so I needed to be careful but it seemed like a good way to put off his questions.

Once again, he pulled the glass away from me.

"Tell me about Bianca," he repeated.

I remained silent and lowered my head, allowing my hair to again fall over my face.

And again, he pushed it back over my shoulder, his knuckles brushing my cheek as he did so. "While your involvement with what happened to Barone may be up for debate, there is no point in denying your involvement in what happened to Bianca. Tell me. Now."

Maybe it wouldn't be a bad idea to tell him a little bit, just enough to appease him. Enough to make him think I was cooperating so he would let down his guard and I could escape. Besides, he'd told me he knew I was involved anyway, so I wouldn't be telling him much more than he already knew.

I twisted my hands in my lap, choosing my words carefully. "Most of Cavalieri village believed Enzo had murdered his wife, Renata. I was told her parents were sick with fear that he would do the same to Bianca, especially after he had kidnapped her right in the middle of Cesare's and Milana's engagement party. So they needed my help in rescuing her from—"

"He didn't kidnap her. He kept her at the Cavalieri estate for her own protection."

"Do you hear yourself? By that same definition, you haven't kidnapped me either. You're only keeping me here"—I raised my arms and curled my fingers into air quotes— "for my own protection."

"Exactly."

I twisted to face him. "You can't be serious."

His brow lowered. "Of course I'm serious. If I hadn't been there tonight, you'd be lying in a pool of blood on your apartment floor with half your beautiful face blown off. I brought you here *for your own protection*. You're welcome, by the way."

This time I was able to break free of his grasp and rise.

With my fists on my hips, I forgot about my disgraceful attire and turned to face him. "Has it occurred to you that maybe those men found me because you screwed up?"

He drummed his fingers on the armrest. "You want to explain your reasoning on that one?"

Warming up to the possibility, I threw back my shoulders and smirked. "That's right, Mr. I think I'm a sexy Italian James Bond. You screwed up. I had cut off all ties. My escape plan was perfect. No one knew where I was hiding out and then within an hour of you waltzing into my life, there are men banging down my door. I hardly think that was a coincidence."

I crossed my arms over my chest as I waited for his response, knowing he had none because I was right. Maybe I would get lucky, and he would feel so stupid and embarrassed for his mistake, he would let me go.

Perhaps if I offered to not breathe a word of his humiliating blunder to anyone he would offer me some money to keep silent, enough to get to America. Surely his reputation as a big badass was worth a few thousand euro?

My smug thoughts were interrupted when Benedict slowly rose.

I had to back up several steps as he towered over me. "Fifty-one days ago you left Cavalieri village on the morning bus for Pescara where you took the 4163 afternoon train to Roma Termini but first getting off at Sulmona, Avezzano and Arsoli then back on later trains in an attempt to throw anyone off your trail. You temporarily stayed at the Orsa Maggiore Hostel for Women under the name Amy Jones, pretending to be a tourist from Milan, before moving to the furnished apartment where I found you earlier tonight."

He stepped forward, forcing me to take another two steps

back as he relentlessly continued. "You rented the apartment with a wire transfer from a bank account in your real name located in Sicily and used your Cavalieri employment documents as proof of previous employment. I can only assume you thought that after two weeks, no one was coming after you."

My back slammed against the wall.

He raised his forearms, caging me in. "Babygirl, there wasn't a single fucking second, from the moment you left Cavalieri village, that I didn't know precisely where you were and what you were doing. You just weren't a priority for me until now. And those idiots found you tonight because of your own mistakes, not because I thought I was—what was that again—a sexy Italian James Bond who screwed up."

Staring at the bright colors of his unique tattoo, I licked my dry lips. "I may have gotten a little carried away with my accusations."

"Is that supposed to be an apology?"

I shrugged one shoulder. "I hardly think, after all that has happened, that I owe you an apol—"

He cupped my chin and forced my head up. "Looks like I'm going to have to teach you another lesson."

Despite my best efforts, my lip quivered as my eyes filled with tears. "Please, not another lesson."

I was just so tired and confused and overwhelmed. So much had happened in the last few hours I didn't even know how to begin to process it all.

He leaned down and kissed the top of my head. "We'll save that lesson for later."

With that, he swept me into his arms and carried me out of the room and back into the naughty pagan bedroom.

Settling me in the center of the bed, he swept the covers

over me. The cool sheets were so soft I couldn't resist wriggling my hips as I settled deeper into the bed.

Benedict left the room, turning off the light as he went.

I turned on my side, rubbing my cheek against the soft cotton of the pillowcase, my eyes drifting closed.

They sprang open seconds later when Benedict returned.

A dark shadow loomed over me, there was a rustle of fabric, then the mattress dipped as he got into the same bed.

I sat up, clutching the blanket to my chest. "What are you doing?"

"What does it look like I'm doing? Lying down."

"You can't sleep in here. With me!"

"And yet, here I am."

His arm snaked around my middle and pulled me down to lie beside him.

I tried to rise up again, but his hand on my breast through the thin silk of the pajama top stopped me cold.

"Go to sleep, *angioletto*. We have a long day tomorrow."

"There must be another bedroom in these private quarters."

"There are three," he muttered, already half asleep.

I tried to rise again. "Then I'll sleep in one of those."

He tightened his grasp, this time pulling me back against him as he turned on his side. "No. I'm not letting you out of my sight. Go to sleep."

"Benedict, we are in the Vatican. We can't sleep in the same bed together, we're an unmarried couple! The Bible says, *but if they cannot exercise self-control, they should marry. For it is better to marry than to burn with passion.*"

His breath ruffled my nearly dried curls as he nuzzled my neck. "Did you want me to wake up a priest to marry us?"

The air in my lungs seized. I was fairly certain he was

taunting me but with him I could never be certain. I wouldn't put it past him to do just that to prove a point. "Of course not."

"Then be a good girl and go to sleep."

My back stiffened. "I couldn't possibly fall asleep next to a strange man."

"Babygirl, I've shoved my cock down your throat. I'm hardly a stranger anymore."

Thankful for the darkness so he couldn't see the blush burning my cheeks, I said, "You know what I mean. There is no way I will fall asleep like this."

He flipped me onto my back and straddled me as he captured my wrists and stretched them over my head. "I have plenty of *creative* ways to wear you out."

I yanked on my wrists. "I'm suddenly feeling very tired."

His lips quirked. "I thought you might be."

Releasing my arms, he moved to lie behind me, only this time his fingers deftly unbuttoned the top pearl buttons of my borrowed pajama top and slipped inside to cup my bare breast. He shifted his hips and his hard cock pressed against my lower back.

I gasped and stiffened my limbs, trying my best not to move.

He pulled me closer. "That's right, babygirl. Any more trouble from you tonight and I'll break at least four of the Ten Commandments in this bed getting to know you further in a *very* biblical way."

Between the warm strength of his arms and my fevered brain trying to figure out which commandments he meant, I finally fell into an exhausted sleep.

Although I would not have slept a wink if I had known what he had planned for me.

CHAPTER 17

BENEDICT

"That's sacrilegious! I won't do it!"

Liliana backed away from the garment I held as if she would burst into flame if she even touched it.

I stalked toward her several steps. "You will do as you are told," I ground out.

She shook her head as she backed around the dining table. "Not this. I'm not risking hell for you."

In no mood for this bullshit, I ran a palm over my jaw and beard, attempting to rein in my escalating temper.

A miserable night's sleep didn't help.

I'd spent a career falling asleep on hard-packed dirt floors, thin straw mattresses full of bugs, a foreign prison cot or two, in a few ditches, and even once in a drainpipe with a sniper rifle while I waited for my target.

And any one of those times, I'd gotten more sleep than last night in a one-of-a-kind, outrageously luxurious four-poster bed with fucking Charlotte Thomas Bespoke thousand count

Egyptian cotton sheets with goddamn 22-karat gold woven into the fabric just to be obnoxious.

And it was all her fault. The adorably stubborn pain in my ass who was currently having a temper tantrum.

All I could think about was how I wanted to grab her by the hips and grind my aching cock against her stomach while I sucked that pouting lower lip into my mouth and sank my teeth into its sweet, pink fullness.

There were at least a dozen times throughout the night where I came close to waking her up just to fuck her.

And I wasn't talking about a gentle squeeze on the hip to waken her.

I was talking about rolling her onto her back, licking her pussy to get it wet enough and then driving straight in, to the hilt, with my cock … to waken her.

Once, I came close.

My hand had slipped between her legs to tease her clit.

She moaned in her sleep and arched her back, rubbing her cute ass against my cock. But when I grasped my shaft and edged it between her cheeks to press it against her tight back hole, she whimpered in pain in her sleep.

Realizing she must still be sore in that hole and wanting her fully awake the first time I sank my cock in her pussy, I rolled away and spent a sleepless night thinking of all the depraved things I wanted to do to my little captive, all while forcing her to call me daddy.

My new favorite kink.

Of course, this all meant I was now in a foul mood and my already low patience threshold was nonexistent.

Cornering her, I held up the nun's habit. "If I have to take off my belt, bend you over this table and tan your naked hide first, then fine, but trust me, you will wear this."

"Why can't I just wear my own clothes?"

"I had them destroyed."

She ran her hand through her hair. "Why?"

Placing a hand under her chin, I lifted her face to meet my narrowed gaze. "I'm not in the habit of having to explain myself, but I thought it would be obvious. It's usually a bad idea to keep bloodstained clothes after committing a murder."

"I didn't shoot him, you did!"

"You were involved, and let's not go down the path of who shot whom and when before either of us have had a *caffè*."

At my reference to Barone's shooting, her gaze shifted away and some of the fight left her.

But not all.

She pleaded. "Can't we find some other clothes for me? There must be some I could borrow?"

My lips twisted. "Yes, because the Vatican is known to be crawling with women. No. It's part of my plan. Put it on. I'm done arguing with you." I shoved the hanger of garments into her chest.

She clasped them, freeing me to turn to the breakfast tray to pour both of us a *caffè*. As I returned with the cups, she turned hopeful eyes in my direction. "Maybe I could just wear the black dress part without the veil?"

I held out a cup. "No. You'll wear the whole outfit."

She grimaced at my outstretched hand. "I don't like a plain *caffè*. I drink *caffè macchiato* in the morning."

Fortunately, the staff had anticipated such a request. Drinking both my own and her caffès, I turned back to the tray to make her *caffè macchiato.*

"Can you just tell me why?"

Seeing that the fastest way to end this would be to appease

her curiosity, I slammed the empty cups down and stormed back toward her.

Yanking the hanger out of her grasp, I tossed it aside and forced her against the wall. "Francesa Morvillo, Emanuela Setti Carraro, Barbara Asta, Graziella Campagna, Rita Atria, Angela Fiume, and little Caterina and Nadia Nencioni."

Her eyes teared at the names I recited.

I didn't have to tell her who they were.

Most Italians, especially someone from Sicily, recognized victims of the mafia.

It was hard to miss their deaths since many were either killed in violent car bombs or brutal daylight shootings. But this list was especially heartbreaking.

I cupped her cheek and swiped at her tears with the side of my thumb. "All women and girls. All violently killed."

She sniffed. "Why are you telling me this?"

"Because unfortunately, babygirl, *unlike you*, they were innocent."

A tremor ran over her body at the stark honesty of my words.

I straightened and continued to stare down at her. "The mafia has no problem killing innocent women and children when they get in the way. So they definitely will not hesitate to kill a woman with blood on her hands. Yesterday should have been proof enough."

She didn't need to know my suspicions that Dante, the man she supposedly worked for, hadn't been the one to send the kill squad after her.

For now, it served my purpose for her to assume her boss had turned on her and wanted her dead.

"I need to get us both the fuck out of Rome for now. Driving a car isn't safe. Taking a train, surrounded by the public, will be." I reached behind me, picked up the hanger and handed it to her again. "And this is how we are going to do it."

She swallowed and slowly nodded.

Hugging the hanger to her chest, she turned to leave the room.

I stopped her with a hand on her shoulder. "Where do you think you're going?"

She swiped at her eyes and sniffed. "I'm going to the bathroom to find my bra and panties and put on the nun's habit like you just said."

Turning her around to face me, I unhooked the first button on her pajama top. "Nice try. Not after that little temper tantrum. You'll change right here in front of me."

Her mouth fell open. "Here? Out in the open? What if someone from the staff comes in and sees me?"

I couldn't help my slight smirk as I took a seat and leaned back. "Then I guess that man will have quite a story to tell in confession this week. If I were you, I'd hurry before they come back for the breakfast tray."

"Can I at least go and get my underwear?"

I folded my hands before me, tilting my head to the side. "I regret to say they were burned with the rest of your clothes."

"Burned? There wasn't any blood on them!"

I shrugged. "Just being thorough. I did keep your boots though. I tore the other heel off for you."

There was no point in mentioning I was looking forward to the kinky vision of her wearing a nun's habit with no panties or bra underneath, a pair of over-the-knee black suede boots completing the look. Add a whip and she'd make a fortune online.

Refusing to look at me, she yanked three high-backed

chairs out from under the table and lined them up as a makeshift screen.

She snatched the black long-sleeved tunic off its hanger and pulled it over her head, having quite a struggle to remove the pajama top underneath.

"Need any help?"

With an angry huff, she responded by turning her back on me to pull the white wimple and coif over her head and tie it off in back. "No. And don't think I didn't notice you chose a Benedictine habit."

As she reached for the black veil, I rose to pour her *caffè macchiato* adding just a dash of milk to her espresso. "I assure you, it was purely a coincidence that I chose a sect of nuns whose entire existence revolves around their veneration and devotion to a man named Benedict."

Emerging from around the chairs, she accepted the *caffè macchiato*. "First off, their devotion is to God, secondly it is *Saint* Benedict, a man known for his humble nature and dedication to service and sacrifice. A definition that hardly applies to you."

I brought my hand to my heart. "Saint? Stop, you'll make me blush. I mean, I know you're grateful to me for saving your life, but saint is—"

She choked on her sip of *caffè macchiato*. "I can definitely see why people have spent the last fifty years shooting at you. Urgh, this needs sugar."

I snatched the cup and saucer from her hand. "Fifty? Christ, woman, how old do you think I am?"

With a wide-eyed look, she shrugged one shoulder. "I don't know, sixty-five? Seventy?"

I knew what she was doing and I wasn't biting. Tossing a teaspoon of sugar into her cup, I tried to hand it back to her.

"Try forty-six and keep up with the sass and I'll show you just how young that is by dragging you into the bedroom."

She scrunched her nose. "More sugar. It's not my fault. I mean your hair and beard are white and gray. And sass? Who says sass anymore?"

"The white hair is from dealing with women like you over the years."

Which wasn't entirely true.

My *angioletto* was turning out to be quite unique.

One moment she was all spit and fire, the next vulnerable, submissive, and scared. Just when I had become convinced she was a liar using sex to distract me, I became equally convinced of her relative inexperience in the bedroom.

She worried about offending God by wearing a stupid piece of clothing and yet supposedly had no issue helping try to kill my brother.

I wasn't used to not having a target figured out. It both infuriated and intrigued me.

I added another teaspoon and looked at her.

She shook her head.

I added another.

Another shake of her head.

I added two more.

She shook her head again.

By now my back teeth ached at just the thought of drinking such a cloyingly sweet concoction, which immediately made me feel old. Damn her.

I shoved the cup at her and walked away. "No more sugar. Drink it and like it."

With her back turned to me, she lifted her cup to drink her liquid sugar. "I don't know what your plan is, but it's obvious you don't know a lot about nuns because there is no way one would travel with an unmarried man on a train," she called over her shoulder.

Folding down the collar of my black shirt, I responded, "Oh, I can think of one scenario where they would."

The cup fell from her fingers and smashed into pieces on the mosaic tiles the moment she caught sight of the white Roman collar I had put on to turn my black slacks and shirt into a priest's clerical attire.

CHAPTER 18

BENEDICT

I did not anticipate how difficult it would be to keep my hands off her.

It was alarming how many times between the Vatican and the train terminal I had to stop myself from putting a hand around her waist or on her lower back to guide her through the crowd or to just bring her closer to my side.

To do so would draw immediate attention. The human mind was a curious machine. The ordinary blurred into white noise. However, it only took the slightest gesture or look for the primal side of the brain to take notice and send up a warning flag.

Most often, the person themselves wasn't even sure what they saw, only that it looked *off*.

Fortunately, Liliana behaved.

I was sure my pep talk about all the innocent women violently killed by men just like her boss helped.

She kept her head bowed, her face mostly hidden by the

veil, and her mouth shut. To the average observer, she seemed a shy and reserved nun, unaccustomed to being out in public.

After we boarded the train, I appealed to the porter for privacy to give us time to reflect and pray as I showed him our tickets for a private car in advance. Seated in the private car, we remained seated and silent until the express train pulled away from the station.

It was only then that I rose to lock the door to the cabin and pull the shade. To have done so while passengers were still looking for a seat would have invited suspicion.

As I sat on the bench and finally relaxed, I watched some of the tension leave Liliana's shoulders. "So we're safe?"

I nodded. "For now, yes."

"Where are we going?"

I rubbed my jaw and beard. Studying her, I tried to decide whether to actually tell her or to lie. I had deliberately been avoiding telling her our destination and steered her away from any train signage for the same purpose.

The only point in lying would be to postpone the inevitable. We would be arriving in just over three hours.

"Cavalieri village, then on to the winery."

Liliana shot out of her seat and bolted for the cabin door.

I snatched her around the waist and pulled her down onto my lap. "Where do you think you're going?"

She struggled in my grasp. The heavy folds of her tunic hampered her effort to kick out at me. "Off this train!"

With an arm over her thighs to restrain her, I said, "It's an express. Was it your plan to jump from a moving train?"

"If it meant getting away from you, then yes!"

The veil blocked my view of her face. I pulled it off her head, taking the coif with it, which loosened the bun she had put her hair in. "I'm afraid I can't let you do that."

"I can't go back there. They'll kill me."

"Who will?"

She turned to face me, her eyes wide and wild. "The Cavalieris!"

The corner of my mouth lifted as I reached up to pull the elastic band which held her hair in the ruined bun.

Her locks tumbled over her shoulders in a soft wave of black silk. Smoothing it away from her face, I said, "Have you forgotten that I am a Cavalieri?"

"No. You tried to kill me too! You're probably only taking me to the winery because it will be easier to dispose of my body there than in Rome."

I nodded. "You're not wrong. I know from experience it is way easier to get rid of a body in a rural area than in an urban one. Plus it's far less likely to be found. And you have way more options for disposal. There is burial, tossing off a cliff, the pigs ..."

Her complexion lost all color.

Placing both of my hands on either side of her face, I said, "Babygirl, I'm not going to kill you. You are far more useful to me alive. I've already told you that."

She swallowed. "I don't believe you. Besides, what happens when you have all your precious information and I'm no longer *useful* to you?"

I lowered my gaze, breaking eye contact.

The truth was, I hadn't figured that part out yet.

It was extremely unlikely she would be able to safely return to her old life.

There was always the option of handing her over to the authorities, but even then, she wouldn't be safe from the threat of assassination as a *pentita*, if she had even the slightest amount of inside information about a mafia family's

159

operations.

There is always the ranch.

I pushed the thought away.

There wasn't a chance in hell I was taking the woman accused of helping almost kill my brother up to Northern Italy to my horse ranch, no matter how tight her cute little asshole was or how sweetly she swallowed my cock.

Setting her on the bench across from me, I scowled. "Let's start with you actually being useful first. Tell me about the nuns who raised you."

That bit of information she had let slip last night was particularly striking and I wanted to know more.

She played with the edge of the veil on her lap.

"Liliana, I asked you a question."

Her lips thinned. "I heard you."

"Then answer me."

"I don't want to."

"I didn't ask if you wanted to, tell me about the nuns."

Keeping her gaze averted, she stroked the serviceable woolen batiste cloth, remaining silent.

Apparently it was time to remind her that I was not a man to be ignored.

Without warning my fingers wrapped around her wrist.

In one move, I pulled her across the narrow aisle and back onto my lap, except this time I had her stretched out on her stomach over my thighs.

So she could not scream and alert the porter, I laid my palm securely over her mouth with one hand, while I flipped up her voluminous skirts with the other.

Her legs kicked out, which only drew my attention to the erotic view of her black-suede-encased calves, slim thighs, and bare ass.

Knowing it was all hidden under a nun's habit just added an extra kink.

I leaned over her squirming body and growled, "Apparently, it's time for another lesson in manners from daddy."

Her response was muffled by my hand. She breathed heavily through her nose as she threw her head back and tried to scream.

Squeezing my fingers over her mouth, I reached for my gun and laid it on the bench, out of her reach. "Scream again, and I shoot the first person who comes through the door."

Her eyes widened as she stilled.

"Are you going to be a good girl and not scream?"

She nodded.

"I mean it, Liliana. You scream and I shoot. It's that simple. You want more blood on your hands?"

Her eyes filled with tears, trying to shake her head "no" but prevented by my grip.

After another moment, I slowly pulled my hand away from her mouth, ready to pounce if she were lying.

She pressed her hands against the bench and tried to push up off my lap.

My hand on her lower back over the bunched-up skirt kept her in place.

She begged. "I won't scream, just let me up."

I caressed her ass cheek with my hand. "I have several problems with that statement."

With my free hand, I grabbed her jaw and turned her head to face me. I wanted to see the look in her eye while I punished her. I raised my arm and brought it down with a loud smack on her naked ass cheek.

She opened her mouth, her body jerking.

I gave her a stern look. "Remember, no screaming."

She pulled her lips between her teeth and whimpered instead.

"My first problem is you didn't say please."

I spanked her again, this time on the other cheek.

Liliana rocked on my lap, struggling to contain her cries.

After rubbing her injured cheeks, I lifted my arm and brought my palm down on her vulnerable cheeks again. "My second issue is you didn't say you were sorry."

"I'm sorry," she whispered.

I shifted my grip on her jaw to use my index finger to cover her lips. "Shhh, don't talk while daddy is speaking. And that brings me to my other point."

I spanked her several times on each cheek, not forgetting to strike the tops of her thighs. By the time I was finished her cute ass glowed a charming cherry pink and was hot to the touch. "You didn't say daddy."

The tears flowed freely down her cheeks by now as she keened and mewed, swallowing her own cries.

Running my hand in tormenting circles over her punished skin, I asked, "So, babygirl, you want to try that apology again?"

She nodded. I released her jaw to stroke her hair. "Yes please, daddy. I'm very sorry for ignoring your question. I promise I'll be a good girl and answer."

Her flesh was warm against my palm as I caressed the soft curve of her ass, the top of her leg. My fingertips teased the sensitive skin of her inner thigh.

Liliana clenched her ass cheeks, her breath hissing on a sharp inhale.

After giving her a quick spank, I commanded, "Relax your bottom and open your legs for daddy."

A shiver ran down her spine but she separated her legs slightly.

There was no way I could come close to doing what I wanted to her in this train car but that wouldn't prevent me from assuaging my curiosity. Slipping my left hand between her legs, I shifted it up her leg, until the tips of my fingers teased her pussy lips.

Her hips wiggled the closer I got.

My right hand, which had been resting on the back of her head, twisted in her hair as a warning.

She stilled.

I slipped my two middle fingers deep between her legs and had to stifle my own groan, not wanting to give away too much of my own emotion.

Fuck.

She was wet.

My naughty little girl was wet from her punishment spanking.

My fingers thrust back and forth, teasing her.

Liliana moaned and buried her head in her hands.

"Such a wet pussy. I wonder if I should forget about asking you any questions and instead just pull out my cock so you can ride it the rest of the way to Abruzzo."

She stiffened. "Please don't, daddy. Please just let me answer your questions instead."

There was that shy inexperience mixed with misplaced religious guilt.

My poor babygirl didn't realize this wasn't an either/or situation.

It was more a now-and-then-later scenario.

I would get my answers and then, as soon as I had her alone at the winery, I would fuck her pretty pussy raw.

Giving her swollen clit a final caress, I pulled my fingers free from between her thighs and allowed her to rise from my lap.

The moment she sat across from me with her flushed cheeks and hair falling in a tangled mess around her shoulders, I captured her tear-filled gaze, slid both middle fingers into my mouth, and sucked them clean.

Her eyes widened above her burning cheeks.

Adorable.

"Now, where were we? Oh, yes. The nuns. What happened to your parents? Why were you there?"

With her gaze averted, she replied in a voice so hesitant and soft, I had to lean forward with my forearms on my thighs to hear her.

"My father was a *capo mandamento*. He was killed on his way to the *Commissione Interprovinciale* twenty-five years ago. My mother wasn't supposed to be in the car with him, but she was nine months pregnant with me at the time and he didn't want to leave her at home."

Her hands shook as she wrung them in her lap.

My gut twisted while I listened, already knowing where this was headed.

She swallowed and continued. "She hung on only long enough to give birth to me. I was immediately transported to a convent in Ispica where I was raised by the nuns."

Ispica was on the furthest southern point of Sicily, as far as possible from the mafia centers in the north while still keeping her in Sicily.

"It was a convent dedicated to the Madonna, so the nuns named me Liliana after the Virgin Mary's symbolic flower."

If her father had been a *capo mandamento*, it meant he had not only been the boss of his own *cosca*, or mafia family

164

within its own territory, but was chosen as the representative leader of multiple territories.

Twenty-five years ago meant the *Commissione Interprovinciale* he had been on his way to attend was the one called to elect a new *capo dei capi,* boss of bosses, of the entire Sicilian mob after the then-current leader had been assassinated in a car bomb.

A new leader was always chosen from the assembled *capo mandamento.* Whoever killed her father saw him as a rival, a threat. Which meant if Liliana's father hadn't been killed, he'd likely have been chosen as the *capo dei capi.*

That was the *Commissione Interprovinciale* which put the Agnellos, specifically Dante's father and now Dante, in power.

Goddammit.

She isn't just some random female who accidentally got in over her head with the mafia.

She's fucking mafia royalty.

CHAPTER 19

BENEDICT

*T*he dull thud of the Range Rover locks hammering into place made her jump.

Not bothering to take my eyes off the curving road which led to the Cavalieri winery, I said, "Don't even think about it."

Liliana crossed her arms over her chest and sank lower into the passenger seat.

After leaving the train, we got into the Range Rover Alfonso had left at the station for me. Not wanting to cause the women any undue trauma, I called Matteo and warned him I was bringing Liliana onto the property.

He, Cesare, and Enzo would make sure Amara, Milana, Bianca, and Gabriella were at the hospital with Barone when we arrived.

With each twisting curve of the road, I could feel Liliana's anxiety rising and caught her hand drifting toward the car door handle in my peripheral vision.

"What exactly would be the plan? Assuming you survived jumping from a speeding car and missed the potentially rocky roll down the side of the mountain. Head to the next village dressed as a nun and beg for alms?"

"I hadn't thought it through."

Tightening my grip on the leather steering wheel, I said, "You didn't think a lot of things through."

I didn't have the full story yet, but I knew enough to be pissed she'd allowed herself to be put in this vulnerable position.

It was clear from what little she told me about Bianca that she had been manipulated into thinking she was helping her, not harming her.

Which had me wondering, what else had she been manipulated into thinking?

Two armed guards nodded and rushed to open the iron gates to the property at our approach. Ever since the shooting, we were not taking any chances with security.

Liliana's breathing had become shallow and erratic.

The pretty pink blush my earlier spanking had brought to her cheeks was replaced with an ashy paleness. The harsh black tunic she was wearing wasn't helping but at least she had taken off the wimple and veil, so it didn't look like I was driving a nun to her execution.

Knowing we had a few minutes before we reached the main house, I thought to calm her, but didn't know what to say. Any platitude I could think of was a straight-up lie.

Everything was not going to be fine.

I could not guarantee that she would be safe here.

And the rest of my family was definitely not going to be understanding about why I brought her here.

Frustrated, I reached for the Roman collar and yanked it off, before unbuttoning the top few buttons at my collar.

Dammit, now she had me nervous.

When we pulled up to the main house, all was still and quiet. The winter was already a time of low activity at the winery but with Barone's near-death experience, a somber cloud had settled over the usually boisterous place.

After getting out, I circled around to open her door. The moment I pulled on the door handle, I realized she had locked it.

I tapped on the window. "Liliana, open the door."

She shook her head.

"Babygirl, you are only delaying the inevitable and annoying the shit out of me while you're at it. Open the damn door."

I tried the handle again.

Locked.

I had wanted her to obey on her own, but clearly that was not going to happen.

Reaching into my pocket, I flicked the lock button on the keyless entry fob and pulled on the door handle before she had a chance to re-lock it.

With the door open, I leaned against the interior door-frame. Crossing my arms, I gestured with a nod. "You have one second to get your ass out of this car before I reach in there and drag you out by your hair."

She gathered her thick locks up in her hand and twisted them into a low ponytail over her left shoulder, out of my reach. "Don't you dare! Take me back to Rome."

"No."

"Take me to the train station then. I'll make my own way."

"No."

"You can't make me stay here!"

"What's the matter, *angioletto?* Was facing the victims of your actions also one of those things you had not thought through? Your favorite book says, *repent, therefore, of this wickedness of yours,* does it not?"

Her dark eyes filled with unshed tears. "Why are you doing this to me?"

I leaned into the interior. "With some targets, facing the consequences of their actions is enough to break them. Trust me, babygirl. What I am doing now is a kindness. There are far more gruesome ways at my disposal to break you."

The muscles in her throat contracted as she swallowed and tightened her jaw, trying unsuccessfully to blink away tears.

Giving me a watery false smile, she said, "A target. I almost forgot that is what I am to you. Thank you for the reminder."

There was absolutely no fucking reason why that should have hurt. Why that technically true statement of fact from her pretty lips should have twisted my gut into a knot.

Or why her crestfallen, broken baby doll expression should make me want to grab her to my chest, hold her close and tell her that everything was going to be okay, because I was there to protect her.

Clearing my throat, I stepped back. "Out of the car. Last warning."

She gathered up her heavy skirts and, ignoring the hand I held out to help her alight, stepped awkwardly from the SUV.

The moment I turned to escort her into the villa, its arched entrance doors slammed open.

Like the avenging Tisiphone, Amara flew toward us with her fellow goddess Furies Alecto and Megaera, in the form of Milana and Bianca, following close behind.

In my defense, I assumed they were only going to scream at Liliana.

Something she more than deserved.

I was wrong.

Amara launched herself at Liliana, claws bared.

With her clenched fists full of Liliana's hair, she screamed, *"Puttana! Ti uccidero!"*

Fuck.

Liliana cried out, raising her arms to protect her face while also trying to dislodge Amara's grip.

As I lunged forward to break them up, I was set on by Milana and Bianca.

Milana faced off with me. "Don't you dare defend this bitch. Barone almost died! We've been through hell these last few days."

Bianca gestured wildly behind her. "She tried to poison me! She's lucky we didn't give Amara the keys to the gun room."

Christ. I knew better than to think they were exaggerating.

There wasn't a doubt in my mind that it had been a topic of discussion over their espresso and pastry this morning whether they would just tear Liliana limb from limb or shoot a hole in her the next time they saw her.

By now, Amara and Liliana were on the ground, rolling over each other in strange, alternating flashes of somber black and bright emerald and gold.

Although not showing yet, I treated Milana as if she were already in labor when I gently cupped her shoulders and moved her to the side. I then pivoted away from Bianca and rushed to stop the fight.

"Ladies! Stop this instant!" I bellowed.

I was ignored. Nothing but high-pitched shrieks and a truly impressive string of colorful curse words polluted the air.

When she had rolled on top of Liliana, I attempted to snatch Amara around the waist from behind, but her silk dress allowed her to slip through my grasp like an eel. Which was unfortunate, because she chose that moment to draw her arm back and punch Liliana right in the eye.

"Dammit, woman! I said stop!"

Milana's voice called over me. "Punch her again!"

Bianca cried out, "Use your nails, girl!"

With a stern look of warning over my shoulder, I pointed to them both. "Not another word."

Just as I was making another attempt to separate Amara and Liliana, there was a shout of alarm from the main house. "They're here!"

Matteo, Cesare, and Enzo bolted toward me.

"About fucking time," I growled. "This is what I was trying to avoid."

Matteo shrugged. "Our bad."

While Cesare herded Milana and Bianca out of the way, Enzo and Matteo reached for Amara's arms while I was able to grab hold of Liliana.

We wrenched the squirming, hissing women apart.

Amara fought Enzo and Matteo's grasp as she continued to yell. "How dare you show your face here, you backstabbing whore. I hope he brought you here to kill you! I hope he feeds you to the fucking pigs. It's more than you deserve for what you did."

Milana called out over Cesare's shoulder. "You tell her, Amara!"

Cesare pulled her to his chest. "That's enough from you, *carissima*. Remember what the doctor said about stress and the baby."

Enzo handed Amara off to Matteo and went to restrain Bianca as she stormed past a distracted Cesare.

Bianca reached up to take off her earrings. "My turn!"

Enzo dropped his shoulder into her middle and lifted her onto it. "The hell it is, *tesoro mio.*"

Bianca raised up on her torso and shook her fist at Liliana. "She tried to kill me! It's an eye for an eye!"

Cesare carried Milana across the yard to their home while Enzo kept Bianca over his shoulder, marching over to the lane that would take them back to the cottage they shared at the edge of the vineyard.

Both women's shouts of protest could still be heard.

Amara shrugged out of Matteo's grasp and leveled her narrowed gaze on me. "I want this woman out of my sight and off my property by nightfall. Get whatever information you need from her and then *get rid of her,* or I will."

Matteo palmed her shoulder and turned her away. "Come on, we're late for the hospital."

She broke free of his grasp and turned on Liliana again. "Did you hear that, bitch? The hospital. Where the man I love is still fighting for his life *because of you.*"

After sending Matteo a warning look, he nodded and with gentle force, took hold of Amara again and guided her toward the stables where Alfonso had emerged at the sound of fighting.

Amara ran to him. He gave her a hug and spoke softly to her as he gestured over her head to Matteo to open the car's back passenger door.

Moments later, all three were rushing out of the yard in a bulletproof SUV, a second guard vehicle behind them, to the hospital.

A strange stillness after the storm settled on the open courtyard.

Liliana trembled against my side, shuddering in my tight hold.

Turning my attention to her, I curled a finger under her chin and raised her face to inspect the damage. There were a few scratches and fabric burns around her neck and one just under her jaw.

Amara's punch fortunately missed Liliana's eye and glanced off her cheekbone. There was a harsh red mark and a faint bluish-purple bruise already showing under the skin.

She remained quiet and still under my inspection of her wounds.

Alarmingly quiet and still.

A bare stalk of a twig was tangled in a clump of her hair. Isolating the tangled curls, I carefully freed the twig and tossed it aside.

She continued to stand before me, completely silent, just staring blankly straight ahead.

My hands fisted at my sides with my effort to resist the urge to offer her comfort.

While I had not intended for her to be physically attacked by the girls, the entire point of this trip was not only to regroup someplace where I could discuss the situation with the others without fear of being overheard, but to also force Liliana past the breaking point.

There were faster ways to get to the truth, torture being one, but they were less reliable.

Having your target willingly give you the information after an emotional epiphany or more accurately an emotional breakdown was far more desirable and yielded more accurate details.

Unable to stop myself, I reached to cup her cheek.

She flinched at my touch.

Gabriella appeared, wearing a bright fuchsia-and-orange silk dressing gown with a matching turban, holding a *Negroni Sbagliato* with an orange wedge as if she had chosen her drink to match her outfit. Something I would not put past her.

Giving the courtyard a sweep of her arm, she said, "What did I miss?"

CHAPTER 20

AMARA

The darkened SUV windows added to the forlorn atmosphere outside as we raced past bare trees and brown fields. In the distance, the Apennine mountains were already a forbidding gray under their cover of snow.

Soon the storms would reach the valley basin.

It used to be my favorite time of year.

From the procession of the statue of the Virgin Mary through the village to the church for the *Immacolata Concezione* which began the season on December eighth, to the *Presepe Vivente* in the piazza with all the farm animals gathered around the empty manger waiting for baby Jesus, to the lighting of the *N'doccia* torch on Christmas Eve.

This year was going to be magical … until that night.

I stared down at my hands. They were filthy with a few scratches here and there. Dark brown crescent moons of dirt were caked under several of my fingernails.

But I didn't see any of it.

All I saw was blood.

Barone's blood.

Each night I was tortured by visions of finding him leaning against his desk in the study, blood blossoming into a large, macabre rose in the center of his chest from the single bullet wound.

I didn't remember crying out for help.

I just remembered screaming.

Screaming and screaming and screaming until my throat was so hoarse, I was reduced to choking sobs.

When I'd pressed both hands to the seeping wound, he'd wrapped his arm around my waist and said, "Don't worry, *dolcezza*. It will take more than a bullet to separate me from you."

Then his eyes had closed and for one sickening moment, I thought I'd lost him.

By then everyone had come running.

His brother Benedict, who had a startling amount of knowledge when it came to gunshot wounds, took charge.

At his command, Rosa ran in with a jar of petroleum jelly which, after cutting off Barone's shirt and jacket, he slathered on both the entrance and exit wounds before applying a gauze bandage.

Before I knew it, we were in the back of one of the winery vans racing to the hospital, while Enzo was on the phone arranging to have the country's best surgeons airlifted from Rome to Abruzzo using the Diamanti helicopter.

The chaos continued at the hospital. Alfonso had to pull me off Barone's inert body as they put him on a stretcher and wheeled him in for surgery. After that it was a string of doctors droning on and on.

Signora Cavalieri, we are doing everything we can to save your husband.

The bullet traveled through the chest wall, collapsing one lung, and fracturing two ribs.

Signora Cavalieri, do you understand? The path around the bullet collapsed because the tissue is elastic, so we have to be careful since it seems to have had an upward trajectory toward the heart.

The occlusive bandage at the scene contained the damage and allowed the lung to partially re-expand.

Signora Cavalieri, we're pleased to say the surgery was a success. Your husband is a strong and stubborn man. He's going to pull through just fine.

At that point, I broke.

I stood and cried, "I'm not Signora Cavalieri! That amazingly strong, wonderfully stubborn man tried to ask me to marry him over and over again." I then pounded my palm against my chest. "And I wouldn't let him because I selfishly wanted the timing to be perfect."

Milana had stood and tried to hug me. "Amara, don't—"

I swiped at the tears. "Why did I do that? Why was I so afraid to say yes? I might have lost him." I threw my arm back toward the swinging surgery doors. "I could still lose him, and he'll never know that I would have said yes!"

Bianca joined Milana and they both hugged me as my shoulders shook with my racking sobs.

Milana ran her hand over my back in soothing circles. "Don't be ridiculous. That man knows how much you love him."

Aunt Gabriella cupped my cheek. "My darling girl, you are looking at this all wrong."

I'd sniffed and raised my head off Milana's shoulder to look at her expectantly.

She smoothed my hair off my forehead. "You probably saved his life by saying no."

Enzo crossed his arms over his chest and smirked. "I can't wait to hear this."

Aunt Gabriella shrugged. "It's simple. A Cavalieri man is too stubborn to die before getting what he wants. Barone wouldn't dare shuffle off this mortal coil before getting a 'yes' from Amara."

In a weird, comforting way, I realized she was right.

And when he finally woke up from surgery and I was able to see him, Barone agreed.

"*Dolcezza*, I've told you before. You're not getting rid of me."

Since then, I'd spent most waking hours by his bedside. Only leaving at his own insistence to get a little sleep at home before returning.

As we pulled up to the special parking spaces reserved for our security detail at the hospital, I smiled to see all the candles, flowers, and bottles of wine left at a makeshift shrine at the base of a statue of the Madonna in a small grove of trees next to the hospital's main entrance.

Word had spread rapidly throughout Cavalieri, and residents from all over the small city had started to show up at the hospital and hold vigil almost from the first hour of his surgery.

The staff loved all the attention. Because of Barone there was a constant stream of sweet platters piled high with *caggionetti, scrippelle,* and *parrozzo.* As well as heated dishes of *baccala* with potatoes, *capone di Natale ripieno,* and *branzino al sale.*

Grateful as the villagers shared their Christmas feasts with them as a thank you and encouragement to take good care of their *Don Cavalieri.*

An angry shout from Barone had Matteo, Alfonso, and me

running down the corridor toward his private room. We got there just in time to see two nurses trying to get Barone to release his grip from around a doctor's throat.

"What is going on?" I yelled as I crossed the threshold.

"Signora Cavalieri, thank God you're here!" cried one of his nurses.

Repeated attempts to tell them I didn't deserve the respectful title had been ignored, with Barone's encouragement, I was fairly certain.

Running over to the bed, I wrapped my arms around Barone's upper arm, taking comfort in the thick, hard muscles and display of healthy strength. "Barone, release him this instant."

Through clenched teeth, Barone said, "Tell him to let go first."

I looked down to see the doctor had a death grip on Barone's chest tube.

The doctor choked out, "Don Cavalieri, I have to remove your thoracotomy tube. It's procedure."

Giving him a sympathetic look, I laid my hand over his grip on the long, plastic tube and said, "I think you should do as he says and let go."

The doctor released the tube and Barone let go of his throat.

Before anyone could stop him, Barone wrapped his hand around the tube and pulled it out himself. Throwing his head back and letting a rumbling growl escape through his clenched teeth before tossing the slightly bloody tube into a waiting metal dish.

A nurse scurried around the bed with a bandage in hand. She paused before touching him, giving me a nervous glance.

Sensing her fear, I directed her to leave the supplies with me. "I'll take it from here."

With a gratified look, they and the doctor left the room with Matteo and Alfonso following to smooth things over.

After stepping into the attached bathroom and scrubbing the dirt and blood from my hands, I located a pair of gloves and slipped them on. Focusing on my task, I chastised Barone. "You really should be nicer to them. They are just doing their job."

He frowned. "What are they going to do? Throw me out? I paid to build this hospital."

I cast him a glowering look.

He sighed as he ran his hand down my back to cup my ass. "All right, *dolcezza*. I'll say I'm sorry later. I'll even buy the good doctor that new MRI machine he's been not-so-subtly hinting about."

I finished with his bandage, pulled off and tossed out my gloves, and turned to look at him.

The moment I did I burst into tears. Again.

Truth was, I had barely stopped crying for days now.

Without saying a word, he wrapped his arm around my waist and guided me up onto the hospital bed with him, tucking me into his side.

I tried to pull back, objecting. "Your stitches."

He placed his hand on the back of my head and pushed it down onto his bare shoulder. "Fuck my stitches."

My palm rested over his heart, above his bandages. I would never tire of hearing its strong, steady beat. For the hundredth time, I whispered, "Will you marry me, Barone?"

His chuckle vibrated deep inside his chest and against my cheek. "I've already told you ... no."

Ever since the shooting we had reversed roles. I proposed

marriage, sometimes several times a day, and Barone always said no.

He hugged me closer, kissing the top of my head. "I've told you before. I won't let this bullshit ruin the special proposal you wanted. I'm going to give you one and it won't be with me lying in a fucking hospital bed with a fucking chest wound."

My fingertips traced circles over his heart. "And I've told you, I don't care about any of that anymore. It was stupid of me to want some perfect memory. I could have lost you."

He cupped my jaw and swiped at my tears with his thumb. "You didn't and you're not going to. I'm too stubborn to die."

I laid my hand over his and smiled.

His brow furrowed when he caught sight of my banged-up hand. "What happened?"

I curled my fingers into my palm. "It's nothing."

He just looked at me. "If you think I'll let a little thing like a bullet wound stop me from getting my belt and pulling you over my lap, you're in for a painful surprise, little one."

He moved his hand down my back to give my ass a warning squeeze.

"Benedict is back. He brought that woman with him."

He smiled. "I know."

My mouth dropped open. "You know?"

"Of course I know. I know everything."

Rolling my eyes, I said, "I'm going to ignore that. Why didn't you tell me?"

"You were supposed to be here when she arrived, so it didn't upset you." He tapped the tip of my nose. "But I guess you were late."

He then wrapped his hand around mine and kissed my

fingertips. "Can I assume she didn't receive the customary Cavalieri warm welcome?"

I leaned up on my elbow. "How can you ask such a thing? She is responsible for almost getting you killed."

"Possibly. Benedict is not so certain."

"She poisoned Bianca."

He tilted his head as he tucked a lock of hair behind my ear. "Again, we might have gotten that part wrong, too. I trust my brother's judgment and you should trust mine, babygirl."

With a frustrated sigh, I settled my head back down on his chest, grumbling, "I refuse to be nice to her."

His hand caressed my back. "Fair enough. In the meantime, I believe you owe Santa a cookie."

When I turned my head to look up at him, he winked.

The children in the hospital were convinced Barone was *Babbo Natale.* So to their delight we had arranged to have a delivery of gifts and sweets sent to the hospital for all the sick children as well as those who were visiting sick adults.

Barone had agreed to dress up in a Santa Claus outfit so he could be wheeled into the common area in a wheelchair the staff had decorated to look like a sleigh. Even though he grumbled about the wheelchair, I could tell he loved every minute of it.

Still, I had to make certain promises to get him to agree to stay seated and follow the doctor's orders and not try to walk around on his own, greeting the children.

"Only you would think about that at a time like this."

He moved my hand from over his heart and down his bare abdomen to slip it inside the waistband of his pajama bottoms. "I'm *always* thinking about it."

I slid out of the hospital bed and rushed over to lock the door and close the small window blind. Then, returning to his bed, I gingerly crept back on it to straddle his lower legs. As I reached for the ties to his pajama bottoms, I gave him a cheeky grin. "Fine, but if that heart monitor goes off, I'm stopping."

Barone gripped the ECG cables attached to his chest and tore them away from the sticker patch electrodes connecting them to the monitor. "What heart monitor?"

I tried not to smile. "You know an alarm goes off at the nurses' station when those detach."

He smirked as he grasped his hard shaft in one hand and placed the other hand behind my head, guiding it down. "No one would dare unlock that door."

My breath teased the head of his cock. "That was very naughty of you, *Santa*."

"Open your mouth and I'll show you what a Bad Santa I am."

CHAPTER 21

LILIANA

The ice rattled in Gabriella's glass as she approached Benedict. "Really, Benedict, what the hell were you thinking, bringing that girl here?"

I shrunk back behind him.

You didn't have to live in Cavalieri village long to know about Barone Cavalieri's infamous sister-in-law, Gabriella De Luca.

I once heard a businessman in the Cavalieri Enterprises offices describe her as a cursed diamond; beautiful and unique in an entrancing way, but too dangerous to possess.

And I couldn't agree with him more. It wasn't that she was mean or vicious, although you never wanted to be on the sharp end of her tongue. There was just always a frenetic energy about her whenever she came into the offices.

I'd never seen anyone move and talk with her confidence and self-assurance.

Especially around such large, intimidating men like the Cavalieri men.

Benedict brushed dirt off his thigh. "I was *thinking* the boys would have done as instructed and gotten the girls out of the way before I arrived."

Gabriella waved her hand. "Oh, was that why Matteo was being such a nuisance this morning when I insisted on Amara and Bianca showing me the new wine label designs and marketing research."

Benedict rubbed his forehead. "Yes, Gabbie. That would be why."

Her eyes narrowed. "You know I hate being called that. It makes me sound like a mangy poodle."

He gave her a hug and a quick kiss on the cheek. "That's precisely why I do it."

She stayed in his arms as she rested her palms on his chest and gave him a sexy wink. "It's a good thing you're good looking. If any other man tried calling me that I'd cut off his balls."

Get your hands off my man.

Wait. Where did that just come from?

My stab of jealousy wasn't just alarming, it was confusing.

He was definitely not *my man.*

My captor. My tormentor. Possibly my murderer, but definitely not my man.

I barely even knew him.

And he and Gabriella made a much more logical couple. They were closer in age. Both obscenely rich and connected. They clearly liked one another. He even had a cute nickname for her.

It wasn't as cute as mine, *angioletto*, but it was okay.

There I went again. Stop it, I internally screamed.

Benedict turned and gestured to me. "Liliana, come here. I want you to meet Gabriella."

Um, no.

Folding my hands in front of me, I kept my head slightly bowed and didn't move. "We've met."

Gabriella turned her piercing gaze on me.

My cheeks heated under the intense scrutiny. It was worse than being caught out by Mother Superior at the convent.

She stepped toward me. After taking a leisurely sip from her drink, a testament to her master skills in intimidation, she said, "Well, well. I have to admit you certainly caught me by surprise, Signorina Fiore, not a small feat. I'll be sure not to underestimate you in the future."

At that I did look up, getting caught in her gaze.

Was that a threat?

I swallowed back the tears threatening to fall. I just wanted to curl up into a little ball and disappear. Never in my life had I prayed harder for a hole to open in the earth.

Facing these people was torture.

Especially since I couldn't tell them the real reason I'd done what I did....

If only they knew.

It was odd. I didn't even really know any of them and yet, the fact they all hated me with such a blinding hot rage cut me to the core.

The Cavalieris may have a reputation for being a powerful and wealthy family who were dangerous to cross, but they were also known for their extreme generosity, kindness, and loyalty not only to one another but to the people in the village who were all treated like family.

Losing the respect of people like that hurt.

Still, it angered me to be judged so harshly ... even if it was justified.

If only they knew.

Gabriella reached out and lifted my chin. "What? Nothing to say for yourself?"

I wrenched my face out of her grasp. "I'm here against my will. I don't owe any of you anything."

She laughed. "There's a spark. I was getting worried. Can't start a fire with a damp piece of wood."

Gabriella cast a glance over her shoulder. "Benedict, I'm sure you have things to do. Leave her with me."

Benedict shook his head. "Gabbie, you don't understand what a handful—"

Completely ignoring his objection, she put her arm around my waist and guided me toward the front entrance to the main house. "Posh, you men always cause such drama. We girls will be fine. You have guards posted everywhere. She's not going anywhere. Now shoo."

Moving alongside Gabriella as if I were nothing more than a tiny leaf being carried off in the wind, I looked helplessly over my shoulder at Benedict, who didn't even protest.

He just let her sweep me into the dark interior of the house.

The moment my eyes adjusted, I came face to face with the scowling countenance of an older, matronly women whose silver hair was pulled severely back into a bun and whose arms were crossed under her substantial bosom. Everything about her screamed disapproval.

Gabriella handed the woman her empty glass. "Don't scowl like that Rosa, it will cause wrinkles. Yes, we all know who she is and we're all angry but that is no excuse for bad manners. Be a dear and have a tray sent up to my rooms."

She then turned to me as she propelled me toward a large central staircase. "I think it best if we eat in the privacy of my rooms. No point in putting you on display like a circus freak."

"I'm not really hungry."

"Then it's a good thing there will be liquor. Come."

Down a beautiful hallway lined with amazing artwork and small side tables displaying gorgeous, expensive vases and statuettes, she pushed open a pair of doors, revealing a living room space with French glass doors leading out onto a wrought iron balcony.

Gabriella sauntered through the living room into a stunning, white marble dressing room.

If I closed my eyes and imagined what the dressing room of a famous actress from the fifties would look like, this would be it. It was all sparkling crystal, gold, and marble with lots of mirrors, white furniture, and a massive vanity covered in expensive perfume bottles and Chanel makeup.

She sat on a white tufted ottoman, pulled out a second one from beneath the vanity, and patted it. "Sit."

Feeling terribly awkward and filthy dressed in my unrelentingly awful black tunic that was now covered in dirt and dust, not to mention my broken-heeled boots, I shook my head. "I really shouldn't. I should go find Benedict."

Twisting her torso, she gave me a once-over with her eyes and nodded. "God, you're right. Rosa will kill me if you track any more dirt in here. Take it off."

My eyes widened. "What?"

She rose and crossed to a paneled wall and pressed some hidden latch. The panels each swung open, exposing a hidden closet. After rustling through several hangers, she selected a deep purple dressing gown and held it out to me. "Here. This will do until your suitcase is brought up."

Without reaching for the hanger, I clutched at the collar of the tunic and said, "I don't have a suitcase. This is all I have to wear."

Gabriella rolled her eyes. "Of course you don't. God forbid one of these men ever bring a woman home with a decent wardrobe. I'm beginning to think your clothes just fall off and are forgotten the moment they enter the damn room."

My brow furrowed. "For your information, Benedict burned mine!"

She shoved the hanger against my chest. "Thank God for that. Now change."

Snatching the hanger before it fell, I said, "I'm confused."

She gestured at my tunic. "I was worried *this* was a choice."

I pulled at the tunic again, even more self-conscious than before. "No, it was Benedict's idea," I grumbled under my breath like a child who had just been scolded.

Gabriella sat before her vanity again and looked at me in the reflection of her mirror. "It's a good thing. You could hardly play the proper villainess in such a dingy, uninspired outfit."

Caught off guard, I had no idea how to respond to my wardrobe not being evil enough.

Before I could say anything, she was hustling me behind a changing screen when we heard a discreet knock on the outer suite door. "That's our drinks. Go."

When she returned holding a porcelain and wood-edged tray, I was still standing in the middle of the dressing room.

She set the tray down with a bang between the two sinks. Gesturing with a wave of her hand, she said, "What's this?"

I cleared my throat. "I'd prefer to stay in what I have on."

On the tray was a pewter platter with a wedge of cheese, dried figs, some cold sliced meats, and crostini. Next to it were two crystal glasses and a matching ice container with silver tongs and a linen-wrapped bottle of prosecco, a small bowl of sliced oranges next to it.

After dropping several cubes of ice in each glass, Gabriella poured in an ounce of Campari and a heavy splash of sweet vermouth. She then topped off each glass with prosecco before dropping in a juicy slice of orange.

Picking up each glass, she handed one to me before taking a sip of hers as she sat on her ottoman and crossed her legs, her bright dressing gown falling in elegant folds around her. "So is this some form of sackcloth penance for your sins?"

"No, I just don't plan on staying so I don't see the point in changing."

"You're lying."

My lips tightened. "I'm getting tired of everyone in your family calling me a liar."

She shrugged. "Then maybe you should stop lying."

I shifted from hip to hip, standing in the center of the dressing room holding the drink but refusing to sip from it.

She turned back to the vanity and patted her décolletage and neck with a pink, perfumed puff. "I'm assuming Benedict knows."

"Knows what?"

"That you weren't responsible for shooting Barone."

I wiped my fingers, wet from the glass's condensation, on my tunic after adjusting my grip when I almost dropped it. "How do you know that?"

Her concentration was divided as she focused on applying a thick fringe of false eyelashes to her right eye. Catching my reflected gaze in the mirror, she said, "I can't talk to you in that awful nun's habit. You're giving me flashbacks to Sister Justina and her paddle. Change first."

With a defeated huff, I moved to stand behind the ornate gold filigree changing screen.

Although I would die first before admitting it, it was a

huge relief to peel off the heavy tunic and replace it with the cool silk of her dressing gown. Securing the purple sash around my waist, I emerged and opened my mouth to ask her again.

Gabriella's gold bangle bracelets rattled on her wrist as she raised one manicured finger, stopping me. "Have a few bites of cheese and drink some of your *Negroni Sbagliato* first. I won't have my fine bartending skills go to waste. And you are already on Rosa's shit list, so there is no point in insulting her further by not eating her carefully prepared food."

Perching on the edge of the ottoman, I selected a small piece of cheese and a fig, then took a sip of the drink she prepared. Of course, my stomach would betray me by loudly growling the moment food hit it. I clenched my abdominal muscles, but it growled again.

Gabriella sent me a knowing smirk as she attached the second false eyelash. When she was finished with her makeup, she removed her turban.

Her beautiful black hair with its hints of gray fell in soft waves over her shoulders. After giving her hair a quick fluff, she picked up her drink and turned her attention back to me.

"Now. No more lies. I'm not one of the men. You can't bullshit me. Tell me."

That businessman I'd overheard at the office was right. There was something dangerously entrancing about Gabriella. Like one of those cobras that mesmerized you right before they struck.

I gripped my glass so tightly I was worried it would crack.

The silence stretched on.

I would say it caused tension in the room, but it was clear the only person who was tense and nervous was me.

She leaned forward and patted my knee. "You're stubborn.

I like that about you. I'll start. If I thought for a second you were even slightly involved with hurting Barone, trust me. They would never find your body."

A shiver ran down my spine. I believed her.

What was it with this family and their threats about body disposal?

It was like they didn't even bother with the inconsequential details of *how* they were going to murder you. They'd rather make chitchat about the *fun* way they were going to forever damn your soul by disrespecting your mortal remains.

My knees tightened as I gripped my glass. "Okay."

I didn't know how else to respond.

She nodded, so I guessed that was the proper response.

"But I know you are innocent, so now the question is, why are you letting the men think you are guilty? You must have a very good reason. You have to know the danger you are risking by not speaking up with the truth."

The ice in my glass shifted, the cubes melting. I watched the last of the prosecco bubbles fizzle to the surface. My chest tightened.

Everything ached.

I was so very tired.

Tired of lying.

Tired of bearing this burden alone.

Still, she was basically a Cavalieri. I couldn't trust her. Could I? "What makes you think I'm innocent? You all know what I did to Bianca."

"Benedict already explained that to us."

Shocked, I stared at her.

He what? How? When?

Her red lips lifted at the corners. "Don't look so shocked,

darling. I don't know what the two of you have been doing for the last twenty-four hours but apparently talking hasn't been one of them."

My tangled hair fell forward over the sides of my face to cover my humiliation at her casual declaration.

How much did she know?

Had Benedict told her about what happened in the tub last night?

Did she think I was a whore for doing *that* with a man I barely knew … and at the Vatican no less.

"Oh, your hair. It's a mess."

Snatching a brush from her vanity, she rose to stand behind me.

Vigorously pulling its bristles through my snarled curls, she continued. "If you had talked, you'd know in a heartbeat the man has a very interesting past, which is a cute way of saying he's dangerous as hell. And not that 'sexy, tall, dark, and handsome with a dangerous vibe' sort of dangerous, although he does have that going for him. But in that 'probably knows a thousand ways to kill you with his pinkie finger' sort of dangerous."

There it was again. That strange stab of jealousy as she spoke so intimately about Benedict.

Knowing better than to talk, I kept my mouth shut as she yanked and pulled on my hair without mercy.

"Darling, this hair is gorgeous, but terribly fifteenth century. A fashionable girl like you needs something with more style."

I smoothed a section over my shoulder. The nuns at the convent had always insisted on cutting my hair in a demure style with a length long enough to allow for it to be pulled up into a serviceable bun appropriate for a proper young woman or wife.

"Anyway," she continued. "A man like that would not bring a viper back to the nest. If he truly thought you were guilty, you'd have been dead before you even hit the ground. That's one. But it's also obvious you were manipulated into thinking you were helping Bianca. And by those nasty pieces of work she called parents."

My resolve weakened. It was so exhausting having everyone think the worst of you.

My voice was soft and low. "I really did think I was helping her."

Gabriella patted my shoulder as she brushed all the dirt and occasional twig out of my hair until it shone again. "Of course you did, darling. Now to that other nasty business—"

I held my breath.

"We both know you're more involved than you'd like to be, but I can tell you feel terrible about it."

My lower lip trembled, the rest of my resolve crumbling beneath her unique combination of straightforward, harsh kindness. "Why do you think that?"

She took her seat on the ottoman again. Lifting the glass out of my hands and setting it aside, she clasped her warm, soft hands around my chilled ones. "Because you didn't fight back. When Amara attacked you. You didn't fight back, darling."

The tears which had been threatening to fall finally slipped down my cheeks.

She clucked as she reached for a tissue and patted my cheeks. "No tears. They ruin the complexion. Now, tell Aunt Gabriella everything."

CHAPTER 22

BENEDICT

The Americans called it good cop, bad cop.

After whispering *you know what to do* to Gabriella when I hugged her, I headed to the stables to wait.

While it wasn't safe to discuss my suspicions about Dante on the phone, I was able to convey my thoughts on Liliana's actions regarding Bianca and a plan on how to gain her trust through Gabriella to the others.

Amara attacking Liliana was not part of the plan.

More bothered to see her in distress like that than I cared to admit, I decided to make myself useful while I waited. After changing into a pair of dark denim jeans and a sweater, I marched into the stables. The smell of fresh straw and horses immediately soothed me.

I missed my own ranch up north.

Unlike humans, horses were uncomplicated, beautiful, loyal creatures.

They didn't send mixed signals about their innocence or

play manipulative games with the truth. They didn't make you doubt your own sanity or question your judgment by appearing guiltless one moment and guilty as sin the next.

And they certainly didn't lure you into wanting to betray everything you stood for just to protect them regardless of what they may or may not have done and hang the consequences.

Already knowing my way around, I unlatched the worn cabinet and drew out the curry comb, body and dandy brush, and soft cloths. After tossing them into a wooden bucket along with some apples, I headed to the first stall, which housed the *Cavallo Romano della Maremma Laziale* black mare I gifted Barone with last Christmas. At fifteen hands, with a docile yet lively temperament, she was a beauty. I had named her Cleopatra for that very reason.

Running my hand along her thick neck and smooth, arched back, I greeted her in soothing tones. "Hello Cleo, my girl. Miss me?"

Seeing that she had not been out in the muddy winter fields recently and was already groomed, I reached for the dandy brush. Starting at her neck and shoulders, I used short, flicking motions to softly brush her coat, being careful to avoid any whorls.

She snorted and gently nudged my shoulder as I worked.

I smiled and patted her flank. "You're welcome, sweetie."

As I silently worked, Alfonso, Matteo and Amara returned from the hospital. While I was anxious to check on Barone, I knew better than to impose while Amara was there. I would check in on him later, after visiting hours were finished.

Amara slipped out of the back passenger seat and without even sparing me a glance, stormed back into the house. Alfonso followed after tipping his hat to me.

Matteo approached. "She's just upset and worried about Uncle Barone. She'll calm down."

I nodded and continued to brush Cleo.

He continued. "Sorry about earlier. I should have had them out of the house."

I glared at him over the horse's back. "You think?"

"How was I supposed to know she'd attack Liliana? She seems so sweet."

My hand paused in my ministrations. "Have you seriously not been paying attention to what these women are capable of? Bianca's right. We're damn lucky she wasn't armed."

Cleo turned her head and snorted her displeasure. Realizing that apparently today was my day to be ordered about by all the females in my world, I continued to brush her coat.

Having heard the car pull up, Cesare and Enzo strolled into the stables.

Enzo laid a hand on Matteo's shoulder. "How's Papà?"

He smirked in response. Counting off on his fingers, he responded, "Judging by the pissed-off doctor, terrified nurses, and the noises coming from behind his locked hospital room door, I'd say he was just fine and ready to come home tomorrow."

Cesare laughed. "So the chest tube's out?"

"Crazy bastard insisted on pulling it out himself. And that's not all he pulled out."

Enzo held up his palm. "TMI."

"I'm just saying, if you don't get him out of there soon, don't be surprised if you have to buy that hospital a new wing for putting up with his randy bullshit."

Cesare rubbed his forehead. "We'll just add it to the roof we agreed to buy the church after Renata's funeral."

My jaw clenched. "That was money well spent."

Enzo nodded as he reached for an apple to feed Cleo. "Amen."

Cesare leaned against the stall wall and crossed his ankles. "I have about one hour before Milana wakes up and realizes I'm gone, so talk fast."

Tossing the brush in the wooden bucket, I motioned with my head for them to follow. We all crammed into Alfonso's small office in the back of the stables. Just before I began, Alfonso walked in.

Taking off his cap, he tossed it on a hook. "Make yourselves at home, boys," he said, as he shoved Cesare's shoes off his desk where they were propped up.

I slapped Alfonso on the back. "The villa may have ears."

He nodded. "Understood."

Crossing my arms over my chest, I began. "Are we all on board with my conclusion about Liliana and Bianca?"

They nodded but my gaze was specifically on Enzo.

He met mine. "I haven't explained it to Bianca yet."

"Yeah, I picked up on that."

"But I will. She can be a little … hotheaded, but she actually liked Liliana and was confused by the whole thing, so your conclusion makes sense. Especially knowing Bianca's parents."

Cesare used the toe of his boot to open Alfonso's desk drawer and pulled out a half-empty bottle of Scotch. "That still leaves Papà's shooting and her spying for Dante."

Alfonso held up his hand. "What the hell?"

Cesare shrugged as he unscrewed the bottle. "Come on, Alfonso. We all know about your secret stash." He took a swig and passed it to me.

I raised the bottle and took a healthy gulp, craving the burn.

I still wasn't entirely certain of my motives for what I was about to do.

The logic made sense and my gut told me something was off.

The problem was it wasn't just my gut doing the talking.

Terrible things happened to a man when he listened to his cock.

It had never been a problem for me. Until now.

After passing the bottle, I said, "I'm not saying that Dante Agnello is not involved but from the beginning I've questioned why. None of this made sense. Using Liliana as a spy. A young female? That's not their usual style. And it makes even less sense now that I know she's fucking mafia royalty."

I then filled them in on who Liliana's father was and the circumstances of his death. Even though he was dead, with the value the Sicilian mafia put on family ties and lineage, anyone who married her would have an advantage through his association with such a formerly powerful man's daughter.

It was similar to the devotion they held for being a godfather.

Since its very beginning, the Sicilian mafia had used the sacrament of baptism as a way of securing family ties and strengthening influence through a form of ritual kinship.

The godfather would be a *compare*, or co-father, to the child and would often gift the family with jewelry, property, and money. It was nothing more than a power exchange or worse, a form of bribery. Usually the money was nothing more than a loan to be called in later when the child was of age, with an arranged marriage to another of the godfather's *children*.

All to create an interlocking, impenetrable web of influence through blood ties and marriage.

It was one of the primary ways the mafia had survived for over two hundred years.

It was so corrupt and out of hand, the Catholic Church had recently taken the radical and unpopular step of banning the practice of naming godfathers on the island of Sicily.

I shook my head as I rubbed my beard in thought. "And then shooting my brother like that? What's the upside? Where's the payoff?"

Enzo leaned forward, resting his forearms on his legs. "We were getting too close to his organization. He knew we were asking questions. We dismantled his land-grab scheme and took out his best hit man. It was retribution plain and simple."

"What if that's what someone wants us to think?"

His gaze narrowed. "What do you mean?"

"I think someone was hoping we'd be so pissed and worked up that we wouldn't stop to ask any questions, we'd just take things at face value. I'm starting to think someone wants us to take out Dante for them. It especially makes sense when you consider how that kill squad in Rome didn't even pronounce Dante's name correctly, but wanted me to think they were sent by him."

Cesare leaned back in his chair. "That's fucked up."

"Stay with me. The whole reason why Renata and her parents were worked up was because Dante walked away from the deal. A pissing match against us wasn't worth it to him."

Enzo nodded thoughtfully. "You're right. Hell, Dante made that clear after Papà warned him off after that warehouse sale was stopped. The rest that followed was more about Renata's greed, not Dante."

Warming up to the subject, I said, "And about that. It all seemed to unravel remarkably quickly. Bianca's parents, the crooked cops, and that bastard Nevio. They all seemed to be worked up into a suspiciously organized frenzy for a group of inept people who didn't trust one another."

Alfonso took a swig from his bottle. "*Santo inferno!* I think you're right. Someone's setting you boys up to take the fall."

Matteo reached for the bottle. "The question is, who? It's not like we have someone on the inside of his organization who can give us the scoop on who's making a play for Dante's throne."

Enzo looked at me. "Or do we."

At that they all looked at me.

I knew what they were thinking.

I was thinking it as well.

There was no getting around it.

No matter how I felt about the situation.

Liliana was our in.

Matteo shook his head as he handed the bottle back to Alfonso. "I don't like it. We can't trust her. And we still don't know why she was spying in our offices or who she answers to."

Gabriella chose that moment to enter the office. "Hello, boys."

I straightened. My stomach tightened as my fingers curled into a fist, bracing for what she learned. "Well?"

She took the bottle from Alfonso, wiped the top with the sleeve of her dressing gown and took a sip. After grimacing and commenting on how much she hated Scotch, she said, "What do you want first? What she said, or what I think?"

We all spoke at the same time. "What she said."

She rolled her eyes. "Typical."

After a dramatic sigh, she continued. "Liliana said Dante Agnello's holding her godfather, a man named Salvatore Giovanni Mangano, hostage. And that she was told she had to come to Cavalieri village to spy on us and filter private information about the business to Dante, or Salvatore would be killed. The last piece of information she gave them was Barone's advance schedule, which included the Christmas party, the day before she tried to help Bianca. Then realizing her mistake, she skipped town."

It was actually worse than I thought.

Suppressing the urge to storm up to the villa, whip off my belt and punish her ass for not telling me all of this the very moment she laid eyes on me, I rasped through clenched teeth, "And what do you think?"

Gabriella waved her hand as she scoffed. "Well, it's obvious. The girl's being manipulated. Those nuns did her no favors with that fucking sheltered upbringing. Any idiot would know that a man like Dante would not send a foolish girl to collect information that was readily available. That poor thing's been twisting herself into knots with guilt over Barone's shooting because she passed along the date of a Christmas party that half of Italy knew was happening, for fuck's sake."

Working herself up into a lather, she snatched the bottle back from Alfonso and took another swig. Coughing past the fiery burn she continued. "And don't get me started on the godfather bullshit. Especially since she has only been hearing these supposed hostage instructions straight from the hostage, not Dante."

Alfonso wrenched the bottle from Gabriella's grasp. "That's enough of this for you."

He then exchanged a look with the rest of us. "I don't know about all of you, but I sure as fuck would like to know more about this Salvatore Giovanni Mangano and what place he holds in Dante's organization."

CHAPTER 23

LILIANA

I stared at the gathering clouds slowly sweeping down the surrounding mountains as I waited for Gabriella to return from her errand.

There would be snow in the valley before too long. The hazy, muted light outside and the somber, heavy feel to the atmosphere matched my odd mood.

While it felt good to finally tell someone the truth, I couldn't shake the awkward feeling that I had overshared so Gabriella would like me, acting like some pathetic nobody trying to curry favor with the popular girl in school.

A sound in the hallway drew my attention, but once again, the door to Gabriella's suite did not open. She had been gone for over half an hour. I wrapped my arms around my middle and tucked my legs up on the sofa. The queasy, uneasy feeling increased.

The moment I confided in her, she had rushed out for the purpose of telling Rosa about dinner and getting us fresh ice for more drinks. It wasn't like I knew her well, but Gabriella had never struck me as the domestic type to be worried about giving meal planning instructions to the household staff.

Once again, I stared at the partially open door.

I wasn't fooled by the temptation.

It was just a pretense.

It was like opening the cage door for a bird with clipped wings.

It gave the illusion of offering freedom but that was not the reality. I had no money, no identification, no transportation, and there were at least ten guards and two security gates between here and the end of the Cavalieri property line, which was at least five kilometers away from the villa.

Not to mention that I was dressed only in a borrowed silk dressing gown.

Despite commenting on not only Benedict's but apparently *all* the Cavalieri men's inclination to ruin the wardrobes of any female in their vicinity, she was no better.

When she left, she took my nun's habit and broken boots, muttering under her breath about tossing them into the fire bin outside.

I covered my eyes with my hand.

Had it been a mistake to tell her about Uncle Salvatore?

Guilt and uncertainty twisted my stomach. I hugged my arms around my middle tighter as a chill raced over my spine, despite a cozy fire across the room.

I wished Benedict was here.

The bitter irony of that thought was not lost on me. Neither was the pure unbelievability of it.

Still, I wished he was here right now.

Despite all his scowls and threats, there was something undeniably reassuring about his brute strength and the possessive way his arm wrapped around my lower back and pulled me close to his side.

As much as I hated to admit it, there was a protective daddy-vibe to it, but in that dirty, sinfully wrong way.

Just as I was about to rise to go find him, Gabriella burst through the door holding a fresh bowl of ice.

Her cheeks had a bright flush to them. The crisp winter-wind scent of having just been outside clung to her, as well as the smoky fumes of Scotch as she smoothed her hair and said breathlessly, "Sorry, that took longer than I expected."

Her eyes were brighter as well.

Oh my, was she drunk? I glanced down at the watery *Negroni Sbagliato* I'd barely drunk since I wasn't used to drinking alcohol.

It couldn't be these, it must be the Scotch I smelled on her breath. I couldn't imagine why she had nipped into a bottle of hard liquor during her errand, but I wasn't going to judge.

Before I could comment, she swept her arm out. "But I have an excellent excuse. I brought a guest!"

Milana walked through the door.

I flew off the sofa, backing up against the nearest wall, holding a throw pillow in front of me as a makeshift shield. "If you come near me again, I'll scream!"

Not that anyone within fifty kilometers would give a damn, but I'd still do it.

Milana held out her left palm and then raised a large, pink metal makeup case in the other. "I come with a peace offering."

Uncertain what to think, my gaze shifted from Gabriella to Milana and back.

Gabriella pulled the throw pillow from my grasp. "Please, what are you going to do, feather fluff her to death?"

After setting the makeup case on the coffee table between us, Milana sat on the sofa arm and clasped her hands in her lap. "Listen. I'm not going to say I'm sorry."

Well, that settles that.

My mouth dropped open. I was completely at a loss for words after her bold statement.

She grimaced. "That came out wrong. Let me try again. Amara is my closest and dearest friend. We all believed that you had hurt her by hurting Barone." She tilted her head toward Gabriella. "I've since been informed we were incorrect in our assumptions."

My head swiveled to Gabriella, my fisted hands on my hips. "You told her?"

Gabriella shrugged and adjusted the clasp on one of her bracelets, as if this conversation was of only mild interest to her. "Of course, I told her."

"I told you all that stuff about my godfather in strict confidence."

Milana's bark of laughter brought my attention back to her.

She covered her mouth and waved her hand in front of her face as she struggled to contain her laughter. "I'm sorry. I'm not laughing at you, I promise. It's just, the idea of telling Aunt Gabriella *anything* in confidence is ridiculous."

Gabriella's eyes narrowed. "Just for that, Cesare is going to surprise you with that Bulgari Diva's Dream necklace from their new Roman collection. The eighteen karats rose gold one with the rubellite, mother-of-pearl and pavé diamonds that you were eyeing the last time we were in Milan."

Milana waved her hand at Gabriella. "You *literally* just proved my point."

With a huff, Gabriella crossed to the drink tray and picked

up the silver tongs. "You are boring Liliana. Get to the good part. Who wants another drink? No one? Just me?"

Milana turned back to me. "As I was saying, while I won't apologize for having my friend's back, I do apologize for the misunderstanding and hope you will forgive me."

I tucked a lock of hair behind my ear. "Of course. Please, there is no need. I'm not exactly innocent in all this."

Gabriella called out from the dressing room lounge. "Yes, you are! Stop with that Catholic nun guilt bullshit!"

My cheeks burned.

With a tilt of her head, Milana called over her shoulder, "Thank you Aunt Gabriella!"

Then after giving me a wink, she continued. "Amara headed straight to her office after visiting with Barone but as soon as I'm done here, I will speak with her and Bianca and tell them everything. I think Bianca will be touched you were actually trying to save her."

My shoulders stiffened.

She crossed the room and grabbed my chilled hands. "Don't look so frightened. It's going to be okay."

I swallowed past the dry fear in my throat. "It's really not, but I appreciate you saying so."

Picking up a wavy curl, she said, "You'll have a better outlook after your makeover."

"My what?"

Her arm wrapped around my waist as she guided me into the dressing room, snatching up her makeup case along the way.

She pushed me down onto the ottoman in front of the vanity mirror as Gabriella swept a towel over my shoulders.

Milana said to Gabriella, "We have to hurry. I only have

about an hour before Cesare returns. He thinks I'm taking a nap."

"I shudder to think what that man is going to be like when you are further along in your pregnancy."

"I'll probably need bolt cutters to prevent him from chaining me to the bed … and not for the fun reasons."

While they were chatting, they stared at my reflection, tilting their heads this way and that.

Milana swept my hair forward over my shoulders. "I agree. You have beautiful hair, Liliana, but it's just too much. It overwhelms your face at this length but don't worry, I've been cutting my friends' hair for ages. You're in good hands."

Feeling as though I was once again rushing into something to be liked and accepted by the popular girls, I nodded. "I suppose you're right. It could be fun to change things up."

Milana clapped. "Gabriella was right. I'm glad I listened to her."

As she turned to open her makeup case to fish out a comb and a pair of sinister-looking scissors, I wanted to ask what Gabriella had been right about but didn't want to seem desperate for a compliment.

Gabriella handed me her drink. "Hold this." She then reached over my head for a cloth bag of hair clips Milana was dangling from her fingertips.

Again tilting her head from side to side, she folded my hair in half until it appeared shoulder length and clipped the ends to the top of my head on one side. "What do you think of a sassy bob? With a sharp angle. Shorter in the back, longer in the front. It would look very Parisian and stylish."

I opened my mouth to respond, but then realized she wasn't talking to me.

Milana reached into the clip bag and took smaller sections

of hair and clipped them at various lengths down the other side of my head. "That might be too extreme for her. I was thinking more of a layered look. Something with a little bounce and movement but keeping it still a bit long."

At this point they both paused and stared at me in the mirror's reflection.

The clip claws pulled at my scalp as I struggled to figure out how I was supposed to answer. "I'm not sure—"

Gabriella took her glass from my hand and surveyed both looks from the front. "Both would look lovely."

Leaning against the vanity counter, Milana said, "What would best suit your personality?"

Without even thinking, I blurted out, "I don't have a personality."

They exchanged a look as I lowered my gaze and died a thousand deaths for being so stupid as to say that out loud.

"Oh, sweetie. Of course you do," assured Milana, patting me on the side of my shoulder.

I gave her a wan smile. It was too late to take it back so I might as well be honest. "It's nice of you to say so, but I really don't. It's okay. I've accepted it."

She frowned. "Don't be silly. Other than that unfortunate misunderstanding ages ago when I thought you were a poisoning murderess—"

"You mean an hour ago?"

"Exactly. *Ages ago.* Before that I thought you were very sweet and kind … and you were always great about getting coffee at the office."

With a sweep of her arm, the ice in her glass rattled as Gabriella scoffed. "Milana, you just compared the poor girl to a golden retriever who's good at playing fetch."

"Well then you say something nice about her."

I raised my palms. "It's fine, really. I'm not looking for pity. It comes with the territory when you're an orphan raised by nuns in a convent. They sort of frown on expressions of individuality." I shrugged. "It didn't help that my only option for university was an all-girls Catholic school run by more nuns."

Milana's eyes widened. "I'd rather die. I've always said I'd have done anything for a chance to go to university. Turns out, I didn't mean *anything*. It's not like I was boy crazy or anything but still, who wants to be surrounded by that many girls—and nuns—all the freaking time."

Having overshared enough for one day, I wasn't going to tell them it was far better than the alternative. Especially since they only just stopped thinking I was a poisoning murderess.

I didn't want them to swing to the other extreme, thinking I was an ungrateful, cold-hearted goddaughter.

Everything I told Gabriella was the truth.

Uncle Salvatore had contacted me through an unknown number saying Dante Agnello was holding him against his will. At first it didn't make sense, since he was Dante's *vice capo*, his most trusted advisor and right-hand man.

Before he could explain, the phone was torn away and another voice told me that unless I wanted his blood on my hands I was to travel to Cavalieri village and get a job at Cavalieri Enterprises. Apparently they had *arranged* for the previous assistant to quit, leaving an opening.

For months it was phone calls in the middle of the night, cryptic emails, and secretive drop locations where I would leave copies of land permits I had covertly stolen.

Then the pressure increased.

I started getting calls from my uncle that ended with his tortured screams, begging me to send him better information, but there was none, at least nothing that I could find.

The best I could do was a few photos of some of Barone's private emails when he left his computer screen on one day—but they weren't about anything in particular—and his private schedule for the fall.

Then Renata's parents contacted me.

Telling me they knew about my godfather and how they wanted to help me get him back if I would help them get their daughter back.

I was desperate to end the torment and truly believed them when they said Bianca was being held against her will. Otherwise, I never would have agreed to put the sleeping meds in her caffe.

The problem was … all this made me sound like an innocent, devoted goddaughter who was desperate to help her beloved godfather, my loving Uncle Salvatore.

And I was nothing of the sort.

I hated my Uncle Salvatore.

He wasn't even my real uncle.

He just insisted I call him that, which only made the way he touched and looked at me all the creepier.

I didn't always feel this way.

I was dumped off at the convent when I was only a few hours old, and it wasn't until I was about six years old that I learned I was there because of the beneficence of my godfather. The nuns never missed an opportunity to tell me how he paid for everything.

At first my lonely, little girl heart was thrilled to learn there was someone out in the world who cared about me. I wrote him long letters filled with foolish chatter about my accomplishments, hoping to make him proud, each time asking when he would visit.

He never came. Not once.

Not until I turned eighteen and he learned from Mother Superior that I was leaving the convent.

He showed up in a rage. I overheard him screaming at her. At the time, I didn't understand what he meant. He just kept saying, over and over again, *the bitch isn't dead yet, I need more time, you have to keep her here, that's what I paid you for.*

When he stormed out of the office, it was the first time I had ever seen him in person.

Instead of introducing himself, or giving me a hug, or telling me how much I looked like my dead mother, he pinned me against the wall and shoved his hand between my legs over my school uniform.

He then sneered. "You had better still be a fucking virgin or there will be hell to pay."

I was so shocked and scared, it didn't even occur to me to speak, let alone scream.

Before I even knew what was happening, he removed his hand and reached inside his jacket to pull out a gun. He pressed the barrel against my temple. "I asked you a question, goddaughter."

"Yes," I whispered. "I'm still a virgin."

He lifted the gun away from my temple and smacked my head with the edge of the handle.

The wound bled immediately, trickling over my eye. "Good. See that it stays that way."

Three days later, a black sedan showed up to take me to an all-girls' university.

It was only later I learned he was referring to his wife.

My beloved godfather, *my dear Uncle Salvatore*, was biding his time until his current wife died so he could force me to marry him.

So no, I hadn't been doing Dante's bidding to save my uncle.

I'd been doing it out of guilt.

I didn't want the death of another human being on my conscience.

My uncle had also told me that if I didn't comply, Dante wouldn't be above bombing the convent where I grew up.

The nuns may have been distant and poor substitutes for a true mother and father, but they were the only family I knew. I couldn't let that happen.

Adding to my guilt was Gabriella thinking and telling the rest of the Cavalieris that I was only acting out of desperation to save a loved one.

Now I was going to have to keep that pretext going until I could get my uncle out of this mess and then figure out a way to get myself away from him.

The whole thing was depressing to even think about.

Perhaps Milana was right, maybe a makeover was just what I needed.

Breaking through my morbid turn of thoughts, Milana asked, "Let's start with what you studied at university."

"Educational studies."

"Oh! So you want to be a teacher! We can work with that personality type."

"Actually, that's education. Educational studies is a degree in studying the theory of learning and how it is impacted by culture."

Gabriella patted my knee. "I think I'll go refresh my drink."

Milana rolled her eyes. *"Porca miseria!* No offense but that sounds boring as hell. Come on, you have to meet me half-way! What's your zodiac sign?"

"I'm not sure. The nuns didn't really—"

"*Madonna santa*! Enough with the damn nuns! When were you born?"

"May sixteenth."

"That makes you a Taurus," she said, pulling out her phone. "Okay, personality traits of a Taurus. It's an earth sign, so you are hardworking, loyal, steadfast, and focused."

I put my chin in my hand. "I'm sounding more and more like a golden retriever."

"Don't give up yet. You're also stubborn with a jealous streak."

Okay, that cut a little close, I thought, thinking of my spike of jealousy seeing Benedict with Gabriella.

Her eyes lit up. "Oh, naughty! Turns out, Taurus is a hedonistic, sensual sign. Your erogenous zones are the throat and neck area and just below the ear. Meow! Kinky."

My hand touched my throat as a blush crept over my cheeks. There was no stopping the erotic memory of all the times Benedict had held me by the throat to kiss me ... or other things.

Completely unaware of my discomfort, she continued. "And you like romantic bubble baths with essential oils and the sultry feel of silky sheets."

"It does *not* say that!"

"It totally does!"

She showed me her phone.

I couldn't believe my eyes.

It was right there in black and white as part of some women's magazine article about what zodiac signs are like in bed.

Milana gave me a sly smile. "I think we just found your

personality. Turns out under this prim and proper demeanor you, Liliana, fly a sassy freak flag!"

I stared at my reflection in the mirror.

I didn't think it was true ... but wanted it to be.

I liked how Milana, a popular girl, was looking at me with new interest and approval.

In a flash, I was no longer the boring convent girl.

No longer the golden retriever.

Taking a deep breath, I said, "Let's go with the angled bob."

CHAPTER 24

BENEDICT

*B*arone sat up straighter in bed as I entered. "You had better be hiding a pair of bolt cutters in that duffel bag to break me out of here."

After tossing the duffel bag onto his hospital bed, I said, "It's been less than a week since you suffered a serious, life-threatening injury."

Barone flipped the blankets to the side to ease first one leg, then the other over the edge of the bed. "Did you bring me clothes?"

I shook my head and placed my palm over my heart. "It would be gravely irresponsible for me to encourage—let alone assist—in making such a rash decision as to leave the watchful care of these knowledgeable doctors, especially for an older man of your advanced years."

He slanted me a nasty look as he pulled the duffel bag closer. "Advanced years? I'm a year younger than you, asshole."

I leaned against a nearby wall and crossed my arms, tilting

my head. "Yeah, but physically, I'm way younger. It's not your fault. I chose a life of danger and intrigue which has given me the body and stamina of an ageless Roman god whereas you chose the life of a businessman. It's natural you'd get a little soft after all those years behind a desk."

Unzipping the duffel and pulling out boots and a pair of jeans, Barone said, "An ageless Roman god?" He rolled his eyes. "I changed my mind, put the bullet back in me."

I placed a hand on his shoulder which he covered with his own. After a pause, he said, "I know, it was a close one."

In our own typical male way, we had just told one another all we needed to say. That we loved each other and the possibility of losing him had scared the hell out of both of us.

Without waiting for him to even try what we both knew would be at best a painful, at worst an impossible, task, I bent and helped push his feet through the pants legs.

While he lifted his hips and zipped them up, I pushed the left boot over his heel and propped his foot against the top of my thigh to lace them up. "In all seriousness, are you sure you're good to leave?"

"They took out the chest tube. We both know after that it's just a matter of giving it time to heal."

I gave him a skeptical look. "They?"

"Me, they, same thing."

I dropped his left foot and started on the right.

"We both know I can't stay here. Whether you're right or wrong about Dante, whoever did this could return to try and finish the job. I need to be on my own land … surrounded by my sons and guns. Besides, I'm going fucking crazy knowing Amara is there alone. She is my responsibility. I need to be there to protect her if something else happens."

"Spoken like a true Cavalieri."

With a hand braced on the hospital bed sidebar, he stood. After a slight sway, he righted himself and nodded to me with a half-smile. "Speaking of a true Cavalieri, interesting tactic bringing Liliana Fiore straight into the hornet's nest like that," he said, letting the hospital gown fall off his shoulders.

My jaw tightened. Rifling through the duffel, I tossed him a charcoal gray flannel. "I'll fill you in when we're in the car, but the situation was … misunderstood."

He slid one arm then the other into the shirt. After I helped him pull it over his shoulders, he took over buttoning it. "It's good to know. I had plans for her."

My gaze narrowed. "What the fuck is that supposed to mean?"

Without looking up, he continued to button his shirt. "What do *you* mean?"

The threat was out of my mouth before I even had a chance to think. "Don't even think of trying to fuck her."

"If Amara didn't cut off my dick for that, Milana definitely would. Besides, Amara's the only one for me. I couldn't imagine even looking at another woman. I meant Liliana is smart. I had planned to move her up within the company to something with more responsibility."

Barone's hands paused, his gaze meeting mine, all signs of our mild, teasing humor gone. "That's one helluva misunderstanding if you're now playing the role of knight errant for the girl."

Not wanting to explain myself, I grabbed the empty duffel and headed toward the door. "I'm not. It's complicated."

He followed me. "It's complicated? Who are you, a sixteen-year-old girl posting on Facebook?"

"Keep talking and instead of breaking you out, I'll tell the nurses you need a sponge bath and are requesting one of the male nurses because you prefer a stronger touch."

Staying behind me as I prepared to open the door and check the hallway, he said, "You win."

After determining the hallway was empty, we turned left, in the opposite direction of the nurses' station.

"I bribed an orderly to prop open a door on the west side next to the alleyway. I have a car waiting there."

Ten minutes later we were racing toward the winery while I filled him in on my theory about Dante and how I was convinced we were being framed as part of a power play scheme.

Neither of us spoke about Liliana again beyond me imparting what Gabriella learned, for which I was grateful. I had no desire to explain my actions regarding Liliana, especially since I didn't really have one.

* * *

AFTER SNEAKING Barone in through the kitchen and up to his suite of rooms, I returned to the lower level to face the music with the rest of the family.

They were seated in the dining room sharing a meal. The chair at the head of the table was noticeably empty. Thank God, it wouldn't stay that way.

All conversation ceased the moment I entered. I knew from a text I received from Gabriella that with Milana's help, she had smoothed things over with Amara and Bianca regarding Liliana.

Judging from the frosty glare I received from Amara, Liliana was on her way to forgiveness but I still had some penance to do.

I inhaled a deep breath and braced myself for more of her anger when she learned I helped Barone break out of the hospital against medical advice.

Gripping the back of the nearest chair, I met Amara's sulking look. "Sorry I'm late. You know what a pain in the ass, backseat driver Barone can be. He insisted we take the SP11 when it was obvious the SP5a would have been faster."

It took a moment of stunned silence for them to realize I was discussing routes home from the hospital before the table erupted in shocked exclamations.

Amara rose from her chair so suddenly she knocked it over.

Running around the table, she launched herself at me.

I wrapped my arms around her as she hugged my middle and whispered, "Thank you for bringing him home."

With a pat to her back, I said, "He's upstairs and yes, Dr. Pontano is already on his way to check him out, just in case."

After giving me another squeeze, she hurried off to be with Barone.

The mobile phone she left behind danced and bounced on the table as it rang.

Enzo glanced at the screen and grimaced. "That will be the hospital calling to inform us about the *breakout*."

He straightened Amara's chair and answered her phone as he stepped into another room to chat with the no-doubt infuriated administrators and doctors.

Before taking a seat to enjoy a generous portion of *cervo in padella* made from the deer I hunted just before Christmas, skillet-roasted my favorite way with juniper berries, garlic, and Marsala wine, I looked to see where Liliana was seated.

She was not there.

Bianca leaned her chin on her hand and asked, "Looking for something?"

Milana nudged her and winked. "Or *someone?*"

Uh oh.

My tactically trained mind considered the battle scenarios.

One, they harmed Liliana and buried her body somewhere on the property.

Two, they reconciled and accepted her into their formed sisterhood and were now teaming up against me.

Three, it was door number two and as a consequence, they aided her in an escape.

My mind could continue processing war scenarios, but it just got worse from there.

Gabbie lifted her glass. "It's about time you remembered you brought a guest here. You've been neglecting her all day."

My knuckles whitened from my hard grip on the back of the chair. "She isn't a fucking guest, she's my—"

All three women leaned in.

Fuck.

Almost fell for that.

"Where is she? Why isn't she down here?"

Gabbie shrugged. "We tried to persuade her to join us, but she was very nervous and shy so unfortunately we couldn't convince her."

The knot in my stomach eased slightly.

Milana picked up her glass of water. "Which was a shame, I really wanted to show off her makeover."

My brow furrowed. "What makeover?"

Bianca clinked her wineglass with Milana's water goblet. "You really outdid yourself with this one. It's a complete transformation."

My chest tightened as my anger rose. Through clenched teeth, I asked again. "What makeover?"

There were a thousand reasons why I shouldn't give a flying fat rat's ass whether the girls decided to play dress-up with Liliana and what color lipstick she was now wearing— except that I did. She was beautiful just as she was, there was no need for any *complete transformation.*

Gabbie nodded sagely as she tore off a piece of semolina bread crust from the slice in her hand. "Although I'm a little worried we may have made a mistake."

Not caring about the edge to my voice, I barked, "Why? What mistake? Did you hurt her?"

The women exchanged a quick look before Gabbie batted her thick eyelashes and drawled, "Oh, nothing like that, darling. I only meant she's a bit"—she shrugged— "naive and inexperienced to look as eye-catching and glamorous as she now does ... *and be among men."*

Bianca gestured with the hand holding her wineglass. "Very true. We're going to have to give her some lessons on how to flirt and handle a man's advances or it's going to be like sending a poor lamb to sleep among a pack of wolves."

The blood pumped so furiously through my veins I could feel it pulse against my skin. In my brain, there was nothing but a screeching primal scream that drowned out their words.

The fact they were family was the only thing preventing me from grasping the edge of this dining table and tipping it over in anger.

Matteo looked from me to the women and back. He waved his hand to get their attention. "Maybe we should change the subject."

Milana nodded, presumably in agreement, but then turned

to me. "I just have one quick question. Where are her panties?"

Dammit, I'm in hell. God is punishing me for all the kinky shit I did to Liliana at the Vatican.

With all eyes turned to me, I cleared my throat and said, "As I'm sure you are aware, we ran into a situation in Rome, and I was forced to dispose of her clothes."

Milana's eyes rolled. "A *situation in Rome* where you had to *dispose of her clothes?* Is that what the kids are calling it nowadays?"

Cesare snort-laughed but then raised his palm and mouthed, *Sorry,* before covering his mouth. His shoulders continued to vibrate with his chortles.

"They were torn and there was blood," I ground out.

Gabriella rose and gave me a condescending pat on the back. "Don't, dear. Now you're just making it too easy for them."

Bianca chimed in. "Don't worry, Uncle Benedict. I took care of it. I loaned her a beautiful sky-blue silk peignoir set of mine. You should have seen her face when she saw the matching thong."

That was it.

Something inside my brain snapped.

Without caring what they thought, I stormed out of the room in a rage to find Liliana.

I only barely registered Gabriella's knowing parting shot. "Told you, girls."

CHAPTER 25

BENEDICT

Taking the stairs two at a time, it was only when I got to the upper level that I realized I had no idea where Gabriella had put Liliana.

Undeterred, I threw open the door of every bedroom I knew was previously unoccupied on that floor, until I got to the only handle that was locked.

Closing my hand into a fist, I pounded on the door. "Open up, Liliana."

There was no response.

I pounded again. "I know you're in there. Open the damn door."

After a long pause, there was a faint fluttering on the other side. "I'm really tired, Benedict."

"I didn't ask if you were tired. I told you to open the door."

"Please, can we just talk in the morning?"

I rubbed my hand over my beard, taking a look down either side of the corridor. I'd be damned if I would stand here talking to a fucking locked door like some besotted teenage boy.

Fortunately, the one thing Gabriella did right was give Liliana the room next to mine.

Unlike the rest of the family, I only occupied a single bedroom with a private bathroom on the far back wing of the villa. The wing had a specially built private staircase entrance which led off the iron balcony that wrapped around the upper level.

Marching through my bedroom, kicking off my boots while I was in there, I exited through the single glass door. The bite from the frigid cold mosaic tiles against my bare feet only spurred me on as I made my way along the narrow balcony.

Keeping to the shadows once I reached the double French glass doors to her suite, I tested the brass handle.

Both annoyed and yet pleased that it was unlocked, I slipped silently inside her room, obscured from her view by the curtain.

Pushing the heavy royal blue and gold brocade aside, I observed her standing before the lit fireplace with her head bowed. The glow from the fire was the only light in the room.

Anxious to see what damage the girls had done to her with their well-meaning makeover, I ordered, "Turn around."

Liliana let out a startled scream as she turned and fell back against the marble mantle. "How did you get in here?"

Now backlit by the orange flames, her face was cast in shadow. "Come here."

"You need to leave."

With my gaze focused on her, I reached behind me, shoved the curtain aside, and felt for the light switch I knew was there. The light was a vintage brass dome with amber glass flush to the ceiling. It only brightened the room slightly above candlelight … but it was enough.

My lip curled at the sight of her hair. "Take it off."

Her hand smoothed the side of her hair to rest on the curve of her neck. "What?"

As my gaze took in the heavy eye makeup with the fake eyelashes and over-glossed lips my anger grew, and I stalked toward her. "I said, take it off."

She circled around the small love seat. The room given to her did not have a separate living room. Instead, the rather large bedroom had a small, attached lounge space with a fireplace and a private bath.

"Take what off?"

"That fucking wig," I ground out.

Even the idea of her playing dress-up for a night and covering up her beautiful long hair pissed me off.

My anger was irrational and misplaced, and I didn't give a damn.

Again she smoothed the side of the impossibly short wig that barely reached her shoulders. "It's not a wig."

The deep breath I took as I was forced to ask her to repeat herself barely affected the thin grasp I had on my patience.

It had to be a wig, no woman in her right mind would hack off all that long, silky hair on a whim. She had to be playing dress-up.

"Come again?"

She rounded behind the tufted chair and pushed out her chin. "It's not a wig. I asked Milana to cut my hair."

I shifted my gaze to the carpet for a moment as I clenched my fists so hard, they shook. Inhaling through my nose, I tried to calm the fuck down. Internally counting.

One, two, three, fou—

ZOE BLAKE

"What the fuck were you thinking, chopping off all your beautiful hair?" I raged.

She blinked, once more touching her hair as if feeling for the locks that were no longer there. "I could tell they thought I was boring and old-fashioned because of my hair and how I was raised. I wanted them to think ... it doesn't matter what I wanted."

She stamped her foot. "It's none of your business why I cut it. It's my hair, I can do with it what I want."

Storming toward her, I grabbed her upper arms before she had a chance to skitter away. "No, it isn't."

She tried to pull away. "Are you crazy? Yes, it is!"

I spun her around and dragged her across the room to a stand-up mirror in the corner across from the bed. Wrapping my left arm around her waist to anchor her in place, I speared my fingers into her hair from behind, giving the soft strands a sharp tug.

Liliana cried out and tried to pry my grip away from her head.

"Drop your arms," I ground out.

After she obeyed, I moved my fingers over her skull again, feeling for pins or any sign that it was a wig.

When I was satisfied that she had truly done the unthinkable, my dark gaze captured hers in the mirror, taking in her heavy eye makeup and bright crimson lips.

Because she already had large, stunning eyes with naturally thick eyelashes and full lips, the added makeup gave her features an artificial *anime girl* effect.

As I stood there saying nothing, she fidgeted before pushing out her lower lip and stubbornly muttering, "It's my hair."

I was about to cross a line.

Technically I'd crossed it last night but I could justify it then.

All was fair in the fog of war.

As far as I was concerned, at the time she was my captive and a suspect in my brother's attempted murder, and I needed information.

It was as black and white as that.

Now things were more of a stormy gray.

She was no longer my captive and yet, strictly speaking, she was not free. I knew she was not directly involved in my brother's shooting but that didn't mean I no longer needed information from her.

And none of that had anything to do with what I was now about to say and do.

Something I had never done with another woman.

Something I never planned to do with a woman, especially given my age.

Something that was likely to throw my well-ordered life into chaos under the best of circumstances, let alone the worst.

Compared to my height and thick, muscular frame, her body appeared small and fragile. I supposed the intent of the harsh angles of the stylish haircut was to give her an edgy, more glamorous appearance.

Instead, she'd gone from looking like a broken little doll whose softly rounded face was overwhelmed by a mass of thick, raven's-wing hair, to a tiny woodland fairy who looked lost and scared.

Either way, one thing was clear. She wasn't safe out there in the world alone.

Even once I straightened out the mess she had gotten herself into with Dante.

The girls were right. She was too easily manipulated and taken advantage of.

She was a lamb thrown among the wolves.

Fortunately for her, every pack has an alpha to fight off the rest.

Tightening my grip on her hair, or rather, what was left of it, my gaze narrowed as I stared at her reflection. "You're going to march into that bathroom and wash off all this whore makeup and if you ever fucking butcher your beautiful hair like this again, I'll take my belt to your ass, do you understand me?"

Tears formed in her eyes. "You're being very mean. I'm your temporary prisoner. You can't tell me what I can and can't wear or dictate how long my hair should be."

My jaw clenched. "The hell I can't. Haven't you figured it out yet, babygirl? There is nothing *temporary* about this." I nodded toward the bathroom. "Now, go and do as you're told."

Her brow furrowed and she crossed her arms. "I won't. I like it. Gabriella and Milana looked at me like I was a freak from another century because of my stupid long hair, and because I was raised by nuns. Milana says my new look is sexy and Parisian."

I closed my eyes briefly, shaking my head. "You silly little fool. Is that why you let them chop off your hair and do all this nonsense to you? So you could pretend you're something you're not, just to fit in?"

Her eyes flashed as her shoulders stiffened. "So what if I did? What's wrong with wanting to look different? To imagine I look like a stylish French femme fatale even if it's just for one silly afternoon. What's wrong with wanting to fit in? With wanting people to like me?"

My fingers dug into her shoulders so I could turn her to

face me. "It's another fucking lie, that's what's wrong with it. It's not the real you. It's a bullshit facade to please someone else."

She hitched her shoulders up to her ears. "You're hurting me."

I refused to lighten my grip. "Good. This is why you are in the trouble you're in. A person who doesn't see value in themselves is an easy target for manipulation."

Pivoting her back around to face the mirror, I demanded, "Look at yourself."

Her lips thinned, her head stubbornly averted.

I wrapped my hand around her throat and turned her head back, forcing her gaze forward as I growled, "I said look at yourself. Is this the real you? The person you were meant to be?"

The side of my thumb slid over the crimson gloss of her lipstick, smudging it.

She tried to move her head. "Please!"

I tightened my grip, leaning in close to rasp in her ear. "Stop struggling. I'm admiring the *new and improved* you."

It was ludicrous now to think I'd wondered if her innocence was just an act, if she was truly a talented whore in disguise.

Just to see the stiff, uncomfortable way she was holding her lips, it was obvious she wasn't used to wearing heavy gloss lipstick, let alone any of the other trappings of a more high-maintenance glam appearance.

That won't stop me from teaching her a lesson.

With a tilt of my head, I studied her reflection. "Something's not right." I grasped the gold chain to her cross. "Here it is. Can't have such an *old-fashioned* accessory with your modern, sexy look."

The point of the cross pinched the center of my palm as I ruthlessly snapped the thin chain off her neck and tossed it in a glass dish on the nightstand.

Liliana grasped at her throat as she cried out. "My necklace!"

"I'll get you a new one. Maybe a cubic zirconia *cornetto* to match your new personality. A fake copy of the real thing with the promise of sex."

She looked at me, stunned and hurt. "Why are you doing this?"

Raising my shoulders, I held out my hands, palms up. "Doing what? I'm admiring the new you."

"You're acting like I sold my soul to the devil so I could turn tricks on the corner. It's just a haircut!"

Turning her again to face me, I leaned in close. "But that's the point, Liliana. It's not just a haircut. For other women, maybe, but not for you. You did this to impress someone else —to pretend you're someone you're not— and I have a problem with that."

She sniffed as she placed her palms against my chest, trying to push back. "Why?"

I scanned her face. Even with smeared lipstick, ruined mascara, and shoulder-length hair, she was stunningly beautiful. "Because you are already perfect just the way you are. You have no idea how angry it makes me to think you don't know that."

She pushed harder against my chest as she shook her head. "This is just another one of your interrogation tricks. Besides, you don't get to judge me for wanting to improve myself."

Her shoulders squared as her chin jutted out. "I didn't like the boring person I was forced to be by the nuns. This is the real me. Bold and sexy. Ready to take on the world."

My hand lowered to my belt buckle. "You're lying and I'm going to prove it to you, right now."

The brown, worn leather belt slid out from the denim belt loops. Although butter soft, its weight would carry quite a sting against her delicate skin.

"What are you going to do?"

I snapped the belt around her neck. "You wanted to look like a whore. I'm going to treat you like one."

Looping the tongue through the buckle, I pulled until it rested against her throat. Not enough to choke her, just enough to apply tension. With my hand gripping the belt just below the buckle, I forced her to her knees. "Now open your mouth."

"I'll scream."

"No one will come. They know better than to interfere."

Her palms pressed against my upper thighs. "I'll bite you again."

The corner of my mouth lifted as I bent down. My lips grazed hers. "That's what the belt around your neck is for, babygirl."

She inhaled sharply.

Straightening, I lowered the zipper of my jeans and pulled out my already hard shaft. After giving it a few pumps with my fist, I straddled her hips with my feet and positioned the head of my cock a breath away from her lips. "Open."

Her lower lip trembled as her gaze fixed on my cock.

I tugged on the end of the belt.

The movement jerked her forward.

My cock slid against her cheek. Then, when she opened her mouth on a shocked gasp, I slipped inside her wet warmth.

Her muffled cry sent a delicious vibration up the underside of my shaft.

The sting of pain from her fingernails driving into my thighs only heightened my pleasure. "That's a good girl, take daddy's cock down your tight throat."

She whimpered as I thrust in deeper.

With a shift of my hips, I moved closer, transferring the belt loop to my left hand and reaching for the back of her head with my right. "But you're not daddy's good girl anymore, are you?"

Her big, adorable eyes blinked up at me as her red lips stretched around the thick base of my shaft, leaving a crimson stain on my skin.

"You're my dirty little whore now."

Liliana tried to jerk her head back but my grip on the back of her head prevented her.

I smirked. "What's the matter? Don't like that new endearment for your new look?" I twisted my fingers in her hair, missing the way I was able to wrap her long locks around my fist several times.

Still, it was sexy as fuck the way her angled bob slipped over her cheeks in soft waves and moved with her head as she sucked my cock. And at least there was still enough hair to grab.

Increasing the pace of my thrusts, I watched my swollen length disappear into her small mouth, her struggle to swallow me deeper.

Her tears smeared her mascara even more, her black eyes and smudged red lips making her look like one of those beautifully sad peridot clowns.

I pulled up slightly on the belt, tilted her head back, and

lengthened her throat. "Get ready, baby. All good whores swallow."

My balls tightened as I pulled out and fisted my shaft. Another day, I would continue to thrust into her throat until finishing, but tonight I didn't trust myself not to hurt her. I was too angry, too worked up, and too fucking turned on.

Keeping a tight grip on the belt, I gripped my own flesh and worked it hard as I growled, "Keep that mouth open," just as she tried to close it.

When she reluctantly obeyed, I shot a hot stream of come onto her tongue.

Liliana closed her eyes and started to close her lips again as she pulled back with a cry.

I yanked on the belt. "Open."

With a sob, she opened her mouth again and I finished coming into her mouth.

"Now swallow it."

"Oo I ave oo?" she asked around my warm come pooled in the center of her tongue.

I leaned down and swiped my thumb over her lip and pushed a drop inside. "Yes."

Keeping my thumb inside her mouth, I said, "Swallow."

There was a gentle suction sensation on my skin as she did as I commanded.

I pulled my thumb out and loosened the belt from around her throat before pulling it free. "So did you like learning what it means to be *bold and sexy?*"

CHAPTER 26

LILIANA

I hated it.

I'd die before admitting it to Benedict.

Nothing about this look was me.

I finally understood why people in those reality makeover shows always appeared so horrified at the idea of receiving a free new wardrobe. It was because every piece of clothing picked out for them was for the person others thought they *should be*, instead of the person they *were*.

Just like in the show, this makeover was done with the best of intentions, and I honestly thought I *should* be this person too. But I was so not.

It wasn't Milana's fault. She did an amazing job with my hair. It really did look stylish and bouncy and pretty and … and I didn't like it. I wanted my long hair back and deeply regretted telling her to cut it *all* off.

Every time I tried to talk it was like my lips were glued together, and there seemed to be this constant gummy ridge of extra gloss on the inside rim of my lips. It was so gross.

And I couldn't stop raising my hands to rub at my eyes from all the heavy mascara, lash inserts and liquid eyeliner they had on them. Each time I blinked something new flaked onto my eyeball, driving me crazy.

Earlier in Gabriella's suite, Bianca had come in and hugged me and said all was forgiven and she knew how manipulative and cunning her parents could be and that she thought it was sweet that I had actually been trying to help rescue her.

Then she hauled out all these clothes for me to try on.

Including lingerie, although with all the tiny hooks and buckles, scraps of lace, underwires and corset bindings, the couture pieces looked more like deceptively beautiful torture devices.

Each bra hurt more than the last.

And these thongs she gave me? How were these even considered panties? It was like I was being cut in two by a piece of waxed butcher's twine.

I never thought I'd actually thank the nuns for instilling in me an appreciation for a serviceable cotton bra and panty set. I would do anything to go back to what I used to consider my *naughty* simple purple silk set.

But I would die first before admitting it to *him*.

He loomed over me. "Get up and go wash that crap off your face."

I stared at his hands as he folded the belt in half before scrambling to my feet and racing to the bathroom. Without waiting for the water to get warm, I scrubbed my face raw with ice cold well water from the tap before also brushing my teeth.

My skin was slightly shiny and my cheeks bright pink by the time I was finished.

It felt blessedly clean.

It took me a moment to find him in the dim bedroom when I returned.

For half a second, I hoped he had left.

Quite the opposite.

He was now standing before the fire. The belt was lying folded on the bed nearby. In his hand he held a solid stainless steel ball from the game of Tic-Tac-Toe displayed on a nearby side table, rolling it between his fingers.

I crossed my arms over my middle so I could rub my upper arms. "Will you leave now?" I whispered. My voice was hoarse from sucking his cock.

Without looking up from the fire, he said, "No."

"You can't keep doing these 'interrogation techniques' on me. I told Gabriella the information you wanted. You have to let me leave now."

He leaned his forearm against the mantle, staring deeply into the flames. "I'm not letting you go."

Forgetting my intention to stay an arm's length away, I rushed up to him. "What's that supposed to mean? You have to let me go. I've done everything you asked me to."

His dark gaze flashed up to mine, the hand resting on the mantle curling into a fist around the steel ball. "That's the problem, Liliana."

I twisted my hands as I paced away. "I don't understand."

"Are you a virgin?"

I swung back to be confronted by his intense glare. "Why … why would you ask me that?"

He stepped toward me. "Answer the question."

The back of my knee bumped into a small table as I slid my left foot behind me. "Tell me why you're asking me first."

His upper lip curled, exposing his teeth as if he were a

wolf snarling. "Keep up the games, babygirl, and see what happens."

After skirting around the table, I continued to back away from him. "I'm not playing any games. I don't see why you need to know."

"Answer the fucking question," he barked.

I started at his sharp rise in tone. "No! Of course not. That would be silly at my age."

He continued to stalk me around the room. "You're lying. Again."

"Am not."

He lowered his brow before saying, "Then I guess we'll see."

Madonna santa! He didn't mean ...

Before I could run, he grabbed my arm and swung me in an arc until I found myself bent over the love seat's arm.

My borrowed silk peignoir and nightgown were pushed up over my lower back in a blink, exposing my basically naked ass since the stupid thong offered absolutely no coverage whatsoever.

I cried out in protest as his fingers slipped around my thong and pulled, easily snapping it off.

Locking my elbows in an attempt to rise, I pushed up and looked over my shoulder.

I saw him push two middle fingers into his mouth. When he pulled them free, they were glistening with his spit.

My eyes widened. "What are you—"

He kicked my feet apart and slipped his hand between my legs.

"Stop! Get off me!"

His fingers pressed between my pussy lips as he caressed my clit, gently swirling his fingers in a circular pattern.

My hips bucked in a failed attempt to stop my body's response to his touch.

He leaned over my body and kissed my shoulder. "There's daddy's good girl."

My cheeks flamed. I knew he was referring to the humiliating rush of wet heat made all the worse by my dark pleasure at him once again calling me *daddy's good girl*.

For the first time, his fingers entered me.

Before, he had only teased at the entrance.

My mouth opened as I rose on my toes. I clawed at the fabric of the sofa and tried to force my brain to focus and figure out if he could actually finger me deep enough to learn if I was still a virgin.

When he added a third finger, he pushed in harder and deeper.

"Ow! Ow!" I cried out from the pressure of him forcing my tight passage to open.

"Shhh," he soothed, running his palm in circles over my lower back. "Just a little further, little one."

My forehead pressed against the fabric of the sofa as I squeezed my eyes shut. My inner thighs clenched and I braced for more pain when he pulled his hand back and thrust in again.

There was a twinge of pain as his fingers pushed in deeper.

Benedict stilled.

My shoulders stiffened as I held my breath.

The only sound in the room was the crack and pop from the fire and then a low, blasphemous curse from Benedict.

He pulled his fingers free, and I felt strangely empty and cold despite the warmth in the room.

His hand moved to my hip where it stayed for several moments.

Neither of us moved or spoke.

When he finally did speak, his voice was low. His words clipped as if he were biting off the ends in anger. "Do you have any idea how close I came to fucking your virgin cunt last night in that tub?"

I winced at his crude language.

When I tried to rise, he put pressure on my lower back. "Stay where you are and answer me."

I hated being in such a vulnerable position, like I was a child waiting for a punishment. I licked my lips. "I stopped you."

He stormed away.

At first I was relieved, but then I realized it was to retrieve his belt from the bed.

"You stopped me by begging me to fuck you in the ass instead, where I already know you were also a virgin. Goddammit, Liliana," he raged.

Hazarding a glance over my shoulder, I straightened and watched as he pushed a hand through his hair and paced.

"I was a good girl. I did what you told me to do. I don't know what I did wrong."

He turned sharply to stare at me. Reaching out, he tipped me back over the arm of the love seat and ran his palm over my exposed ass cheek. "That's the problem, *angioletto.*"

I huffed and pounded my fist against the sofa cushion. "You keep saying that and I keep telling you I don't understand."

He smoothed his palm over my other ass cheek right as I heard the metal jingle on his belt buckle.

Out of the corner of my eye, I watched him refold it in half. Horrified, I blurted, "Wait!"

He moved to stand at my side, so I was pinned between his hard body and the back of the love seat. "Time for some harsh *understanding.*"

He then raised the arm holding his belt and lowered it with sharp force until the leather snapped across both of my cheeks.

I screamed from the painful impact.

He raised his arm again, this time striking me slightly lower, on the under curve of my ass.

I kicked out my legs, squirming in an attempt to rise. "It hurts! Stop!"

He struck me again and again before he paused to say, "Do you not see the pattern, babygirl? You allowed yourself to be manipulated into spying on us. Manipulated into harming Bianca."

Another painful thrash from the belt. With this one I absorbed the pricking hot pain as a physical manifestation of the guilt I still felt over my involvement with her poisoning, despite her forgiveness.

This time the belt struck my upper thighs. "No more! Please!"

"No, you'll hear this. Then you went and chopped off your beautiful hair in a pathetic attempt to be liked."

The agonizing truth of his words matched the blistering pain that radiated over my skin, seeming to pulse in waves.

"You allowed me to manipulate you as well. Dammit," he raged before throwing the belt across the room.

I sniffed, missing how I used to be able to hide behind a dense cascade of hair. Now, the shorter length still covered my face, but only barely, making me feel even more exposed and vulnerable. "I'm sorry! I didn't mean to. It won't happen again."

My back muscles trembled as he ran his hand over my spine. "We both know that's yet another lie, but I know now it's not your fault, babygirl. It was how you were raised."

He went down on his haunches at my side and smoothed my hair away from my face. "It's okay, daddy's here now and I'm going to make sure you keep your word."

My hand brushed at my tears before I pushed on my elbows to rise.

He laid a hand on my shoulder. "Not yet, little one."

I frowned as my stomach clenched. "What do you mean you're going to make sure I keep my word?"

Rising, he walked a few steps over to my untouched dinner tray and picked up the small glass pitcher of olive oil. Then, on his way back to me, he picked up a small decorative bowl and dumped the six round stainless-steel balls from the decorative Tic-Tac-Toe game into it. He placed the bowl on the low table to my right and poured the entire pitcher of olive oil over the metal balls.

He moved to stand behind me.

I nervously tried to fill the silent void. "I wasn't raised to lie if that's what you're saying, quite the opposite in fact."

Air hissed through my teeth as he rubbed my still throbbing, punished skin. "I know. You were raised to be an obedient good girl. The problem is, they sent you out into the world without anyone to watch over and protect you."

He leaned over and reached for one of the olive oil-coated metal balls. As he picked it up and held it over me, the olive oil dripped on the top curve of my ass ... and in between.

Oh, no.

My torso bucked up. "Benedict! You're not going to put that inside of me, are you?"

He pushed the metal ball between my cheeks and slowly rolled it down until it pressed against my tight back entrance. "That is precisely what I'm going to do."

I clenched my back hole as tightly as I could. "You can't! That's ... you can't!"

He spanked my ass.

"Ow!"

Too late. I unclenched.

He pushed the metal ball inside of me.

The heavy weight pressed against my sensitive inner muscles, stretching them. "Take it out!"

"Do you want another spanking?"

"No."

"Then be a good girl and take your punishment."

Through tear-filled eyes I watched him reach for another metal ball. My shoulder blades tightened as I held my breath.

Again, he forced my cheeks apart and rolled the metal ball between them until he pressed the ball against my tiny hole, forcing it inside of me.

He stroked the puckered ridges of my hole with the tip of his finger. "It is in your nature to want to please and submit. You fight it but only when you think you are doing something wrong or sinful."

The metal balls shifted, rattling in the bowl when he reached for another one.

I moaned. "Please, not another one."

Ignoring my plea, he pushed a third heavy metal ball inside of me. I could actually hear it tap against the other two inside of my body.

My toes curled. The weighted balls were painfully

stretching my inner muscles while making me feel as if I were slowly being impaled. "It really hurts."

He caressed my lower back then reached for another ball. "Just a few more."

I whimpered. "They won't fit. Please, no more."

"Trust me. They'll fit."

He held the fourth ball against my asshole. "Tell daddy to push the ball inside of you."

I rocked my forehead against the sofa cushion. "I can't."

"Little one, this is part of your punishment. Now tell daddy to punish your little asshole with this metal ball."

"Please don't make me."

"Did you want me to get my belt again?"

I inhaled sharply. "Please daddy, punish my little asshole with the ball."

"Good girl."

My hips pushed out, and I threw my head back and groaned as he forced the fourth ball inside of me.

"It's full! It's full!"

His fingertip caressed my punished hole. "You obviously need guidance and discipline."

My only warning was the clang of metal against the bowl. Then the dreadful pressure of yet another ball pushing against my hole. Sweat broke out on my brow as my stomach clenched and twisted with each intrusion.

He went down on his haunches by my side again. "Which is why I'm keeping you."

Keeping me?

He held the final ball to my lips.

I was so grateful he wasn't going to push it into my ass, I opened my mouth without question and let him slip it inside. The earthy tang with only a hint of the sweet taste of the olive oil coated my tongue as I struggled to move the heavy ball around in my mouth without chipping a tooth on the metal.

Benedict stroked my cheek with the backs of his knuckles. "That's my good girl. I want you to feel something in all your cute little holes, plus I can't have your screams bringing the family to our door."

My screams?

He moved to stand behind me again, then his hand pushed between my stretched-open legs. "Brace yourself, babygirl."

Placing a hand on my left ass cheek, he slowly pushed two fingers into my tight pussy from behind.

I screamed around the metal ball in my mouth as I rose on my toes. The balls in my ass made it feel like he was pushing his entire fist inside of me.

He vibrated his fingers, hitting a sensitive nerve inside me that made my eyes roll back in my head. Leaning over me, he reached his arm around my torso to cup my breast, pinching my nipple.

I was overwhelmed by his intense masculine strength pinning me down.

The heavy weight of the balls in my bottom, the one in my mouth, and his fingers inside my pussy made it feel as if I were no longer in control of my own body which, in an odd way, gave me the freedom to let go.

Of everything.

Any guilt over how what we were doing was wrong and twisted, any confusing emotion over how I felt about what he was doing or why he was doing it—all of it was gone.

All that was left was the deliciously wicked sensation of floating in a turbulent sea of raging, lava-heated waters. The waves crashed over me, stealing my breath, each one stronger than the last. One after the other.

The pressure in my lungs built. Waves crashing. His hand moving, faster and faster. No oxygen. My head spun. More waves. The water getting hotter. I couldn't breathe. Faster. Hotter. It was coming. The darkness. The light. Breath.

I came so hard stars burst behind my eyelids and I almost choked on the metal ball.

I was only partially aware of Benedict releasing my nipple and holding his palm in front of my mouth, coaxing me to spit the ball out as if asking a child to spit out a hard candy.

"*Brava ragazza.* Now push back on your bottom."

My cheeks grew hot. I knew what he wanted but it was so embarrassing. "I can't. I'll just go into the bathroom and do it."

He ran his hand over my pussy. "Then I'll fuck your cunt instead."

I looked over my shoulder. "What?"

He quirked a brow. "I wasn't going to take your virginity with you bent over a sofa arm with some game balls shoved up your ass, but if that is your wish ..."

Squeezing my eyes shut, I bore down and pushed the metal balls into his hand.

If I thought having them inside of me would make accepting his cock easier, I was wrong. The moment his cock-head pushed against my entrance, I knew it would be painful. His cock was so much bigger and thicker than the metal balls.

His hands gripped my hips. "The only thing sweeter than watching your lips stretch around the base of my cock is watching your cute asshole swallow my cock."

I moaned as the increase of pressure and pain morphed into a darkly intense, sinful pleasure.

Running his hand up my back he grasped my hair and pulled me upright to a standing position with my back against his chest. The movement pushed his cock deeper inside my ass.

"Ow! It's too deep!"

"You'll take it and like it. You're lucky I'm not taking my belt to you again now that you've deprived me of the pleasure of wrapping my fist around your hair while I'm fucking you from behind."

My feet were lifted off the floor as he wrapped his arm around my middle and leaned back slightly while he drove into me. His hand shifted down to tease my clit again.

I moaned at the sensation of his fingertip sweeping the still sensitive nub.

With my head against his shoulder, he rasped in my ear. "You're going to be a good girl and come again so daddy can fill your little asshole with his come."

"Yes, daddy," I breathed, and then did as I was told.

But at that moment, I swore it would be for the last time.

CHAPTER 27

LILIANA

*T*hrough a slit in the bathroom door, I strained to survey the darkened bedroom.

I had lingered so long in the shower my fingers were pruned. I then delayed further by drying my hair the slow way on low heat.

Instead of the sleek, straight bob style Milana had painstakingly created with a flatiron, it now fell around my face in soft, bouncy waves.

Although I still regretted my hasty decision, the haircut was growing on me. The less severe style with the breezy, tousled curls suited my personality, such as it was, better.

Taking a moment to listen, I didn't hear any movement. As much as I might be tempted, I couldn't hide in the bathroom all night. With a deep breath, I swung the door open.

He was gone.

My heart fell.

Which was stupid.

Of course, I wanted him gone. Why would I want to face

him after the incredibly degrading, kinky sex we just had? My gaze slid to where my dinner tray had been. Thankfully, it was also gone. Along with the Tic-Tac-Toe game balls.

I closed my eyes in mortification.

I literally let that man shove a decor object up my ass. And liked it!

What is wrong with me?

Maybe Benedict was right.

I'd never had a solid handle on who I was as a person. I supposed that came with the territory of being an orphan. It didn't help that my father was a notorious criminal who died a violent death. The nuns weren't exactly keen to make sure I felt a connection to my dead parents. They refused to even allow me to display a photo of them let alone talk about them.

I seemed to keep expecting someone to tell me who I was and what I was supposed to do with my life. The problem was, knowing I needed to change that about myself and actually having the courage and strength to make the change happen were two very different things.

The bedroom door opened, and Benedict stepped inside. He had changed into a fresh pair of jeans and a loose-fitting white T-shirt. The V-neck collar gave tantalizing glimpses of the mysterious tattoo on his chest. His hair was wet so he must have also taken the time to shower.

I grabbed a throw pillow from the love seat and held it over my chest, covering up my now hopelessly wrinkled borrowed silk nightgown. "I thought you'd left."

He crossed to the bed and laid what he was holding on the blanket as he gave me a wink. "You're not that lucky."

I faked a yawn. "I'm really tired."

He shook out a gorgeous, quilted, brown velvet dressing robe with a shawl collar and held it up to me. "You're shorter than Barone's first wife so this will drag on the floor, but it'll be nice and warm."

Snatching the pillow from my hands and tossing it back on the love seat, he handed me the dressing gown.

Before I could say anything to accept or reject it, he held up a long, white cotton nightgown with a scalloped eyelet trim. It would have been a very conservative nightgown except the cotton was so soft and sheer it was practically see-through.

"We'll need to roll up the sleeves on this. I couldn't find a pair of socks, so I'll just give you a pair of mine to wear. Get dressed."

Shaking my head, I placed both items back on the bed. "First, I worked at Cavalieri long enough to hear the rumors. I'm not wearing the clothes of Barone's murdered wife. Second, there's no reason to get dressed. What I'm wearing is just fine for going to bed."

He tapped the tip of my nose. "First, strictly speaking he didn't murder his first wife. And she fell ill before she had a chance to wear any of this. Second, you're not going to bed. Not before I feed you."

"I'm not hungry."

"I didn't ask if you were hungry. I said I was going to feed you. Now get dressed."

"Why can't I just wear this?"

The moment the question was out of my mouth, I knew I really didn't want anyone to see me in the scandalously clingy silk nightgown Bianca had loaned me. It left very little to the imagination, even if I did have the peignoir as a cover.

Benedict placed his hands on my hips and pulled me against him.

He leaned his face close until our lips almost touched.

"Because, you adorably kinky little girl, I'm going against my nature and trying to be a gentleman here. If you parade around in the same gown I fisted at your lower back while I forced olive oil-coated balls up your ass, the uncivilized beast in me will return."

Santo inferno!

"I'll change."

"Good girl."

Scooping the nightgown, socks, and dressing gown into my arms, while taking note there were several other items in the pile he brought, I rushed back into the bathroom. Worried he would burst through the door at any moment, regardless of if I locked it or not, I hurried.

I caught a glimpse in the mirror before exiting and was mildly annoyed at how much the brown velvet of the dressing gown made the copper highlights in my hair glow. Why couldn't he have chosen something ugly to at least leave me something to complain about?

The socks were in my hand. "These are too big."

He tilted his head as his lips thinned. "You're just going to be stubborn every step of the way, aren't you?"

I frowned. "It's not stubborn to simply state a fact."

Once more wrapping his large hands over my hips, he lifted me off the floor and carried me to the bed. Yanking the socks from my hand, he reached to grab my foot.

I tucked it under the hem of the long nightgown. "What arc you doing?"

He glanced up with a furrowed brow after snatching my foot and pushing one of the socks over my toes and heel, all the way up to my knee. "Have you noticed how often you ask me that question?"

The second sock was pushed onto my other foot all the

way up to my knee as I smirked. "Maybe you should ask yourself what you're doing wrong that I feel the need to constantly ask you it?"

He slid his hands up on either side of my hips and leaned in as his gaze focused on my mouth. "Or I could just invest in a mouth gag."

My eyes widened. Sliding under his arm, I jumped down from the bed.

Already knowing that any further objections would be met with an obstinate no, I followed him silently down to the villa kitchen. It must have been late because the household was quiet and still. As I hopped up onto one of the stools surrounding a marble kitchen island, Benedict rummaged in the refrigerator.

"Any requests?"

"I already told you I'm not hungry."

"Eggs it is."

I rolled my eyes and let out a dramatic sigh which he ignored.

It was oddly comforting to sit in the cozy kitchen and watch him cook.

The kitchen was silent except for the occasional low chime from a nearby clock, the clink of a pan, or click from an oven knob turning. There was a soothing, domestic rhythm to it all. I had been deprived of such a pleasure growing up, having never been allowed in the convent kitchen.

With a deftness that was surprising given the size of his large hands, Benedict cracked four eggs into a bowl and seasoned them with pepper and a dollop of cream after placing two ramekins into the warming oven.

When he removed the ramekins and reached for the olive

oil, he looked up and gave me a knowing wink before pouring a generous dollop at the bottom of each one.

My cheeks burned at the inference.

There was no way I was ever going to look at olive oil again without thinking about what we did. I would have to move out of Italy.

He poured two eggs into each ramekin, put them back in the oven and turned the broiler on. While we waited, he reached into the bread box and cut us two thick slices of freshly baked *Pane Spiga*.

When he pulled the ramekins from the oven, he went back into the refrigerator and removed a bright orange block of *bottarga*. I licked my lips.

I'd only ever had it once before, on a dish served at a lunch party at the Cavalieri offices. Such a savory food item was far too decadent to be served at the convent.

Using a grater, he grated the salted and cured fish roe on top of the eggs. After hand shredding a few leaves of parsley, he centered the ramekin on a plate and slid it in front of me with a fork.

My stomach took that moment to growl.

I wrapped my arms tightly around my middle.

The corner of his mouth lifted, but to my relief he said nothing, simply reached into a cabinet for two wineglasses and poured us both half a glass of a really intense red wine which I was sure came from some insanely expensive Cavalieri vintage that the family treated like a cheap table wine.

Forking up egg from his own dish while standing next to me, neither of us spoke as we ate.

It would be polite to thank him or say it was good or even ask him where he learned to cook, but I was concentrating too much on swallowing without choking instead of noticing how he smelled like spicy soap and leather, to worry about small talk.

When we were finished, he took the dirty dishes and stacked them in the dishwasher. After draining both his wineglass and my mostly untouched one, he led me back upstairs.

The moment we reached my bedroom door, I was turning to finally thank him for the food when his arm wrapped around my back and propelled me forward.

"That was my bedroom door."

"No, it wasn't."

"Yes, it was. I know because it's across from the table with the ceramic *Orazio Pompei* yellow and blue apothecary vase with the woman on it. I was very careful to take note because I didn't want to get lost."

Benedict shouldered open a door further down the hall. "You're adorable."

Leading me inside, he flicked on the light switch. It took less than a second to realize I was in his bedroom.

"Oh no." I swung around and walked right into the wall of his chest.

Gesturing with his chin, he said, "Get into bed, *angioletto*. It's late and we have a long day tomorrow."

"I will as soon as you get out of my way so I can go back to my room."

He stepped forward, forcing me to back up until my butt hit the edge of the mattress. "You're sleeping here, with me, where I can keep an eye on you."

With my gaze trained on the center of his chest, I shook my head. "Nope. That barely worked when you were holding me prisoner at the Vatican, which is literally a fortress, but it's not going to work again now. We are in the middle of nowhere. The entire villa is surrounded by guards, and I have no money, no ID, no clothes of my own, and *no shoes*! I'm obviously not going anywhere."

Without responding, he folded his arms over his chest.

"What if Gabriella let me sleep on the sofa in her suite?"

"No."

"How about I—"

"No."

"You haven't even heard what I was going to suggest."

"Fine."

"What if I—"

"Still, no."

"You're impossible!"

"And I'm also tired and losing patience which means I'm about to get grumpy."

"About to," I mumbled.

"What was that, babygirl?"

"Nothing." I sighed. "I'm not winning this argument, am I?"

He wrapped his hand around my neck and pulled me close to kiss the top of my head. "Nope."

With another resigned sigh, I moved to climb into the bed under the covers when I felt a sharp tug from behind.

Benedict pulled the dressing gown off my shoulders.

I crossed my arms over the sheer nightgown, knowing he'd see my nipples if I didn't. "What if I'm cold?"

"Then I'll keep you warm."

"I just remembered, I'm not cold," I said as I scrambled underneath the covers.

While he was kicking off his shoes and moving about the room, I arranged the extra pillows to create a modesty barrier between him and me. Better late than never.

When he shrugged out of his T-shirt and reached for the

zipper of his jeans, I squeezed my eyes closed and pulled the covers up over my chin. Ignoring his amused chuckle.

By the time he turned off the light, I was already pretending to be asleep and focusing on my pretend deep-sleep breathing. So I was unprepared when he whipped away the pillow wall from behind me, wrapped his arm around my middle and yanked me into his embrace.

"Hey!"

He tightened his grasp. "Just count the Ten Commandments I'll break with you and go to sleep," he murmured against my neck.

My mouth opened on a shocked gasp.

How did he know that was what I was doing last night?

The man really was the devil.

And once again, I never would have fallen asleep if I had known what awaited me in the morning.

If I spent much longer as his captive, I would never sleep again for fear of the coming dawn.

CHAPTER 28

BENEDICT

"Get on the helicopter."

"No!"

"Liliana, I'm not going to tell you again."

"This is insane! They will kill us both."

"I've already told you. That is not going to happen. I have a plan."

She crossed her arms. "Forgive me if I don't have a lot of confidence in your"—she held up her fingers and did air quotes— "plan."

"Did you seriously just air quote me, woman?"

"Your *plan*"—she again put plan in air quotes— "so far has gotten me shot at, almost killed jumping from a balcony, almost pancaked as roadkill on a Vespa, attacked and my eyes nearly scratched out." She lowered her voice. "And other *unmentionable* consequences. I'm over your plans."

I gestured to the pilot, indicating I needed a moment. I wrapped my fingers around her upper arm and dragged her away from the spinning helicopter blades.

I could have just dragged her onto the helicopter, but they were sensitive aircraft, and I didn't want to risk her struggling and making the pilot nervous about how she'd behave during the flight.

Before I could speak, Barone stepped out onto his bedroom balcony holding an espresso. He raised it in salute and called down. "Need any help?"

I called up without taking my eyes off Liliana. "I'm perfectly capable of handling my woman, thank you, brother."

Liliana's mouth dropped open as her hands fisted on her hips. "I'm sorry, your what?"

Just then there was a flash of color as Gabbie appeared on her own balcony on the other side of the villa, in one of her signature, brightly colored dressing gowns and matching turbans.

She leaned over the railing. "What's going on? Benedict, do you need help talking to Liliana again?"

I closed my eyes.

Fuck.

Maybe she didn't pick up on the subtle—

"Again? What does Gabriella mean by again? Did you ask Gabriella to pump me for information yesterday? Was that all a setup?"

I rubbed my beard. Dammit.

Before I could respond, Cesare and Milana strolled up from their grotto home which was connected to the side of the villa.

Milana called out to Liliana. "Oh! I love it curly much better! Way more *you*!"

Liliana called back. "Thank you! I was worried you'd be mad I washed the style out so soon."

SEDUCTION OF THE PATRIARCH

Milana waved her off as she crossed the courtyard from several yards away. "Not at all. You do you. Besides, the tousled, wavy look is softer and more flattering for your facial features."

Amara, who had apparently joined Barone on the balcony, called down. "Morning Milana! And I agree! Liliana, you look really nice."

Liliana looked up and gave her a shy wave before calling up, "Thank you!"

Milana then pointed to Liliana. "Where did you get that outfit? It's so retro vintage. I love it."

Liliana smoothed her hand over the brocade boatneck sheath dress and matching twill blazer in mustard yellow as she looked at me, unsure, I was certain, how to answer.

I had given her the outfit to wear after raiding Barone's dead wife's closet again.

I never liked Angelina. I had found her to be bitter, judgmental, and sanctimonious. Still, no one deserved to die from such a horrible, agonizing disease like she had. At least her more conservative taste in expensive clothes was being put to good use.

Angelina was, in no small part, the reason why I'd handed over the Cavalieri empire to Barone despite being the older son and entitled to a larger share. For a time, I had defied our father and turned my back on the family legacy.

Preferring instead to search for excitement and adventure rather than tied to the land.

It was Barone who stepped up. He sacrificed everything for the family. Marrying a woman he didn't love and giving up any dream of his own to stay and work the vines and grow the family fortune, securing our legacy for generations to come.

I finally wised up and did my part later ... but always from the shadows.

The violence and blood left in my wake would never allow me to step back into the light.

Through clenched teeth, I interrupted. "Ladies! In case you've failed to notice, there is a massive helicopter with a spinning blade over my shoulder."

Liliana's eyes narrowed. "That's no reason to be rude."

"That gives me every reason to be rude. We have to leave."

"*You* have to leave. I'm not going anywhere."

"We are not having this discussion again."

She threw her hands in the air. "What discussion? There was never any discussion. There never is."

Gabbie called out from the balcony. "You tell him, Liliana."

I pointed up at her. "That's enough from you. Back inside." I then swept the villa with my arm. "All of you. This is a private conversation."

Baron wrapped a possessive arm around Amara's waist and led her back into their room. Gabriella blew Liliana a kiss then flashed me a very unladylike chin flick with a cheeky grin before disappearing inside.

Cesare was already holding the passenger car door open for Milana as they prepared to leave for the office.

When I returned my attention to Liliana she turned her cute face up at me with her lower lip thrust out. "You were the one who told me I needed to be more assertive and stop allowing people to manipulate me."

"I meant other people, not me."

She grinned. "Well, I guess that backfired on you, didn't it, because I'm taking your advice starting today."

I folded my hands in front of me and pressed my finger-tips against my lips, taking a moment to choose my words carefully. "*Angioletto*, the only way I'm going to save your godfather is if we go to Sicily. I can't do that without you."

Since with only a few inquiries last night we learned that Liliana's dear Uncle Salvatore was actually the notorious rat bastard Salvatore Giovanni Mangano, *vice capo* to Dante Agnello.

There was now very little doubt in my mind that he was actually the one behind all of this. I just needed to make a few more inquiries to confirm it.

Unfortunately, none of them could be made from here.

I needed to go into the belly of the beast.

And Liliana was my ticket in.

She may not have realized, but I knew how valuable an asset she was in Sicily.

I wish I could say I hated lying to her, but I didn't. Never once had I ever claimed to be a moral man and I had no intention of becoming one now.

I was ruthlessly effective because I was feared, and I was feared because I was ruthlessly effective. I always did what I had to do to get the job done. Always.

If lying to Liliana about wanting to save her piece-of-shit godfather was what got her on this helicopter and to cooperate with me, then lying was what I was going to do. It was better than the alternative … which I was about two seconds from employing if she continued to disobey me.

A strange expression crossed her face. She then broke eye contact and bit her lip. Her shoulders hunched as she stepped back. All deception and hesitation markers.

My gaze narrowed.

It almost seemed as if she were fighting because she didn't want me to save her godfather. It was an irrational theory. She was in this mess because of her desire to help him.

Why would she not want to save him now?

Would there ever be a time when I had this woman figured out?

She was half my age and half my size and yet she was still running circles around me.

It was damn embarrassing.

Even my own family could see it.

I needed to get this situation under control.

Liliana lowered her gaze. "I just don't see why you need me?"

That is one helluva loaded question.

The untimely thought popped into my head. I shook it off. That was for later.

Knowing I was getting nowhere fast, I sighed. "I'm sorry, babygirl."

She tilted her head. "What for?"

"If you didn't like plan A, you're really going to hate plan B."

Her eyes widened as she backed up a step and raised her palms to ward me off. "What's plan B?"

Using the side of my hand, and careful not to strike her too hard, with a swift, decisive motion I struck at her ninth pressure point in the carotid sinus, causing an overreaction of her vagus or heart nerve which led to a dramatic spike followed by a sudden and immediate drop in blood pressure.

I caught her unconscious body before she hit the ground.

Matteo ran up with our bags.

He looked from me to the unconscious Liliana in my arms and back, then shrugged. "Probably for the best. The take-off in a helicopter is always the worst."

As I cradled her in my arms and headed toward the helicopter the pilot jumped out to open the door.

"What happened?" he called out over the roar of the propeller blades.

Stepping into the cab, I arranged Liliana on my lap then pulled the harness over us both. "She fainted. Poor thing hates flying."

The pilot nodded and climbed back into the cockpit.

After Matteo and I both put our headsets on, the pilot asked, "All set?"

I gave him a thumbs-up.

He nodded. "Very good, Signor Cavalieri. We should be in Punta Raisi, Sicily in two hours."

CHAPTER 29

BENEDICT

"*I* can't believe you hit me!"

"I did not hit you. I applied strategic compression to a known pressure point to achieve a momentary state of unconsciousness for a targeted result."

She squirmed on my lap, but I refused to release her. "Same thing."

"Agree to disagree. One is done with pinpoint precision to remain in control of a situation. The other is the barbaric response of someone who never had control of the situation in the first place."

Matteo piped up over the headsets. "Give it up, Liliana. The man literally gets into peoples' heads for a living, there is no winning an argument with him. Trust me. I've spent a lifetime trying."

I lifted up one ear of her headset and said for her ears only, "Well, there is one way for you to win."

At that I bucked my hips up slightly so she could feel the hard ridge of my cock under her thighs and gave her a wink as my hand shifted to rest between her thighs just under the hem of her dress.

Her mouth dropped open as her cheeks turned a very pretty pink.

Casting a glance in Matteo's direction, she wrapped her small fingers around my larger wrist and tried to dislodge my hand.

I squeezed her thigh in response and moved my hand higher. I then lifted her headset a second time and said, "Try to move my hand again, and I'll finger-fuck you right in front of my son."

She immediately released my wrist and folded her hands primly in her lap.

I wouldn't of course.

There was no fucking way I would ever let another man, not even my son, witness the glory that was Liliana in the throes of an orgasm. Her orgasms were like witnessing an angel discovering how deliciously fun sin could be and being there the moment she tumbled straight out of heaven's clouds into my arms.

As we cleared the main coast of Italy and crossed the Tyrrhenian Sea toward Sicily, Liliana's anxiety was palpable.

In a gentle, rhythmic motion, I shifted my hand up and down her forearm in a slow caress. At my first touch she tensed but after a few passes of my hand, she was lulled into a passive reaction.

It was then I checked her pulse. It was erratic and elevated.

When I looked up, Matteo was watching us both. He had picked up on the strange signals Liliana was giving off as well.

He silently nodded.

We agreed that when we landed in Sicily he would watch over Liliana while I dealt with Dante.

If anything went sideways, he was to get her off the island as quickly as possible on a Pershing 108 powerboat we had secretly docked at a private marina to the south, in Aspra, a small town outside of Palermo along the coast. By arriving via helicopter to the north, it was our hope Agnello's men would assume we'd leave the same way, buying us some extra time if necessary.

He also knew not to wait for me.

Through the small triangular windows, the concrete disgrace that passed for an airport, *Punta Raisi,* came into view. Part of the Sack of Palermo, when the mafia destroyed centuries of mature orchards, vineyards, and ancient villas to build poorly made concrete buildings through corrupt building projects meant to improve Sicily's infrastructure after the war.

Punta Raisi was their crown jewel.

Built in the worst possible location for an airport because of the crosswinds, but perfect for coordinating shipments of heroin to America, known euphemistically as the "Pizza Connection." You could say what you wanted about them, but no one ever said the mafia didn't have a sense of humor.

Matteo flipped open the leather satchel between his feet. "Did you want the Mateba Hunter Magnum or the Beretta 92?"

I side-eyed him.

The corner of his mouth lifted. "Stupid question."

Reaching into the bag, he took out the heavy .44 caliber revolver and handed it to me.

Air hissed through Liliana's clenched teeth as her back stiffened.

The night I took her captive I had used a much smaller, older Smith and Wesson Model 19 .357 revolver with a long, polished nickel barrel. Although still an intimidating gun, it looked like something out of an American Western movie. That was by design. Everything I did was intentional.

The gun I was holding now was a .44 Magnum and was far more terrifying and intimidating because Liliana was not my intended audience … or target.

While we hadn't announced our arrival, we already knew we'd be presented with a welcoming party the moment we landed. We had limited information resources in Sicily because multiple mafia factions had such a stranglehold on every aspect of society there, but we had learned that much.

I reached up and stroked her head, smoothing her hair, which was growing on me. "This is all going to be over soon, babygirl."

Her large eyes were pools of darkness. "Yes, but to what end?"

Matteo saved me from the difficult answer.

He checked his own magazine clip before handing me a handful of extra bullets.

The pilot's voice came over our headsets. "Landing in five, sirs."

He was under strict instructions to barely touch down before he lifted off again the moment we disembarked, just in case there was trouble.

Matteo fastened his gun holster under his arm and tucked his gun inside before shrugging back into his blazer. There was a noticeable bulge. The Beretta was not an ideal gun for concealment, but then, that was the point.

Leaning to the side, I did the same.

Liliana continued to watch on with silent, haunted eyes.

There was nothing I could say to her in this moment.

Her role in this macabre theater was still undetermined.

Time would tell.

The one thing I was certain of, was she wasn't in any mortal danger or I never would have brought her. She was worth too much alive to them.

And to me.

I tightened my arm around her. I couldn't think about that right now. It would cloud my judgment. My family needed to come first. Even as I thought it, my mind screamed ... *liar.*

The moment the helicopter landed, Matteo and I put our first plan of attack into play.

The various maintenance crew and airport staff quickly scattered after we touched down and two men in cheap suits pulled up in a black sedan and alighted, guns conspicuously drawn.

Matteo turned to me. "How sweet. They sent a welcoming party."

I recognized the driver immediately from security footage filmed at the Cavalieri winery the night of Barone's shooting. *Sonofabitch.* This was going to be easier than I thought. "You know what to do."

Matteo gave me a quick salute, opened the door, and helped Liliana out, then reached for the bags. Bending low to avoid the whipping blades, they moved across the tarmac toward the gaping entrance of a nearby open hangar.

He moved in front of Liliana as he dropped the bags he was carrying and raised his left arm and waved. "Hello gentlemen. Are you the Uber I ordered?"

The driver smirked as he held his Glock sideways up to Matteo's chest. "Very funny, dickhead. We were told you were an old man."

Matteo rubbed his jaw. "You shouldn't have said that. It annoys the shit out of him when you call him old man."

The second guy, who was too busy leering at Liliana's tits to pay attention, looked up. "Who?"

From behind him, I said, "Me."

I fired one bullet into the companion's head, taking half of it off.

That's what he gets for trying to kill my brother.

My primary focus had not been the man who pulled the trigger, but rather the one who ordered the hit.

That being said, if the man was dumb enough to stroll up with a gun drawn on my girl and my son ... well then ... play a stupid game, win a stupid prize.

The companion dropped onto the dirty, cheap cement like the sack of useless meat he was.

Before the driver had even fully registered what had happened, Matteo grabbed the Glock out of his hand, unchambered the live round and dropped the magazine onto his dead friend's lifeless body.

Through it all, Liliana just stood there.

Still and pale, as if she were an angel carved out of white marble, cursed to stand guard over the horrors in a cemetery.

I pushed her behind me and fisted the front of her dress in my left hand to pull her close.

After a moment's hesitation, her hands pressed against my back.

A rush of air entered my lungs as my heart began to beat again.

Shifting my hand to her hip, I gave it a quick squeeze, then released her to focus on the task at hand, reassured that she'd stay close behind me. If I could have, I would have spared her that first part, but the element of surprise was essential.

One of the essential rules of engagement was, never assume the enemy you saw was the only enemy around.

If we had assumed it was a fair fight of two on two, and met them head on, we may have walked into a trap if there had been a second kill squad lurking.

Matteo used the lifeless man's coat to wipe the blood splatter off his boots.

I smirked. "Did I get you?"

He shrugged. "Not as bad as you could have, considering the angle."

The driver's eyes bulged. "What the fuck?"

I raised my gun and tapped the heavy barrel against his forehead as I forced him to his knees. "Hey! Language. There is a lady present."

I had dropped the f-bomb countless times in Liliana's presence but that didn't mean I would tolerate scum like him doing so.

"Who are you guys?"

Matteo tilted his head to the side. "Didn't you get the memo? He's the old man, I'm his son, and behind him is the fucking mafia princess you're here to collect."

The driver pointed to Matteo. "He said fuck."

I banged him on the forehead again with the heavy barrel of my gun.

"Ow!" he complained as he rubbed the burgeoning red spot.

"He's allowed. You're not."

Matteo reached inside the man's jacket and pulled out his wallet and phone, handing them to me.

I flipped the wallet open. "Let's see who we have here. Alessio Ettore. Well hello, Alessio. Let's have a more formal introduction, shall we? I'm Benedict Cavalieri and this is my son, Matteo."

Matteo gestured with his guns. "But you can call us by our nicknames. Mine is *Fuck Around* and his is *Find Out*."

I shook my head, trying not to laugh. I'd taught him well.

Using conflicting emotions during a confrontation made it difficult for an adversary to read your intentions. It put them on their back foot and lowered the chances they would remember the details of a prepared lie.

After pulling his identification out, I held it up. "I hope you don't think this is rude, Alessio. May I call you Alessio? Good. But I'm going to keep your identification, Alessio, so I know *exactly* where to find you—and your family—if you lie to me. Let's begin."

He waved his palms in the air next to his head. "No. No. No. Why would I lie?"

"Who sent you?"

"Dante."

I opened his phone and clicked on the photo app. "Tell me, which one of these beautiful children do you want me to shoot first?"

Liliana's grip on my suit jacket tightened.

I reached back and squeezed her hip.

Alessio's eyes bulged again. "What do you mean?"

"I warned you not to lie to me, Alessio. And you just lied. So now I'm asking you, which one of your children do you want me to kill?"

"I'm not lying."

"Dante himself did not send you. You did not hear the words come out of his mouth."

His shoulders hitched to his ears. "No. Not in that way. No. It was Salvatore. His *vice capo* was who told us to come, but he speaks for Dante, so Dante told us to come."

There was a short gasp behind me.

"Where is Dante now?"

"I can't tell you that."

Matteo looked at the phone and pointed with his gun. "I think you should kill that one."

Alessio arched his neck. "Wait, which one? Not the boy, right? One of the girls? The fat, ugly one?"

Matteo and I shared a look. Fuck, this guy was a piece of shit. We'd be doing his daughters a favor at least.

I banged Alessio on the head again with the barrel tip of my gun. "You're not focusing, Alessio, and that offends me."

He waved his hands again. "No! No! No offense! I'll tell you! He's on the *Alina Odyssey*."

The *Alina Odyssey* was his yacht, named after his American girlfriend. It was probably docked somewhere in Palermo. It wouldn't be too hard to find.

I nodded to Matteo as I turned to Liliana.

Her complexion was a troubling ashen shade. I wrapped one arm around her shoulders and pulled her in with a hand against the back of her head as I said, "Cover your ears, babygirl."

She did as she was told.

It was unlikely her palms did much to muffle Alessio's screams for mercy or the gunshot that ended his life but at least this time she didn't see it.

Matteo tapped me on the shoulder and held up the black sedan keys he found in Alessio's pocket. I nodded before sweeping Liliana into my arms.

Matteo walked ahead of us and opened the back passenger door.

I bent low and stepped inside, still holding her close. Matteo slipped behind the wheel and drove us to the private

Donna Franca Suite we had reserved at the Villa Igiea Hotel in Palermo about a half an hour away.

* * *

BY THE TIME WE ARRIVED, our private concierge handed me a sealed cream envelope.

SIGNOR CAVALIERI,

I WOULD BE HONORED if you and your guests joined me for dinner.

DANTE

CHAPTER 30

LILIANA

"*Zolfo sugnu*," I murmured.

"What does that mean?"

I started at Benedict's deep voice.

My knuckles whitened from my grip on the slightly weathered iron railing of the elegant terrace.

As if in a trance, I didn't object earlier when we parted in the hallway with Matteo heading to his own room and Benedict ushering me into his with a proprietary hand on my back.

When we crossed the threshold, I had passed through the luxurious suite and beelined straight to the glass doors for the terrace, ignoring the elegant, sea-inspired decor of the suite. Perhaps I could appreciate the unique stiffened rope-knot chandelier and the cobalt blue geometric lines of the clean white walls at a later time.

Crossing the terrace's clay tiles I looked out over the sparkling water and inhaled the briny, earthy scent of the salt water, the wind whipping my short curls against my cheeks. I closed my eyes and tried to pull tiny vestiges of warmth from the sun's weak winter rays.

I had so desperately wanted to feel as if I were home and finally safe.

But I didn't.

It would be easy to blame Benedict and the staggering display of violence I just witnessed, but I knew that would be just an excuse.

His hands appeared on either side of mine on the railing, and he enclosed me in his arms from behind.

There it was … the warmth I had been expecting when we touched down in Sicily … the warmth I had been seeking in the scent of the warm, salty breeze.

The feeling of safety.

The feeling of home.

There were things I needed to think through.

Horrible, dangerous, life-changing things.

These past few months, I had been holding on to this hope that all I needed to do was to get back to Sicily and everything would be fine. As if everything that was happening was just some storm that needed to pass, or a nightmare I needed to wake up from.

Each time I received a call from my godfather, I would get twisted and tense, holding my breath waiting for him to say it was over, that whatever he had done to incur Dante's wrath had been forgiven by my acts of penance—that I was finally free and safe.

That I could come home.

But each time, with each call, I was drawn deeper into the nightmare.

Then Benedict found me.

That should have been the most nightmarish moment of all and yet it wasn't.

He could have killed me.

He should have killed me.

Suspicion alone would have justified it and Lord knew he had the skills to carry it out and his family had enough money for him to have completely gotten away with my murder. It wasn't as if I had anyone in my life to miss me.

But he didn't. Quite the opposite in fact. He *saved* me.

How fucked up does my life have to be that the safest I'd ever felt was in the arms of the man sent to kill me?

It was easier to pretend moral outrage when it was a kinky sex game.

It wasn't an emotional wound.

It was just him pulling my hair and making me call him daddy, right?

It wasn't me feeling cared for and protected for the first time in my life.

It wasn't me sleeping through the night curled up in his arms, warm and safe, compared to a lifetime of cripplingly lonely nights spent in a bare, cold room at the convent.

It wasn't me wondering what it would feel like to be a part of a big family like the Cavalieris, to be surrounded by all that noise and laughter and arguments and teasing and love all the time.

It wasn't me marveling at how a man as big and terrifying as Benedict could be the first person to truly *see* me, enough to get angry over the idea of someone taking advantage of me.

I needed to stop these spiraling thoughts.

They were beyond dangerous. For all I knew, *he* was also manipulating me. I could be falling into his trap. Getting me to doubt who I was deep inside, then detaching me from the only home I'd ever known. Making me think his family could be mine.

Still ... it was so tempting.

I leaned back against the comforting strength of his chest as my gaze was drawn to his hands gripping the railing beside mine. In this light the faded, purplish-white scars slashing over his knuckles were more visible.

Fighting scars. Violent scars.

A tiny spot of crimson on my cuff caught my attention. Blood.

I tilted my head and studied it more closely. I couldn't be sure if it was from the first man or the driver. Probably the first man. This was the second time this week I had gotten a stranger's blood on me.

I wasn't sure if there was an etiquette about these things but it didn't seem right that I should be staring at the final drops of oxygenated blood from another human being ... and I didn't even know their name. At the very least, I should know their name.

Or perhaps it was fitting.

After all, we were in Sicily.

And being in Sicily, I rasped the words against the dry wind. *"Zolfo sugnu."*

Benedict nudged my neck. "Babygirl? You said it again. What are you saying? I can't make it out."

"You wouldn't understand."

"Try me."

I ran my fingertip over the spot of blood. It had already dried. Seeped into the fabric, like the history of violence on the shores of Sicily.

"I tried to tell you before. I'm not Italian. I'm Sicilian. You may think it is the same thing but it's not. We think differently. It's hard to explain. It's something in the soil, in the air, in the centuries of being ruled by invaders."

I turned within his arms and looked up at him. "Despite my family history, I've seen more violence with you in these last few days than I have in my whole life."

He flinched but didn't apologize.

I didn't expect him to.

Looking him in the eye with what most would have mistaken for boldness but which I knew was more pragmatism, I asked, "Are you worried about me?"

His eyes scanned my face. "Yes."

I stared back.

He didn't have kind eyes. They were too sharp, too intelligent to be kind. Yet at the same time he never seemed to look down on me or through me.

It wasn't that he was studying me so much as he was attempting to understand me. At first, I figured it was just for the information I could provide but once he'd gotten that, I realized it was more than that. It was deeper.

Not anything deep like he was looking into my soul. That would be too romantic or, God forbid, religious for a man like him.

It was more that he was trying to figure out how I thought, as if that were the key to understanding me. As if that were the key to understanding anyone.

It was as if he viewed people through a lens based on the decisions they made throughout their lives.

These last few days, I'd been glad of the difference in our ages. As someone older, stronger, and more experienced, he had a way of making me feel as though he were in control of the chaos around me. I didn't think I would have felt the same way if he had been my age.

Deep down, I knew I was too young to understand *him* and too naive to know if his way of putting people onto tiny slides to be viewed and judged was good … or a terribly cold and analytical way to live.

It only increased my paranoia that this could all be part of an elaborate manipulation on his part to trap me into betraying my godfather and Dante.

I played with the button on his shirt. "It's what I'm trying to tell you. If you were Sicilian, you wouldn't be. We have this funny way of internalizing things we cannot control, a sort of generational fatalism that helps us survive."

The ends of my hair stung my cheek as they whipped against my skin. Such a strange sensation. I had no idea my hair could hurt. It had always been secured in a tight bun or ponytail when in the wind.

His warm hand pushed my curls away from my face as he cupped my cheek. Tilting my head back, he asked again. "And what does *zolfo sugnu* mean?"

"It's an old Sicilian saying left over from when there were sulfur mines. *'I am just sulfur.'* It means I have no control over what is happening to me. I am nothing."

He frowned. "Don't say that."

"Why not? It's true."

"Just don't."

"You're the one always yelling at me to tell the truth."

His thumbs caressed my cheekbones. "Yes."

"So, *zolfo sugnu.*"

He stepped closer, pinning me against the railing. His voice growing harsher. "Stop saying that."

"Zolfo sugnu. Poisoner."

"Stop."

"Zolfo sugnu. Murderess."

"Babygirl."

"Zolfo sugnu. Mafia princess."

"I'm warning you."

"Zolfo sugnu … whore."

"Enough."

His mouth slammed down on mine.

I wasn't sure why I baited him into kissing me, only that I wanted him to.

And I immediately regretted it.

CHAPTER 31

BENEDICT

*a*nd just like that, I was fucking done.

With all of it.

If it weren't for my brother and her piece of shit godfather, I'd toss Liliana over my shoulder and head back to the airport and fly her home to my ranch this very night. The very second I handled this bullshit with her godfather and Dante, I was taking her back there.

Whether she liked it or not.

I didn't give a damn that I'd only fucked her twice and not even properly yet.

She was mine.

I was keeping her.

My lonely broken doll.

My little lost angel.

She was not cut out for this violent and bloody world, full of self-serving people who only wanted to use and manipulate her—including me.

With me, she at least would be safe and protected.

And loved.

I wasn't sure if I was capable of falling in love, but I had a strong feeling that if it were possible, it would be with her. And only her.

My hand shifted from her cheek to the back of her head as I wrapped my arm around her waist.

Thrusting my tongue between her lips, I crushed her to me so fiercely I feared I might crack one of her delicate ribs.

The edge of my teeth scraped against hers as I devoured her like a man starved. Swinging away from the banister, I lifted her off the ground and reached for her knee, wrapping her leg around my waist.

She clung to me, wrapping her other leg around me, and encircling my neck with her arms.

Biting her lower lip, I growled, "That it's, baby. Hold on to me."

I meant it in more ways than one as I carried her into the suite. I tilted my head to the right and captured her mouth again, thinking about fucking her on the pale blue lounge sofa, but then fearing we may shatter the glass coffee table in front of it in our zeal.

Besides, with what I had in mind, I needed a bed.

With her in my arms, I turned to the right into the main bedroom. Near the bed, by the time her feet touched the floor, I was already dragging the borrowed blazer off her shoulders and reaching for the zipper in the back of her dress.

She wrenched her head to the side and breathlessly said, "Benedict, I—"

I didn't want to hear it.

My hand on her jaw, I pulled her head forward for another kiss while I forced her dress over her hips and down to her ankles. Pushing her back onto the bed, I kicked off my socks and shoes and tore off my suit jacket.

After unbuttoning the first few buttons of my dress shirt, I pulled it over my head.

My gaze narrowed as I stared at her soft skin and the gentle swell of her breasts over the edges of the lace cups of her bra. Every stitch of clothing, right down to the damn pair of panties on her body, was borrowed.

When we left here, we would stop in Milan and buy her a new wardrobe. The idea of providing for a woman was a novel one for me and I liked it.

Or perhaps I would take her straight to the ranch and give her nothing but my old sweaters and T-shirts to occasionally cover her nakedness with until she got used to the fact she was now mine. Just in case she still had thoughts of trying to escape me. That idea also had merit.

Liliana moved up onto her elbows and inched deeper back onto the bed. Her lips were already swollen and a crushed cherry red. The wary look in her dark eyes told me she instinctively knew this time was going to be different.

Smart girl.

My hands lowered to my belt buckle.

The muscles in her thighs tensed seconds before she pushed off on her heels and flipped onto her stomach, preparing to bolt off the bed. Anticipating her reaction, I raised my arm and gave her cute ass an open-palm slap.

"Ow!" she cried out.

As she reached around to cover her ass, I wrapped my hands around her hips and flipped her onto her back as I yanked her to me closer to the edge of the bed. "Not so fast, little one."

Her lower lip trembled. "I think I ..."

I sank my closed fists into the mattress on either side of her hips. "Started something you can't finish? I agree, but it's too late now." My mouth captured hers again, tasting her fear.

After breaking free, I commanded, "Take off your bra."

Liliana swept her knees beneath her and leaned up. "Can we—"

"Talk about this?"

She looked up at me hopefully.

I unbuckled my belt and whipped it from the pants loops. Folding it in half, I said, "No. Do as you're told."

Lowering her head, she reached behind her and fumbled with the bra clasp.

I could have helped but she looked so damn sexy with her wind-tousled hair, pink cheeks, and submissively bent head. I especially loved the way the curves of her breasts jiggled and swayed with the movement of her arms as she struggled to obey my command.

When the clasp finally released and her breasts spilled free, I fell on her like a mad man.

Wedging my knee between her legs, I latched on to her breast as I pressed my hips down onto hers. Sucking the sensitive nub deep into my mouth, I cupped her other breast and squeezed, appreciating her moan, and arched back.

My hand then ran over her gently curved stomach to slip my fingers inside the thin silk of her panties. Her hips bucked the moment the tips of my two middle fingers skimmed her pussy lips.

Reaching between us, she wrapped her hand around my wrist. "Wait."

Applying pressure, I pushed between her lips until her clit pressed against one of my fingers. "Shhh, baby. I know you're scared, but daddy's here."

Despite my cock being hard enough to pound nails, I had to rein it in.

With my *angioletto* being a virgin, this was already going to be painful for her, especially given my size.

I inhaled the honeyed vanilla scent of her skin as I moved my mouth over her abdomen. "Fuck, baby, I could eat you alive."

Slipping off the bed, I kneeled on the floor and ripped her panties off. With my head between her legs, I grasped the tops of her thighs and pulled her to the edge until her sweet cunt was within a breath of my mouth.

She leaned up on her elbows. "Benedict, we have to stop. This is moving really fast, and I ..."

I kissed the soft skin of her inner thigh. "Babygirl, I've already fucked your tight asshole twice."

Her cheeks blossomed into a fierce blush. "You shouldn't talk like that. It's sinful."

My hand slid down her pussy lips to tease her puckered hole. "Careful. You look so pretty when you blush, I might have to do worse than just talk about it."

I leaned in close so she would feel my breath. "Maybe I'll even lick your cute hole again just so this time I could see your reaction as my tongue flicks and teases and ...."

Liliana covered her face with her hands and fell back. "You have to stop!"

She tried to slam her thighs closed and twist her hips but I was having none of it. Taking pity on her, I focused only on her clit as I pushed first one then two fingers inside her. Preparing her for my cock.

The primal, possessive beast in me was pleased to feel how wet and ready she already was, but if she was going to take my cock for the first time, I would need her sated and relaxed from an orgasm and her inner muscles more stretched and open.

Twisting my fingers inside of her, I flicked her clit with the tip of my tongue, savoring her nectar. I flattened my palm over her stomach to still her writhing, evasive reaction to my ministrations. I knew she was lost when she stopped trying to fight me.

I moved my tongue faster, applying a little more pressure as I listened to the pace of her breaths and felt how her body responded to variations in my touch. When I knew she was ready, I added a third finger.

Liliana moaned and thrashed. The covers wrinkled where she fisted her hands into them. "It's too much."

Twisting my fingers at the same time that I thrust, I kept my voice a low growl, knowing the vibrations would add to her pleasure. "Open your legs wider for daddy, baby. I need to push a fourth finger in."

She whimpered. "No, daddy."

Fuck.

My other hand lowered the zipper of my jeans and pulled out my cock. I had kept it restrained so I didn't lose control but hearing her call me daddy without being told to just brought me damn close. I squeezed my flesh and pumped it hard, trying to ease the pressure.

Ignoring her plea, I forced a fourth finger into her tight cunt at the same time.

"Don't stop!" she screamed, her thighs tightening against my shoulders, her hips rising off the bed.

I held her tight, following her movements with my mouth, still sucking on her clit, not breaking contact.

Her interior muscles rippled and clenched around my fingers as her back bowed and she cried out her release.

Wanting, no, *needing*, to feel her release around my cock, I pulled out my fingers, wrapped my hands around her hips and pushed her further back onto the bed to cover her body with my own.

I then spread her legs wider so I could push my hips between them. Using her own cream as lubrication, I leaned up on my knees, grasping my shaft and positioning it at her entrance.

Bracing my forearm near the top of her head, I pushed my fingers into her hair and kissed her forehead. "This is going to hurt, *angioletto*. Don't be afraid, after this you'll truly be mine."

I gritted my teeth as my balls tightened, already anticipating the hot clench of her body around my flesh, when her body stiffened under me, and her fingernails dug into my upper arms.

The adorable blush drained from her cheeks.

Her pale lips moved, but no sound came out.

"Baby?"

She became like a frightened wet cat.

Kicking, clawing, and biting.

With little effort, I pinned her wrists over her head. "What the fuck, Liliana!"

I knew she was a virgin, but Christ, just last night I was balls deep in her ass and the night before I was the same down her throat, so she could hardly claim maidenly fright.

"Fear not, for I have redeemed you; I have called you by name, you are mine," she rasped with wide, tear-filled eyes.

"What?"

"Non temere, perché ti ho redento; ti ho chiamato per nome, tu sei mio."

It was then I recognized the Bible verse. Isaiah 43:1. For one twisted second, I wanted to tell her that it was a beautiful passage reminding believers of God's compassion, and not some cudgel of organized religion, but stopped before I used the Big Guy as a wingman to get laid.

I wasn't exactly a religious man but even I had lines I wouldn't cross.

I pushed her hair back from her face. "Babygirl, shhh. It's all right."

The tears overflowed her eyes and streamed down her cheeks. "*Zolfo sugnu.*"

"I told you to stop saying that."

She shook her head. "If you do this. If I let you. Then *zolfo sugnu*. I'll have no chance at a family. A home. I'll have nothing. I'll *be* nothing. *Zolfo sugnu.*"

This was also not the time for a lecture on how her worth as a woman was not tied to a thin membrane that had no evolutionary purpose beyond the fragile egos of small-dicked men.

I cursed as I rolled off her.

The second I did, she shimmied off the bed and ran into the bathroom, slamming the door shut behind her. She was damn lucky I didn't chase after her and kick it open when I heard the lock slide into place.

I stood and stormed through the hotel suite into the adjacent bedroom and attached bathroom. Turning the silver lever to start the shower, I tore off my jeans and stepped under the chilled stream of water, knowing it would do nothing to calm my anger or hard-on.

Dante had better hope he had the right answers for me tonight.

With my primal lust still raging and unsatisfied, I now needed an outlet and would be out for blood.

CHAPTER 32

BENEDICT

"Well, this isn't awkward at all," murmured Matteo.

"Shut the fuck up," I barked.

He saluted. "Shutting the fuck up."

I gazed at a silent Liliana as we continued to ride down in the elevator in silence. The heightened color in her cheeks was the only indication she heard Matteo.

Once again, she was wearing the clothes of a dead woman.

This time the outfit was a slightly too long, red-and-cream herringbone striped skirt with a matching off the shoulder crimson sweater. It was the perfect outfit to show off the way her new haircut accentuated the curve of her jaw and high cheekbones, her big eyes, and the slope of her shoulders.

And fucking Milana and Gabbie knew it when they packed it for her. Damn them.

A delicate strand of pearls hung around her throat. Missing was the gold cross I tore off her in a fit of anger and lust like a fucking Neanderthal.

She didn't know it, but the cross was tucked safely in my wallet.

I had every intention of replacing it at the first opportunity.

Again I stared at the pearls. They were a classic symbol of elegance, innocence, and purity.

And all I could think about was giving her a very different kind of pearl necklace.

Clearing my throat, I spoke to Matteo. "You know what to do when we're on the boat?"

He glanced between Liliana and me and raised an eyebrow in an unspoken question.

I stared back at him, refusing to answer.

He shrugged and responded. "Affirmative."

If my suspicions were correct about Dante and Salvatore, Liliana's godfather, then three steps would happen in rapid succession when we arrived on the yacht.

Step one, an excuse would be made to separate Liliana from me.

I would put up an objection, as would be expected, but would ultimately agree to it if Matteo accompanied her.

Assuming my opponent would have planned for this, step two would then occur, in the form of a distraction they would create to lure Matteo away from Liliana.

And if I was right, that was when the most crucial step would happen.

* * *

THE TENDER CUT its engine and approached the stern platform of Dante's forty-meter, limited edition luxury Benetti B. YOND yacht, named the *Alina Odyssey.*

One of two men dressed entirely in black holding semi-automatic Beretta PMXs shifted the gun he was holding to his side and held out his hand to Liliana as we prepared to disembark.

Keeping my legs wide for balance, I stepped between them and onto the platform.

I then held my hand out to Liliana.

She hesitated at first, but then took it.

Staged at the top of the platform between the two backlit staircases was a large infinity pool jacuzzi whose constant rush of water masked what I was about to say.

Pulling her close, I rasped in her ear, "I don't give a *fuck* that you think you are now among family. Hesitate again when I reach out to you and there will be hell to pay, understand, little one?"

Her shoulders stiffened as she nodded imperceptibly but it was enough.

I was confident she had been around me long enough to know it wasn't an idle threat.

The other man stood in front of Matteo and me. "We have to check you for weapons."

Matteo unbuttoned and held open his brown suede jacket. "My pleasure and don't worry." He winked. "I won't tell your boss you failed to do so back on the dock."

I rubbed my beard and shook my head, hiding a grin before also opening my double-breasted gray-check sport coat.

We both knew there was a reason the men back at the dock "forgot" to check us. If I had to hazard a guess, these two men were supposed to have "forgotten" to check us as well.

Unless …

Matteo looked over at me.

I nodded.

Finished with Matteo, the man moved to stand before Liliana. "Arms up."

Without even taking my eyes off the man frisking me, I warned, "Lay one finger on her and I'll break your body into so many tiny pieces it won't even make a splash when it hits the water."

The man paused and then, as if assuming he must have somehow misheard me since he was the one holding the gun, reached toward her again.

I cleared my throat to subtly get his attention and this time all I did was look at him.

He backed away. "I'm sure she's fine."

Matteo buttoned his jacket before he placed a hand on the man's shoulder. "Good choice. He wasn't kidding. Plus I would have fucking laughed my ass off watching it happen."

I offered my elbow to Liliana. We strolled up the short staircase to cross the open stern deck of the massive yacht, where we ascended another small staircase and crossed polished teak flooring into an elegant cocktail lounge.

A tall man with wavy black hair reaching just past the rolled collar of his navy wool sweater had his back to us at the bar.

Rather than be fooled, I was impressed. It was a classic manipulation tool.

It showed balls to turn your back on an enemy.

Showing him the respect he at least deserved in his own territory, I said, "Don Agnello, I presume?"

The man himself turned with a knowing grin, his arm outstretched. "Call me Dante, please. You must be Benedict Cavalieri."

I shook his hand. Keeping my arm around Liliana's waist, I offered, "I assume you are acquainted with—"

My captive.

My possession.

My angioletto.

My future ...

"—Signorina Liliana Chiara Fiore."

She stiffened.

I squeezed her hip reassuringly.

Dante took her hand and raised it to his lips, kissing the back. "I have heard wonderful things but never had the pleasure. Signorina, welcome. Our fathers were great friends. I hope that we may be as well."

The moment he released her hand, Liliana wiped it on the side of her skirt. If he noticed, he didn't say anything as he turned to my son. "And you must be Matteo."

Matteo held out his arm and the genial smile on his lips didn't reach his eyes. "If I must."

They shook hands.

Dante cupped his hands together before him. "I thank you for accepting my invitation to dine. We still have a few hours before dinner and I would prefer to discuss business beforehand so that we may enjoy our meal."

I smiled indulgently. "Agreed."

Dante turned to Liliana. "My staff have prepared one of my finest staterooms for you to rest and relax in while the men talk. There is chilled champagne and strawberries. If that is not to your liking, you have only to ring and they will bring whatever you like. I promise we will not keep a beautiful woman such as yourself waiting too long."

Liliana's hand reached up to grasp the lapel of my tuxedo jacket. "I don't think ..."

Playing the part, I shook my head. "I don't stand on such antiquated precedent. I'm fine if she stays. After all, I did go to a great deal of trouble to … *acquire her.*"

Liliana hissed through her teeth as she caught my intended implication meant for Dante.

I refused to look down, knowing the pain I would see in her eyes and uncertain if I would be able to bear it. This was an absolutely essential element of the plan, and it was crucial that Liliana know absolutely nothing about it.

Dante's gaze narrowed slightly. The corner of his mouth lifted. "May I remind you that Liliana is of Sicilian blood? As far as I'm concerned, she is family. A sister. If you need to hear it, ancient hospitality rules, of course, apply. You have my word, no harm will come to her while she is under my protection."

I took a step closer to Dante.

The three guards near the perimeter closed in.

Dante raised his arm and they stopped.

I smiled. "Let's be very clear. She's under *my* protection and *all* that implies. Understood?"

Dante raised his chin. "Is that so?"

I didn't respond, just met his gaze.

Finally he nodded. "Understood."

I returned his nod. "And Matteo will keep her company. Nonnegotiable."

Before Dante could object, Matteo stepped forward and offered his arm to Liliana. "Sounds like a plan to me. Come on, Lili. Let's go check out this stateroom and get into trouble."

Before leaving, he took the bartender by surprise by stepping behind the bar and snatching a bottle of Patrón x

Guillermo Del Toro Añejo Tequila and two shot glasses. "For the road," he said with wink.

He was playing the role of the carefree *bon vivant* well. We both knew any attempt to put them at ease about me was pointless. My reputation would precede me.

Fortunately, Matteo's exploits were still extremely well hidden.

As far as anyone knew, as my only son he was blowing through the Cavalieri money while making a half-assed attempt to earn his keep by showing up at our headquarter offices a few days every couple of weeks.

I knew it was part of the act, but I still called out. "Don't let her have more than one shot."

Liliana looked back at me over her shoulder as Matteo took her by the hand and led her away.

Steps one and two complete.

CHAPTER 33

BENEDICT

*D*ante gestured for his bartender to move aside as he placed two snifter glasses on the silver marble bar and then reached into his white linen trousers for a set of keys.

Unlocking a glass cabinet behind him, he retrieved the crystal bottle of *L'Esprit de Courvoisier Cognac Lalique Decanter*, removed its gold-plated stopper, and poured two glasses, sliding one toward me.

After cupping the bottom of the glass in my palm and swirling the expensive amber liquid to warm it, I inhaled the rich vanilla and dried fruit notes.

As he picked up his own glass and stepped out from the bar, I gestured with a nod toward his guards. "Perhaps we should send the kids out of the room before the adults start talking."

Dante's gaze swept over his guards then back to me.

I hid a smirk. "Trust issues? Understood. How about I start?"

Setting my glass aside, I braced my foot on the lower rail of a barstool and lifted my gray wool slacks to expose my ankle holster and removed my Glock 43.

A guard raced forward to grab it from me.

I then reached behind my back and removed the Tanfoglio GT27 I had tucked into my waistband.

The guard grabbed that as well.

Keeping my gaze on Dante, I slipped my hand in my boot and removed the double-edged Smith and Wesson fixed blade boot knife I had hidden there.

Dante took a sip of his brandy. "Anything else?"

I grinned. "There is an adorable hot-pink taser hidden between Liliana's breasts." I slanted a deadly look at his guards. "But I highly recommend no one attempt to retrieve it. Then of course whatever fun toys Matteo may have on him."

The guard tried to speak.

A look from Dante silenced him. "All of you. Leave. Now."

After they departed Dante leaned his back against the bar as he frowned. "I'd say it was clever of you to sneak those weapons past my guards, but we both know there was barely any attempt at concealment."

I leveled a look at him. "We both know why I'm here."

He nodded. "I do. You think I ordered a hit on your brother and in retaliation you've already killed two of my men. I appreciate you accepting my offer of a civil discourse before further blood is shed."

Before he could say more, I stated, "It's not an exaggeration to say, had I done otherwise, you would never have heard the bullet."

He inhaled through his nose as he ran the edge of his thumb over the smooth crystal edge of his glass. "No, your reputation is ... well ... let's just say even with my extensive contacts and resources I'm assuming I was only able to learn a fraction of what you're capable of and it was enough."

I returned his gaze. "I'm sure I don't know what you're talking about."

He rubbed the back of his neck. "Was that bit about the Liechtenstein monarchy true?"

I shrugged as I took a sip of brandy.

"Then there was that intriguing story about the tourist boat sinking in Lake Maggiore."

I shook my head in mock sadness. "Yes, terrible tragedy."

He copied the gesture. "Agreed. Always a shame when a boat full of spies from multiple countries suddenly sinks in a freak storm. Especially when you learn its passenger list contained a few misbehaving Russian oligarchs who were illegally buying land, villas, and hotels in the area."

I shook my head, casually leaning an elbow against the bar. "Yeah. I hear they never found their bodies, but the good news is everyone else on board survived."

Dante nodded. "I think my favorite was your secret involvement with the Vatican scandal over the cardinal, the femme fatale, and freeing that hostage nun who was held by jihadists."

"Pure speculation. I'm a simple horse farmer from up north."

He nodded. "And I'm just an accountant from Chicago."

We both raised our glasses in a mock toast and drank.

I reached into my jacket pocket for a pen and wrote on a cocktail napkin.

Your yacht is bugged. Talk on deck.

I held it up to Dante.

He read it and nodded. "Benedict, can I interest you in a cigar on an upper deck?"

"Indeed."

After selecting a Diamond Crown Maximus, I accepted the brass cigar cutter and clipped the end before swiping a wood match and holding the flame just under the tobacco to light it from the heat of the flame so as not to burn the leaf.

The moment the end glowed a bright orange, I lit the cocktail napkin on fire and waited until it was only ash.

We moved from the enclosure to take another set of stairs to an upper deck overlooking the marina.

The sky was a fiery wash of jewel tones—topaz, amber, amethyst, and ruby—as the sun set over the marina. With the mild winter temperatures and calm water, our voices would carry more easily across the water but at least we wouldn't be recorded.

Dante took a long drag off his cigar, his gaze following a beat-up turquoise fisherman's boat returning to port. "I didn't order any hit on your brother. We had our differences but shooting a man in his home like that is not my style."

I tapped my cigar, ashing it over the side. "I know."

Dante threw his head back and laughed. "You know? Just like that. You trust my word on the matter."

I blew a smoke ring. "It has nothing to do with trusting you. You gave me the proof a few minutes ago."

Dante turned his back on the view. Leaning his elbows on the railing he said, "This I have to know."

Indulging him, I said, "You said I killed two of your men."

He placed his cigar in the corner of his mouth and nodded.

I met his gaze. "Not five."

He frowned.

312

I explained. "A kill squad in your name was sent after Liliana a few nights ago."

With a low curse, he turned back to stare down at the water. After several minutes, he said, "Who?"

I took a drag on my cigar, watching the glowing end flame to life then return to a burning simmer. Slowly blowing the fragrant bluish smoke into the evening wind, I finally said, "You already know who."

He rubbed his eyes. "Fuck. He wasn't my choice as a *vice capo*. More of a compromise to the old guard. He's been a pain in my fucking ass from the beginning." Sparing me a glance, he smirked. "I shouldn't be telling you that, but something tells me you already figured that much out."

I smirked back.

He shook his head. "The rumors about you don't even come close, my friend."

"Salvatore knows the two men he sent in a desperate attempt to dispatch me, my son, and Liliana at the airport before I even reached you didn't work. By the way, they were also the idiots he sent to kill my brother, so I've handled that loose end for you. You're welcome."

He took a long drag from his cigar. "I haven't said thank you yet."

I rolled my cigar between my fingers and laughed. "By now, he's realizing I haven't shot you in the head out of revenge for my brother with the gun your guard *accidentally* missed when he patted me down, which means Salvatore's plan to frame the Cavalieris for your murder has completely failed."

"Why your family?"

"He couldn't risk trying to frame one of the other mafia families. There are too many ritual kinships through marriage and godparents, not to mention business dealings, past and future. The war it would trigger would be messy and bloody. He'd take your throne but all that would be left would be bones and ashes."

"So there was your family. Conveniently on the other side of Italy. No"—he quirked a half smile at me— "*obvious* mafia connections, but with the open secret of bad blood over that land permit mess and Enzo's wife's death."

Speaking around the cigar in the corner of my mouth, I said, "Just so."

"Why go after his own goddaughter? He's raised her since she was a baby."

"*Paid* to have her raised. There's a difference."

"All right. *Paid* to have her raised. Where does Liliana fit in? She's beautiful, intelligent, the daughter of a revered former *capo*. As her godfather and guardian, there are any number of lucrative marriage prospects he can arrange for the girl. Why kill her?"

With a brush of my hand, I flicked away a piece of ash from the cuff of my jacket. It was a sleight of hand diversionary tactic, a precaution in case my face gave away even the slightest microaggressive emotion at the idea of Liliana being bartered off like a side of beef.

That Dante was discussing sliding her about like a pawn on a gameboard, precisely the way I, myself, considered doing not seventy-two hours earlier, was immaterial to me.

The situation had changed.

She was mine now.

And no one, *fucking no one*, was going to take her from me.

"I've always measured a man by his actions and the decisions he makes, not his excuses. The fact is he tried to kill her

314

and used some local goons pretending to be Agnello soldiers to do it. The rest is immaterial."

We both stood there in silence, smoking.

He took a sip of his brandy, then studied the swirling liquid. "This isn't the eighties. I can't just shoot the bastard in the head at the next *Commissione Interprovinciale*. There is nothing but your speculation that points to him. And there is already unrest within the organization since I took power, over my attempts to move us toward—less complicated business pursuits."

I lifted the cigar to my mouth then paused. "'There is nothing more difficult to take in hand, more perilous to conduct, or more uncertain in its success, than to take the lead in the introduction of a new order of things.'"

Quoting Machiavelli's *The Prince* back to me, he said, "'Men should be either treated generously or destroyed, because they take revenge for slight injuries – for heavy ones they cannot.'"

Placing a hand in my trouser pocket, I turned to him and leaned a hip against the rail. "*The Prince*, the true mafiosi bible."

He did the same. "And if memory serves, not a bad read for a spymaster either."

I tilted my head. "Touché."

He tossed the remainder of his cigar into his extremely expensive brandy, extinguishing it with a hiss. "If you kill Salvatore—and while as a guest on my yacht no less—you will leave me no choice but to kill you and your son. Regardless of what I may suspect."

Facing him, I took a slow sip of my brandy, savoring it before responding. "I'd love to see you try. Fortunately—*for you*—I won't put you in that position."

"How so?"

"I've only left him two options open. Salvatore will show his hand tonight at dinner. He didn't go to all these lengths to become Don to give up now."

Step three.

Dante rubbed his neck. "You realize even if you prove Salvatore ordered a hit on your brother as part of an assassination plot"—he gestured between us— "we still have a problem."

I did.

While under reasonable circumstances it would be considered a positive thing to expose corruption and stop a potential coup plot within your ranks, not so within a mafia outfit.

I'd exposed a severe weakness within Dante's leadership.

His *vice capo*, his second in command, had planned to assassinate him and frame a powerful family in Italy for the deed.

All without his knowledge.

In addition to killing Salvatore and anyone within his ranks loyal to him, Dante would need to silence anyone who knew about the plot or risk appearing weak and ineffective.

Unless I could come up with a plan that solved both of our problems.

CHAPTER 34

LILIANA

*H*e went to a great deal of trouble to acquire me.

Acquire me.

Acquire me, like I was some rare mushroom he had to search out online for a freaking pasta dish.

Matteo leaned over as we followed one of Dante's henchmen down the narrow hallway to the stateroom and whispered, "Don't."

Without turning to look at him, I whispered back. "Don't what?"

"Whatever you're spinning in that pretty little head of yours, just don't."

At that I did turn.

Take away the silver beard and hair and Matteo was the spitting image of his father. Apparently he also inherited his Svengali-like mind-reading skills as well.

Matteo winked. "It comes in handy with women."

He responded as if I said those thoughts out loud.

What the hell?

The rest of the way to our stateroom, I concentrated on trying to remember every Old Testament verse on castration I could think of, just in case.

The moment the door closed, I crossed my arms over my chest. "Acquired me?"

Matteo crossed to the small bar in the corner and set the bottle of Patrón x Guillermo Del Toro Añejo Tequila on its surface. "I'm not discussing this with you, Lili. Drink?"

He pulled out the stopper and poured two shot glasses. One all the way, one only about halfway.

I uncrossed my arms and approached him. It was hard not to like Matteo. In addition to Benedict's devastatingly handsome looks, he also had his charm and dark humor. I eyed the glass skeptically. "I've never had tequila. What does it taste like?"

"Never had tequila? That's a tragedy we must correct immediately."

He held out the halfway filled one to me, which I took between two fingers.

He continued. "By rite of passage, your first experience should be the cheap rotgut shit, to really feel the burn. That's the good stuff." He tilted the bottle and surveyed the etched label. "I'm afraid I'm going to spoil you with this elitist crap, but it can't be helped, needs must."

Despite our dire circumstances and my anger at Benedict, I smiled as I lifted the glass and sniffed it. "It smells like lemon, petrol, and pepper."

Matteo smirked. "See, you're a natural. It will taste just like that, sort of like a limoncello but less sweet."

I eyed him doubtfully. "Like a limoncello?"

He nodded. "But less sweet. Salute!"

"Salute!"

Matteo tossed his entire shot back.

The moment the liquid hit the back of my throat I choked and tried to lower the glass.

Matteo tilted the bottom. "Drink up, buttercup. It's bad luck not to finish a shot."

I finished the glass then, between gasps and chokes, I rasped, "That ... did ... not ... taste ... like ... limoncello!"

He patted me on the back. "I know. I can't believe you fell for that. My father is right, you are far too innocent for the real world, let alone this den of vipers."

I propped my palms on my knees and bent over, trying to catch my breath. "Am not!"

He leaned against the bar. "I can see down your sweater. Cute bra."

With a cry, I pressed my hand against the center of my chest and straightened, frowning at him. "A gentleman would not have looked."

All teasing humor suddenly left his eyes.

He stormed toward me with such fierce intensity I dropped the shot glass on the floor and actually turned to run. The sudden change in him triggered my flight response. Tripping over my slightly too large, borrowed heels, I didn't get far.

His fingers wrapped around my upper arm and swung me around until I was pressed against the stateroom door.

He placed a forearm over my head and leaned in.

Unlike with his father, where I would feel a confusing mixture of fear and desire in a situation like this, all I felt in this moment was fear.

His dark gaze narrowed. "A gentleman would not have looked? Are you fucking kidding me with that?"

I flinched and lowered my head at the harsh edge to his tone. My stomach clenched as I curled my fingers in my skirt. Realizing how badly I wished Benedict was here right now.

"Look at me," he barked.

Startled, I looked back up at him.

"Where is the taser my father gave you?"

Uh oh.

I bit my lip. "I, well, um ..."

"Where is the fucking taser, Liliana?"

I twisted the fabric of the skirt at my sides. "Back at the hotel."

"Why?"

When I didn't answer, he asked louder. "Why?"

My vision blurred with tears. "It was awkward tucked inside my bra, and I was afraid it would drop out."

"We're on a motherfucking boat filled with pieces of shit criminals and the one goddamn weapon my father gave you so that you could protect yourself, that would hold these bastards off long enough for him or me to get to you in time, you left at the hotel because it felt funny tucked in your fucking bra?"

I winced at every curse word. "Please don't curse at me like this."

He slammed his fist on the door over my head. "I'll curse at you however I fucking please, Lili. Do you not understand what is happening here?"

He paced away, running his hand through his hair only to abruptly pivot and turn back to me. "Can't you see how much he cares about you? Jesus fucking Christ, Lili! Do you know what he will do to me if you get hurt?"

Who was he talking about?

He couldn't possibly be talking about Benedict?

He held his palms up near my face as if he couldn't decide whether he wanted to choke me, shake me, hug me, or all three. "I need you to listen very carefully. You may not understand the reasons behind what we are doing, but you have to trust me. My father and I really are trying to get you out of this alive. These mafia organizations have empires larger than most third world countries and women are just one more asset to be traded and bartered."

Benedict had warned me of the same thing.

Zolfo sugnu.

I was nothing but a pawn.

It was a timely reminder. I had come dangerously close to giving Benedict my one and only *asset*, as Matteo put it, without negotiating anything in return.

That was how this whole game was supposed to be played, wasn't it?

Without knowing it, he had also warned me away from his own father.

I'd started thinking of Benedict as my protector.

I'd even started to think I might be falling in love with him.

How stupid was that?

The captive falling for her captor.

It had probably been part of Benedict's plan all along.

He had been practically taunting me with it this whole time.

Telling me I was too easily manipulated.

Here I was thinking he was the first person to truly *see* and *understand* me when in reality he was pointing out the weaknesses in my character he was openly exploiting.

I swallowed before swiping at the tear on my cheek. "I understand."

"I hope that you do because I'm saying this for your own protection. This man who you think is your only family … these people who you think you share a connection with just because you are all from Sicily … none of them give a damn about you. But my father—"

The door against my back vibrated as someone furiously pounded on it.

I shot away and turned to Matteo. "What should we do?"

It was obvious from the way the person knocked that something was wrong.

He didn't look a bit surprised at the turn of events.

He poured another shot and gave me a wink. "Show time."

Kicking back the shot, he then answered the door.

A beautiful blonde practically fell over the threshold. "Thank God! I need your help!"

Something about her seemed off. I looked closely as she launched herself at Matteo, crying although there appeared to be no tears.

The purple and black bruise under her eye *shimmered*.

It was eyeshadow! My mouth opened on a gasp.

I stretched out my arm to point at her and said, "Matteo, she's fa—"

A stern shake of his head stopped me.

He stared intently at me for a second before grasping the woman by the shoulders and exclaiming with exaggerated emotion, "My God, you poor thing, what has happened to you?"

She rolled her eyes as she pushed back her shoulders, brushing her breasts against his chest. "He's gone mad! He hit me and I'm afraid he'll hurt my sister too! Please, I'm desperate! You must help me!"

She pulled on his sleeve as she moved toward the door.

My awestruck gaze shifted from Matteo to the "damsel in distress."

Matteo called out, "Of course I will help save your sister. Liliana, I must leave you here alone, but I will return."

He let himself be dragged over the threshold, slamming the door in his wake.

I stood in the center of the now eerily silent room.

Placing my hand over my eyes I sighed.

Obviously we just leveled up in this twisted game everyone seemed to be playing but me.

With nothing to do but wait to see where my pawn player was told to go next, I might as well enjoy the sunset. As I headed toward the terrace, the stateroom door opened again.

I turned and needed to grab hold of the back of a nearby chair to keep myself upright. "Uncle Salvatore?"

He swung his arms open wide as two armed men swept into the room and closed the door, blocking it. "What, no hug for your loving godfather?"

Acidic bile burned the back of my throat as I stepped from around the chair and approached him. Keeping my arms at my sides, I leaned into him as he hugged me.

Pressing me too tightly and for too long, his hand ran down my back and over my hip. Suppressing a shudder of revulsion, I squirmed out of his embrace. "What are you doing here? I thought ..."

My gaze wandered over his perfectly tailored sharkskin silver suit. It, along with the flashing gold rings on his fingers, gel-slicked, dyed black hair, and deeply tanned complexion which gave his chemically whitened teeth an extra glare, all complemented the Hollywood mafia aesthetic perfectly.

He hardly looked like a man who had been taken hostage and tortured in some hole these last six months.

Lowering my voice, I finished. "I thought Dante was keeping you prisoner in some hole somewhere."

He slapped me.

My hand went to my cheek.

"He is Don Agnello to you. Show some respect."

I lowered my head. "Yes, godfather."

"And is that liquor I smell on your breath?"

I lifted my palm to my mouth and breathed then sniffed. "I only did half a shot to taste it."

He sneered. "So you're a whore now."

My head reared up. "No! I only did it to be polite, like I was taught."

Uncle Salvatore's beefy hand fisted my sweater and yanked me forward. "Oh yeah? Then where's your gold cross? Where's the sign of your faith?"

My hand went to my neck, my cheeks burning with humiliation as I thought of Benedict and last night.

Him tearing the cross from my throat.

Him pushing his cock into my mouth.

Him fucking my ass from behind.

Then from earlier today when I almost let him take my virginity.

Not to mention all the sinful things I let him do to me at the Vatican.

I was a whore.

"I must have lost it."

"That better be the only thing you lost, goddaughter!" He sneered as he looked down the gap in my sweater, caused by his grip, at my exposed breasts.

Without having to ask what he meant, I nodded. "It is. I swear."

"And now she swears too."

I closed my eyes. "I meant, I promise. Yes. I'm still pure."

I'm still an *asset.*

"Good."

I had to ask. "I don't understand. Has Don Agnello forgiven you? Are you okay now? Can I stop?"

Please, please, please say that I can stop.

I wanted this to all be over.

In a flash, I realized that everything I had just been chastising myself about while hardening my heart against Benedict was bullshit. He hadn't been the one betraying me. My godfather had!

In his own heavy-handed, arrogant way, Benedict had been trying to protect me this whole time.

Benedict was right. I wasn't meant for this world. My heritage be damned. I didn't care who my father was or that I was considered a mafia princess. Apparently, I didn't inherit any of his genes because all I wanted was a quiet life somewhere away from all the games and danger and manipulation and lies and violence.

My godfather moved more deeply into the stateroom. "Grow up, Liliana. There was never any situation with Dante. I said that to get you to do what I asked without question."

To manipulate me.

"Did you order the hit on Barone Cavalieri?"

He raised his arm. "You want another slap?"

I hunched my shoulders as I flinched and backed away. "No."

"Then don't ask questions that are none of your concern."

"His brother, Benedict Cavalieri, almost killed me in revenge. Dante … I mean Don Agnello sent a kill squad to Rome after me as well. They all think I'm involved."

"If you had stayed put like you were told and not run, then no one would be suspicious."

"I had to leave. Those people lied to me. They said they were trying to save their daughter. That Enzo Cavalieri had kidnapped her. None of that was true! I knew the Cavalieris would blame me for putting that stuff in Bianca's drink."

He motioned to one of his henchmen who stepped forward and pulled a chair out from the small dinette set in the corner. Salvatore sat, crossed his legs, and adjusted his pinky ring without offering me a seat. "Well, you've caused me a great deal of trouble. Now I have to call in favors to save you."

I wanted to point out that I wouldn't be in this situation if he hadn't lied to me about being in mortal danger thus forcing me to spy on the Cavalieris in the first place, but I remained silent.

I folded my hands in front of me and kept my head bowed. "I'm sorry, Uncle Salvatore."

"Fortunately for *you*, your loving godfather has come up with a solution to get you out of this whole mess and back in the good graces of Don Agnello."

My stomach clenched.

Without even hearing it, I knew his solution for *me* was somehow going to benefit *him*. Apparently I was catching on to this game.

I also knew that no matter what it was … I would have no choice but to obey.

He was my godfather and the *vice capo* in one of the most powerful mafia organizations in Italy.

In Sicily, that meant, for all intents and purposes, he had the authority to do whatever he wanted with me, especially since I had no money or other family or friends to run to for help or protection.

Not even the law would help me. The mafia was the law in Sicily.

Closing my eyes, I braced for the worst. "Yes, godfather?"

"Before dinner, you're going to spread those pretty legs and convince Benedict Cavalieri to fuck you."

CHAPTER 35

BENEDICT

*A*s I made my way to the lower deck and Liliana's assigned stateroom, I passed Matteo in the hallway. His suede jacket was torn, and the corner of his lip was bleeding.

I smiled. "Did everything go as I suspected?"

He touched the corner of his mouth with the tip of his finger and grimaced. "Just so you know. Always being able to think two moves ahead of everyone else is one of your more annoying qualities."

I adjusted the torn sleeve of his jacket and patted his arm. "Three moves, actually."

"You just proved my point and yes it did. And you wouldn't believe who they sent to provide the distraction. Antonia Fichera. Anyway, Salvatore entered the stateroom soon afterward."

"And?"

Matteo sighed. "And you were right. He's going for option one."

My hand curled into a fist. "Of course, he is. Fucking coward."

If I could have spared her this I would have, but it was necessary.

To secrete her away on my ranch in the north would have only prolonged the problem.

The mafia never forgot a slight or a transgression. Ever.

The head needed to be cut off the snake, quickly and cleanly, if Liliana was ever going to live a life without having to look over her shoulder.

It became immediately clear to me in Rome that Salvatore had become desperate.

A desperate man was rash and unpredictable. His actions usually caused collateral damage in the form of innocent victims.

The perfect example would be any number of over-the-top mafia killings from the eighties. Car bombs, semi-automatic weapons used with hundreds of bullets fired on a public street in the middle of the day when a single man with a knife could have been sent in the dead of night. All overkill. All with innocent victims.

Salvatore knowing Liliana was an asset for later, yet still willing to kill her now, told me he was on the edge.

What Salvatore needed was options.

As Sun Tzu taught in *The Art of War*, always allow your enemy hope. An enemy with nothing to live for fought with despair. An enemy with a future, a path to freedom, on the other hand...

The key was to give him options, and for that I needed Liliana.

"Call the others. Let them know."

He nodded. "And you?"

I patted him on the shoulder as I continued down the hallway without responding.

He called after me. "A gentleman never tells, I get it."

* * *

SHE WAS SITTING PRIMLY on the end of the bed when I entered.

Keeping my gaze on her, I closed and locked the door. "I passed Matteo in the hall. Apparently there was some excitement in my absence and he had to leave you. Are you okay?"

She stood and smoothed her skirt. As she raised her head to face me, I noticed one cheek was slightly more flushed than the other.

The bastard slapped her.

I sucked in a breath and internally counted to ten. Reminding myself of the long game. While nothing would give me more satisfaction than to tear this yacht apart until I found Salvatore so I could break his neck with my bare hands, Dante was correct.

Even if he knew my reasons why, he would be forced to start a war with us just to save face. A war where innocent people would be caught in the crosshairs.

Salvatore would get his.

Very soon.

Fortunately, one of the things that made me so deadly and feared throughout my career was my patience.

When a hothead killed, it was sloppy and quick.

When someone with patience killed … it was slow, methodical, and painful.

My attention turned back to my girl.

Her smile was forced. Her eyes too bright. "Yes. Some

woman burst in claiming her boyfriend or someone had hit her. Matteo went to handle it. I've been worried."

"He's fine. It's been some time since he had a good fist-fight, so it made his day."

She pulled her lips between her teeth and nodded as she lowered her head. "I need to tell you something."

I approached her slowly. Stretching out my arm, I smoothed her hair back off her face. "Tell me later."

Her shoulders stiffened. "I can't. It's important. It's about—"

Fuck.

This needed to happen, and I couldn't let her talk about it.

Her godfather tried to kill her once. He had only stopped because he thought of another use for her. He wouldn't hesitate to renew his original plan if he thought she had betrayed him.

Since this room was likely bugged like the rest of the yacht, it wasn't like I could just slit my palm with a knife and squeeze some drops of blood on the sheets.

Besides, I wanted it to happen.

Yes, I wanted it as well. Badly.

This played perfectly into my private plan.

What better way to claim Liliana unequivocally as my own than to have her so-called mafia godfather think it was his plan that forced us together?

That I was certain the second part of his plan was to have me murdered on my wedding day was immaterial. As far as her bloodthirsty world would be concerned, it was a sanctioned match and therefore, untouchable.

She would be mine.

I tucked a finger under her chin and lifted her head as I wrapped an arm around her waist, pulling her close. "I only want to talk about what almost happened earlier, *angioletto*. And what is going to happen now."

She rested a palm against my chest. "What do you mean?"

My cock lengthened as I pressed the hard ridge against her stomach.

Her eyes widened and she tried to back away.

My arm around her waist stopped her.

"We're finishing what we started. Now it's your choice."

Her pulse fluttered at the base of her throat, her fingers clenching around my shirt.

My tongue flicked over my lower lip. I yearned to taste it. I leaned in close, until my breath mingled with hers. "I can try my best to take this slow and sweet."

I moved my hand to push inside her soft curls. Twisting my fingers, I tilted her head back and kissed along her jawline until I nipped at her earlobe. "Or you can tell daddy you want to be a *bad girl*."

She inhaled sharply, holding her breath.

The tip of my tongue teased the curve of her ear. "That you want daddy to hold you down and fuck your tight pussy until you scream even as you fight him."

Her breathing returned in fast, ragged gasps.

I knew what my babygirl needed.

Her upbringing, confusion, and guilt were warring with her need to please and submit.

They were tearing her apart inside. There would be plenty of time later to teach her how to think for herself. How to make her own decisions and not be manipulated, but not tonight.

Tonight she needed me to take charge.

Tonight she needed me to be the bad guy so she would not have to shoulder the guilt of an immoral act.

Tonight she needed me to be the daddy, so she could at least lie to herself and say she fought the inevitable.

"Do you want that, babygirl?" I rasped against her lips as I shifted my hand to wrap it around her throat. "You want daddy to take you hard and rough?"

She stared up at me and slowly nodded once.

I flicked my tongue over her lower lip. "I need you to say it, baby. It's important. I want to get this right for you. If so, tell me now. Slow and sweet? Or make it hurt?"

Blood pulsed through my cock as I waited what felt like an eternity for her shy response.

Finally, she whispered, "Make it hurt, daddy."

A red haze dropped before my eyes as a rush of possessive, primal lust like nothing I had ever experienced before in my life rushed over me. My last rational thought was a genuine fear that I might accidentally injure her in my zeal to fuck her senseless.

The sweater she was wearing didn't stand a chance. I tore it to shreds. The metal clasp on her bra bent and snapped as I tore it as well.

No doubt frightened, Liliana cried out and turned, only to fall onto the bed.

She crawled on her knees to get to the other side.

I grabbed at the skirt she was wearing and ripped it off her hips. As she kicked at me, so went her heels.

"Benedict—" she pleaded, on her back in the center of the bed, now wearing only a pair of panties.

I kicked off my loafers and sent the buttons of my shirt flying as I tore it off. Reaching for my belt buckle, I said, "That's daddy, to you."

"Daddy, please, you're scaring me."

I whipped the belt off. "Good. Now get on your knees and get over here and suck my cock."

I lowered the zipper on my jeans and pulled out my cock. The only way I wasn't going to tear her in two was if I eased the growing tension of my arousal with her wet mouth.

Liliana moved to her knees and crawled across the bed to me.

I placed my hand on the back of her head and guided her to the head of my shaft.

She opened her lips and I pushed inside her warm, wet mouth.

Throwing my head back, I let out a guttural moan as I pushed my hips forward.

While she concentrated on swallowing my cock, I unfurled my belt and raised my right arm.

Her beautiful eyes looked up just in time for me to bring the belt down on her pretty ass.

Since I kept my left hand on the back of her head, her scream vibrated up my shaft. "Keep sucking."

She sank down onto her ankles.

"Get back up on your knees now or I'll turn you around and fuck your ass dry."

Liliana whimpered but did as she was told, rising back up to her knees on the bed.

I raised my arm a second time and the moment the head of my cock touched the back of her throat, I swept the leather belt down on her ass.

She cried out a second time as her teeth sank into my shaft. Not deeply, but just enough to add a darkly erotic sting of pain. "Careful, babygirl," I warned.

After I warmed her with several more swipes of the belt, I pulled my cock out of her mouth and ordered her to lay on her back before I slipped out of the rest of my clothes and joined her on the bed.

Turning her to lie on her left side facing me, I pushed my thigh between her legs and palmed her pussy with my left hand. Pressing two fingers inside her wet warmth, I said, "Where are daddy's fingers?"

Her left hip lifted off the mattress. "Inside me," she moaned.

I kissed the soft, vanilla-scented skin of her neck, then bit down. "Where?"

"Inside my ... pussy."

"*Brava ragazza*. That's daddy's dirty girl."

I pumped my fingers in and out, opening her tight muscles as I pulled her pert nipple into my mouth.

Her fingernails dug into my upper arm.

I thrust my fingers in and out harder as I used the pad of my thumb to tease her clit.

Her legs clenched around my thigh. I knew she was close.

Rising, I moved to shift between her legs.

Liliana panicked. "No. I can't. I can't!"

She rolled away.

Before she got to the edge of the bed, I reached out and grabbed her hair and wrenched her back. Pushing her on her back, I forced her legs open and wedged my hips between them.

Her arms struck out as she fought me. "No!"

Easily capturing her wrists in one hand, I pinned them over her head. Using my free hand, I grasped my shaft and positioned it at her slick entrance.

Before pushing inside, I caressed her pussy with the head of my cock, running it up and down in slow, sweeping circles, each time applying more pressure.

Liliana swept her head from side to side. "Don't. Don't. Please, don't."

"I'm sorry, babygirl. Daddy has to make you his."

I thrust forward straight to the hilt.

Liliana cried out.

I held tight as she bucked her hips and thrashed beneath me. "Take it out! Please! Take it out!"

It took every ounce of willpower I possessed to hold on to her and not thrust while her body clenched tightly around my rigid flesh.

Knowing I would be the first and only man to ever experience the exquisite, pleasurable torture of her tight cunt squeezing my cock dry finally had me understanding why they called it the *little death,* because I was fairly certain I was touching heaven right now.

My mouth crashed down on hers to silence her cries as I pulled my cock out slightly and thrust back in. Swallowing her scream, I did so again and again, relishing the vibrating ripples up my shaft from her clenching and unclenching muscles.

Still she continued to fight me.

And I fucking loved her for it.

She bit my tongue and wrenched her head to the side as she twisted her torso.

I moved my hand to her breast and pinched her nipple, increasing the pace of my thrusts. "That's it, babygirl. Fight me."

Her hips bucked as she arched her back and moaned. "Yes. Oh! Oh! Yes!"

Releasing her wrists so she could use her arms, I kissed her neck and used my hand to force her knees open wider, pounding into her unchecked with more violence as my balls tightened and the pressure in my cock increased.

She wrapped her arms around my torso and raked her nails down my back. "Harder, daddy!"

I leaned up on my knees and threw her legs over my shoulders.

Through clenched teeth, I rasped, "Fuck, yes, baby. Take it. Take my fucking cock in that tight pussy of yours." I spanked her ass a few more times. Just to push her over the edge, I teased her dark hole with the pad of my thumb.

She fisted the covers. "Don't stop! Don't stop!"

"That's it, babygirl. Come for daddy. Come now!"

Nothing about her first time was soft or sweet or gentle.

Everything about it was violent and dirty and wrong.

And us.

CHAPTER 36

BENEDICT

Scooping her into my arms, I carried her into the shower.

Under the warm spray of the water, I held her close ... and waited.

After several minutes her body jerked as her knees buckled.

My arm tightened around her middle and I clasped my hand to the back of her head, holding her close to my chest, over my heart while she sobbed.

I kissed the top of her head. "Shhh, babygirl. It's going to be okay."

She clung to me, trying to shake her head. "No, it's not. You don't know. He told me he would kil—"

I framed her face with my hands and gazed into her eyes.

Fuck, I would have given every drop of blood in my veins if I could have taken away just a fraction of the remorse and guilt I saw reflected there.

So much pain for someone so young and innocent. It only hardened my resolve to get her the fuck away from all this greed, cold cruelty, and violence as fast as I could.

I was going to hide her away up in the mountains with me.

Like a precious little fairy not meant for human eyes.

I was going to do everything in my power to create a world of beauty and warmth for her, where she felt protected and loved. Even the idea of spoiling my adorable little baby-girl rotten brought a smile to my face. I couldn't fucking wait to show her my ranch and the horses and to see her face when she first set eyes on the stunning views from our bedroom window.

I wanted to tell her all of this.

But couldn't.

Because I didn't know who was listening.

And because I needed her reactions at dinner to be genuine.

We were still in enemy territory and in order to get her out of here safely, I needed to be yet one more person who was manipulating her for their own ends.

For the first time in my life, I prayed to a God I never knew I believed in for her to forgive me in the end and realize I was doing this for her.

"Babygirl, I know you're tired of all the games and the manipulations. I know you're scared. I know you just want it all to be over. And I know I haven't given you many reasons to trust me, but I'm asking you to anyway. I need you to trust that I know you better than you think I do. I need you to trust that I would never have allowed you to do something you would regret. Do you understand what I'm saying?"

Her shoulders hitched as she sobbed. "You're wrong. I know I shouldn't, and it's probably one of the countless mistakes I've made over the last few months, but you're the *only* one I trust. That's why I need to tell you—"

My mouth caressed hers as my tongue slipped inside, tasting the salt of her tears despite the spray of the shower. Careful not to deepen the kiss, knowing her lips were already bruised and swollen from my earlier kisses, I pulled back. "Not another word, Liliana. I mean it."

"You don't understand, I need to warn you—"

I cupped her jaw and placed my thumb over her lips. "Trust me, little one. There is nothing you can say that daddy doesn't already know. Understood? Now be a good girl and let me finish washing this tragically short hair of yours so we're not late for dinner."

Her lower lip pushed out in a pout but she stopped trying to speak.

* * *

AN HOUR later we exited the stateroom and headed toward the upper deck for dinner with Dante and his officers.

Liliana was dressed in another previously unworn designer outfit compliments of Barone's dead wife. This one was a stunning cobalt blue gown that hugged her curves. Since it was a bit too long for her shorter frame, it trailed well past her heels, creating a mermaid silhouette with sequined blouson sleeves in a lighter blue covering her slender arms.

She resembled a 1940s movie siren. Especially with how she had curled her shorter, shoulder-length hair into tight waves and kept her makeup simple with a black cat-eye liner and matte red lip. The entire look was elegant and stylish while still conservative.

It suited her perfectly.

And all I could think about was tearing the dress to shreds, trashing those curls with my fingers, and smearing her lipstick with the tip of my cock.

Before we entered the room, Liliana stopped and turned to me. "Do we have to do this? Couldn't we just have dinner at the hotel or better yet, leave the island?"

I rubbed my palm in a soothing circle over her lower back and leaned down to whisper in her ear. "When I get you back to the hotel, the only thing I'll be eating is your sweet pussy."

She lowered her head so her angled bob slipped over her cheeks, only slightly obscuring them. "What happened was brought on by a traumatic set of circumstances. It will not be repeated. *Let not sin therefore reign in your mortal body, to make you obey its passions.*"

It was adorable how she quoted from the Bible whenever I pushed her sexual limits.

I moved my hand lower to cup her ass. *"You can be sure of succeeding in your attacks if you only attack places which are undefended."*

With that I pressed two fingers against the fabric of her dress to tease the crease of her bottom just below the curve.

She rose on her toes, pushing her arm behind her in a fruitless attempt to brush my arm aside as she gave a cute little cry. "Oh!"

I chuckled. "Careful babygirl, I have my own bible. It's called *The Art of War.*"

Before the blush left her cheeks we continued to the bow where the dining room offered a stunning, panoramic view of Palermo's harbor. Just before we entered, I pulled her aside, looking as if I were adjusting the back clasp of her dress.

"Remember what I told you, *angioletto.*"

She inhaled a slow breath and held it for a second before releasing it. "No matter what happens, trust you."

"Good girl."

Her lips thinned as she cast me a sullen look. "You realize you sound like the snake to Eve?"

I ran my hand down her back. "You know that was the best sex she ever had."

She turned her head so the edge of her jaw grazed the tops of my knuckles. "You're terrible."

My hand moved possessively to the curve of her waist. "The worst. I'll show you just how bad later."

None of this fooled me. I knew she was terrified.

She'd tried several more times to talk to me after our shower. I knew she was desperate to convince me to leave the yacht and Sicily.

At the very least, it proved I was right.

She wasn't a little fallen angel.

She was a little lost angel who'd had her better nature taken advantage of.

There wasn't a doubt in my mind she truly thought she was helping Bianca that day and she had absolutely no idea of Salvatore's plans to shoot Barone when she handed over that schedule or she would have warned him as she was trying to warn me.

It was why it was so easy to accept what was about to happen.

What man wouldn't want to claim such a sweet creature for his own?

* * *

Dressed in a similar Armani tuxedo, Dante crossed the dining room to greet us both as we entered. "My compliments to your tailor," he quipped.

I ran a hand over the side of my tuxedo jacket. "And mine to yours."

It was a shame we were enemies only united against a common foe. I was beginning to like the guy.

Turning to Liliana, he once more took her hands and kissed the back of both. "You look charming, Liliana."

"Thank you, Don Agnello."

He tilted his head. "I've told you, call me Dante."

Her smile faded. She removed her hands and folded them in front of her. "I'm sorry. I was told not to be disrespectful."

Dante's head lowered as his brow furrowed.

He flashed me an icy glare.

When I matched his, he immediately realized it was obviously not on my command.

A mutual realization dawned. Salvatore.

The muscles between my shoulder blades tightened at the thought of that bastard dictating to *my girl*.

Easing the tension, Dante said, "Whoever told you that was mistaken. If they have an issue with how you address me, they can come and see me. Let me introduce you to the rest of the guests."

Matteo joined us as we made the rounds. It was a select but influential group.

Dante was sending a subtle message to Salvatore who suspiciously had yet to arrive.

The men in attendance were mostly *capo mandamento* from the surrounding territories as well as Dante's *consigliere* and *reggente*.

If we were not here, a person would be forgiven for

SEDUCTION OF THE PATRIARCH

thinking this was a *Commissione Interprovinciale* called to select a new high-ranking position … like a new *vice capo*.

A bulging man with two black eyes walked in with the only other female in attendance, a conspicuous blonde in an inappropriate black cocktail dress cut too low on top and too high on the bottom.

I was the farthest thing from a prude and had no objections to a woman dressing however she liked—except when it came to the length of my babygirl's hair, which I was making her grow back as quickly as humanly possible—but there was also common sense.

You didn't throw a raw steak into a den of lions and expect them to remember their table manners.

Matteo turned his head to appear to look at something over his shoulder. "Manfredi Viscuso, *soldati* loyal to Salvatore and his girl, Antonia Fichera. She's the one they used for the distraction earlier. I see she ditched the fake black eye."

I raised my Scotch to my mouth to cover what I was saying. "So are the ones you gave her boyfriend real?"

Manfredi glared in our direction while Antonia gave Matteo a once-over and winked. "You look pretty good in a tux, Matteo."

Matteo looked between her and Manfredi. "I see you and your girlfriend share eye makeup tips. Is he wearing your panties too?"

Manfredi stepped toward Matteo, but then seemed to stop himself.

It wasn't lost on me that her suggestive look seemed to bother not only Manfredi who suddenly grabbed her by the upper arm and dragged her over to the bar but also two other men in the room, both *capos* of competing territories and according to my intel on the Agnello organization, both married.

It seemed Salvatore trying to kill him and steal his throne wasn't Dante's only ticking time bomb.

I hazarded a glance in his direction and wondered if he knew it.

CHAPTER 37

LILIANA

*A*ll that was missing over the dining room door was the inscription *Lasciate ogne speranza, voi ch'intrate* and I'd literally be in Dante's *Inferno* entering through the gates of hell. How ironic.

Every introduction.

Every bit of small talk.

Every seemingly innocent compliment or side comment was like the sting of the hornets and wasps, representing the sting of a guilty conscience, from the *Divine Comedy*.

And that was the black heart of it.

Not a single person in this room could claim a clean conscience, not even me.

Fuck him or I kill them both.

That was the ultimatum I had been given.

The moment my godfather walked through the door appearing not just healthy but arrogant and smug, I knew I had been manipulated. Again.

Then he made his demands and I had never felt more worthless in my entire life.

I was worse than a pawn in a dangerous game.

I was the King's Pawn. The first move in chess where the pawn was always thrown out into the middle of the board as bait to start the game. His gambit of shooting Barone Cavalieri to frame Dante didn't pay off so now what? He was going to somehow blackmail Benedict through me? Or worse, try an even clumsier attempt to frame Dante by killing Benedict and Matteo?

I'd had it drummed into me my whole life that I would have no value as a "good wife" and would throw away my chance to be a mother if I opened my legs and tossed away my "gift" to my husband as if it were garbage.

Logically I knew it was an antiquated notion but growing up with no real family or anyone to love me, a good marriage had always been my only chance at having a family of my own, so it was important I not jinx it. Especially since it was always understood my godfather would have a say in who I would be "allowed" to marry since he controlled the purse strings.

And yet, I didn't hesitate.

I didn't even have to stop and think about it.

I would gladly play the whore if it meant saving Benedict and his son.

Even if it meant throwing away my chance at a husband, a family, and a future of my own.

I had almost torn his family apart by playing an unwitting role in the attempt to kill his brother. I wouldn't be responsible for causing that warm and loving family any more pain.

The only problem was ... thinking I was ready to play the bold, seductive femme fatale in the story who was ready to seduce the hero to foil the villain, versus actually seducing the hero, were two very different things.

Benedict had stormed in, my tarnished knight in shining armor.

And in that amazing, over-the-top, usually infuriating, intimidating, incredibly arrogant way of his, he immediately understood what was happening without me even having to say a word and took complete control.

And oh my did he take control!

I was still blushing to think of the dirty things we'd just done … and said.

I was going to have to drive to the other side of Italy to find a priest for confession when the time came just so I didn't risk *ever* running into the father on a market day at the piazza. I couldn't even imagine how many *Hail Marys* and *Our Fathers* I was going to be given for this one.

I was going to be on my knees for days.

My blush deepened when a very erotic double entendre popped into my head, thinking what Benedict would probably say had he heard me say that out loud. I sighed internally. I'd just have to add that to the list for confession.

Before I got to confession, though, I had to survive this dinner.

Benedict refused to allow me to discuss anything about my godfather's possible plans with him.

Not. One. Word.

It was as if he thought the walls had ears or something.

My only hope was stopping my godfather before he caused too much damage.

I was briefly hopeful when he wasn't in the room when we arrived for dinner but that was dashed when he arrived just as we were seated.

After giving Uncle Salvatore a hard look, Dante said, "Friend, have you finished what you came for?" He motioned to the seat to his left.

I let out a small gasp and gripped the arm of my chair, casting a glance around the table to judge the rest of the guests' reactions. No one reacted. Was I seriously the only one who caught his dark inference?

Dante's dark gaze found mine and winked, while my godfather gave a noncommittal response about business in the south holding him up.

Benedict's hand moved to my upper thigh where he gently squeezed my flesh without even looking in my direction, a not-so-subtle message that he had caught the exchange between Dante and me.

I reached for the glass of red which the silent server had just poured and gulped half of it down, listening with half an ear as Dante talked to Benedict about the wine being aged for five years, how the grape was a *Nerello Cappuccio,* and how the vine grew on Mount Etna so the volcanic soil gave it a pleasant, earthy, floral fruitiness or whatever.

I just hoped it got me drunk.

I'd never been drunk before but now seemed like a good time to start.

Again, without even looking at me, Benedict gently pulled the wineglass from my grasp and held it in his own.

Darn it.

Knowing it was for the best didn't assuage my pique.

As Dante was pulled into a conversation with one of his capos, Benedict turned to me. "We will discuss that wink you two shared later."

Mesmerized, I watched Dante tear a piece of bread in half and hand Salvatore a piece.

Blinking to break my own stare, I turned to Benedict. "It was nothing."

"In the future, little one, I'll decide what is and what is not *nothing* when it comes to flirting exchanges between you and other men. Spoiler alert, any exchange will always be considered flirting and therefore handled with swift retribution."

The servers arrived and placed antipasti plates in front of each of us as the main server cleared his throat and announced to the guests, "For your enjoyment, the chef has prepared a *milinciani sott'ogghiu cu cucunci antipasti* served with a small wedge of *Piacentino Ennese* with fresh bread."

As I prepared to make do with the piece of saffron and black peppercorn pecorino cheese and bread and avoid the popular Sicilian preserved eggplant dish since it contained caper berries, Benedict caught the attention of a passing server.

Lifting my plate he handed it to the server and made a quiet request so as not to embarrass me in front of the other guests. "Kindly return this to the chef and request an antipasto for the lady that does not contain any capers."

The server nodded. "Yes, right away sir."

My stomach did a flip. He remembered I didn't like capers. It may be a silly, inconsequential thing to some, but I'd never had anyone who'd cared enough about me to even notice I didn't like capers, let alone to actually do something about it if I were served them.

Before I could thank him, there was a shout from the other end of the table. "I see you are comfortable in taking the privileges of a husband, Benedict Cavalieri."

Those warm and fuzzy stomach flips quickly turned into twisted knots as my godfather stood up and tossed his napkin on the table.

At the same time, that gorilla of a bodyguard who was always with him, Manfredi Viscuso, shot out of his chair and left the room. I feared he was after a gun or reinforcements.

Was this his lame plan? To provoke a fight over dinner?

I leaned forward and attempted to diffuse the situation. "I don't like capers, godfather. He was just being a gentleman."

Uncle Salvatore pointed his pudgy, gold-ring-encrusted fingers at me. "You shut your mouth. No one is speaking to you."

Benedict quietly folded his napkin and slowly stood, buttoning his tuxedo coat. He leaned down and kissed the top of my head and whispered, "Sorry you had to hear that, babygirl."

I fought back the tears in my eyes.

It was hard to believe that only a few days ago I thought this amazing man next to me was my enemy and the one spitting vile venom across the table at me was my family.

He nodded to Dante. "My apologies for disturbing your generous hospitality and this fine table with such boorish behavior, Don Agnello."

Uncle Salvatore's jowls vibrated as his eyes bulged.

Just then Manfredi returned holding something white bunched up in his hands.

Before my horrified eyes, he thrust his arms open.

Without thinking, I screamed and jumped up—throwing myself in front of Benedict as I squeezed my eyes shut, bracing for the impact of the gunshot.

CHAPTER 38

BENEDICT

I grabbed Liliana and spun her behind me.

Later I would bend her over my knee and spank her with my bare hand until her skin glowed for risking her life to save mine. Then I would kiss her senseless for the selfless act of what had to be love whether she knew it yet or not.

It was fine.

I was used to being several steps ahead of everyone else in the room.

Which was why I knew Salvatore's *soldati* didn't have a gun, but he did have something that was going to humiliate and hurt my babygirl—at least in the short term.

The male guests stared uncomfortably at the reddish-brown stain smeared on the white sheet while the only other female in the room, Antonia Fichera, cackled as she said in a stage whisper, "Looks like I'm not the only whore at the feast."

I clenched my right hand into a fist, reminding myself that

this grim scene needed to play out if my plan was going to work.

Exchanging a quick look with Dante, I focused on Salvatore and played my part. "What the fuck is this?"

Salvatore snagged the sheet and lifted it to make sure everyone got a good look.

That was when Liliana peeked around my back and let out a small cry. "Uncle Salvatore, what have you done?"

Salvatore pointed a finger at me again. "Who is the boor now? Rutting between my goddaughter's legs. Forcing himself on her."

I surged forward but an arm across my chest stopped me.

Matteo urged under his breath. "Let it play out."

He was right.

I reached back and grasped Liliana's hip to assure myself she was still safe behind me.

In full rage, Salvatore turned to Dante. "Don Agnello, this pig has disrespected my family and your hospitality. You should have shot him like a dog when he killed Pietro and Alessio and accused us of trying to kill his brother. Now he insults us by forcing himself on my goddaughter under your roof. Let me honor you by making an example of him and his son. We will show these Cavalieris what it means to cross us."

It was clear Salvatore was concerned with what we might be telling Dante about his involvement in the attempt on Barone's life and possibly what his henchmen may have told us before we dispatched them at the airport, so his new plan was to get rid of me and Matteo and cut his losses.

And apparently he had no issue with publicly humiliating Liliana to make it happen.

What better way to destroy her reputation and discredit anything she could say against you than by branding her a whore in front of anyone who mattered. Afterward, she would have no one in the organization willing to protect her from anything he wanted to do with her ... or to her.

I had my suspicions as to why and it disgusted me.

Liliana tried to push around me. "No! That's not true! He's lying. I seduced him!"

"You hear that! He turned her into a whore! Liliana, you have disgraced me enough with your disgusting behavior. Get away from that man and get over here with your family where you belong," Salvatore commanded.

Pushing my fingers under her hair, I wrapped my hand around her neck, tilted her head back, and captured her gaze. One hard look from me silenced her. I then pulled her close to my chest.

Keeping my voice low and even, I said, "You talk to me, Salvatore, or the next word you say to her will be your last."

Salvatore's complexion turned purple as he yanked on his bow tie in an effort to loosen the button at his collar. "Do you hear how he speaks at your table, Don Agnello?"

While the capos were distracted trying to prevent Salvatore from stroking out and the servers scrambled to remove the bloody sheet from the table, Dante flashed me an annoyed smirk.

I lifted one shoulder in a slight shrug. The last comment was off script but there was only so much a man could take before enough was enough, even if it was my fucking plan.

Liliana gripped my lapel and looked up at me as she pleaded, "Benedict, you have to leave now. Please. I'll appeal to Dante. I'll convince him I seduced you."

I winked. "Remember what you promised." Before returning my attention to the matter at hand.

Dante's *consigliere,* a man named Giovanni, stood. "There will be quiet in the room. Don Agnello is ready to speak."

I took my seat. Then, making sure to keep my gaze on Salvatore, I opened my legs and drew Liliana between them and sat her on my right thigh with my arm wrapped around her waist.

Salvatore fell into his own seat with a grunt, batting away Manfredi's hands as he tried to fix his bow tie.

Dante steepled his fingers and appeared to consider. "My dear friend Salvatore is correct. The false accusation of our organization's involvement in the cowardly attempt against Barone Cavalieri's life in his own home and the blood spilled in vengeance cannot go unanswered. Honor demands a response."

Salvatore rose and buttoned his tuxedo jacket as he motioned to Manfredi. "Thank you for this honor, Dante. Their bodies will rot—"

Dante raised his hand. "I wasn't finished." He motioned for both of the men to sit.

Salvatore's lips thinned. He sat without unbuttoning his tuxedo jacket, causing it to buckle and bunch awkwardly around his waist.

If I weren't the secret mastermind pulling the strings behind this farce, I would find it fascinating how Salvatore's ego allowed him to think a man of my reputation and resources would just calmly sit here and let a buffoon like him pass moral judgment on me.

Dante took a deep breath and said, "So when Benedict Cavalieri pledged to me that blood could only be healed with blood, I agreed."

Salvatore's beady eyes lit up as he licked his lips and

exchanged a look with two different capos across the table. Matteo, Dante, and I all took note of who.

Dante laid a hand over his heart.

Turning to Salvatore he said, with a solemnity that would have rivaled the best American actor in Hollywood, "Which is why Salvatore, my friend, I know you will not begrudge your Don for taking on the privilege reserved for a godfather and her departed father, may he rest in peace in God's good graces, for announcing that Benedict Cavalieri will wed our Liliana Chiara Fiore."

CHAPTER 39

LILIANA

*U*ncle Salvatore shot out of his chair so abruptly it stuck to his hips. "*Vaffanculo!* This is heresy! You have stolen my sacred right and honor as her appointed godfather."

Dante rose. Splaying his fingertips out, he leaned on his hands as he surveyed the table with narrowed eyes.

All conversation ceased.

He then turned his icy glare on Uncle Salvatore. "Are you daring to question the authority and judgment of your Don, *my friend*?"

Once again, I was astonished to see that no one seemed to react to Dante's repeated, malicious use of the word *friend*.

There had always been a ludicrous hypocrisy regarding the close ties between the Sicilian mafia and the Catholic Church, with the former even claiming the Virgin Madonna as their patron saint.

Still, for supposed men of faith, you would think they at

ZOE BLAKE

least knew enough of their Bible to recognize when their leader was making blatant references to Judas.

Uncle Salvatore groped for a cloth napkin from the table and swept it across his sweating brow. "No, of course, Don Agnello. I was just overcome for a moment. I am not questioning your decision. You spent a great deal of time in America, perhaps you were not aware that it is customary to allow the godfather of the woman to arrange such things."

The men around the table shifted their chairs back and turned their shoulders toward Dante to await his response. The change in mood was palpable. Even I could tell what little support Uncle Salvatore might have had in the room was gone the moment he challenged Dante.

Dante signaled to his *consigliere* to speak, as if to respond himself would be beneath his dignity. "It was brought to our attention that two members of our organization, Pietro Gallo and Alessio Ettore, violated their *omertà* by accepting an outside hit contract on Barone Cavalieri without approval from Don Agnello."

Uncle Salvatore shifted several steps backward toward the exit.

Giovanni continued. "These were not *men of honor*. Unfortunately they died quick, ignoble deaths so we may never know why they dishonored their oath."

Uncle Salvatore stopped where he stood and exchanged glances of badly concealed curiosity with Manfredi.

Dante nodded and took over. "That does not mean their blood debt must not be paid. Benedict Cavalieri has come as an emissary of his family to seek peace. To avoid further bloodshed, I offer the hand of Liliana Fiori in marriage as well as a sizable dowry to secure a spiritual kinship between our families. The wedding will take place five days from now at the Cavalieri Winery Estates in Abruzzo."

My fingernails dug into Benedict's upper arm.

Five days?

That didn't give me much time to backtrack all the grand speeches and declarations.

Somehow I would need to get to Dante right away and explain to him the real situation and how obviously Benedict and I were not actually going to be getting married.

Benedict tightened his grip on my waist as we both stood. He nodded to Dante. "Thank you, Don Agnello. Since I am sure you have much to discuss with your associates, my new bride has agreed to show me and my son the sights of Palermo."

I bit my lip. Uh oh. I really needed to stay on the yacht and speak with Dante.

Looking up at Benedict, I said, "Actually, if you and Matteo just wanted to go, I'll stay and—"

Benedict swung me into his arms and talked over me. "What was that? You want a *cannolo* first? How can I say no to such a beautiful face?"

Someone called out, "Spoiling her already!"

"Hey! 'Leave the gun, take the cannoli,'" shouted another, to a round of raucous laughter.

It was always odd to me how much the Sicilian mafia adored the American *Godfather* movie, even going so far as to mimic the dress and lingo. I never saw the appeal. It made Americans think mafia life was all my beloved homeland had to offer.

As Benedict carried me out of the room there was one final catcall. "You know what they say about nuns and the cream filling!"

Then someone sang out a lyric from a famous old Sicilian Carnivale song. *"Ogni cannolu è scettru d' ogni Re ... lu cannolu è la virga di Mosè."*

Matteo followed at our side, shaking his head. "My Corsican isn't great. Did that old man really just belt out at the top of his lungs, 'Every *cannolo* is the scepter of every king ... the *cannolo* is the penis of Moses'?"

* * *

EVERY TIME I tried to speak, Benedict silenced me with a look.

Down the hallway.

Across the upper deck.

The lower deck.

Down two sets of stairs.

If he didn't let me talk soon, we'd run out of boat!

No small feat since we were on a freaking yacht.

When we reached the stern platform, I dug in my heels.

This time the guards didn't hassle us, but instead offered respectful nods as they helped load our apparently already packed garment bags.

Matteo climbed into the waiting tender first and turned to offer me his hand as Benedict stood on the edge of the platform with his hand at my back.

I backed away. "I'm not going with you."

Benedict applied pressure to my back. "Of course you are. Matteo, careful she doesn't slip on the hem of her dress."

I pushed back against his hand and sidestepped his hold. Aware of the listening guards, I smiled and said through clenched teeth, "I'm tired. You two go have fun."

"Well, if you're tired, darling, then I'll drop you off at the hotel," said Benedict, stepping toward me.

I tapped my foot. "Did I say I was tired? I meant ..."

Darn it. I couldn't think what I meant.

Why was he making this so difficult?

Obviously it was in both of our interests that I stay behind and talk with Dante privately.

Glancing over my shoulder at the guards, I closed the distance to Benedict. Reaching up to wrap my arms around his neck, I said loudly, "I need a kiss before you leave."

Then as my lips were close to his, I whispered, "You can go. You don't have to protect me anymore. Now that Dante is involved everything will be fine. I'll explain to him how my godfather manipulated the situation with that horrible bloody sheet display. I'll make him understand there can't possibly be a wedding."

The wind had picked up across the water, whipping a curl across my cheek.

Benedict brushed it back with his warm palm as he whispered back against my lips in a slightly louder, almost-stage whisper. "I'm afraid that's not going to be possible."

My stomach clenched.

What now? I was getting so tired of this twisted game. Bracing myself for what new fresh hell of lies and betrayal that Benedict had uncovered, I asked, careful to keep my voice low, "Why not?"

He gave me a quick kiss. "Because it was my idea that we marry."

"What?" I shouted.

He lifted me by the hips and literally tossed me into Matteo's arms.

Benedict then leapt into the tender, and it had pushed away from the stern platform and was racing toward the

Palermo marina before I even had a chance to catch my breath.

When we reached the shore and I was certain my voice would not carry over the water, I turned to Benedict. "You said that for the guards' benefit, right?"

He shrugged out of his tuxedo jacket and draped it over my shoulders. "Who's hungry? I'm starving."

Pushing my arms into his jacket I couldn't help but notice how the sexy scent of his cologne clung to the lingering warmth. "You haven't answered my question."

Matteo stretched his arm out in the direction of the music and lights. "What's down there?"

I turned to see where Matteo was pointing. Casting a glance around the harbor to get my bearings, I said, "We're at the end of *Via dei Cassari* so that must be the music from the *Mercato della Vucciria*. After eight in the evening the open-air market becomes one big party with food vendors, music, and drinks, so it attracts a huge crowd. The tourists love it."

Benedict grinned as he untied his bow tie and unbuttoned his collar. "I heard food."

Matteo smiled as he did the same, then shrugged out of his jacket and rolled up his shirtsleeves. "I heard drinks."

I looked between them and grimaced. "Did either of you hear tourists?"

We marched up the slight hill to the market, following the sound of the live music and laughter. After all the tension, drama, and uncertainty of the last few days the normalcy of it all was surreal.

It was like that moment in the movies after the action crew saved the world and emerged from the sewer or a crashed, top-secret government spy plane, blinking into the bright sunshine while the rest of the world was just going about its business having no idea they came within a few seconds of being vaporized.

As we crossed into the *Piazza Caracciolo*, we stopped at a cafe booth where Matteo ordered a *Birra Messina* beer and Benedict an *Americano Perfecto*.

Wanting to appear sophisticated, I straightened my shoulders and channeled Gabriella. I flashed the barista a smile and waved my hand with a twist of my wrist the way I observed Gabriella do it and said, "And I'll have a *Negroni Sbagliato*, darling."

Benedict wrapped his arm around my middle from behind and pulled me against his chest. "Cancel that. She'll have a *Crodino* spritz."

I jerked to try and break his grasp.

He wasn't budging.

Folding my arms over my chest, I pushed out my lower lip. "I can order a drink with alcohol. I'm not a child."

He kissed the top of my head from behind as he leaned to the side to say close to my ear, "Trust me, babygirl. I know you're definitely not a child, but I also know you're not used to alcohol and you've had more than enough with those gulps of wine on an empty stomach."

When we got our drinks, Matteo asked about what was further along where the music was much louder.

I averted my eyes, not wanting him to pick up on the fact that I had actually never been allowed to visit that part of the market. "Oh, that part is the *Piazza Garraffello*."

I mimicked Gabriella's dismissive hand gesture again. "It's surrounded by a bunch of run-down buildings, and they mainly dance there and play a bunch of loud DJ techno music. It's not really my scene. Plus it's filled with pickpockets and criminals who prey on the tourists."

Matteo grinned. "Dancing, pickpockets, and criminals. Count me in. I'll see you two future newlyweds later."

Reaching into my drink I tossed an ice cube at his retreating back.

Turning to Benedict, I said, "I know you were just teasing, but I'd feel better if you just confirmed that you weren't serious when you said you were the one who told Dante we were getting married."

The crowd crushed us together as we approached the food stalls. They were a ramshackle mix of wooden tables, food carts and even just baskets propped up on cinder blocks.

Vendors called out to each passerby, trying to wave them in, luring them with the smell of frying oil, garlic, salt, and spices permeating the air.

Even though most of the food vendors were technically illegal setups, all the food was freshly prepared and, in some cases, deliciously indulgent.

In many ways it represented the best of Sicilian culture. We weren't about fancy, high-end, cloth-on-the-table restaurants with famous Michelin-starred, classically trained chefs, but rather a ramshackle gathering of tables behind which stood an old grandmother in a kerchief and apron, her gnarled, arthritic hands preparing the ingredients for the secret seasonings for *pane con le milza* from a family recipe passed down over fifty years while the next generation worked the fryer oil.

Benedict held me close, using his height and bulk to make sure I wasn't jostled in the crowd. "So what should I try first?" he asked.

Again, ignoring me.

With a resigned sigh, knowing there was no way we would be able to have a conversation in this crowd anyway, I surveyed the various vendors. Passing over the *panino con le panelle, sfincione,* and *pezzi di rosticceria,* I continued to survey the various colorful menu options.

Along the way, Benedict stopped in front of a smoking grill of long white tubes wrapped around small bunches of parsley and onions. The vendor raised a knife and sliced a lemon in half, then dramatically squeezed the juice over the skewers, making the grill sizzle and pop and sending a fresh plume of fragrant citrus and black pepper-scented smoke into the air.

He pointed. "What about this dish?"

I held a hand over my mouth as I looked at the *stigghiola.* "Only if you want to see me vomit. I can't stand even watching someone eat tripe."

Benedict turned me away from the stand. "No lamb intestines on the wedding menu. Noted."

I frowned up at him. "You keep teasing, but this is serious. Dante said five days which means he's already having his *consigliere* call associates and tell them to be at the Cavalieri winery for a wedding by the end of the week. We need to tell him *tonight.*"

He took the empty paper cup from my hands and tossed it in a nearby garbage can. "You haven't eaten. Pick a stall or I'm going to pick something for you."

Worried he'd find the one healthy thing in the entire piazza, like roasted chestnuts or the boiled octopus, I rose on my toes and spotted one of my favorite foods and headed in that direction.

I stopped in front of the *friggitore di strada* with his huge, churning cast-iron vat of boiling pork fat. The golden-brown rice balls bobbed in the oil as the fryer jostled them with his slotted spoon.

As I leaned in close to see if the stall offered only the *carne* Bolognese sauce or if they also offered my favorite, the *burro* béchamel sauce with cheese and ham, I was bumped from behind.

Benedict's ever-present quick arm around my waist saved me from an extremely painful hand in the oil vat. He squeezed me tight. "How in the hell did you survive out in the world before you met me, little one?" he admonished lightly.

My heart flipped.

There was plenty of evidence to show that I obviously had barely done so.

It was painful to think I would soon be returning to that lonely existence. I realized the world would feel not unlike this piazza without Benedict around.

Loud, chaotic, crowded, and full of strangers, some of them dangerous.

He ordered a plate full of *arancini* balls with extra *burra* sauce and on the way back to the relative quiet of the harbor we also picked up a plate of chickpea fritters and two cannoli garnished with candied orange peels and pistachios.

Moving away from the chaos of the market, we walked back to the harbor. Benedict found a cozy spot on an elevated patch of grass under a Bismarck palm.

Once he sat down and stretched his long legs out, he angled his arm behind me with his palm in the grass so I could lean back.

My first bite into a still warm and crispy *arancini* ball was heaven as the fragrant saffron blended with the earthy starch of the rice and the creamy saltiness of the *burro* sauce. I let a small moan escape as I enjoyed the savory treat.

He leaned forward. "Can I have a bite?"

I held the fried rice ball up to his lips and watched as he sank his teeth into the spot where my mouth had been.

My tongue flicked out to lick my lower lip as if I were tasting the same bite.

It was silly to think such a simple thing was erotic. I meant, the man took a bite of street food. No big deal.

He placed his lips where mine had been while the edges of his teeth teased the outer edge of the ball, not unlike how he teased my nipples, before he pulled the bite into his mouth and savored it, then swallowed.

I barely noticed when he took the rest of the food from my hand and lifted me off the grass.

Adjusting his jacket around my waist against the growing chill of the evening, he pulled me close as he placed a hand under my chin. "I'm taking you back to the hotel."

I looked past him to the twinkling lights of the harbor. "But it's such a pretty view and we can hear the music."

He winked. "Little one, if those are the sounds you make when you bite into a fucking ball of rice and if that is the look on your face just *watching* me do the same, then I'll be damned if I'm letting anyone watch the food porn that is going to happen when I feed you those cannoli."

My cheeks burned.

As he grabbed my hand and led me off the grass and back onto the walkway, I asked, "Are you ever going to answer my question about the wedding?"

CHAPTER 40

LILIANA

"*L*iliana is right. The whole idea is preposterous," stated Bianca as she placed a Castelli ceramic bowl filled with steamed broccoli rabe and garlic on the table. The bowl, decorated with bright lemons and bunches of grapes along its sides, added a colorful touch to the table.

I waved my hand close to my side, saying in a low voice, "I don't think I used that word."

This is getting out of hand.

Amara followed with a scarred wooden cutting board on top of which was a long loaf of golden-brown *Pane di Altamura* bread. From the nutty, sweet aroma wafting from it, I could tell it was still warm.

I smoothed the tablecloth and moved a dish of olives out of the way so she had room to set it down. "I agree with Liliana," she said. "The idea is crazy."

I twisted in my seat as she pivoted to return to the kitchen. "Actually, I never used that word either."

This is like the worst game of telephone ever.

Where the heck is Benedict with that wine?

Enzo came into the dining room carrying a heavy cast-iron pot with steam rising from under the loose-fitting lid.

As he set it down in the center of the table and lifted the lid, he said, "Liliana has a point. It would be ludicrous for the two of them to get married, but Uncle Benedict is right. It has to be a real wedding, or they will smell a rat and the plan won't work." He turned to Bianca. "We could always get married."

Bianca paused in setting out a small stack of sterling silver serving utensils. She sent him a questioning look. "What was this now?"

He wrapped his arms around her waist. "Why let a good party go to waste? We already announced the engagement. We could let them think it was Benedict and Liliana getting married and then switch out at the last minute before they walk down the aisle. What do you think, *tesoro mio?*"

She wrapped her arms around his neck and leaned in close and said very sweetly, "At the risk of sounding like a bridezilla, I'm going to have to insist—on top of not wearing my dead sister's wedding dress—that I also not be asked to be a stand-in bride at a fucking gangster wedding."

She cast me a quick side glance. "No offense, Liliana."

I raised both palms up. "No worries."

I then leaned over slightly and, keeping my gaze forward, whispered out of the side of my mouth to Matteo at my left. "Dead sister's wedding dress?"

He leaned toward me and whispered back. "You didn't hear the one about the gambling priest, the gun, and the whore?"

My mouth dropped open as I turned wide eyes on him.

He smirked. "Tell you later."

"Besides," continued Bianca, "you promised me *at least* a six-month engagement."

Enzo's hand moved to cup her ass. "I promised you I would wait out a *no more* than six-month engagement to finally make you my wife and that was nine weeks ago; or more precisely, sixty-seven days, nine hours and thirteen minutes ago."

Milana and Cesare walked in at that moment, both carrying matching crystal cruet sets each with extra virgin olive oil and aged balsamic vinegar which they set on opposite ends of the table.

Cesare then held out a chair for Milana and said to her, "We could do it."

Milana turned her face up to him. "First of all, hell will freeze over before I get married in a church. Second of all, I know you did not just volunteer up *my* wedding to be some rush job, slapdash mobster affair. It's bad enough everyone in the village knows you already knocked me up because that crazy bitch tried to kill me." She glanced at me. "No offense, Liliana."

My tension rose as I tried to force my tight lips into a smile. "Nope. No worries."

Matteo leaned in close to me and patted my hand. In a stage whisper he said, "The crazy bitch she is referring to is the aforementioned whore, not you, because it was Bianca, not Milana, you tried to kill."

I spoke through my clenched teeth, awkwardly keeping my forced smile. "Yeah, caught that. Thanks, Matteo."

I knew his dark humor was his way of trying to make me feel part of the family because everything was supposedly forgiven and forgotten but it wasn't that easy with me. The guilt and shame over the misguided part I played in harming this wonderful family still plagued me.

Cesare grabbed Milana's chin and tilted her head to face him as he placed his hand over her stomach and gave her a hard kiss on the lips. "Yeah, I did."

"That wasn't meant to be a 'check out the fruits of my God-like Cavalieri sperm' moment for you," she teased.

He raised his eyes and his arm to the ceiling as if appealing to the gods. "Too late. Bask in my greatness all ye mere mortals."

Milana laughed and threw a cloth napkin at his face.

Cesare caught it one-handed while pulling out the chair next to her and sitting, then placed his arm over the back of her chair, edging her close. "And what is this *my* wedding bullshit? Am I allowed to attend?"

She appeared to consider it. "I haven't decided yet."

Cesare leaned in and said something in her ear that made her blush furiously and giggle.

Matteo stood up to start slicing the bread. "Something tells me he just secured his invite."

The whole table laughed as Barone and Benedict both appeared from a different doorway holding several bottles of wine.

I tilted my head to the side and pressed my fingers to my cheek to make sure it wasn't obvious that I was now blushing at Benedict's appearance.

Dressed casually in a pair of worn jeans and an oatmeal-colored thermal with wooden buttons at the collar and a pair of heavy, scuffed work boots, you'd hardly guess the man was the eldest heir to a billion-dollar wine empire with a family legacy that stretched back to when Italy was literally a kingdom.

With his slightly ruffled silver hair, roguish earring, intimidating height, dangerous past and impossibly arrogant demeanor he looked more like a pirate or one of those mountain men who shun society and could kill bears with their bare hands.

Amara and Bianca rushed to take the bottles from Barone just as Gabriella appeared with a wine opener in time to scold them. "It was just a tiny piece of lead for heaven's sake. He's fine. Fit as an ox. If you don't stop spoiling him, he'll be impossible to live with."

Although Gabriella seemed annoyed, I didn't miss the look of sisterly affection she gave him when she also rushed to take the final bottle of wine from his grasp. It wasn't hard to miss the undercurrent of fear that still ran just beneath the surface of gratitude and love in the room.

That lingering cloud of what if.

What if he hadn't survived?

What if the gunman had continued shooting?

What if? What if? What if?

Barone wrapped his arm around Gabriella's shoulders and gave her a quick, reassuring hug before taking the wine key from her to help Amara uncork the bottles.

A stab of guilt pierced my chest.

I pressed my heels against the floor with the intention of silently pushing the dining chair back. With so much chaos around the afternoon family meal, I was hoping I could sneak away and no one would notice.

The chair barely moved before it abruptly stopped.

I carefully pushed harder, not wanting the legs to squeak.

It wouldn't budge.

Before I could check to see if it was caught on something,

a pair of strong hands settled on my shoulders. I tilted my head back.

Benedict leaned over my chair from behind.

Once again, as if reading my mind, he spoke soft and low so the others could not hear. "Don't even think about it. I would notice." He then kissed me on the forehead and with a definitive shove, pushed my chair back under the table before taking the seat next to me.

Just so I completely got the message, he dropped a hand on my upper thigh.

Glancing around to make sure the exchange hadn't been witnessed by anyone else, I caught Barone Cavalieri's eye.

The breath seized in my lungs.

I hadn't spoken to him since … well … since everything.

When Benedict, Matteo and I arrived back from Sicily it was late morning and he and Amara were still *occupied* upstairs. Apparently he and his brother shared more than just a similar appearance.

Plus, truth be told it wasn't like I was seeking him out, even though it would be the proper Christian thing to do.

I owed him an apology.

Benedict had told me several times over that there were forces at play that I had no idea about and that none of this was my fault, but it didn't feel that way.

Then Barone smiled at me. It was a brotherly, warmhearted gesture just like he did to effortlessly put Gabriella's unspoken fears at ease.

I lowered my head and bit my lip, trying not to smile back. Part of me didn't think I deserved the rush of happiness I felt.

Benedict's fingers pressed into my thigh.

I looked up and met his gaze.

Benedict winked at me. "Don't be getting cute with my brother. Remember, you're mine now."

I pleaded with him in a low voice. "You need to stop saying that. The whole time you were getting the wine they were debating over what a crazy plan this wedding is. *They think you're serious.* You need to tell them that it's just a trap for my godfather Salvatore and we're not really getting married."

Last night over cannoli, Benedict finally explained what he wasn't able to discuss on the yacht.

About how he needed a way to both allow Dante to save face and seem in control of his organization while also irrefutably trapping my godfather in a betrayal.

So they decided to take Salvatore by surprise in announcing our wedding.

Apparently, Benedict believed he'd try again to get rid of Dante but this time he wouldn't trust it to a flunky. He'd do it himself and that was when they'd catch him in the act.

Of course none of this meant it needed to be a *real* wedding.

Rosa entered holding a bowl of fresh ricotta cheese which she set to the side before lifting the lid off the central cast-iron pot and stirring the contents. It was a rich, creamy looking soup with the fresh, herbal scent of fennel.

I lowered my shoulders and sank back into my chair, remembering her look of disapproval from the other day. I had since learned she was the beloved housekeeper of the estate and de facto grandmother. So it probably made sense that she hated me with the fire of a thousand burning suns and would never forgive me no matter what anyone said about my innocence in Barone's shooting.

As she ladled the first bowl and expertly garnished it with

a spoonful of fresh ricotta cheese, Cesare rubbed his hands and reached for it. "This smells delicious, Rosa. What is it?"

She smacked his wrist. "It's not for you. Yet. It's a special dish. Just for Liliana. To welcome her to the family. The first bowl is hers."

All eyes turned to me.

I froze.

Benedict reached for the bowl and placed it in front of me.

Rosa folded her hands in front of her apron and looked expectantly at me.

My hand shook a little as I reached for my spoon, already knowing whatever it was could taste like warm vomit and I would swallow it down like it was the best thing I'd ever eaten.

It was then I realized what soup she had made. It was *maccu ri favi*, a very popular Sicilian fava bean and wild fennel soup.

She had made a taste of home, just for me.

Just for Liliana.

To welcome her to the family.

My vision blurred as my eyes filled with tears. "I'm so sorry!"

Pushing back my chair, I ran out of the room.

CHAPTER 41

BENEDICT

*T*his villa was too damn big with too many rooms.

I finally spotted her through a window, sitting curled up and shivering outside on a chaise in a corner of a walled-in garden terrace accessed through the library.

Snatching the folded soft wool plaid blanket from the ottoman in front of the cold fireplace, I opened the glass door and joined her. I shook out the blanket as I walked and before she could object, I swooped her into my arms and took her seat.

After swaddling her in the wool, I settled her on my lap, brushing back a stray curl that was stuck to her tear-wet cheek. "Want to tell me what that was about?"

She sniffed. "Please don't think I'm having second thoughts about helping you. My uncle is a horrible, hateful man and I want to help you stop him. And I know I owe it to Barone and his family to help."

Liliana laid her head against my shoulder and twisted the

fringed edge of the blanket. "I just … I just can't lie anymore. Even if it's for a good cause. I can't do it."

I brushed my knuckles down her soft cheek. "Who's asking you to lie?"

"Don't tease me, Benedict. Not right now."

Placing a finger under her chin, I forced her to turn to face me. "I'm not teasing you."

She sighed. "Benedict, your whole big plan to trap my uncle. Technically, it's a lie."

With another sigh, she pressed her forehead against my chest. "I sound horribly ungrateful. You've risked your life for me and now I'm being a big baby complaining about a few silly lies. It's just, your family is being so nice and when Rosa said welcome to the family it felt so real, and it made me feel like such a horrible fraud and interloper. And I don't deserve any of their kindness, not after what I've done and definitely not after what my uncle's done and now I'm complaining about—"

Pushing my fingers into her hair, I pulled her head back and with her shocked gasp, slammed my mouth down on hers. Her hands twisted into the front of my shirt as I thrust my tongue inside her warm, sweet mouth.

My arm wrapped around her hip, cradling her closer to my chest as I tilted my head to the other side, deepening the kiss. When I finally freed her mouth, her lips were slightly bruised and swollen.

I traced her lower lip with the tip of my finger. "No one is asking you to lie, babygirl."

A frown wrinkled her brow. "How can you say that? You keep telling your family that we are getting married in four days. You're literally asking me to *lie* in a church in front of your family and a priest and God to play along during a fake wedding ceremony!"

Fuck, she was adorable.

Especially all wrapped up in this blanket.

It was all I could do not to pick her up and just carry her across the field to the helicopter and fly us both back to my ranch right here and now. We could both be naked, wrapped up in a couple of fur blankets in front of a roaring fire enjoying a mountain view by nightfall.

I took a deep breath and cupped her cheek. "When, at any point in time, did I claim it would be a fake wedding?"

She opened and closed her mouth several times before frowning again. "Well ... of course it's a fake wedding. I mean, you didn't have to say it in so many words but ... of course it is ... because ... well, just because of course it is!"

Matteo and the others were always telling me one of my more annoying characteristics was being steps ahead of everyone else in the room half the time. It was a fantastic asset when I was facing down a room full of adversaries who wanted to kill me, or when I was faced with a tense hostage negotiation.

However, not so much when in my mind we were already married and settled on my ranch together, with her carrying our first child, and meanwhile she was curled up in a ball crying because she was feeling lost and confused, thinking this was all just a big farce and at the end of it I was going to toss her out into the cold.

I looked down into her big, beautiful eyes as I gently rubbed my thumb over her lips.

A better man would take this moment to whisper sugar-coated words of love or perhaps even fall on his knees apologizing for causing her even a moment's worry about his devotion and unwavering affection for her.

Too bad for Liliana I was the man who'd come chasing after her, because she was getting none of those things from me.

"I need you to listen very carefully to me, *angioletto*, because if I have to tell you this again, I'm going to take off my belt, put you over my knee, and whip your cute ass until you beg me to shove those metal game balls up your tight little hole just to make the punishment stop, understood?"

Her palms shoved against my chest as her spine stiffened. Turning her head to check to make sure no one had overheard, she jammed a finger in the center of my chest while harshly whispering, "Benedict—uh ... Darn it."

I tightened my lips to keep from smiling. "Luciano."

Her brow furrowed. "What?"

"My middle name. It's Luciano. That was what you were searching for, correct?"

She huffed and pushed the tip of her finger against my sternum. "Benedict Luciano Cavalieri, you should not say such shocking things to me when your family could be listening."

"Trust me. Once you get to know them, you'll learn they are not that easily shocked."

"I'm not going to get to know them! I'm heading back to Sicily as soon as it's safe. Don't you see how absurd this is? We shouldn't be pretending to get married. We don't even know each other's middle names."

"Yours is Chiara."

She huffed. "That's not my point. Show-off."

I reached between us for my belt buckle as I looked at her inquiringly. "Is your point that you don't want to listen and are choosing my belt? I still owe you a spanking for that stunt you pulled back on the yacht when you risked your life jumping in front of that bullet for me."

She rolled her eyes. "I owed you for saving my life in Rome and besides, it doesn't really count as me risking my life when I technically jumped in front of a stupid balled-up sheet."

Wrapping my hand around the back of her neck, I pulled her closer. "It sure as fuck does count. You didn't know he didn't have a gun at the time and if I ever—ever—catch you risking your sweet, beautiful life like that again you won't sit for a week."

She tucked her chin and mouth beneath the blanket.

"Good girl. Now, it's time we get a few more things straight. In four days' time, you will be in a real church, standing in front of a real priest, saying *very real* vows promising to love, honor and *obey* me in a real wedding."

She lifted her chin above the blanket and opened her mouth.

"And before you get yourself in trouble," I continued, "by saying something that might anger me, like talking about an annulment. Let me assure you, when that priest says, 'until death do us part,' that means God Himself will have to pry you from my cold, dead hands."

After tightening my hold, I flipped her under me so we could stretch out on the chaise.

As I braced my forearm next to her head, I reached inside the blanket.

Slipping my fingers inside the collar of her dress to touch the warm skin of her breast, I said, "And once we are man and wife, buckle up, babygirl, because there will be nothing holding me back from enjoying this sweet little body of yours."

Her eyes widened. "You've been holding back?"

The corner of my mouth lifted as I ground my hard cock against her hip. "Like you wouldn't believe."

"Wait." She wiggled out from beneath me. Rolling off the chaise onto the tiles and getting to her feet to pace away from me. "I need to think."

Adjusting my now painfully erect cock before rising, I swept the discarded blanket off the ground and placed it on her shoulders. "Fine but do it inside. This isn't Sicily. It's far too cold in Abruzzo for the dress you're wearing, and it will be significantly colder in the Dolomites."

She cast a confused look over her shoulder at me as I ushered her over the threshold back into the library. "For starters, it's not my fault you wouldn't let me take any of my own clothes when we left Rome. And second, the Dolomites? As in the mountain range so far north it's practically in Austria?"

After closing and locking the library doors which led into the villa in case any of my family came looking for us, I crossed to the fireplace. I flipped open the ceramic box which contained the matches and said, "For future reference, I have a very strict policy of not stopping to pack an overnight bag when getting shot at by an inept mafia kill squad."

I lowered onto my haunches and lit the already prepped fire.

With her hands tucked inside the blanket, she gestured to me. "Can we double back to the Dolomites and why it matters that it's colder there?"

Before answering, I adjusted a log which shifted as the fire warmed. Then, brushing the dirt off my palms as I rose to

SEDUCTION OF THE PATRIARCH

face her, I said, "It matters because that is where we will be living. I own a manor complex of about fifteen thousand hectares outside San Vito di Cadore, about eighteen kilometers from Cortina d'Ampezzo, not unlike this one. It has a comfortable chalet, stable, and other buildings where I raise champion horses. You'll like it there."

She spread her arms wide. "Are there any more details you wanted to tell me about this life you have all planned out for me? Any children? If so, how many? Am I allowed a job?"

Not appreciating her tone, my eyes narrowed as I crossed my arms and leaned to the side of the fire against the mantle. "As a matter of fact, yes. If you're not already pregnant with my child, my hope is you will be by the end of winter. I'd love to have as many children as you want because I think you are going to make a wonderful mother and I missed out on a great deal of Matteo's upbringing. I'm sure you've figured out that money is not an issue with this family, but if you wanted to work for your own fulfillment I wouldn't stand in your way. Barone mentioned he had some Cavalieri projects you'd be great for."

Her gaze focused past me to stare at the flames inside the fireplace as they caught and slowly grew in intensity. For several minutes the only sound in the room was the crackle and hiss of the fire. I watched her watching it.

The silence stretched.

Another man would have gotten impatient and demanded she speak.

Another man might have tried to plead his case or fill the silence.

Or worse, another man might have second-guessed his plans and backtracked.

I did none of those things.

Call it obnoxious arrogance, but I was already three steps ahead of my babygirl. I could practically hear her thoughts.

What was worse, I knew I was partially to blame for her current confusion and anger. After all, I was the one who encouraged her to start standing up for herself and stop allowing others to manipulate her.

Although in my defense, even at the time I told her that, it didn't include me.

Fortunately, that was only the first step.

Step two was her thinking she needed to leave me to achieve that.

Step three was proving her wrong.

Of course, this was all just playing out in my mind. To actually start the game, my adorable queen would have to make the first move.

CHAPTER 42

LILIANA

*O*ut of the corner of my eye, I scanned the room, then shifted closer to the door, placing a large leather armchair between me and Benedict before I took a deep breath, pushed out my chin, and said, "No."

I braced for his booming yell, my stomach clenching as I edged my right foot back, preparing to bolt for the door.

He tilted his head to the side and studied me for a moment before responding. "No."

I frowned. "Wait. Is that no with a question mark like you are double-checking that I said no, or are you saying no back?"

He grinned. "I'm saying no back."

"You can't say no back."

"And yet I just did."

I paced away. "You were the one who told me I needed to stop letting people manipulate me."

"Step one."

"What?"

"Nothing, continue."

Reaching the other side of the room, I turned and paced back. "I've been thinking about this a lot. And you're right. So many things that happened over the last few months and even the last few days would not have happened if I had recognized when I was being used."

I shrugged the blanket off, warming up to my subject.

Pointing to the center of my chest, I said, "I may technically not be to blame for my uncle's sins, but if I had been a stronger person with a stronger sense of self maybe I could have done more to stop him."

Taking a deep breath, I turned to face him. "So I'm taking *your* advice. I'm not going to let myself be pushed into something I'm not ready for. Even though you didn't, strictly speaking, *ask* me to marry you, more told me I was marrying you. My answer is no."

I took another breath as I paced away. "I know you and Dante are just doing this as some kind of master plan to trap my uncle and save me from his retribution, while also preserving Dante's authority, but there has to be another way."

I was rambling because I didn't want to admit the real reason.

But maybe becoming a stronger person was about facing your fears and owning up to how you felt.

I twisted my hands, my eyes filling with tears again. "This is actually harder than I thought it would be. As unbelievable as it sounds, I think I actually might be falling in love with you."

I cleared my throat. "But I can't be sure. I suspect someone with a stronger personality who knows their own mind would be, but I'm not. For all I know I could be confusing love with a fucked-up blend of abandonment, damsel in distress, and daddy issues."

I swiped under my eyes. "I think I need to learn to stand on my own two feet. Otherwise, I'd feel like I was using you to avoid the scary prospect of having to face the world alone."

With my fingernail I picked at a loose stitch along the seam of the leather armchair to avoid eye contact with him as I waited for him to respond.

Braced for the gut-wrenching heartache was more accurate.

All I wanted to do was curl up in a ball and cry.

Then I'd figure out what to do next about finding a job, a place to live ... Clothes.

I had absolutely no idea why he was offering marriage, but I knew it couldn't possibly be out of love. It was probably out of guilt for taking my virginity. His family had already paid enough for my sins. He shouldn't have to be saddled with me for life as well.

He straightened and stepped toward me. "What do you like to drink?"

"It's a little early in the day for me."

"I'm not pouring you one. I mean what's your favorite drink? I've already observed you don't like wine and you apparently didn't enjoy the *Negroni Sbagliato* Gabriella made you."

I smoothed the skirt I was wearing to cover my unease before lifting one shoulder. "How do you know I didn't enjoy it?"

"Babygirl, if you think I didn't interrogate Gabbie and Milana to make sure you were sober and of sound mind before deciding to chop off all your beautiful hair, then you haven't been paying attention."

I tapped my foot and turned my attention back to the thick thread poking out along the leather seam. My cheeks warmed at the idea of him being all growly and protective over the possibility that the girls had gotten me tipsy before convincing me to pull a pseudo-Britney Spears. "I don't really know what I like to drink. I haven't tried much besides wine."

He seemed to consider my response as he rubbed his beard and nodded. "When we were at the Vatican, I noticed you admiring the Pinturicchio frescoes. Who's your favorite artist? Renaissance aside, with your imagination I would have pegged you as more of a Baroque or Neoclassicism fan."

Suspicious of his intentions, I leaned my hip against the chair and stared at him. "Is this some kind of trap?"

"I admit some people can be a bit judgmental about the Baroque period but—"

"You know what I mean." I waved my hand at him. "You're taking my refusal awfully well. Why aren't you more *you* about this? You know, stomping and growling and yelling."

"Just answer my question. Your favorite artist?"

I threw my arms up. "I don't have one yet. I wanted to finally go to a museum while I was in Rome but was afraid to leave my apartment too much. Why are you asking?"

He leaned his hands on the back of the chair opposite from mine. "We've already established you don't like capers but do like *bottarga*, have to be forced to eat your vegetables, love *arancini* and have a bit of a sweet tooth and a fondness for your home cuisine."

My mouth opened and closed as I tried to think of a response, but none came.

How did I respond to the revelation that an intimidating beast of a man like Benedict Cavalieri who, while in the middle of unraveling a mafia assassination plot involving the attempted murder of his brother, also had the time to notice that I had a sweet tooth?

He pushed off from the chair and prowled toward me.

I fell back as I raised my hands, prepared to fight him off if he tried to pull me into his arms.

He didn't.

I shouldn't feel disappointed that he didn't, right?

After all, I was telling the man I didn't want to marry him. And I didn't, right?

Because it would be absurd to marry a man I met barely a week ago. Right?

Benedict slowly circled me as he scanned me with his dark gaze.

I spun around with him, trying not to turn my back on him in case he was waiting for a vulnerable moment to snatch me and toss me over his shoulder.

He wasn't.

Dammit.

No. I should be happy he wasn't.

He tilted his head to the right, then the left before saying, "I'm going to say Chanel would be best. Gabbie's the expert so we'll double-check with her, and of course the girls will tease you for not picking an Italian designer …"

"Chanel? I don't understand. Is this another one of your interrogation tactics?"

He continued to circle me. "You didn't think I was going to take my girl to Paris and not spend an obscene amount of money spoiling her rotten, did you? It's going to be fun showing my nephews how it's done," he said with a wink.

"I'm not going to Paris with you, Benedict. I just told you I was leaving for Sicily to be on my own."

Stopping in front of me, he crossed his arms. "You'd prefer

somewhere else? You mentioned wanting to feel stylish and French so I took that to mean you might enjoy seeing Paris, but I'm fine visiting anywhere."

What the hell? How was this man so deep inside my head? "I did?"

"You did."

I frowned, trying to catch up to the conversation. "Did you have me investigated or followed or something?"

His brow lowered as his gaze intensified. "No."

The atmosphere in the room changed in an instant, like that charged second immediately following a lightning strike when everything seemed to be shocked into suspended stillness.

My gaze skittered to the right as I slid my hips along the back of the chair. "Were you recording me this whole time in case I confessed something about Barone?"

His head turned slightly in my direction. The deceptively simple gesture stopped my heart with terror.

When he responded, I knew it couldn't only be in my imagination that his voice had taken on a lower, deeper edge. "No. I was listening as you talked."

I swallowed and edged closer to the door. "No one listens that closely to me when I talk. I'm not that interesting."

He slowly unfolded his arms.

My gaze was drawn to his large, powerful hands.

My breath hitched because I knew precisely what those hands were capable of.

He stalked forward. "If you think that, then I must not be showing you enough attention."

My brain melted trying to even conceptualize what it would be like to have Benedict pay more attention to me. With my back pressed against the door, I reached behind me and tried to turn the knob. Locked. My fingertips splayed around the knob feeling for a key or button.

He leaned his forearm over my head, lowering his head to whisper against my ear. "It's locked, babygirl."

The adrenaline raced through my veins so intensely I was lightheaded. I licked my lips as I stared at his mouth. "Will you unlock it?"

He reached up and stroked my cheek with the backs of his knuckles. "Eventually."

I struggled to keep from closing my eyes and leaning into his touch. "What if I said please?"

His chuckle was a dark vibration I could practically feel emanating from his chest, he was so close. "Oh, you'll say please, all right."

I swallowed.

He wrapped his hands around my jaw and tilted my head back. "But first, you and I are going to come to an understanding."

His mouth captured mine. Swallowing my gasp, his tongue swept inside. As his hand fisted my hair, his arm wrapped around my middle, lifting me off my feet.

My fingers dug into his upper arms as I tried to push back, but I was no match for the strength of his arms as he carried me to the massive, cozy sofa in front of the fire. The moment my body hit the soft leather surface, his followed to pin me down.

Pushing his knee between my legs, he yanked the hem of my dress up.

I wrenched my head to the side. "Wait. We can't do this again. That one time was the only time. I need to save myself for my future husband."

His fingers ripped my panties off as he reared up over me.

His breathing was deep and uneven from our kiss. "Dammit, woman. How many times do I have to tell you that I am that man? We are getting married this Sunday. Let me put it in language you'll understand. *If a man seduces a virgin who is not betrothed and lies with her, he shall give the bride-price for her and make her his wife.*"

Shocked to my core I pushed against his chest. "No fair! You can't quote from the Bible!"

He unfastened his belt and lowered his zipper. "All's fair in love and war, babygirl."

Pulling out his cock, he fisted the thick length before bracing his forearm near my head and pressing his hips between my legs. He pushed the head of his cock against my already embarrassingly wet entrance.

My fingers curled in his shirt and I held my breath, bracing for the same pain I felt before.

His lips caressed the skin below my ear. "Trust daddy, baby."

His body shifted as he drove his hips forward, thrusting his cock deep inside of me.

I squeezed my eyes shut, clenching my teeth, but there was no pain. He shifted and thrust again.

My eyes sprang open. "Oh!"

My inner muscles contracted around his shaft, sending a ripple of pleasure up my spine. There was something about his weight pressing down on me as his cock filled me.

It was so *consuming*.

He bit my earlobe. "You feel that cock, baby? It's yours. Just like I am. I want you to use me."

Certain I hadn't heard him correctly, I threaded my fingers into his hair and pulled to get his attention. "What?"

Grabbing my wrists, he pinned them over my head and

slowed his thrusts, grinding his hips against my clit each time he pressed in to the hilt. "You heard me. I want you to use me. Especially since I have every intention of using you."

He leaned down and kissed the edge of my jaw, rasping, "I'd buried myself in the shadows and on the edge of society for so long, I'd forgotten what it felt like to live."

I raised my right knee and tilted my hips as I shamelessly pulled on his shirt, needing to feel his skin.

He raised up, yanked off his shirt, and tossed it aside before claiming my mouth again. As he did so, he reached between us and tore the collar of my dress. He wrenched my sleeves and bra straps down, exposing my shoulders and the tops of my breasts.

He licked and laved at my nipple. "Not only am I going to use this sweet body, I'm going to enjoy rediscovering the sensual pleasure in art. The delicious decadence in food."

He punctuated each sentence with a hard, grinding thrust. "The erotic sight of expensive silk lingerie caressing your skin."

I moaned as his hand moved between our bodies to swirl his fingertips against my clit.

I raked my nails over his chest before curling my fingers into his chest hair and pulling.

The way he was slowly, methodically driving into me was maddening. It was as if I were staring at a massive wave that just kept rising and rising, cresting but refusing to crash onto the shore.

His voice was a dark growl as he ran the sharp edges of his teeth along the curve of my breast. "I'll be damned if I'll be denied the wicked delight of being the one to get you drunk for the first time."

He moved to lean over me, vowing, "Or to not be the man

standing by your side when you first lay eyes on the glowing lights of Paris from the Pont Alexandre III over the Seine at sunset."

His intense gaze held me as captive as if he still held my wrists. He cupped my cheek then shifted his hand to wrap it around my throat, increasing the pace of his thrusts.

My fingers stretched around his wrist, my mouth opened on a cry.

My body strained to adjust to the violence of the impact of his cock as he hammered harder and harder into me. The head of his cock kept touching a bundle of nerves that sent a warm rush of pleasure racing over my limbs.

Keeping his gaze on me, he growled, "So go ahead and use me, babygirl. Use me for my cock, for my money, for the protection I can offer. Call me daddy or sugar daddy. I don't give a fuck. As long as you understand I'm calling you mine. And we *are* getting married this Sunday whether you like it or not."

Without waiting for a response, his mouth slammed down on mine just as the wave finally crashed, drowning me in the dark waters of his sinfully tempting life of hedonistic pleasure.

CHAPTER 43

LILIANA

There was a collective sigh as all five women took a step back and looked at me.

I self-consciously swept my hand over the boat-neck collar with my right hand before adjusting the wide satin headband.

Gabriella. Oops. Aunt Gabriella, as I was told to now call her, stepped behind me and carefully attached the trailing tulle veil to the headband. "Does it feel secure? Not too heavy?"

I turned to face her. "No, it's fine. Is it straight?"

She waved her hand with a twist of her wrist, her signature gold bangles jangling. "Darling, you're going to make me smear my perfect eye makeup. You look beautiful."

She looped an arm around Rosa's waist and gave her a side hug. "You outdid yourself, Rosa. Using Benedict and Barone's mother's dress was a genius idea."

Rosa clasped her hands together. "I'm so glad the pretty white satin had not yellowed."

Bianca bent low and fluffed the flared, full-length ball-gown skirt. "So gorgeous. Liliana, you were made for this classic style."

Apparently having more money than God Himself in Italy meant the Cavalieris could have had any major haute couture designer drop everything and sew me a wedding gown within a few days, but I refused. The very idea of having that much fuss, expense, and attention on me practically caused me to break out in hives.

Fortunately, Rosa had come up with the perfect solution. She had found Benedict's mother's wedding dress from the mid-1950s in storage. It was a similar style to the infamous wedding gown that Audrey Hepburn never wore since that was all the rage at the time. I decided not to take it as an omen.

While Milana finished securing the small, cloth-covered buttons down the back of the fitted long-sleeved bodice, she sighed. "You have the perfect shape for this dress. Nice boobs with a cinched-in waist."

Amara angled her head. "Fortunately the full skirt hides the necessary last-minute alterations and doesn't make your hips look big."

I smoothed my hands over the dress. "I was just about to ask. It looks okay? Nice and smooth? You can't tell?"

Bianca laughed. "They were a helluva something borrowed! Let's hope the priest doesn't find out what's under your skirts," she said with a wink.

Amara covered her eyes. "One of these days, Father Luca is going to excommunicate all of us."

Since it was bad luck for me to look in a mirror, I would have to take their word for it.

The last thing I needed was more bad luck.

Today was going to be difficult enough with my uncle here and Benedict's insane plan to trap him into exposing himself to Dante as the traitor who tried to kill Barone.

I still didn't fully understand why we couldn't just let sleeping dogs lie and walk away from the whole thing, but Benedict insisted that both I and the rest of his family would not be safe until my uncle was dealt with.

And I trusted him.

Sort of. I was still unsure about us getting married *for real*.

I had lied to Benedict. Again.

I didn't *think* I might be falling in love with him.

I knew I was *already* in love with him.

Hopelessly so.

I just didn't want to admit it, knowing I would sound like a silly schoolgirl with a sexy daddy crush. So I'd tried to be strong and walk away.

Admittedly I hadn't tried very hard, but I had at least tried to do the responsible, rational thing.

And in his usual, extremely arrogant, over-the-top, seductive way, he, for lack of a more refined term, *persuaded* me to say yes to his, also for lack of a better term, marriage proposal.

He hadn't offered me love but maybe that was too much to ask for someone like me.

He had offered a life, a home, the possibility of children … a family.

And who knew, maybe one day I would become the type of person he could love.

So here we were, getting married.

I swallowed as I placed a hand over my stomach.

Actually getting married.

This was actually happening.

I was marrying a man I barely knew.

I breathed deeply through my nose.

A man who a week ago I thought wanted to kill me.

Yup. It was fine. Everything was just fine.

The girls around me kept talking and fussing with my gown and veil.

And bonus, my wedding was a trap for my murdering uncle.

Oh, no, did it again. I allowed myself to be manipulated into a huge, colossal mistake.

I grabbed my middle as panic cramped my stomach.

Before anyone had a chance to notice, there was a knock on the door.

After answering, Rosa approached us with a silver tray. On it were five palm-sized black velvet boxes and a larger one the size of a hand. In the center of the tray was a vellum card with my name scrawled on it.

Rosa lifted the card. "It is Benedict's handwriting."

That simple statement did not help my panic. I'd known him for such a short time, I'd never actually seen him write anything down. What kind of foolish, illogical woman marries a man before she sees his handwriting?

Pressing my hand into the stitch forming in my side, I forced a smile and accepted the card.

My angioletto,

Right about now, you're thinking of running. There is no point, little one.

I found you once. I'd find you again.

So we can marry now in front of family.

Or later, with you tied up and over my shoulder in the basement of the Vatican.

Your choice. Either way, you <u>will</u> be my bride.

- Benedict, your very soon to be husband

WELL. What did I expect? A love poem?

Was it weird my stomach still fluttered at the caveman possessiveness of his tone? He may not love me in the traditional sense, but you had to at least like someone a whole heck of a lot to threaten to commit multiple crimes just to make them your wife, right?

Amara smiled. "What does it say?"

I flattened the card to my chest as my cheeks burned. "Oh, you know. The usual groom stuff."

Milana picked up one of the black velvet boxes. "Can we open the presents?"

I looked at the back of the card. There was an additional note saying he had gotten the gifts for the girls on my behalf and the larger box was for me.

We each took a box, counted to three, and opened the lids together.

There were several audible gasps.

I stared in wonder at the dual pendant nestled on the black velvet pillow. It was a beautiful, intricately carved silver cross. Dangling next to it was, at first glance, what looked like a small, four-petal flower designed with emeralds, but I realized they were actually basil leaves.

Above it was another small note in Benedict's handwriting.

To replace the one I broke.

Gold was too cold.

My baby should have the warmth of platinum next to her skin.

Bianca ran up and hugged me. "Oh my God, Liliana, this is unbelievably thoughtful."

Amara did the same as her eyes teared up. "I don't want to crush your veil, but I just have to hug you!"

Milana shooed her away. "Give the girl room to breathe." She then rubbed my back. "So sweet. I love it."

Rosa held up her jewelry box and placed a hand over her heart. "I will wear it always." Then kissed my cheek.

It was then I finally caught a glimpse of what each of them held.

They had a much larger version of the emerald basil pendant set in platinum. In the box I could see a silver card with beautiful calligraphy on it. "Can I see the card?" To cover up the fact that I was apparently supposed to know what was written on them, I said, "I want to make sure they got the note right."

To my Cummari, my chosen sisters.

It is a Sicilian tradition to give a basil plant, but I wanted to give you something we could pass down as a legacy to our daughters.

- Liliana (soon to be) Cavalieri

A lump formed in my throat. I handed the card back and turned to face away from the room as the girls chatted animatedly and helped one another put their necklaces on.

I laid a hand over my chest to calm my racing heart and stared up at the ceiling, willing myself not to cry.

A few nights ago, I mentioned in passing to Benedict the unique Sicilian word *cummari*. It described the special bond between close female friends, your chosen sisters. I said that it was traditional to gift your new *cummari* a basil plant. I then confessed I hoped one day the girls would consider me a *cummari*.

At the time, he had given me a kiss on the forehead and shaken his head, saying he didn't understand why I couldn't see what others saw in me. Then I changed the subject and didn't think anything more of it.

Aunt Gabriella came up behind me.

She reached for the pendant in the box I was still holding.

After gently pushing my veil aside, she draped the necklace chain around my neck and secured it before leaning close and whispering so the others couldn't hear.

"It has always been my experience that only a man in love listens to the little things."

I reached up and touched the necklace which had already started to warm against my skin.

She patted my arms. "Come, we have more surprises for you!"

I sniffed. "No, please! You've already done so much."

It really was too much. So many times I wanted to blurt out that it wasn't like it was a *real* wedding, but everyone was going out of their way to make me feel special and welcome and I didn't want to ruin their fun.

As we headed down the main staircase, I spied Barone waiting for us in the hall.

I missed a stair and had to grab the rail. My heart pounded in my ears with each step we took toward his imposing figure. By the time we reached the main level, my hands had grown so cold I couldn't feel my fingers.

Barone smiled down at me and looked at the other women. "Ladies, would you give us a minute?"

I bit my lower lip to keep from shouting out, *don't leave me alone with him.*

Amara leaned up and whispered something in his ear.

He winked and said, "I'll meet you there after I'm finished

with Liliana," before giving her a playful pat on the butt as she giggled and walked away.

After I'm finished with Liliana? What is that supposed to mean?

I clasped my numb hands together before me as I kept my head lowered.

"I have something for you in my study."

My eyes widened.

His study.

Wasn't that where he was shot?

I slowly raised my head to look at him.

Was this a trap?

Some kind of twisted revenge game?

Was I about to complete a divine retribution circle by getting shot in the same spot in a freaking wedding gown after he had gotten shot the night he was supposed to propose to Amara?

Was that what Amara had whispered to him?

Was he going to meet her after he had finished killing me?

I wondered if I screamed loud enough whether Benedict would hear me. I wasn't even sure if he was still in the villa or at the church by now. Even with all these out of control thoughts about his brother killing me in cold-blooded revenge filling my mind, I still knew deep down that I wanted to run to Benedict for protection.

I guessed that was what most would consider a true test of my feelings.

Barone placed his hands on his thighs and bent over slightly to look me in the eye. "I'm not sure where you went in your mind just then, but I have to say it was fascinating to watch. No wonder Benedict finds you so endearing."

Benedict finds me endearing?

He then smiled and I had to admit, it was charming. Like

the kind of charming that made me think that maybe he wasn't going to shoot me between the eyes while I was wearing his mother's wedding gown right before marrying his brother after all.

He said, "You should probably know that despite being his favorite—and only—brother, I'm fairly certain Benedict would hunt me down like a dog and finish what your uncle started if I harmed a hair on your head. Not that I want to. Come on."

Feeling a little silly for the bonkers rabbit hole I tumbled down, I followed him into the study.

On his desk was a large white box.

Barone said, "We couldn't possibly replace what you lost as a child but I'm hoping that after today you will consider us family."

He then lifted the lid to the box. Inside was a gorgeous bouquet of fresh Zagara blossoms.

The sweet, citrus scent of the orange blossoms filled the room. In Sicily, Zagara blossoms carried significant symbolic and traditional meaning at weddings but mostly for me, it was a piece of home that I didn't think I'd have on this day.

"Benedict learned that in Sicily, it was customary for the bride's parents to give their daughter a bouquet of Zagara blossoms for good luck on the day of her wedding. I know I'm a poor substitute, but I hope—"

With tears blurring my vision I launched myself into his arms.

Wrapping my arms around his neck I hugged him as I cried, "Thank you! Thank you so much!" I sniffed. "I know I don't deserve any of this. Your forgiveness or your kindness, but I—"

He pulled back and looked at me with a frown. "You look

like a smart girl. You probably should have figured out by now that this wedding was not Benedict's *only* option to shut down your uncle and appease Dante Agnello."

He reached into the box and handed me the bouquet with a wink. "It just happened to be the only option that got him what he really wanted. *You.*"

Wait. What?

CHAPTER 44

BENEDICT

Taking my place near the altar, I surveyed everyone seated in the nave, awaiting the start of my wedding ceremony.

This was going to be the worst goddamn wedding ever.

Half the wedding guests looked like the most-wanted list from the *Direzione Investigativa Antimafia* division.

The church was probably crawling with so many listening bugs from law enforcement they likely had one up the statue of the Virgin Mary's ass.

Not to mention each mafia family insisting on their own security details doing a sweep of the church beforehand to make sure that everyone was keeping to tradition and not stockpiling any weapons behind the crucifixes or pews.

There were even goons swiping each guest with metal detector wands before they entered to ensure all the invited mafia families obeyed the *no guns in the church* rule.

Salvatore had made sure to position Manfredi as one of

the goons, so I already knew how that was going to play out. Fortunately, we had our own clever work-around.

Matteo arrived and escorted Dante Agnello and his American girlfriend, Alina, up the aisle. They were flanked by two bodyguards. At least those were the two in view. There were an additional three watching Alina that I assumed Dante didn't want anyone to know about.

Appearances were an important part of the ritual kinship aspect of this ceremonial peace between the Agnello organization and the Cavalieri family. It wouldn't look good if he ordered his capos and their wives to attend but kept his girl safe at home.

I didn't blame him. I had six Cavalieri security guards in secret positions with the sole purpose of guarding Liliana. And those were just the ones watching my girl. Between them and the ones watching over the others, it was fair to say half the "guests" on the Cavalieri side were on the payroll.

After securing her seat, Dante caught my eye and nodded before heading to the back of the church.

Matteo joined me at the altar. "Dante agreed to walk Liliana down the aisle instead of Salvatore. He'll inform Salvatore of the bad news."

I didn't even try to hide my smirk.

Salvatore would definitely be out for blood after the final insult of being denied the prestigious honor of escorting the bride in front of such an exalted audience, especially as her so-called godfather.

It was bad enough her wedding would end in bloodshed. I wasn't going to force her to begin it by walking down the aisle on the arm of that monster.

The string quartet in the balcony of the church began playing the pre-ceremony music, "Suite No. 3 in D Major" by

Johann Sebastian Bach as Father Luca entered from a side door behind the altar and took his place in front of the altar.

My brother slid in next to me just as the back doors of the church opened to prepare for the bridal party.

I squinted at him. "Cutting it a little fucking close. Was attending your only brother's wedding keeping you from something?"

Father Luca cleared his throat as he kept his eyes on his Bible.

"Sorry, Father."

Barone reached under his tuxedo jacket to tuck in his shirt as he said out of the corner of his mouth, "One perk of taking a bullet, my girl has been insatiable for my cock."

Father Luca cleared his throat again.

Barone lifted his hand. "Sorry, Father," he whispered.

I tilted my head in his direction and whispered back. "You better get that girl down the aisle before you knock her up, or worse, someone steals her from you."

He rolled his shoulders then folded his hands in front of him. "What the fuck do you think I've been trying to do these last few months?"

Father Luca raised his finger to his lips and shushed us.

We said in unison as we raised our palms up, "Sorry, Father."

After a beat, I shrugged and said, "I don't understand what's taking you so long. It only took me a few days to get my girl to the altar."

Barone turned to me, hands on his hips. "Are you fucking kidding me? Half of Italy's mafia elite are sitting in the pews. Her dress has—"

Father Luca cleared his throat.

Barone and I both looked at him, then I turned my head to

see Matteo on his phone and frowned. "What are you doing? Don't disrespect the church. Put your phone away."

He whispered back. "I'm applying online to become a minister of the Universal Life Church so I can marry you and Lili in the parking lot when Father Luca kicks our asses out of here for being the sacrilegious bastards we all are."

Father Luca slammed his Bible shut and glared at us all as he let out a long-suffering sigh.

Duly chastised, we all schooled our features to look more appropriately pious as I placed my hand over Matteo's phone and slowly pushed it down out of sight.

Barone leaned in and whispered, "I paid for the roof. You can pay for the new steeple."

I reached my right arm across my middle and shook his hand. "Deal."

The string quartet began playing the opening notes for Pachelbel's "Canon in D minor."

The wedding procession had begun.

Amara, Milana, Bianca, and Gabriella looked beautiful in matching azure blue gowns. Being an artist, keen on color selection, Bianca had thought to research and learned that blue was a meaningful choice in Sicilian weddings, symbolizing loyalty. They each carried small bouquets of Zagara blossoms which would match Liliana's larger bouquet.

Once they were up the aisle there was a pause and the music changed.

While I knew most of the guests turned expecting to hear the typical opening strains of "Marcia Nuziale" as the bride entered, I had made a change.

It started with a long, plaintive note from a violin. Sad and sweet.

Then Schubert's tranquil melody, "Ave Maria," floated through the church just as Liliana appeared.

I knew a pounding, annoyingly upbeat wedding march would not suit my little lost angel on this day. Something serene with a bit of melancholy would be perfect.

I thought of her when I heard this song. How it was supposed to be so innocent, so virginal, and yet there was a touch of dark sorrow hidden behind the light melody.

Damn, only a week and this woman was already turning me into a lovesick poet.

God, she looked beautiful ... and terrified.

Her steps slowed, then her back stiffened and her lips thinned.

My hand curled into a fist at my side as I watched her obvious distress.

I wished I had the confidence to know if it was the situation, her godfather, bridal wedding jitters, or me.

For the first time in my life, I wasn't arrogantly three steps ahead of the room.

I couldn't read her mind.

Suddenly, I found the idea that I wasn't absolutely certain Liliana would make it the last hundred steps to reach me untenable.

Then Liliana came to a jarring halt as she encountered the scowling glare of her godfather who chose to sit at the end of an aisle just for that purpose.

That was it.

There was a wave of stunned gasps across the church as I broke protocol and stormed down the aisle.

My poor babygirl's face lost all its color and her dark eyes widened at my approach.

Dante, already guessing my intention, nodded gallantly, and stepped aside.

Liliana swayed, her arm reaching out. "Did you change your mind?" she asked, her voice barely audible.

Towering over her, I cupped her cheek. "Quite the opposite, babygirl."

Deliberately moving to the side to block her view of Salvatore, I placed a protective arm around her lower back and guided her to the altar. When we got there, I kept my arm around her waist and turned her to face me.

Father Luca leaned forward and said, "You're supposed to face me for this part."

Without taking my eyes off her, I responded, "Just say the words, Father Luca."

Liliana gave a worried glance between me and the priest. "Shouldn't we do as he says," she whispered.

The corner of my mouth lifted. "Babygirl, from this moment on, the only man you need to obey is me."

She blushed prettily and bit her lip at my pronouncement, clearly still nervous.

Pressing my palm against her back, I pulled her closer to my chest and without any regard to the hundred or so people watching us, leaned over and rasped in her ear, "Don't worry, I'm here. Just be a good girl and say 'I do' and this will all be over soon."

Liliana gave a slight nod and said, soft and low, "Yes, daddy."

Her mouth dropped open with a gasp before she covered it with her hand as she blushed scarlet red.

It had been just loud enough for poor Father Luca to hear it and to stumble to a stop at a very unfortunate part. "—you have come together—"

And it was in that moment, for the first time in my life, I truly prayed.

God, I don't know what I did to deserve this precious angioletto, but I swear I will love, honor, and cherish her until the day I die and into the afterlife.

Liliana buried her head in my shoulder in embarrassment after I tightened my arm around her and motioned for the priest to continue.

This was the best goddamn wedding ever.

CHAPTER 45

BENEDICT

*T*he very moment I broke our kiss, I hustled Liliana into an antechamber off to the side of the altar.

I knew we only had a second before the others arrived.

Cupping her jaw, I gazed down at her. "Are you ready for this, wife?"

She blinked up at me. "That sounds so odd … wife. I'm your *wife*."

"Well, get used to the sound of the word because I'll be showing you the definition of it real soon," I said with a wink before giving her a quick, hard kiss on the lips just as Barone arrived.

"At least Amara and I had the decency to sin in the parking lot in the back of the car like good Christians," he teased before hugging me and then clasping Liliana's hands and giving her a kiss on each cheek and congratulating her.

He then turned to me and said, "The others are in place." Concern darkened his eyes. "Is she ready for this?"

Liliana frowned as she stood between us and placed her hands on her hips. "Hey! I'm right here!"

Barone gestured with his head. "Less than a minute as a Cavalieri and she's already got the attitude down. You're screwed." He reached into his jacket pocket and pulled out a folded piece of white paper. "By the way, any idea why Father Luca just handed me this invoice from the Vatican for a glass shower door?"

Liliana gasped and covered her mouth as her cheeks blushed a pretty pink.

Before I could respond, Salvatore waltzed through the door with Manfredi behind him.

"Is this where the godfather is finally permitted an audience with the new queen?" He sneered.

Liliana stiffened.

I reached behind me and squeezed her hand before responding. "I'm going to be honest with you, Salvatore. This is a shit three-step plan."

Barone crossed his arms and leaned on the table behind us. "I'd have to agree. Probably worse than the one where I get shot, but of course, I'm a little bit biased about that one."

Salvatore's gaze narrowed as he reached into his tuxedo jacket and whipped out his Glock. "You want to say that again?"

I exchanged a glance with Barone and shrugged. "Sure. It's. A. Shit. Three. Step. Plan."

Salvatore gestured with the barrel of his gun between him and Manfredi. "Really, asshole? I don't know how they do it in Abruzzo, but in Sicily, the man with the gun has the best plan."

Moving slightly more in front of Liliana, but not so abruptly he'd notice, I said, "Let's test that theory. Step one.

You tell everyone you came back here as the devoted godfather to congratulate your beloved goddaughter only to find that I was holding her at gunpoint, having always intended to use her as bait, never as a bride."

Liliana's fingers curled into the back of my jacket. I knew I was cutting close to the bone when it came to her deep-down fears about this wedding.

Willing her to hold on, I continued. "So you kill me in a fit of revenge and tragically your beloved goddaughter gets caught in the crossfire. Taking care of two loose ends. How am I doing so far?"

Salvatore dug into his pocket for his handkerchief and swept it across his brow.

"I'm going to take that as a yes. So let's move on to step two."

Barone interjected. "Is this my dramatic death scene? I love this part."

"Why yes, brother, it is. In step two, Salvatore, acting as the devoted *vice capo,* races to find Dante to inform him of the betrayal and the trap they have all been led into by the conniving Cavalieris. Only to tragically learn that he was too late, Dante was already dead because you had already killed him in revenge for your shooting. At least that is what Salvatore will tell his organization. In reality he's going to shoot you, probably in the head this time just to make sure and then when he sends his lapdog Manfredi to fetch Dante, he'll shoot him the moment he enters the room."

Salvatore stepped closer. "You Cavalieri brothers think you're so fucking smart."

I tilted my head. "Just so we're clear. Is that because I guessed your plan correctly or because we're arrogant assholes from Abruzzo?"

Barone sighed. "You know, it could be both."

I rubbed my beard. "Excellent point."

Salvatore said, "I'm going to enjoy shooting you both in the fucking head."

Barone's shoulders straightened. "Before you do, one last clarification. It was you who ordered the hit on me, right?" He waved his hand. "I mean, we don't have to go into the whole villain speech about wanting to do a power grab from Dante, blah blah blah, we get it."

Salvatore let out a frustrated growl. "Yes, of course it was. Now move out of the way, so I can get a clear shot at my traitorous bitch of a goddaughter too."

My gaze narrowed. "You forgot to ask what the third step was."

"What?"

I repeated, "The third step. You didn't ask me what the third step was."

Salvatore's mouth twisted. "What's the third step?"

I directed my next words over my shoulder. "Liliana? Would you like to show your devoted godfather the third step?"

Barone and I shifted slightly to the side and back.

When she spoke her voice was soft but strong. "Gladly, *husband.*"

Looking resplendent, my avenging angel bride raised her arms, fanning the voluminous skirt of her wedding dress out on each side, almost like angel wings, allowing easier access to the hidden side pockets recently sewn within the folds.

I slid my hand into her wedding dress pocket, gripped the Beretta 92 and pulled it free. Barone did the same from the other side.

After all, we had known no one would think to check the bride for weapons.

Pushing Liliana fully behind me so she could take shelter under the table, I stepped forward and fired, dropping Manfredi with one shot between the eyes.

Leaving Salvatore for Barone who decided on the equally lethal but slightly slower death that had been reserved for him. A shot to the chest.

* * *

I WRAPPED my hand around Liliana's wrist and pulled her out from under the table. "We're leaving."

She dragged her heels. "Wait. Shouldn't we stay and help explain?"

I rounded on her. "Absolutely not. Dante and several of his men were listening with Cesare, Enzo, and Matteo the whole time one room over. They will handle the bodies. Now let's go."

Her fingers curled into fists. "Wait. I need a minute to think. You said some *things* a moment ago. And now the threat is over and technically we're not really married yet until we sign the civil documents."

Dammit. I forgot about the fucking civil registrar.

"There is nothing to think about."

Her head shook violently as she jammed her finger into my chest. "You called me bait! I'm finally realizing I deserve to be more than a pawn or freaking bait."

I wrapped my hand around her neck and yanked her against my chest. "Haven't you figured it out yet, *angioletto?* You are by far the most endearing, adorable, infuriating, intriguing, precious, fascinating, gorgeous creature I have ever laid eyes on, and I cannot wait to experience this bright, beautiful world all over again through your eyes. I'm in love with you."

Her lower lip trembled. "As unbelievable as it sounds, I love you too. And you really want me for your wife?"

I swept her into my arms. "Even better, babygirl," I said with a wink. "I want to fuck you."

Taking advantage of her shocked gasp, I slammed my mouth down on hers, allowing myself a quick taste, before breaking free and carrying her out of the church.

CHAPTER 46

MATTEO

*L*ater that evening.

CESARE AND ENZO charged out onto the terrace, both talking at once.

"Tell him to go to hell!"

"Absolutely not."

I turned and leaned against the iron railing as I looked down at the glowing ember of my cigar. "Heard any interesting gossip?"

Enzo crossed his arms over his chest. "What the fuck, Matteo? You saw the hell I went through with Renata."

Cesare ran a hand through his hair. "You were there for the bullshit we had to deal with during our childhood with our parents and then afterward when Papa was accused of killing our mother."

I took a long drag from my cigar. I nodded but didn't respond.

Enzo threw up his hand and left. After another moment of silence, Cesare did the same.

The French glass door opened, letting some of the wedding music drift over the terrace before Barone slid it closed. Taking a cigar from his inside jacket pocket, he silently clipped the end.

Watching him closely, I handed him the pack of wooden matches.

He struck one along the iron railing and held the flame just below the tobacco, heating it.

The brisk winter air filled with blue smoke and the scent of coffee and cedar.

His chest rose as he took a deep breath. He surveyed the dark fields of the vineyards, then said without facing me, "Your father will put a bullet in Dante's head for even suggesting this."

I tapped my cigar, watching the ash cascade down and then be picked up in the wind. "If an alliance with Dante's powerful *capo* Antonius Fichera is the key to shutting down any misguided vengeance plans for Salvatore's murder, then it's the right step to take. My father will see that."

Barone tilted his head back and blew out a cloud of cigar smoke. "There are rumors ... about the daughter, Antonia. Of course, I'm the first to tell you that rumors, especially salacious ones, are—"

My jaw tightened. "I've met her. They're true."

They didn't have to warn me. I already knew it was not going to end well.

But I was a Cavalieri.

It was my responsibility to help protect the family and our legacy, by any means necessary.

EPILOGUE

ANTONELLA

"*E*lla! Ella! Wake up!"

I rolled over and pulled the blanket over my head. "Go away, Antonia. I'm sleeping."

She yanked the covers off me. "Ella. This is life or death. You have to wake up."

Keeping my eyes closed, I bent in half and grasped for the covers before falling back onto my pillow.

Everything was life or death for my twin sister.

Born three seconds apart, we were worlds different from one another.

With the exception of appearances, we were complete polar opposites.

Propping a second pillow over my face, I groaned. "I mean it, Antonia. I have a presentation in class on Haydn's contribution to the formal conventions of the modern string quartet tomorrow and I need to sleep."

She tore the pillow off my head. "Holy shit, could you be

more of a nerd? I have a serious crisis here and I need your help!"

Knowing she would not let me sleep otherwise, I sat up in bed and pushed my hair out of my face. "What is it this time?"

I was trying really hard, not be judgmental but with Antonia a crisis could be anything from a minor car accident that she caused, to a broken nail, to a fight she had with a friend because they both wore the same outfit to a party.

I loved my sister, but she was shallow as fuck and unfortunately had a reputation to match.

Which made things extremely uncomfortable for me when I was occasionally mistaken for her.

The disgusting things men would say and try when they would grab me around the waist assuming I was my sister made my cheeks burn even now to think about. It was small wonder I never had any interest in a boyfriend and buried myself in books and music.

Anybody would be put off men after such experiences.

"Father is angry at me. And now he's going to punish me *for life*. He says I have no choice. If I don't do as he says, he'll cut me off and kick me out of the house."

I shrugged. "Is that all? He's always angry at you. You know he won't really kick you out."

She paced back and forth at the bottom of my bed. "You don't understand, Ella. It's different this time. I really fucked up."

I leaned forward on my knees and gripped the bottom bed railing. Something in her tone told me this time was different. "What happened? What did you do?"

She waved her hands. "I can't tell you, but I need you to do me a favor."

"What do you mean you can't tell me? What kind of favor?"

She grasped my hands. "Please, Ella. It's just a small favor and I promise it will only be for a few days, just until I can find my boyfriend and convince him to elope with me."

I leaned back and tried to free my hands, but she tightened her grip. "What kind of favor?"

"Father is trying to force me to marry Matteo Cavalieri. So I just need you to travel to the Cavalieri estate and pretend to be me. Please, Ella! I'm desperate!"

This was not a small favor.

But she was my sister.

It was my responsibility to protect her, even from herself.

I fell back and pulled the pillow over my face again.

I already knew this was not going to end well...

To be continued...
Antonella gets caught in her own trap when Matteo comes to claim his new bride. The enemies to lovers saga continues.

Scorn of the Betrothed
Cavalieri Billionaire Legacy, Book Five

ABOUT THE AUTHOR

Zoe Blake is the USA Today Bestselling Author of the romantic suspense saga *The Cavalieri Billionaire Legacy* inspired by her own heritage as well as her obsession with jewelry, travel, and the salacious gossip of history's most infamous families.

She delights in writing Dark Romance books filled with overly possessive billionaires, taboo scenes, and unexpected twists. She usually spends her ill-gotten gains on martinis, travels, and red lipstick. Since she can barely boil water, she's lucky enough to be married to a sexy Chef.

Check Out Zoe's Website

ALSO BY ZOE BLAKE

CAVALIERI BILLIONAIRE LEGACY

A Dark Enemies to Lovers Romance

Scandals of the Father

Cavalieri Billionaire Legacy, Book One

Being attracted to her wasn't wrong… but acting on it would be.

As the patriarch of the powerful and wealthy Cavalieri family, my choices came with consequences for everyone around me.

The roots of my ancestral, billionaire-dollar winery stretch deep into the rich, Italian soil, as does our legacy for ruthlessness and scandal.

It wasn't the fact she was half my age that made her off limits.

Nothing was off limits for me.

A wounded bird, caught in a trap not of her own making, she posed no risk to me.

My obsessive desire to possess her was the real problem.

For both of us.

But now that I've seen her, tasted her lips, I can't let her go.

Whether she likes it or not, she needs my protection.

I'm doing this for her own good, yet she fights me at every turn.

Refusing the luxury I offer, desperately trying to escape my grasp.

I need to teach her to obey before the dark rumors of my past reach her.

Ruin her.

She cannot find out what I've done, not before I make her mine.

Sins of the Son

Cavalieri Billionaire Legacy, Book Two

She's hated me for years… now it's past time to give her a reason to.

When you are a son, and one of the heirs, to the legacy of the Cavalieri name, you need to be more vicious than your enemies.

And sometimes, the lines get blurred.

Years ago, they tried to use her as a pawn in a revenge scheme against me.

Even though I cared about her, I let them treat her as if she were nothing.

I was too arrogant and self-involved to protect her then.

But I'm here now. Ready to risk my life tracking down every single one of them.

They'll pay for what they've done as surely as I'll pay for my sins against her.

Too bad it won't be enough for her to let go of her hatred of me,

To get her to stop fighting me.

Because whether she likes it or not, I have the power, wealth, and connections to keep her by my side.

And every intention of ruthlessly using all three to make her mine.

Secrets of the Brother

Cavalieri Billionaire Legacy, Book Three

We were not meant to be together… then a dark twist of fate stepped in, and we're the ones who will pay for it.

As the eldest son and heir of the Cavalieri name, I inherit a great deal more than a billion-dollar empire.

I receive a legacy of secrets, lies, and scandal.

After enduring a childhood filled with malicious rumors about my father, I have fallen prey to his very same sin.

I married a woman I didn't love out of a false sense of family honor.

Now she has died under mysterious circumstances.

And I am left to play the widowed groom.

For no one can know the truth about my wife…

Especially her sister.

The only way to protect her from danger is to keep her close, and yet, her very nearness tortures me.

She is my sister in name only, but I have no right to desire her.

Not after what I have done.

It's too much to hope she would understand that it was all for her.

It's always been about her.

Only her.

I am, after all, my father's son.

And there is nothing on this earth more ruthless than a Cavalieri man in love.

Seduction of the Patriarch

Cavalieri Billionaire Legacy, Book Four

With a single gunshot, she brings the violent secrets of my buried past into the present.

She may not have pulled the trigger, but she still has blood on her hands.

And I know some very creative ways to make her pay for it.

Being as ruthless as my Cavalieri ancestors has earned me a reputation as a dangerous man to cross, but that hasn't stopped me from making enemies along the way. No fortune is built without spilling blood.

But while I may be brutal, I don't play loose with my family, which means staying in the shadows to protect them.

I find myself forced to hand over the mantle of patriarch to my brother and move to northern Italy...

...or risk the lives of those I love.

Until a vindictive mafia syndicate attacks my family.

Now all bets are off, and nothing will prevent me from seeking vengeance on those responsible.

I'm done protecting the innocent.

Now, I don't give a damn who I hurt in the process...

...including her.

Through seduction and the power of punishment, I shall bend her to my will.

She will be my rebellious accomplice, a vital pawn in my quest for revenge.

And the more my defiant little vixen bares her sharp claws, the more she tempts me to tame her until she purrs with submission.

Scorn of the Betrothed

Cavalieri Billionaire Legacy, Book Five

A union forged in vengeance, bound by hate, and... beneath it all...a twisted game of power.

The true legacy of the Cavalieri family, my birthright, ties me to a woman I despise:

the daughter of the mafia boss who nearly ended my family.

Making her both my enemy...and my future wife.

The hatred is mutual; she has no desire for me to be her groom.

A prisoner to her families' ambitions, she's desperate for a way out.

My duty is to guard her, to ensure she doesn't escape her gilded cage.

But every moment spent with her, every spark of anger, adds fuel to the growing fire of desire between us.

We're trapped in a volatile duel of passion and fury.

Yet, the more I try to tame her, the more she fights me,

Our impending marriage becomes a dangerous game.

Now, as the wedding draws near, my suspicions grow.

My bride is not who she claims.

RUTHLESS OBSESSION SERIES

A Dark Mafia Romance

Sweet Cruelty

Ruthless Obsession Series, Book One

Dimitri & Emma's story

It was an innocent mistake.

She knocked on the wrong door.

Mine.

If I were a better man, I would've just let her go.

But I'm not.

I'm a cruel bastard.

I ruthlessly claimed her virtue for my own.

It should have been enough.

But it wasn't.

I needed more.

Craved it.

She became my obsession.

Her sweetness and purity taunted my dark soul.

The need to possess her nearly drove me mad.

A Russian arms dealer had no business pursuing a naive librarian student.

She didn't belong in my world.

I would bring her only pain.

But it was too late…

She was mine and I was keeping her.

Sweet Depravity

Ruthless Obsession Series, Book Two

Vaska & Mary's story

The moment she opened those gorgeous red lips to tell me no, she was mine.

I was a powerful Russian arms dealer and she was an innocent schoolteacher.

If she had a choice, she'd run as far away from me as possible.

Unfortunately for her, I wasn't giving her one.

I wasn't just going to take her; I was going to take over her entire world.

Where she lived.

What she ate.

Where she worked.

All would be under my control.

Call it obsession.

Call it depravity.

I don't give a damn… as long as you call her mine.

Sweet Savagery

Ruthless Obsession Series, Book Three

Ivan & Dylan's Story

I was a savage bent on claiming her as punishment for her family's mistakes.

As a powerful Russian Arms dealer, no one steals from me and gets away with it.

She was an innocent pawn in a dangerous game.

She had no idea the package her uncle sent her from Russia contained my stolen money.

If I were a good man, I would let her return the money and leave.

If I were a gentleman, I might even let her keep some of it just for frightening her.

As I stared down at the beautiful living doll stretched out before me like a virgin sacrifice,

I thanked God for every sin and misdeed that had blackened my cold heart.

I was not a good man.

I sure as hell wasn't a gentleman… and I had no intention of letting her go.

She was mine now.

And no one takes what's mine.

Sweet Brutality

Ruthless Obsession Series, Book Four

Maxim & Carinna's story

The more she fights me, the more I want her.

It's that beautiful, sassy mouth of hers.

It makes me want to push her to her knees and dominate her, like the brutal savage I am.

As a Russian Arms dealer, I should not be ruthlessly pursuing an innocent college student like her, but that would not stop me.

A twist of fate may have brought us together, but it is my twisted obsession that will hold her captive as my own treasured possession.

She is mine now.

I dare you to try and take her from me.

Sweet Ferocity

Ruthless Obsession Series, Book Five

Luka & Katie's Story

I was a mafia mercenary only hired to find her, but now I'm going to keep her.

She is a Russian mafia princess, kidnapped to be used as a pawn in a dangerous territory war.

Saving her was my job. Keeping her safe had become my obsession.

Every move she makes, I am in the shadows, watching.

I was like a feral animal: cruel, violent, and selfishly out for my own needs. Until her.

Now, I will make her mine by any means necessary.

I am her protector, but no one is going to protect her from me.

Sweet Intensity

Ruthless Obsession Series, Book Six

Antonius & Brynn's Story

She couldn't have known the danger she faced when she dared to steal from me.

She was too young for a man my age, barely in her twenties.

Far too pure and untouched.

Unfortunately for her, that wasn't going to stop me.

The moment I laid eyes on her, I claimed her.

Determined to make her mine…by any means necessary.

I owned Chicago's most elite gambling club, a front for my role as a Russian Mafia crime boss.

And she was a fragile little bird, who had just flown straight into my open jaws.

Naïve and sweet, she was a temptation I couldn't resist biting.

My intense drive to dominate and control her had become an obsession.

I would ruthlessly use my superior strength and wealth to take over her life.

The harder she resisted, the more feral and savage I would become.

She needed to understand… she was mine now.

Mine.

Sweet Severity

Ruthless Obsession Series, Book Seven

Macarius & Phoebe's Story

Had she crashed into any other man's car, she could have walked away—but she hit mine.

Upon seeing the bruises on her wrist, I struggled to contain my rage.

Despite her objections, I refused to allow her to leave.

Whoever hurt this innocent beauty would pay dearly.

As a Russian Mafia crime boss who owns Chicago's most elite gambling club, I have very creative and painful methods of exacting revenge.

She seems too young and naive to be out on her own in such a dangerous world.

Needing a nanny, I decided to claim her for the role.

She might resist my severe, domineering discipline, but I won't give her a choice in the matter.

She needs a protector, and I'd be damned if it were anyone but me.

Resisting the urge to claim her will test all my restraint.

It's a battle I'm bound to lose.

With each day, my obsession and jealousy intensify.

It's only a matter of time before my control snaps…and I make her mine.

Mine._

Sweet Animosity

Ruthless Obsession, Book Eight

Varlaam & Amber's Story

I never asked for an assistant, and if I had, I sure as hell wouldn't have chosen her.

With her sharp tongue and lack of discipline, what she needs is a firm hand, not a job.

The more she tests my limits, the more tempted I am to bend her over my knee.

As a Russian Mafia boss and owner of Chicago's most elite gambling club, I can't afford distractions from her antics.

Or her secrets.

For I suspect, my innocent new assistant is hiding something.

And I know just how to get to the truth.

It's high time she understands who holds the power in our relationship.

To ensure I get what I desire, I'll keep her close, controlling her every move.

Except I am no longer after information—I want her mind, body and soul.

She underestimated the stakes of our dangerous game and now owes a heavy price.

As payment I will take her freedom.

She's mine now.

Mine.

www.ingramcontent.com/pod-product-compliance
Lightning Source LLC
LaVergne TN
LVHW020154270425
809719LV00009B/945